PROUD CAPTIVE, PRICELESS TREASURE

As he walked beside the secluded pool, the sheik caught sight of Bryna sitting on the other side. She was alone and Sharif could not resist giving into the desire to gaze upon her unveiled face. Shielded by the trees, he made his way toward her, stopping when he realized she was crying.

"Why do you weep?" he asked softly.

She hurriedly dashed the tears from her eyes. "Beacuse I am lonely, because I'm in a strange land, because I may never go home again," she answered, feeling oddly defiant.

"Arabia is your home now." Taking her hand, he pulled her to her feet. He drank in Bryna's beauty as the wind whipped her dark hair.

All at once, Sharif's hands tightened and he drew her against his hard, muscular body. Gazing tenderly into her eyes, he murmured her name and lowered his mouth to hers.

Also by Karen Jones Delk

Emerald Queen

Available from
HarperPaperbacks

The Bride Price

Karen Jones Delk

HarperPaperbacks
A Division of HarperCollins*Publishers*

This is a work of fiction. The characters, incidents, and
dialogues are products of the author's imagination and are not
to be construed as real. Any resemblance to actual events or
persons, living or dead, is entirely coincidental.

HarperPaperbacks *A Division of* HarperCollins*Publishers*
10 East 53rd Street, New York, N.Y. 10022

Cover illustration by Diane Sivavec

First printing: January 1992

Printed in the United States of America

HarperPaperbacks, HarperMonogram, and colophon are
trademarks of HarperCollins*Publishers*

10 9 8 7 6 5 4 3 2

To Gail Malone who sparked the interest in Arabia that led me to write this book.

AUTHOR'S NOTE

IN SETTING A NOVEL IN NINETEENTH CENTURY Arabia, I established a difficult task for myself. Little research material was available. Few Europeans of the period traveled on the Arabian peninsula and lived to tell of it. I discovered in the writings of Sir Richard Burton, C. M. Doughty, Karl May, T. E. Lawrence, Wilfred Thesiger and others, a life little changed over centuries.

Though more than one hundred years passed between Jean Louis Burckhardt's wanderings in Arabia and Thesiger's crossings of the Rub al Khali, their depictions of the Bedu and their customs were remarkably similar. I drew from various sources to describe Bryna's experiences in the desert and the simplicity and honor of the Bedouin people.

Because Arab dialects are many and because my source material spanned a century and a half, the spellings in this book may depart from modern Arabic. When possible, I used transliterations by scholars such as Alfred Guillaume, who was the head of the Department of Near and Middle East in the School of Oriental and African Studies, and a professor of Arabic at University of London, and later visiting professor of Arabic at Princeton University.

I must admit that writing this book was a wonderful excuse to learn more about historical Arabia and the Bedouin people. As a child growing up in the humid delta country of Louisiana, I was intrigued by the desert, a fascination which was fueled in my adult life by conversations with friends who were employed by American companies in Saudi Arabia. I hope you enjoy the product of my research as much as I enjoyed writing it.

PROLOGUE

✦✦✦✦✦✦✦✦✦✦✦

Alhamdillah! PRAISE ALLAH, FOR HE IS GOOD! Silhouetted against the pale Arabian sky, Sheik Sharif Al Selim reined his graceful white mare to a halt on the crest of the mountain. Lifting his face skyward, he closed his eyes against the hazy sunlight filtering through the tree branches overhead and savored the moment, breathing deeply of the clean, juniper-scented air.

He grinned as the breeze caught at his flowing aba and headdress and caused them to billow out behind him, exciting the playful young saluki at his side. It was enough on this beautiful day in early spring to set the high-spirited dog racing in circles, yipping joyously.

The morning was filled with birdsong, and around him bushes rustled in the breeze. It was not like the empty places of the desert, where the only sounds were the harsh rush of the wind and the clamor of nomads who passed through the silent sands. Though he was most at home in the desert, Sharif loved the mountains. He preferred Taif, the hideaway of wealthy Arabs, even to his home in Riyadh.

1

"Come, Târiq." Sharif gently urged his horse forward. He guided her down the steep, narrow trail, his mind on his problems.

A man should not be so troubled that his concerns stayed with him even in pleasant moments. Still, the sheik was grateful for the moment of solitude as he tried to collect his disturbing thoughts. His burden was his alone, but on a day like today the yoke of leadership seemed especially heavy.

Tribal sheiks were selected, not born. "An equal among equals," they ruled judiciously with their *majlis,* or council of lesser sheiks. Sharif had been young when he became the leader of his people, chosen not only because his father had been sheik before him, but because leadership came naturally to him. He was a sayyid, a descendant of the Prophet, and equipped with the qualities necessary to govern one of the most powerful tribes in Arabia: courage, honor, wisdom, and *hadhdh*—luck.

However, his luck could be questioned over the past few years. His misfortunes had begun seven years ago with the death of his wife in childbirth. Noorah. Lovely, gentle Noorah. What loneliness her name still brought him.

There had followed seasons of too little rain and senseless rivalries among the desert tribes when they should have been ousting their enemies from their country.

If the tribes could think of themselves as one people, if they could unite as a nation, if they could overcome the treachery of the Ottoman empire, if . . . A grimace of impatience flitted across Sharif's rugged face before he heaved a sigh of resignation. Never mind. *Insh'allah.* It was as Allah willed it.

Life was difficult for the Bedu, the children of the tents, but at least, in the desert, a man knew who his enemies were—the sun and the wind, the scorpion and the snake.

The preoccupied rider scarcely noticed as the mare picked her way daintily down the gentle slope, requiring no guidance along the familiar path. The sheik's mind was on his nephew Zayid, the young man he had chosen as his successor. Having received no news of him for some months, Sharif feared for his safety.

Just last year Sharif's elder brothers, Hamza and Talel, had been murdered by raiders, and he himself had been wounded. When the sheik recovered from his injuries, the intelligence he received regarding the marauders was disheartening. The attackers were from a tribe of low standing. It was not fitting that the powerful Selim tribe should seek retribution upon them.

But he could not forbid the hotheaded Zayid, eldest son of Sharif's elder brother, from setting out alone to avenge the deaths. The young man had vowed to find the raiders, or even two members of their tribe, and kill them. No blood price would be accepted. He would shoot one murderer as his father had been shot and stab the other with a sword as Talel was slain. A tooth for a tooth, an eye for an eye, blood for blood, as it should be. Vengeance would be complete.

Insh'allah, the sheik reminded himself again.

He flexed his broad shoulders as if to shed his worries and realized with a start that he was already at the bottom of the trail. Just below him, through the trees, he could see the home of his beloved aunt, Alima. Though he was eager to see the old woman, he dreaded to emerge from the cool shadows of the forest into the heat that would engulf him. The hour was early, but already heat shimmered on the flat rooftop of the house.

Alima was always pleased with her nephew's company, but she rarely sent for him. Curious as to what prompted her request this morning, he rode slowly down to the dusty road in front of the house.

His aunt, still lovely despite the ravages of age, was too outspoken, some said, for a proper Moslem wife. She had been his ally for many years, befriending the boy Sharif when he entered the household of Malek, his uncle. Today, from the harem, she offered staunch support for Sharif the sheik. He knew her well—her likes, her dislikes, her daily routine. He even knew where to find her in this sprawling villa she had purchased for herself when his uncle had died.

Admitted to the women's quarters by the aged eunuch "guard," Sharif paused beside the door to watch his aunt. The elderly woman, her braided hair streaked with gray, her slight frame showing the effects of a lifetime of idleness, lounged on rich satin cushions, sipping a cool drink. Behind her, a small black slave lethargically wielded a fan. Across from her, Hirfa, a decrepit Bedu serving woman, hunched over a tray of sand, reading Alima's fortune.

Glancing up, the old servant spied Sharif. Immediately she rose and made a respectful obeisance.

"*As salaam 'alaykum*, peace be unto you, revered Aunt," Sharif greeted Alima, his usually stern face lit with a smile. "No, no, do not get up," he added quickly when she prepared to rise.

"*Wa 'alaykum as salaam*, and unto you be peace," she welcomed him, and settled back on her pillows. "You are kind not to require formality from an old woman, my lord, for my bones ache and I am nearly prostrate with heat."

She was about as feeble as his favorite riding camel, the sheik thought to himself, but to his aunt he said, "May there be upon you nothing but health, if God wills, Alima. You look well."

When she beamed with delight, her nephew was glad it was not necessary for women to wear veils before family members. How often he had been warmed by her smile.

He accepted readily the invitation when she patted a pillow beside her, saying, "Come thou hither, Sharif." Rings twinkled on her slender fingers, and her bracelets bumped together with a soft golden clatter as she clapped her hands, summoning the eunuch. "Bring *rubb Rumman* for my nephew."

Instantly the slave bowed and disappeared to fetch some of the pomegranate syrup for which Taif was known.

When Sharif was situated beside her, Alima nodded toward the old crone who stood still before them. "I hope you do not mind, Sharif, if Hirfa finishes reading my future in the sands."

The sheik glanced at her indifferently. Hirfa's dark eyes, crafty and sly, met his, then slid away. He had never liked the woman, but some believed she was gifted with the "sight."

Nodding grudgingly, he gave his permission, but he chided his aunt, "Can your future be different today from what it was yesterday or the day before?"

"Fortunes change." She shrugged carelessly.

"All things are as Allah wills them," Sharif retorted. "What is written cannot be changed."

"Say not that I wish to change my fate, nephew, but that I dislike surprises." When the eunuch reappeared, bearing a tray with a cup of syrup and silver pitcher of water, Alima mixed the two to make a cooling drink. Passing the cup to Sharif, she met his gaze directly. *Bismallah,* she thought as she always did, he is as handsome as Satan himself, and his gray eyes, shockingly light in his sun-bronzed face, seemed to see into a person's very soul.

Thrusting away those vexing thoughts, she teased, "Admit it, nephew, wouldn't you like to know what is willed before it happens? Perhaps we should have Hirfa foretell your future."

"Yes, *sidi,*" the servant agreed eagerly, "it would be a great honor to read the fortune of a leader of men."

Before he could respond, she gathered a handful of sand and allowed it to trickle through her clawlike fingers onto the tray. Then she leaned over it, examining the peaks and valleys of sand.

Closing her eyes, Hirfa began in a singsong voice, "Oh, my sheik, ruler of the tribes of Al Selim, I see long life for you and respect for your wondrous wisdom in the *majlis*. I see *ghazzi*, many raids in the wilderness. You will be triumphant, mighty in battle, and you will take many spoils. Your herds will fill the empty places of the desert."

She opened her eyes and peeped at the man. One black eyebrow was raised skeptically, but he said nothing. Mumbling to herself, Hirfa returned to her inspection of the sands. Her eyes narrowed and the numerous furrows in her forehead deepened. "Joyous news, O Beloved of God," she crooned. "I see a son, strong and manly, who will rule your people after you."

Sharif set his cup on the table with a solid thud and frowned at her ominously. "Zayid rules after me. Know you not I am the father of a daughter?" he asked scornfully. "And my wives are too old to bear children."

"I cannot say how Allah writes your destiny, O master, only that it is written," she replied blandly. "I am but the bearer of news. What I read in the sands is as Allah wills, good . . . or ill."

"What else do you read? Who will bear this son?" Alima asked.

"Enough of this," Sharif protested. "Did you not bid me here because you wished to talk to me?"

Before the woman could answer, Hirfa hastily smoothed the surface of the sand. "If the master wishes to hear no more, I beg to be pardoned, my lady." She moved as if to depart.

"Wait!" Alima's command caused the old slave to stay her quick exit. "Have you told us all, Hirfa?"

"There is nothing else of import, my lady," she mumbled uneasily, refusing to meet Alima's questioning gaze.

"There is more?" Sharif's aunt demanded.

Hirfa hung her head and did not answer.

"Tell us what the sands say, woman," Sharif commanded impatiently. "Then be gone."

"They say that you will value love above honor," the fortune-teller whispered reluctantly. "You will find what your heart wills, my lord, but her bride price will be your honor."

"What? Never!" The man's temper strained to breaking, he jumped to his feet and swept the tray from the table, knocking over his cup and dashing its sticky contents to the floor. "Away with your false words!" he roared. "There is nothing to be valued more than honor. It is better to die with honor than to live in humiliation. And, please Allah, I do only his will, not my heart's. Now leave us!"

Turning his back to collect himself, he did not see the cringing Hirfa scuttle away. Behind him, Alima gestured for the eunuch, who rapidly cleaned the worst of the mess, then dodged from harm's way as Sharif wheeled on his aunt.

"Sometimes you try my patience, Alima," the sheik muttered.

The old woman regarded him imperturbably from her cushion. "As I tried Malek's patience before you. Do not take Hirfa's readings so seriously, nephew," she advised serenely. "I do not."

"Then why do you have her tell your fortune at all?" he grumbled, pacing irritably. His robe swirled behind him, and bits of sand, strewn on the smooth tile floor, grated under his boots, loud in the tense silence.

"To amuse myself. Time passes slowly for a woman alone. But you are not here to talk about my amusements."

"Why did you send for me?"

"To speak of other things," his aunt answered vaguely, her full attention seemingly required to refill Sharif's cup. Setting it on the table in front of the seat Hirfa had so recently vacated, she peered at him shrewdly. "It is not like you to lose your temper, Sharif. What troubles you? Is there news of Zayid?"

He shook his head in mute response.

"No word of Zayid, but always plenty of news about Nassar." Alima sighed.

The man's jaw worked at the thought of his flabby, useless nephew, but he bit back his reply. After a moment he said evenly, "It is my hope Nassar will settle down when he is married next year. In a few months, I plan to send him on hajj, pilgrimage to the Holy City of Mecca. Perhaps when he has earned the title of Hajji, he will wear it with dignity."

"Perhaps," she agreed dubiously. Then, gazing up at the sheik earnestly, Alima said, "I wish to discuss a matter of some importance, my lord."

Sharif nodded attentively and sat down across from her. At last they had reached the reason for her summons. "What is it, Aunt?"

"I wish to speak of marriage . . . for you."

Sharif stiffened and leaned back slowly, increasing the distance between them. "I already have two wives, and I do my duty by them," he stated flatly.

"Indeed, my sheik, no one could doubt it." Her agreement was quick. "When your brothers were killed—may Allah keep such and all hateful things from you—you arranged marriages for their widows among your relations. That was as it should be. And you married Fatmah and Latifeh, the oldest wives, yourself. I am not sure that is as it should be."

"I did what was right," he began reasonably. "They are old—"

"Exactly!"

"And past the age of childbearing," he went on, his voice rising slightly to override his aunt's. "How could I ask anyone else to marry them?"

"So you took the shrews to your own harem." Her voice held more exasperation than sympathy.

Before he glanced away, Alima saw a spasm of pain cross his face. When the man turned to her again, his craggy features looked as if they were carved from stone. "It makes no difference," he said coldly. "I do not seek love from them nor companionship."

"Nor even sons," she interjected emphatically.

"Nor even sons." The soft gray of Sharif's eyes darkened to the steel of restrained anger, but his aunt was not chastened.

"I know you think me a meddling old woman, my lord," she continued doggedly, "and perhaps I am. But, as always, I look to the good of the tribe."

Silently the sheik rose and walked to the doors that opened onto the walled harem garden. Without seeing them, he stared out at the fountain and blooming roses while he weighed her words. Facing her, he said grudgingly, "Very well, say what you will, Alima. You know I trust your opinion as much as I trust some in my *majlis.*"

"I am grateful, Sharif. You have been like a son to me, and I hope you will heed what I say now. You must find another wife, one who pleases you. Perhaps what Hirfa says is true. Perhaps you will have a son who will become a lion of the desert, the leader of the Selims."

"Allah preserve me from another wife!" Restlessly he resumed his pacing. "I treat Fatmah and Latifeh equally, but it is all I can do to keep the peace between them." Suddenly he stopped in front of his aunt to say quietly, "Let me fulfill my obligations to the wives I have. I do not want another."

"You think you will never care again, Sharif"— the old woman smiled up at him tenderly —"but one day you will love again. It will be Allah's great gift to you."

"Allah blesses me in other ways," he countered firmly. "I will never love again."

"We shall see what your future holds, my lord," she concluded their interview just as firmly. "But for now, consider what I have said."

With a black scowl, Sharif whirled and strode

from the harem without another word. Women were *sheytàn*, life's torment, he fumed, even Alima . . . especially Alima, with her knowing smile. Eventually she would learn she was wrong. He would not love again. It hurt too much.

CHAPTER

✦✦✦✦✦ **1** ✦✦✦✦✦

PERCHED ON A BALE OF HAY, BRYNA SAT IN A pool of warm July sunlight that poured through the open door of the stable. In her lap she held a whining puppy as she tended a cut in his forepaw. "Stay still, *mon petit,* just one moment more," she whispered in soft Creole. She wrapped a length of white fabric around his wound.

"Et voilà." Skillfully tying the dressing in place, the girl released the squirming ball of fur and watched with amused satisfaction as the pup balanced on three legs and gnawed irritably at the bandage. She glanced up at the Negro groom who leaned on a broom nearby. "Now, Benoît, you can tell Tetie-Charles that his puppy will be good as new."

"Don't know what is wrong with that boy, always bringing home strays." The wiry old man sniffed.

"Your grandson suffers from nothing worse than a good heart," the girl scolded, but her blue eyes were merry.

"You have a good heart too, mam'selle, and a

way with animals," he grunted approvingly, returning to his sweeping. "But I think you'd better not let Sister Françoise find you in the stable again."

"You are right," she agreed. "Besides, I should go so you can do your work." As Benoît plied his broom, the girl lifted her feet in absentminded cooperation while continuing to gather her bottles and bandage, stuffing them into a dilapidated hatbox.

"Put down your feet, mam'selle. I cannot sweep beneath them if we do not want you to become an old maid."

"If I become an old maid, I doubt it would be your fault," she replied dryly, but she lowered her feet nevertheless.

"Then whose fault? Not yours," he insisted, his broom raising motes to float in the shaft of sunlight. "You will make some man a good wife someday, Mam'selle Bryna, but until then I will not sweep beneath your feet, *oui?*"

"*Oui.*" Smiling, she rubbed her nose, which itched from the dust. Before she could return to packing her medicines, the puppy began to bark, running forward bravely, then scurrying backward with each stroke of Benoît's broom. A mischievous grin on his weathered face, the groom gently extended the reach of his broom so the puppy nearly tumbled over himself in his efforts to escape, causing the old man and the girl to dissolve into laughter at his antics..

Their hilarity was interrupted when a voice trumpeted from the stable yard, "I have looked everywhere for you, Bryna Jean-Marie O'Toole. I should have known I would find you here."

Short, dumpy, and formidable, Sister Françoise strode into the stable, blinking in the dimness. When the girl jumped to her feet to greet her, the nun scolded halfheartedly, "Just look at you. Whatever shall I do with you? You look like a common street urchin, and the Mother Superior wishes to see you at once."

The puppy, attracted by Sister Françoise's tapping foot, pounced with a ferocious growl, sinking his teeth into the hem of her habit. Snarling and whining, he crouched low to the ground and tossed his head back and forth, tugging mightily. His short legs pumped rapidly but did little to propel him backward. Abruptly he lost his grip and his footing at the same time and sat down with a surprised yelp.

Struggling to hide a smile, the woman commanded, "Benoît, collar this fearsome beast and let me take Bryna to Mother Véronique."

Bryna tucked her battered hatbox under one arm and followed obediently. Trotting behind Sister Françoise's broad, black-clad form, she hastily ran her fingers through her straying curls, then belatedly rubbed her hands together in a vain attempt to remove the dirt from them. Mentally she reviewed her most recent misdeeds, trying to deduce the reason for the summons, but she could not. She had not shirked laundry duty, had not skipped mass, had not stolen away for a solitary swim in the bayou. She had not even lost her temper for nearly two weeks.

When she could stand the curiosity no longer, she asked, "Do you know why Mother Véronique wishes to see me, Sister? She hardly ever sends for me unless—"

"Unless you have done something wrong," the woman finished for her. Her round face red with exertion, she glanced over her shoulder at the girl. "Do not worry." She chuckled. "I don't think she knows about the cup of lard you pirated from the kitchen."

"It was for a good cause," Bryna muttered defensively. "I made an ointment for Benoît."

"You are a thoughtful child," the nun replied with a warm smile. "So I will tell you what I know. The reverend mother received a letter this morning. She read it, then sent for you."

Mulling over that information, Bryna scarcely noticed when they crossed the shell-covered drive and approached the Hôtel Ste. Anne, the orphanage that had been her home for most of her life. It was a ramshackle three-story building with huge windows and an incongruously ornate front gate. Its walls, constructed of *briquettes entre poteaux*, or bricks between posts, were in sore need of paint, and the rusting iron fence that surrounded the compound sagged in several spots. The cistern beside the dilapidated laundry shed tilted slightly to one side, and the yard was little more than patches of dusty grass between paths worn by the feet of children.

Chickens scratched in the dirt near the back gate, scattering in alarm as the two women entered.

Scolding noisily, a squirrel leapt from the trunk of an old oak tree and darted across a tiny herb garden to disappear around the corner into the crimson bougainvillea that crept up the side of the house. Along the back of the building, a narrow gallery, its wobbly rail draped with an ancient honeysuckle vine, ran the entire length.

"Here, let me take your medicines until after you have talked to the Mother Superior," Sister Françoise instructed, taking the hatbox in careful hands. "Then you can tell me what all the excitement is about. Do not fear, *cher,*" she said, using the more familiar form of the endearment, "but do not make her wait any longer."

Reluctantly Bryna smoothed her skirt and mounted the rickety wooden stairs. Stopping before Mother Véronique's closed door, she faltered, her hand lifted to knock. Behind her, a bee droned lazily among the pale yellow honeysuckle blossoms, and from the side yard she could hear the laughter of the children. Certain she was about to be chastised for some forgotten sin, she rapped lightly.

"Entrez." A gaunt, stooped figure in black, Mother Véronique stood at the window overlooking the play yard.

"You wished to see me, Mother Superior?" Bryna stood poised warily in the doorway.

The old woman turned, her dark eyes taking in her ward's appearance, and a ghost of a smile crept across her withered face. Bryna was lovely, mannerly, well educated, and nearly grown, Mother

17

Véronique thought affectionately. Yet here she was as she had been so many times in the past. Her dark hair with its hidden lights of auburn tumbled around her shoulders. She wore a rumpled, grass-stained skirt, a smudge on her cheek, and a ready smile. God forgive anyone who tried to break her dauntless will and bright spirit.

"Bonjour, chère." She gestured toward a chair and Bryna obligingly took a seat. Sitting down across from her, Mother Véronique hesitated a moment, then delicately cleared her throat and said, "I have today received a letter, Bryna, from your father."

"Oui." The girl nodded expressionlessly. Stipends for her support arrived regularly from the father she had never known.

"He, er, he sends money and requests that you join him. We are to book passage for you on the first ship to Tangier or Gibraltar."

"Join him?" Bryna repeated incredulously. "After all these years? I will not."

"I fear you must," the old woman said sadly.

"Why?" Hurt and resentment caused the girl's voice to rise. "In all the years since my mother died, he never came for me. Why should I go to him now? Why would you send me?"

"I must. He wants you with him and I do not have the right to keep you, *chère,*" the Mother Superior replied wearily.

"Who has a better right?" Bryna exploded. Her blue eyes flashing, she jumped from her chair and began to pace the small room. "You and Sister

Françoise are my family, my only family since Blaine O'Toole deserted my mother."

"He did not desert Catherine, *chère*. Monsieur O'Toole was a professional soldier—"

"You mean a mercenary?"

"A mercenary, if you wish," the old woman conceded, expelling her breath in a puff, "but he was ready to give up war. Your father is an honorable man, Bryna, and he had one last obligation to fulfill. He could not take Catherine where he had to go. What kind of life would that have been for a genteel Creole girl?"

"What kind of life was it when my grandfather refused to take her in, even when she was ill?" Bryna asked through gritted teeth. "It must have broken her heart to be disowned, to know her child would never be acknowledged by her father. And it was Blaine O'Toole's fault. He should never have married her."

"Do not forget, it takes two to make a marriage. I knew your mother well. Catherine loved Blaine enough to give up everything for him, and he loved her. And, though you may not want to believe it, your father loved you. He called you *la petite maîtresse,* 'the little mistress,' because, but for your blue eyes, you were the very image of Catherine, so dark and slender and graceful. I remember the pride in his eyes each time he looked at you."

"Pride and love are two entirely different things," the girl interjected hotly.

"He loved you, Bryna," the nun countered firmly. "I think even now he must love you in his way, and he wishes to show it."

"He should have shown it long ago."

Accustomed to Bryna's temper, which burned white hot in an instant and cooled just as rapidly, the woman was still taken aback by her vehemence.

Kneeling beside Mother Véronique, the girl entreated, "Please, Mother Superior, Hôtel Ste. Anne is my home. Let me stay with you and I promise I will not be a bother."

"You have never been a bother, *chère*," Mother Véronique murmured in a voice choked with emotion. "You know I have prayed about it for some time now, my dear, but the answer is always the same. There is no room here. The orphanage continues to grow. We have known for a year or more that you must soon leave us."

"Unless I take the veil," the girl corrected desperately.

"Bryna, Bryna." The old nun shook her head, tears brimming in her eyes. "You do not have the calling. You have said so yourself."

"There are other things I could do. I have a little money I have saved from what he has sent me, and I am a passable seamstress. I will take in sewing."

"You are gentle-born and convent-educated. Life is hard for a woman alone, and your choices are limited. You have no calling to the church, no place in commerce. You do not wish to be a governess, and you have no prospects for marriage in New Orleans. Perhaps this is for the best. I knew and loved your mother, and I believe she would want you to go to your father."

Bryna buried her face in Mother Véronique's lap. The coarse fabric of the woman's habit did not muffle the misery in her voice. "He is a stranger. I do not want to go to him, Mother Superior. What will I do?"

The nun smoothed Bryna's tousled hair and whispered comfortingly, "Do not cry, my child. Put aside your anger for a moment and listen to me. Though I cannot explain it, I believe this journey is but the first step of the path God has set you on. No one can know what lies ahead, but I think you must make a new life for yourself."

Bryna lifted a pale, resentful face to her beloved guardian. "I will go," she stated deliberately, "but I will leave my savings with you, because as soon as I am of age, I will return. Then I will make a new life. I will choose my own family. I'll love them and they'll love me. And we will never be apart."

CHAPTER

✧✧✧✧✧ **2** ✧✧✧✧✧

IN A CRAMPED CABIN ABOARD THE PACKET SHIP
Mab, Bryna packed her belongings, moving woodenly between the bureau and her open trunk. A little while ago, the Pillars of Hercules, the mountains
that straddled the Straits of Gibraltar, had been
sighted. Now the journey, which had appeared
frightening and long at first, seemed very short.
Soon her old life would be over and her new one
would begin. The past was the past, even last night.

"So there ye are, Bryna." A feminine voice with
a distinct Scottish burr interrupted her thoughts.

Straightening with a start, the girl turned to face
her cabin-mate. "Aggie, I didn't hear you come in."

"I canna say I am actually in. There's scarcely
room for two people to sleep in here at the same
time, let alone to pack." Agnes Moore chuckled.
"Though I canna say it's much better on deck wi'
most of the passengers oot and aboot."

The middle-aged woman's ample figure filled
the doorway. Her pleasant face was pink from sun
and wind. Gray-streaked strands of brown hair had
been blown from her neat bun and floated on the

breeze admitted by the open door. But Aggie's impressive hat, trimmed lavishly with artificial fruit, did not stir, held in place by a huge bow under her double chin.

"Are ye well, lass?" She regarded her young friend worriedly.

"I am fine," Bryna replied with a wan smile, hoping Aggie would question her no further.

"When I dinna see ye topside, I feared ye were peaked." Although she did not voice it, concern thickened her already considerable brogue.

"I was just finishing my packing. You were wise to do it yesterday."

"Not wise, just experienced," the older woman insisted modestly. "I hope I dinna forget anything." She pulled out her ever-present spectacles and peered through them, her nearsighted gaze sweeping the cabin before lighting on Bryna. "Ye're not still nervous aboot meeting yer father?"

"Perhaps a little."

"No need to fear, lass. True, Blaine O'Toole is a silver-tongued rascal. And I've told ye that he and my Gordon are rivals in the spice trade, but 'tis a fine, friendly competition. Do nae worry, Bryna, yer father is a good and fair man." She nodded for emphasis, causing one of the wax cherries on her hat to slide forward and bob in front of her face.

Absently Aggie batted at the fruit with her lorgnette and concluded, "So leave off wi' yer worryin' and come up on deck. 'Tis a glorious day, and if ye do nae come soon, ye'll miss all the excitement of landing. Gibraltar is a wondrous place."

"The captain said we wouldn't dock for another hour," Bryna protested, unwilling to leave the cabin yet. "I'll be up long before then."

"As ye wish," Aggie agreed reluctantly. Her hand on the door latch, she paused. "Are ye sure nothing ails ye?"

"Nothing." Bryna forced her lips to curve in a bright smile. But when the woman turned to leave, she could not keep from blurting, "Aggie, wait! Have you seen Derek . . . Lieutenant Ashburn this morning?"

"So that's it. Naoo, lass, I've nae seen him. I tried to warn ye," she reminded the girl gently, "he's nae one for good-byes. I daresay flirt and fare-thee-well is more his style."

"I suppose," Bryna whispered, certain she would die from misery.

Aggie looked at her shrewdly, but she asked no questions. Instead she cajoled, "Come up soon, lass. We'll find a good spot near the rail. Perhaps ye might even see some of Gibraltar's apes. Besides, a bit of fresh air will do ye good."

Alone in the cabin, the girl tried to collect herself to go out, if only to please Aggie. She had become genuinely fond of the Scotswoman from the moment they'd met on the dock at New Orleans.

How painful the memories of that day were, even now. Bryna and Sister Françoise had waited amid a flurry of farewells as passengers boarded the *Mab,* a luxurious packet. While Mother Véronique spoke to the captain, nearly all the young wards of Hôtel Ste. Anne fidgeted, sweltering in the hot Louisiana sun, eager for the spectacle of the graceful ship's departure.

Her nearsighted eyes fixed on the ship at the end of the pier, Agnes Moore had marched past them, a massive hatbox dangling from her arm. At first sight she had looked stern and matronly, dressed in a traveling dress of stiff black bombazine, but on her head she had worn an extraordinary fabrication of ribbon and netting, topped by a stuffed bird that seemed to gaze intrepidly forward.

When the woman drew even with the captain and Mother Véronique, her head swiveled under the elaborate hat so the bird seemed to stare at them solemnly. The captain greeted the newcomer immediately with a polite bow and introduced her to the mother superior. After a moment both women, still conversing earnestly, walked toward the waiting girl.

"*Chère,* I would like you to meet your cabin-mate, Madame Moore." Speaking in careful English, Mother Véronique gestured toward the woman. "Madame, may I present Mademoiselle Bryna O'Toole. She is traveling to Morocco to join her father."

"I am pleased to meet ye, Miss O'Toole." Aggie rummaged in her reticule and brought out a lorgnette. Holding the lenses in front of her eyes, she looked the girl over carefully. "Much better. I can see naow. Ah, ye hae yer father's eyes."

"You know my father?" Forgetting manners for the moment, Bryna shot up from her curtsey and regarded the woman with surprise.

"Aye, we're nearly neighbors. My husband owns a shipping business on Gibraltar, and we see Blaine every time he comes over from Tangier. He's a charmin' rogue, and I suspect I'll like the daughter as much as I like the father." The woman's plain round face was suddenly transformed by a dazzling smile. Beaming, she folded her eyeglasses and returned them to her bag. "Just call me Aggie, my dear, and I will call you Bryna, if ye do nae mind."

"Please do," Bryna said promptly, warmed by Aggie's magnificent smile.

"Do nae worry aboot Bryna, Reverend Mother," the Scotswoman reassured Mother Véronique. "I'll watch o'er her as if she were one of my own, and we'll get word to her father the moment we land."

"Merci," the nun murmured gratefully, glad Bryna had already found a friend and a chaperone.

Turning to the girl, Aggie added, "I look forward to sharing a cabin wi' ye, lass. Olivia, my next to the youngest, just married a young man here in Louisiana, and I dreaded the long, lonely trip home. I hae five living children, all of them daughters. My youngest, Cassie, is in Scotland visiting family, so I'm traveling alone, and I dinna ken what I would do withoot a bit of youthful companionship."

"Merci beaucoup, Madame Moore." Bryna felt a rush of gratitude for the woman's kindness.

"Aggie, dear, Aggie."

Efficiently the woman recruited a porter to carry their baggage, then considerately waited nearby as the girl bade farewell to the only family she had ever known.

As the Mississippi's current took the *Mab* downriver, the children jumped up and down on the dock and cheered. Bryna stood with Aggie at the railing, waving until the ship rounded a bend and the city disappeared from view. Then she stood still, looking out at the verdant riverbank, tears blurring her vision. Lovingly she fingered the locket she wore around her neck, a parting gift from Mother Véronique, which contained faded pictures of her parents and a lock of her mother's black hair. She would treasure it forever.

At last her new friend stirred and patted her on the shoulder. "Come, let's explore our living quarters, Bryna," she suggested. "D'ye object to sleepin' in the top bunk? We face a considerable problem, ye see, gettin' me into an upper berth."

"I do not mind." Drawing a deep breath, the girl squared her shoulders and put on a brave smile. "Yes, let's explore. I have never seen a ship's cabin before."

"Good girl." The Scotswoman nodded encouragingly. "Ye must always be open to new experiences, for ye ne'er know which might be the greatest adventure of yer life."

Bryna and Aggie were friends before the *Mab* had passed from the channel into the Gulf of Mexico. While they unpacked in their tiny cabin, laughing and bumping into each other with every move, they got to know each other. Soon Bryna found herself pouring out her story. When she had finished, the sympathetic Aggie seemed even more determined than before to protect her young charge.

Accustomed to caring for others, Aggie had no trouble keeping her word to Mother Véronique. As the mother of daughters, she was well practiced in the role of chaperone, and until Lieutenant Derek Ashburn boarded the *Mab* in Bermuda, she could quell the advances of an unsuitable admirer with a single disapproving stare through her lorgnette.

Bryna had been alone at the railing when Derek arrived at the Hamilton dock on Bermuda. Her breath had caught in her throat at the sight of him. Surrounded by a chattering bevy of females, the wives and daughters of his fellow officers who had come to see him off, he was dashing and handsome in his scarlet-and-black uniform. Raptly, Bryna watched as the British soldier made his farewells, bending to kiss the hand of each woman before he turned and strode toward the gangway without a backward look.

The young man was slender and well-proportioned. He carried himself erectly and his shoulders were lithe and muscular. Curly chestnut hair framed his rather aristocratic face and his hazel eyes were warm and amiable the moment they met hers.

Bryna realized with horror that he had seen her gawking at him. He was not yet aboard, and already he would think she was not a real lady. She ducked her head in embarrassment and quickly turned away, but he had seen the interest in her eyes.

Derek introduced himself to Aggie and her ward at dinner that very evening. Although the Scotswoman could not fault his behavior, she made it clear that she did not like him. Toward her, he was a gentleman, polished and courteous, but there was a hint of flirtatiousness in his manner toward Bryna.

The girl was flattered by his attention. For the first time in her life, she felt pretty. For the first time she was being courted, and for the first time she was in love.

Bryna was ecstatic to spend every waking moment with the young Englishman. During the days they strolled the deck endlessly, their heads close as they talked. In the evenings they played chess or talked in the salon, under Aggie's watchful, myopic eye.

"Can't we get away from that old dragon for a while?" Derek finally asked one day as he and Bryna walked around the main deck. "Our promenade this morning has been no fun with her sitting on that bench. This is the fourth time we've passed her, and she glares at me through those spectacles every time."

"Aggie is not an old dragon," the girl defended her friend laughingly. "She's just looking out for me."

"I don't think she sees well enough to look out for you," he muttered. Bending close, he whispered, "Try to get away after dinner, Bryna, and meet me on deck."

"But what—"

"Please come. I want to talk to you." His breath was warm and stirred the hair over her ear.

"I'll try," she promised, trying to ignore the

29

shiver his nearness brought.

That evening Bryna excused herself from the salon early, pleading a headache, and stepped out onto the deserted deck. The wind was high and cool, whipping her skirt against her legs, and the moon had gone behind the clouds. The girl hesitated a moment for her eyes to adjust to the blackness and wondered whether Derek had changed his mind.

"Bryna." She barely heard her name over the creak of the timbers and moan of the wind in the rigging. Her heart pounding, she turned and saw Derek standing in the shadows.

"You . . . you said you wanted to talk to me?" she stammered, suddenly ill at ease.

"I've been waiting for you, love," he murmured.

Capturing her hands, he drew the girl into the shadows beside him. As Bryna looked up at him, she could not see his face clearly in the darkness, but she knew he was going to kiss her, just as certainly as she knew she should protest. But she did not.

When Derek's mouth met hers, Bryna felt a pleasant surge through her body. She parted her lips tentatively and was gratified when his arms tightened around her. Then she gave up thought and experimentation, surrendering herself to blissful, unaccustomed sensation.

Later, when the young man walked her to her cabin door, Bryna thought she saw love in his eyes, and she believed that she and Derek would be together forever.

She had believed—until last night. Unshed tears burned her eyes and tightened her throat. Closing the lid of her trunk with a bang, she sat down on the narrow bunk that had been Aggie's.

Last night she had been such a fool. She had crept out to meet Derek again while her chaperone slept. This time the night had been serene and perfect. The gentle breeze was surprisingly warm and the full moon was reflected on the water. She had flown to his arms, her lips seeking his this time. Then he had led her to a bench, where they'd sat in silence for a time, their backs against the railing as they listened to soft accordion music floating up from steerage. Nestled against Derek's chest, Bryna sighed contentedly.

"What? A sigh? Aren't you happy, my love?" he asked playfully.

"I'm very happy," she murmured.

"As am I, my darling. I will treasure the memory of the last few weeks. I am only sad it is our last night together."

"Our last night?" Sitting bolt upright, she turned to look at him.

"Well, er, yes." He did not meet her gaze. "The captain says we're right on schedule and should arrive in Gibraltar tomorrow. From there you will go on to Tangier to meet your long-lost father, won't you? After a short visit in Gibraltar, I intend to go home to England."

"But . . . " Still searching his face, the girl shifted on the bench until she was outside of circle of his arms.

Derek raised an eyebrow knowingly and shook his head. "Bryna, surely you knew it must end when we reached our destination."

"I thought—" She suddenly wished the night were not so bright that he could see her.

"I am afraid I know what you thought, my dear," he chided gently. "I can always tell a woman with marriage on her mind, and I'm hardly ready for that."

"I thought you loved me. I even let you kiss me."

"I found it very pleasant, but a harmless flirtation doesn't mean I am ready to give up my freedom."

"Perhaps you supposed it to be harmless, monsieur," she said icily, rising to leave.

"Bryna, listen to me." Derek grasped her arm to stay her.

Without saying a word, she looked down pointedly at the hand gripping her arm. Then she lifted icy blue eyes to his in an unspoken command.

Derek released her arm at once, but he requested softly, "Stay a moment, Bryna. At least let me explain."

"Très bien," she said in clipped tones, going to stand by the rail a short distance away, "I would like to hear what you have to offer as an explanation."

"Damn, this is not going well at all." Wearily raking his fingers through his hair, Derek moved to stand behind her.

"What did you expect?" she snapped at him

over her shoulder. "You took advantage of me."

"I did not take advantage of you, Bryna."

"What do you call stealing kisses on a dark deck?"

"Stolen? I judged them freely given," Derek responded tartly. "Are you truly so naive you do not know what could have happened between us?"

When she refused to answer or even to look at him, the young man took Bryna's arm and gently turned her to face him. His hands on her shoulders, he bent toward her, speaking to her as if she were a child. "I never behaved as less than a gentleman with you. But I never offered more than the time we had together here. I enjoyed our little shipboard romance, didn't you?"

"Shipboard romance?" He felt her body stiffen under his hands. "Is that all it was to you—a way to relieve the tedium of a long sea cruise?"

In the darkness, he flushed at the accuracy of her accusation. He had known he wanted to kiss her, to hold her in his arms, from that first day at the dock in Bermuda. Impatiently he countered with a challenge, "Can you say you did not enjoy our time together?"

When she still did not answer, he continued, "You are very sweet, Bryna, but I cannot wed you or even court you. Try to understand: when I marry, I need a wife with position and influence."

"I do understand." Her face, pale in the moonlight, was set and angry as she stared up at him.

"No, you don't," he disagreed, shaking his head. "I think you're an exquisite, delightful girl, Bryna, but if I cannot marry you, I will not insult you by offering you anything less."

"Do you really think I would consent to anything less?" She drew herself up proudly and glared at him.

"Nothing I say seems quite right tonight." Derek sighed, wishing he could undo the damage of this conversation. "I am sorry if I hurt you."

"I do not need your apologies, Monsieur Ashburn, or your pity," Bryna replied curtly. "Good night and good-bye." With all the dignity she could muster, she turned and walked away.

CHAPTER

✧✧✧✧✧ **3** ✧✧✧✧✧

"SEE THE TALL MOUNTAIN O'ER THERE?" AGGIE pointed across the narrow Straits of Gibraltar toward the purple hills of North Africa. "That's one of the Pillars of Hercules, Jabal Mūsā."

Bryna listened politely, her face set resolutely toward shore. She presented a rigid back to the travelers ranged along the deck behind her, but she was acutely aware of them and grateful that Derek was nowhere to be seen.

"Soon ye'll see something truly magnificent." The woman turned her eyeglasses to the port side of the ship. "Any moment now."

Just then the *Mab* veered toward the coast of Spain, and before them rose a mighty rock that could only be Gibraltar.

"Look at it!" Aggie cried, disarranging her elaborate hat with her lorgnette as she bounced with excitement. "What a bonny sight! And what a fine thing to be home again!"

"It is impressive," Bryna agreed, squinting against the blinding sun. Above them the cliff face loomed, gray and barren against the vivid blue sky.

"'Tis indeed," the Scotswoman agreed proudly. "Its Arab name is Jabal Târiq, after the Moorish sultan who conquered Spain."

"I thought there was a city here." A woman's plaintive voice reached them from down the deck. "I thought we were going ashore."

"We will indeed go ashore, madame," the captain answered heartily, "but I fear you've been misinformed. Gibraltar is not a city, only a small town."

"I do not see how anyone could live in this desolate place," the woman responded dubiously. "It looks as if it is washed by the sea on every side."

"We know better." Aggie winked at her young friend merrily. Barefoot sailors scampered in the rigging overhead, furling the sails as they were lowered. The *Mab* veered again slightly and the tiny town of Gibraltar, built in a cleft between cliff and sea, came into view. Slowly now the ship neared the dock. On shore, the scarlet uniform of the English army and the plaid kilts of the Highland regiment stood out in sharp contrast with the somber black suits of Spanish merchants and the white robes of city Arabs.

"Where can Gordon be?" Aggie fretted, peering anxiously through her lorgnette. "Surely he'll nae be late to meet me." Suddenly the sweep of her spectacles over the dock halted and she clutched Bryna's arm with her free hand. "There he is. That's my Gordon, that handsome man comin' around the warehouse there. D'ye see him?"

"I see him," Bryna affirmed. She spotted the portly man with flaming red hair and whiskers

36

emerging from a narrow side street and picking his way through the dark-skinned crowd. It would be difficult to miss Gordon Moore anywhere, she decided.

Suddenly the girl's gaze fell on a slender young man wearing an English uniform, and her heart gave a lurch. His nonchalant stance and sleek good looks reminded her disturbingly of Derek. Quickly she averted her eyes, her attention returning to Aggie's smiling husband. Gordon stood with his hands clasped behind his back. The picture of a prosperous merchant, he rocked gently on his heels while he waited for the *Mab* to tie up.

Dragging the girl by the hand, Aggie charged toward the gangplank, nearly bowling over the more sedate passengers in her path. She and Bryna were the first to disembark. Gordon stepped forward expectantly, and the couple flew to each other's arms, both talking at once, excitement broadening the burr in their voices.

Unwilling to intrude on the joyful reunion, Bryna lingered near bottom of gangplank. Awkwardly she turned to watch the other passengers disembark. When Derek appeared at the top of the gangway, she whirled hastily and found Gordon inspecting her curiously.

She was a comely lass, the Scotsman decided at once, a bit tall, but she had a fragile look about her with that dark hair and fair skin. He suspected strength and determination were masked by those delicate features that with enormous blue eyes gave her face an almost fairylike quality. Her pale blue traveling dress was modest in cut and very proper, but it did not disguise the curves of her slender figure. At the base of her throat nestled a simple oval locket, engraved with roses. She wore no other jewelry, but she bore herself like a queen.

"Aye, ye're an O'Toole." He nodded approvingly. "I can tell just by looking at ye. My Aggie says ye're a fine lass. Welcome to Gibraltar, Mistress Bryna. I'm Gordon Moore."

"Bonjour, M'sieur Moore, and thank you. I am pleased to meet you at last. Your wife has told me so much about you."

"All of it fond lies. Ye know my Aggie is blind, but did ye know her blindness was caused by love?" With a grin he drew his protesting wife to his side. "I do nae see yer father," he said to Bryna. "If I know Blaine O'Toole he dinna know which boat ye were on or he would hae been here. Do nae worry aboot a thing, lass. We'll take ye to our house and send word to him."

"Merci. How long will it take him to arrive?"

"If he's in Tangier, he should be here within two days. If nae, it may take a bit longer. But no matter, ye're welcome to stay wi' us as long as ye need to."

Across the dock, Derek joined his cousin, Frederick Masterson.

"Welcome to Gibraltar, cuz," Freddie greeted him. "Ready for a bit of fun?"

"I could use some excitement," Derek agreed heartily. "Lord, but I'm tired of serving in every dead little outpost in His Majesty's realm. I am thinking seriously of resigning my commission."

"No." Freddie was shocked. "You'll feel differently after your furlough."

"I doubt it. I haven't had a reasonable assignment in two years. You can't imagine the heat in the Caribbean."

"And you can't imagine the heat in the Mediterranean," Freddie answered blithely. "Well, I vow our casinos will outdo anything they've got in Bermuda."

"You can be sure of it."

"I say, are you still devilish lucky at cards?"

"Devilish lucky," Derek confirmed, conveniently forgetting the stack of IOUs he had nearly bankrupted himself to pay before leaving his last post.

But Freddie had stopped listening. His eyes were on Bryna and her companions. "I say, who is that beauty?" he asked urgently. "Was she on the ship with you?"

"Her name is Bryna O'Toole."

"O'Toole? Is she related to O'Toole Effendi?" Freddie asked excitedly. Then, noting his cousin's puzzled look, he explained hastily, "That's what the natives call Blaine O'Toole. He is one of the wealthiest traders in North Africa. Used to be a mercenary soldier—a colonel, I think. But he's a civilian now and made a fortune in spices."

"How wealthy is this O'Toole?" Derek's tone was casual.

"Wealthy enough to bribe his way into business

in Morocco. No easy task, that. Hear he lives like a bloody king in Tangier."

"Didn't the sultan close the country to all foreigners?"

"He closed the interior," Freddie corrected. "It's risky, but European ships go in and out of Tangier all the time. A few brave and very prosperous kaffirs—that means infidels, y'know—even live there. You never said, is she related to Blaine O'Toole?"

"I believe he is her father," Derek responded dryly.

"Do tell." His cousin whistled under his breath, his gaze still on Bryna. "She's stunning. Can you introduce me?"

"You'd be wasting your time, old man. She's a lovely girl, but rather young and unsophisticated."

"Who cares?"

"Indeed, who cares?" the other man answered slowly. He watched her as she left the dock. There was more to Bryna O'Toole than met the eye, he decided. Throwing a companionable arm over his cousin's shoulder, Derek urged, "Tell me more about O'Toole Effendi, Freddie."

"I will, under two conditions."

"Yes?" Derek regarded the other man warily.

"One, you buy me dinner. Hadn't finished luncheon when your ship was sighted, and I'm famished."

"All right. And two?"

"Two, I'll tell you about him if you will tell me about his daughter," Freddie bargained with a stubborn glint in his eye.

"Agreed." Derek laughed aloud.

"Marvelous. Never know when I might undertake an expedition to Tangier myself. Wouldn't want to miss an opportunity to woo an heiress, y'know."

"I know, cuz, I know."

"We really must find you a decent suit of clothes, old man. Ain't right that you should wear your uniform on furlough, especially if you're thinking of becoming a civilian."

"You can take me to your tailor after you've told me about O'Toole, Freddie."

"After you've bought me dinner," the other man retorted. Then, arm in arm, the cousins strolled to Freddie's carriage.

"My Olivia dinna need this in Louisiana. I thought ye might use it." Aggie held out a simple, elegant hat with a thick lace veil for Bryna's inspection.

"Oh, no, Aggie, I cannot," the girl protested. "You and Gordon have done too much for me already, letting me stay with you, taking me to see the sights and listening to my problems."

"Nae such thing. We've enjoyed yer company the last two days." Aggie patted Bryna's hand fondly. "As for yer problems, if ye're only hurt the once in love, 'twould seem ye're ahead of the game. Besides, Derek Ashburn is nae worth the tears ye've shed o'er him. One day ye'll find a good and true

41

man. Naow go on, lass, try on the hat."

"Merci, Aggie." Bryna smiled and obeyed, turning so the woman could adjust the heavy netting over her face.

"'Tis only a wee thing," Aggie said ruefully, "but it has a veil, which ye're goin' to need in Tangier. Moslems are nae keen on seein' a woman's face, nae even one as bonny as yers. And Islamic law is the law of Morocco, of all the Arab world."

"Señora Moore . . . " The maid's quiet voice from the doorway startled the women. "Your husband asks you and the young lady to come downstairs, *por favor.*"

Whipping the hat from her head, Bryna smoothed her hair and followed the Scotswoman downstairs, where they found Gordon waiting in the hall outside the ornately decorated parlor.

"There ye are, ladies. Come in, come in," he greeted them heartily, ushering them into the room that looked as if it had been whisked from Edinburgh in the twinkling of an eye.

Stopping in the center, Gordon cleared his throat noisily to alert its only occupant. The tall man who stood at the window overlooking the garden, his back to them, turned, and Bryna found herself staring into blue eyes that exactly mirrored her own.

"Bryna, lass, I want ye to meet . . . " Her host foundered, seemingly at a loss.

"Blaine O'Toole, my father," she finished for him, her voice level and expressionless. She stared at the big Irishman with no welcome in her eyes.

"Petite maîtresse, can it be you?" Crossing the rich Turkey carpet in two strides, Blaine took Bryna's unwilling hand in his. "You are beautiful, as beautiful as your mother."

"Merci." She accepted the compliment coolly. Freeing the hand he had captured, she increased the distance between them.

A shadow crossed the man's handsome face, but he forced a charming smile and turned to Agnes. "Hullo, Aggie, m'dear, welcome home. Thank you for looking after Bryna until I could get here."

"It was nae hardship, O'Toole. Ye've a fine daughter."

But neither O'Toole heard. They scarcely seemed to realize the Moores were still present. From opposite corners of the room, they regarded each other intently.

Uncomfortable in the prolonged silence, Aggie fluffed a pillow on the hard horsehair couch and said nervously, "Well, sit down, then. Can I get ye a cool drink, Blaine?"

With effort, the man transferred his attention from his daughter to his hostess. "No thanks, Aggie, Gordon has already seen to my comfort. You've taught him well," he teased.

"Well, then . . . " Meaningfully she caught her husband's eye.

"Ah, yes. Well, then." Gordon took the hint with relief. He tucked his wife's hand in the crook of his arm and led her toward the door, calling over his shoulder, "Aggie and I will leave ye for a while. Ye must hae a lot to catch up on."

"A lot to catch up on indeed," Blaine muttered, watching the couple leave. Turning, he invited, "Won't you sit down, *ma petite*?"

"*Non, merci*," Bryna replied, her chin lifted rebelliously. "I prefer to stand."

"As you wish," the man agreed amiably. Dropping onto a chair, he stretched his long legs out in front of him. "I hope you do not mind if I sit." The smile he turned on the girl was disarming as he asked, "Where do we begin, Bryna O'Toole?"

"Why don't you tell me why you sent for me?" she answered evenly.

"Because I wanted to see you, to have you with me."

"After all these years?"

"Yes, after all these years." He nodded gravely. "I decided 'twas time."

"And you never thought I might not want to come?"

"I thought of it."

"Or that I would have plans for my own life?" she continued in a rush. Her color high, she paced in front of his chair.

"I knew you had no real plans." He dismissed her objections with a shrug.

"What!" Bryna's head swiveled, and she glared at him through narrowed eyes.

"Mother Superior wrote that you were not destined for a life in the church. Thank God," he added incongruously. "And I knew that you had no prospects for marriage."

"Mother Véronique wrote to you about me?"

"Someone had to," Blaine responded dryly, "since you did not answer my letters."

"I never read them."

"So the mother superior wrote me. She was most concerned that you never opened them. I thought it curious, too . . . since you kept them."

"She apparently wrote you a great deal."

"Twice a year, the sainted lady sent me reports on your progress. So you see, I know you better than you think."

"Based on some thirty letters?" Bryna cut in sarcastically. "You do not know me. You might know that I was a good student or that I broke my arm when I was ten, but you do not know me any better than I know you."

"I know you've got a sharp tongue." Bryna's father frowned. His limited supply of patience was dwindling. "I must tell you, *chère,* for all you look like your mother, you certainly do not have her sweet disposition."

"If my mother had not been so sweet, perhaps she could have made you remember your responsibilities," the girl retorted.

"I never forgot my responsibilities." Blaine sprang from his chair and scowled at his daughter.

"Oh, yes." Bryna met his gaze defiantly, showing no inclination to retreat. "You always sent money for my keep, didn't you? Perhaps someday I can repay you."

"With what?" the man roared, bending so his face was close to hers. "Your sewing money? 'Twould be a fine life for the daughter of Blaine

O'Toole. I'm the one who'll be taking care of you, young lady. You might be interested to know that I am a successful merchant. I thought you might be willing, even glad, to share in my good fortune."

Bryna looked singularly unimpressed, but before she could reply, a rap sounded on the door and Aggie peeked into the room. Behind her lorgnette, her weak eyes blinked at the two irate faces turned impatiently toward her.

"Sorry to interrupt," she apologized with a determinedly cheery smile, "but dinner is nearly ready and I thought you might want to freshen up."

"Merci." Bryna swept from the room without a look back.

"It got noisy in here quickly, O'Toole," their hostess said accusingly as Blaine looked after the girl, frowning.

"Ah, Aggie." He sighed. "I've undertaken a great project here, winning over my own daughter."

"Aye," she concurred, "but ye're not likely to win her wi' a display of yer Irish temper."

"She was showing just as much temper as I was," he muttered.

"No doubt. She inherited yer finer points—enormous pride, a quick temper, winsome blue eyes—and she canna sit still when she's upset."

"She's an O'Toole all right." Blaine chuckled despite himself.

"Aye. Since neither of ye are especially forbearin', ye're goin' to hae to gi' each other time. That's what it takes to build love and trust."

"Trust is liable to take a great deal of time," he

remarked soberly. "She's been hurt. I see it in her eyes."

"And I see it in yers, Blaine. I have for as long as I've known ye," Aggie said softly.

He shot her a harassed look, then returned to his post beside the window. For a moment the woman thought he was not going to speak. When he faced her again, his expression was bleak. "I don't think the ache has stopped since I left New Orleans all those years ago. Oh, it ebbs and flows, but 'tis always there."

"And ye always faced it alone."

"Aye. I see now that I left Bryna to another kind of loneliness." Blaine began to pace. "The child thinks I did not love her. I cannot excuse my behavior, Aggie, but I can explain it. I have always planned to have her with me."

"I believe ye, but ye must make Bryna believe," the woman said softly. "And it's been so long."

"Do you think it is too late?" He halted his pacing midstride.

"Naooo." Aggie's watery eyes gauged his apprehension before she added, "But ye must talk to her."

"I will, if she will give me a chance."

"She will." She nodded wisely. "But as I said before, hae patience. And once ye've won her trust, O'Toole, take care ye ne'er let her down again."

"Welcome to Mahgreb al Aqsa, the Land Farthest West," Blaine boomed as their sloop neared the dock. "And welcome to Tangier *la blanche.*"

Blaine loved the panorama of his adopted city, sun-baked and whitewashed, scaling the cliff that rose behind it, but he was hardly aware of it. Stealing a glance at Bryna, who sat silently beside him, he was pleased to see the first signs of interest she had shown since they'd sailed from Gibraltar. During the short passage, her face had been closed and guarded and she had spoken only in polite response to his efforts at conversation. At last he had given up.

Aware of her father's scrutiny, Bryna was grateful for the veil she had donned when they'd neared the coast of North Africa. She had taken care with her dress this morning, selecting a dark, sedate frock with long sleeves.

"Ye may swelter in the heat, my dear, but ye'll be extremely proper to the Arab way of thinkin'," Aggie had assured her.

While the boat tied up, the girl surveyed her surroundings curiously, watching raptly as dark-skinned men wearing turbans and the loose-fitting robes called djellabas milled about. Some of them worked, some waited, but all seemed to be shouting. Loud and strident, the cacophony engulfed the travelers the moment they stepped ashore.

Suddenly, from the heights, a haunting cry rose and hung in the air, seeming to increase in volume as a hush fell over those assembled at the dock. Most of the men turned and walked silently toward the city, disappearing into the narrow streets. After

New Orleans led up to an open gallery. On either side of the hall were a library and a dining room. There was no parlor. Blaine had not wanted one. He chose instead to make the common rooms spacious and cool with high cedar ceilings and to decorate them with colorful native mosaic tiles.

Along the gallery upstairs, four carved doors opened into four splendid bedchambers. Bryna felt a stir of excitement when Fatima opened the one at the far end and gestured for her to enter. She had never had a room of her own.

Poised in the doorway, she did not stifle her gasp this time. The room was huge, almost as large as the girl's dormitory at Hôtel Ste. Anne, and it was beautiful. Here, too, foreign melded with familiar. It seemed as if Blaine had drawn from bazaars and markets around the world to make the room a refuge for his daughter. Colorful mosaics adorned the walls, rich Turkey carpets were spread on the tile floor, and polished brass lamps hung from the blue-and-gilt ceiling. But under latticed windows, open to admit the breeze, was placed a tester bed, incongruous with its rose silk hangings and spread. Later Bryna learned he had imported the bed from England just for her.

After a light lunch of thinly sliced cold lamb, Bryna slept until late afternoon, awakening to the cry of the muezzin. As she bathed behind a rattan screen, she could hear Fatima shambling about the room, lighting a lamp against the dusk, laying out her clothes for dinner.

The girl lingered until her water cooled, postponing another meeting with her father. If they argued again tonight, it was no more than he deserved, she told herself rebelliously. Rising, she reached for a towel and began to rub her body vigorously.

Everyone—Mother Véronique, Sister Françoise, even Aggie—seemed to think she could simply forget sixteen years of neglect, Bryna fumed. Everyone found Blaine charming. A silver-tongued rascal, Aggie had called him. They urged her to hear his side of the story. Well, in the entire twenty-four hours she had known him he hadn't told his story, if he had one, she thought disagreeably.

Although she hadn't really given him a chance. The towel still clutched in her hand, the girl slowed her actions as she guiltily recalled his efforts to draw her into the conversation at dinner last night. And this morning he had been solicitous while she had been silent and unresponsive. I suppose I could listen to what he has to say, she thought grudgingly, but he is not going to charm me. I will have the explanation he owes me.

Downstairs, Blaine wandered restlessly from the courtyard to the library. How could he say what he needed to say to his daughter? How was he to deal with her coldness? True, he hardly knew her, but damn it, she was his daughter, his and Catherine's. Surely the girl had some feeling for him—he was her father.

She looked so much like Cathy, Blaine reflected

sadly, but there was a steel about Bryna that his delicate wife had never had. Bryna was a survivor, he suspected, a strong, unforgiving survivor. He did not know if he could win her love or her trust.

Heaving a deep sigh, the man stepped out onto the terrace. The city sprawled below him, and lights flickered on a hundred rooftops where Arab families gathered in the cool of the evening. There, mint tea was being sipped and stories as old as the desert were being told. Faint laughter carried up to him in the still night, and he listened in a melancholy mood.

He was unaware when Bryna entered the dark room behind him. Catching sight of him through the open doors to the terrace, she did not make her presence known, taking a moment to watch him.

Her father was a virile man, his lithe, muscular body hardened by years of soldiering. His erect carriage, another reminder of his military days, made him seem even taller than his six feet. Blaine's wavy auburn hair was sprinkled with silver at the temples, the only evidence of his forty years. Time and the sun had had surprising little effect on his lean, bronzed face. A network of wrinkles at the corners of his twinkling blue eyes seemed to add to his appeal, as did the lines that played beside his sensual mouth each time he smiled his ready smile.

He was handsome, Bryna had to admit. She remembered almost nothing of her mother, but Catherine's picture revealed a delicate beauty. What a delightful couple they must have made.

"*Bon soir,* my dear. You look lovely this

evening." The man turned.

"Merci," Bryna responded uncomfortably, on her guard as Blaine entered the room, clapping his hands loudly. Instantly Yusef appeared to light the lamps.

When the old servant had gone, her father gestured toward a pair of chairs that flanked a small table and suggested almost shyly, "Shall we have some wine before dinner? I would like to talk to you."

"Très bien." She sat down on one of the chairs, busily arranging her skirt to keep from meeting his eyes.

Blaine poured two glasses of fine red wine. Handing her one, he sat across from her and lifted his glass for a toast.

"Here's to saying what must be said," he offered seriously.

"Oui, to what must be said." Bryna finally met his gaze. Father and daughter regarded each other silently for a moment over their glasses, then awkwardly each looked away.

At last Blaine cleared his throat nervously and said, "There is so much I want to tell you, Bryna."

"Please just tell me this. Why didn't you ever come back for me?"

Blaine nearly choked on his wine at the abruptness of the question, but he managed to swallow and draw a deep, steadying breath. Choosing his words carefully, he said, "I had no way to keep you with me. I did what I thought best."

"By trying to foist me off on my *grandpère?*"

she countered bitterly. "That loving gentleman didn't want me, either."

"'Twas his loss. Mine was that I wanted you with me and I couldn't have you."

"You wanted me so much, you left me at the orphanage thinking no one cared for me but the sisters."

The big man looked pained, but he said nothing in his defense. Encompassed by anger right now, she would not hear his explanation. He only hoped that when the time was right, the wish he expressed in his toast would be granted. Then they would say what must be said. Then and only then could respect and trust and even love grow between them.

Concentrating on the glass she clutched so tightly that her knuckles were white, Bryna did not see the turmoil in Blaine's face. "All these years . . ." she whispered harshly.

"I am sorry, lass," he responded gently, wishing she would look at him. "I always planned to send for you, but I had to do what I thought best for you, the daughter Catherine had borne me.

"I never should have left your mother, Bryna. She was beautiful and so delicate. But I had already accepted my last commission, the one that would pay for a home of our own. Besides, even mercenaries have a code of honor. I was obligated to do my duty—or what I considered my duty—one last time.

"When the news of her death reached me, I . . . I went a little mad for a time. I volunteered for every foolhardy mission. When I was not trying to kill myself in battle, I was drinking, wenching, trying to forget."

"But you could not forget?" While she listened, Bryna's hand rose involuntarily to caress the locket she wore.

"Never." Blaine shook his head firmly. "When I finally came to my senses, I knew I still could not send for you. What would I have done with a wee one? Hauled you from camp to camp? Placed you in the care of camp followers each time I went into battle, praying I would return? You were better off with the sisters.

"I gave up soldiering then and became involved in setting up trade routes to the East. When I began to prosper as a merchant, I did send for you."

"You did?" Guarded but willing to believe, Bryna watched her father.

"Aye, but Mother Véronique convinced me that my life was still too unsettled to bring up a child.

"Now wait—" he cautioned when the girl's mouth dropped open in surprise, "—I'll not hear any angry words about that fine lady. She was right. 'Twouldn't have been fair to drag you halfway around the world and hand you over to a native nurse. You see, I could not remarry, for I've compared every woman to Cathy."

"So you and Mother Véronique decided that if I did not have a mother, I could not have a father, either?" Bryna muttered rebelliously.

"Bryna Jean-Marie O'Toole, look at me," Blaine ordered quietly, rising to stand before her.

Unwillingly she obeyed and was surprised to see tenderness and entreaty in his blue eyes. "You do have a father," he informed her gently, "though not a very good one. I realized recently that you would soon be a woman full grown and I had never known you. I've never told you that I love you. I've never asked you to forgive me."

"To forgive you?" she repeated warily.

"Yes." Silently Blaine awaited his daughter's judgment.

Bryna sat very still, her gaze fixed on the night beyond the terrace doors. At last she sighed and shook her head as if to clear it. "Next to pride and patience, Sister Françoise's favorite subject was forgiveness."

Blaine exhaled in a rush, realizing for the first time that he had been holding his breath. Taking her hands in his, he pulled her from her chair and asked urgently, "Then you'll forgive me, *petite maîtresse*?"

"I will try to forgive you, but I warn you, I do not know if I can forget."

"'Tis not much time, but you have six weeks to find out." He grinned weakly when she stared at him with shock. "That is how long you have given me, isn't it, 'til your eighteenth birthday?"

"Another of Mother Véronique's letters?" she asked ruefully.

"Aye."

"Six weeks may be enough, but it could take longer. We shall see." Unexpectedly her lips curved in a smile. "I wouldn't want to make it too easy for you, Blaine O'Toole."

He swooped suddenly and planted a kiss on top of her head. "Daughter, you're a woman after my own heart. Take as long as you like, *chère,* take as long as you like."

CHAPTER

✧✧✧✧✧ **4** ✧✧✧✧✧

THE HEAT OF THE DAY WAS NOT QUITE OVER when Bryna wandered through the empty rooms of Blaine's luxurious home, the skirt of her pink cotton dress swaying, her bare feet slapping softly on the cool tile floor. Enervated by the heat of Tangier, the girl understood the native custom of kef, rest during the afternoon, but she couldn't sleep. While the teeming city was quiet, she roamed the deserted house.

Accustomed to being surrounded by people at Hôtel Ste. Anne, she was oddly unsettled by her solitude. Here, even the servants napped in the afternoon. Morocco and its customs still felt so alien to her, she wondered if she would ever be at ease.

At last she padded out into the tiny walled garden below the house, burning her feet on the sun-baked steps. She found a shady spot under a tree and plopped down with a mighty sigh, uncaring that she was soiling her skirt. She leaned her head against the puny tree trunk and closed her eyes.

Suddenly it occurred to her that she missed

Blaine. She had seen him off on a business trip at dawn that very morning, but already she missed him. She would not have believed it five days ago.

After a while—she did not know how long—Bryna became aware of the sun, scorchingly hot through the fabric of her skirt. Swatting drowsily at an insect that droned around her face, she opened her eyes to discover the lower half of her body was no longer in the shadow of the tree. She must have dozed off. Shifting to take advantage of the shade that was left, the girl lethargically contemplated going inside.

Yusef appeared on the steps to the terrace and frowned at her. His skimpy gray hair was disarranged so his bald pate showed through, and his clothes were rumpled. Obviously his kef had been disturbed.

"There is a gentleman to see you in the library," he announced. Disapproval dripped from every syllable.

"A gentleman?" Bryna sat up in surprise. "I know no one in Tangier. Are you sure he does not wish to see my father?"

"*Non,* mademoiselle, he insists he must see you right away. I told him you were resting, but he is *Inglayzi*—an Englishman—and he would not understand."

Brushing the dirt from her skirt, the girl followed the disgruntled servant to the house. As her feet met the cool tile floor, she remembered that she wore no shoes, but before she could retreat, Derek Ashburn, handsome in an elegant new suit, was at her side.

"Bryna, I was afraid you would not see me," he greeted her, pressing his lips fervently to her hand.

"What are you doing here, Derek?" she asked, shocked beyond polite conversation. Shaking with sudden anger, she yanked her hand from his. He could hardly think he was welcome after the things he had said to her on the *Mab.* But miserably she realized her fury was directed at herself as much as at him. She had told herself a hundred times in the past five days that she hated the arrogant young Englishman. Yet now that he was here, as attractive in his civilian clothing as he had been in his scarlet uniform, she felt nothing but confusion and an unwanted attraction.

"I came to see you, of course." Seemingly unfazed, Derek bestowed a winning smile upon her. "I've been so wrong, my darling. Will you forgive me?"

"I'm sorry you made such a long trip in vain, Monsieur Ashburn." She swept past him haughtily, displaying more composure than she felt. "I do not think we have anything to say to each other."

"Please, Bryna, just listen to me for a moment." Derek followed her. Her back to him, the girl did not see the flicker of triumph in his hazel eyes when she halted, torn by her emotions.

Taking her by the arm, he gently turned her to face him and lifted her chin until her unwilling eyes met his. A rueful smile on his handsome face, he argued almost teasingly, "You must forgive me, you see. I cannot bear it if you will not."

"Derek, I do not—"

He shook his head as if discouraging a pampered child from an ill-advised deed. Then, placing a finger to her lips to silence her, he coaxed, "Come and sit down so we can talk."

"All right," Bryna agreed reluctantly, hating herself as she allowed him to lead her to a chair. She sat with her head bent, her eyes fixed on her hands clasped in her lap and her feet tucked beneath her skirt.

Kneeling on the floor beside her, the man addressed her earnestly. "Since you left me that night on the boat, my love, I haven't been able to get you out of my mind. I've been in Gibraltar for the past five days trying to work up my courage to come here and apologize for the terrible things I said. You surely know I did not mean them.

"I was afraid of losing my freedom, you see," he explained with just the right amount of amused disbelief in his voice. "Now I know what an idiot I've been. Now I know I want to spend my life with you. I plan to resign my commission and I want to take you with me—as my wife—when I return to England."

He paused, staring at her profile, inviting a response. When she didn't answer, he placed a hand on her shoulder and continued doggedly, "Did you hear what I said, my love? I want to marry you. I intend to ask your father for your hand."

"That night on the *Mab*, you were not willing to wed me or even to court me," she answered, staring straight ahead. "Isn't that what you said? You told me I was not the kind of wife you needed. What were your words? Let me see if I can remember—"

"Forget what I said that night. Forget what a fool I've been." Derek's hand tightened on her shoulder and he said urgently, "Bryna, I'm telling you I love you."

The face she turned to him was dismayed. Derek claimed he loved her, now that it was too late. How could it be true after the cruel things he'd said? She couldn't deny she'd felt a thrill of attraction when she found him here in the library today, but was that love?

"Say you will marry me, Bryna," he pressed.

"I cannot, Derek." The girl's gaze returned to her hands, and her voice was not above a whisper.

She was refusing him? A look of disbelief flitted across Derek's handsome face before he schooled his expression. "Will you always hate me?" he asked, downcast. His grip on her shoulder loosened, and his hand dropped to hang dejectedly at his side.

"I don't hate you." She sighed ruefully.

"You mean there is hope?" he crowed, his countenance brightening. "Then I will call on you. I'll call every day until I win you over. I'll make you love me, Bryna."

"I don't know what to say." Bryna rose and walked to the doors to look out over the garden.

"Say you love me, too." She heard him rise and step toward her. "You know you care for me. Remember all those moonlit nights on the *Mab*?"

"Derek . . ." When Bryna turned, she found him standing very close. He made no move toward her, but he was so near she could feel his warmth. Almost shyly she looked into his hazel eyes and was assailed by memories of being held in his arms. Her heart pounded and her breath was short. "I . . . I do not know what I feel."

"I have overwhelmed you, haven't I, sweetheart?" Derek's voice was low and amused. "I don't think I ever realized how small and fragile you are. Why, you only reach my shoulder! And you're even more beautiful than I remembered. I was a fool to let you go," he said fervently, convincing himself as thoroughly as the girl.

"I shouldn't have been so vehement, darling, but I had to tell you how I feel. I'll go now, but I'll return tomorrow and the next day and the next, until you admit that you love me as much as I love you."

"Please, Derek—" she began to object.

"No, my darling, I will do what I must." Drawing Bryna into his arms, he kissed her tenderly, chastely. But before his nearness had time to cast its spell on her, he released her.

"Until tomorrow, my love."

"Until tomorrow," she murmured, bemused. Perched on the edge of the chair she had recently vacated, she stretched her legs out in front of her. Serious thought was vanquished when she caught sight of her toes, pink under a coating of dust, peeping from under her skirts. A mischievous grin lurked suddenly at the corners of her mouth. He had thought she was small and fragile when she was only barefoot.

Then another fanciful thought occurred to her. In bare feet, she had just entertained a proposal of marriage from the very proper Derek Ashburn. Did he need a wife with only position and influence, or must she also have shoes? The idea of an unshod Mrs. Ashburn struck the girl as very funny, and her shoulders shook with her laughter. She was grateful no one could see her fit of hilarity. The servants would probably think her mad.

She probably was mad even to consider marrying Derek, she realized, suddenly sober. Did he love her or the fact that she was now an heiress? She would give much to know whether his last five days had been spent learning about her father's business.

Sighing deeply, she went into the dusky courtyard. What strange tricks life plays, she mused, sinking onto the stone bench beside the fountain. For years she'd thought no one loved her; now she had a father and a suitor.

She sat, lost in thought, until the call of the muezzin. Night had fallen, she realized. It was past time for dinner, and Fatima had not come for her. In fact, she had not seen any of the servants for some time. Puzzled, she listened for sounds from the house.

Suddenly Bryna's head reeled with the pain from a brutal blow. Lights danced before her eyes, dimming as she slumped to the ground at the feet of her assailant. No one stirred in the house as the rough Arab nudged the girl with his booted foot, rolling her onto her back to be sure she still breathed. Moving unhurriedly, he sliced a piece of fabric from her pink skirt and secured it to the outside of the gate with a small ornate dagger.

"Let there be no doubt," the man muttered grimly. "O'Toole must know Gasim Al Auf has taken his daughter and understand the reason." Flinging the girl's limp body over his shoulder, he stole into the night.

The injured girl lay very still, not daring to stir. Clenching her teeth, she steeled herself against another wave of bitter bile that burned the back of her throat. She swallowed hard and willed herself not to retch. Moving her head slightly, she gasped as an excruciating pain exploded behind her closed eyes. Lights flickered inside her lids again, now bright and red-tinged.

"She's coming around, I think," Bryna heard a female voice exclaim excitedly. The cultured English accent of the speaker cut through a discordant rise and fall of otherworldly wails whirling around her pounding head.

She opened her eyes and blearily surveyed the murky darkness of a tiny, windowless room. Groggily she focused on the fragile, blond-haired girl who leaned over her.

"I say, are you all right?" the British girl asked anxiously.

"I think so," Bryna answered hoarsely in English, stirring tentatively on the blanket that shielded her from the hard-packed dirt floor.

"We've been ever so worried about you. You've scarcely stirred since they brought you in last night."

"Last night? Where am I?" Bryna attempted to sit up but succeeded only in jostling her throbbing head.

"Slowly, dear, you've quite a goose egg," the other girl warned, pressing her reluctant patient back on a filthy pillow.

"Who are you?" Bryna asked curiously. Her nurse was young and obviously a gentlewoman, though her patrician face was streaked with dirt and her hair matted and dirty.

"I am Pamela Hampton-White," the girl responded, graciously offering her hand. "And like you, I am a captive of the slave trader Nejm Al Anwar."

"A slave trader?" Wincing, Bryna lifted herself onto one elbow. "Where are we?"

"We are still in Tangier, but I do not know for how long." Pamela's chin quivered, but she continued bravely, "We are, all of us, to be sold into bondage. Even those poor wretches from among his own people." She gestured toward the opposite corner of the filthy room.

Bryna peered through the gloom, where she discerned a huddle of black-clad Arab women who clung to each other, a tragic chorus that lamented its fate loudly. Their voices rose and ebbed, echoing off the high-domed ceiling of the minuscule chamber.

"We cannot be sold into slavery," Bryna muttered disbelievingly.

"Of course we can," a contemptuous voice disagreed from nearby. "This is Morocco."

"May I present Condesa Theresa Delgado, a noblewoman of Spain." Pamela directed the newcomer's attention to the source of the voice. Bryna twisted gingerly on her pallet to see another woman in European dress, sitting behind her with her back to the clay brick wall. Theresa nodded disdainfully, her demeanor haughty even under these adverse conditions.

"Theresa was captured by pirates."

"They had the audacity to attack my father's yacht," the Spanish girl fumed. "The Conde Tomas Ramone Fernando Delgado, the most powerful man in Ceuta." The nostrils of her aquiline nose flared with indignation.

"Yes, yes, Theresa," Pamela interrupted soothingly, having heard the story a dozen times. "May I introduce . . . " She faltered. "I am sorry, what is your name?"

"Bryna O'Toole."

"How do you do, Bryna," Pamela replied courteously. "I am happy to meet you, whatever the circumstances."

"I am glad to meet you, Pamela," the Creole girl responded inanely, "and you, Theresa." She nodded to the other woman, who obviously took it as her due. Still propped on her elbow, she muttered more to herself than to her companions, "Surely there is a way out of this situation. Some law—"

"You are in the Islamic world now," Theresa scoffed. "The law, the *Sharià,* is the Koran, and the

68

Koran is the word of God. An infidel woman will find no deliverance in Muhammad's law."

Bryna addressed Pamela desperately. "Then what about . . . "

"Nejm Al Anwar," the blonde supplied gloomily.

"Where will I find this Nejm Al Anwar? I must speak to him."

"It will do you no good," Theresa interjected. "The Aribi say he will sell all of us. I will die before I will be sold again."

Theresa's passionate declaration was lost as Bryna cried, "You understand Arabic?"

"Sí." Theresa sniffed disdainfully. "One must to survive in this part of the world."

"Could you translate for me when Nejm comes?"

"There is no need. French is the second language of the Ottoman empire, thanks to Napoleon and the Mother Church. Nejm speaks it."

"Don't worry," Pamela insisted. "Lie down and rest a moment." She gestured toward the insect-infested cushions.

"I think I would rather sit up." Bryna frowned distastefully. Her skin crawled, but whether with real or imagined insects, she didn't know.

"Nejm probably will not come here, anyway," Theresa contributed bitterly. "The only one we are likely to see is the eunuch who brings our breakfast, such as it is."

"Yes," Pamela agreed woefully, "but it is better than being hungry. I get very hungry when I am upset. I've always had a good appetite, but now I feel as if I am starving almost all the time."

"Does the eunuch speak French?" Bryna interrupted unsympathetically. Before she worried about her stomach, she must talk to someone who could correct the error that found her in the hands of a slave trader.

"He speaks a little," Pamela answered, "but you'll soon find out, for here he comes with our breakfast."

Across the room, veils were hastily pulled into place as a black servant entered the room, bearing a kettle of couscous flavored with stringy bits of mutton. Above their face coverings, the Arab women's dark eyes cast spiteful stares at the eunuch's back as he threaded his way to the corner where the infidel women sat.

"*Bonjour*, Mubarak," Pamela greeted him. The eunuch's face lit with a smile.

"*Bonjour*, Mademoiselle Pamela," he responded in a high, piping voice. His French was rough and heavily accented. "Look, I have brought food for your friend." Squatting down beside Bryna's pallet, he thrust a dish of food and a greasy doughnut called a *sfenj* toward her. Then he served the European women.

"Mubarak," Bryna began tentatively, "I need your help. I must speak to Nejm Al Anwar and explain that I am not a slave. I am a free woman, an American."

"But you are a slave, mademoiselle," he said perplexedly. "My master paid a good price to your old master."

"But he was not my master. He had no right to sell me."

"Yet he did. So your fate is as Allah wills. Nejm Al Anwar is your *sidi*, your master, as well as mine." Rising quickly to thwart further argument, the eunuch took the pot to the hungry Arabian women. He set it unceremoniously in the middle of the floor and withdrew, closing the door behind him. The dark-skinned women fell upon their breakfast ravenously, dipping their bowls into the steaming pot, then feeding themselves with their fingers.

"I do think it is a nasty custom," Pamela complained, gingerly following suit, "but one must make do here. There are no knives and forks. But take care to use only your right hand if you wish to get along. The left is considered unclean."

Bryna nibbled at the tasteless food, her stomach churning with every greasy mouthful, but she must eat. She must stay well if she was to survive.

In time Mubarak returned and paused to speak to the native women in Arabic. When he finished they resumed their wailing with renewed vigor. Wincing, he presented himself to Bryna, Pamela, and Theresa.

"So sorry to disturb you, young ladies, but my *sidi* Nejm orders you to make yourselves presentable for the souk," he informed them apologetically.

"What is that?" Bryna questioned, dreading the answer.

"The bazaar," Theresa answered before the slave could, "where we will be auctioned like livestock. Is that not so, Mubarak?"

The eunuch glanced unhappily at Pamela. The dainty blonde's face had blanched at the announcement, and she awaited his answer with tears brimming in her brown eyes.

"Oui," Mubarak said at last, "you go to the auction house. But do not fear. It will be over before you know it."

"I will not go. I will die first," Theresa declared dramatically.

"Please do not speak of such things, mademoiselle," the eunuch begged woefully. "The taking of one's own life is *harim* . . . forbidden."

"Well, if we must go to the souk, perhaps you could bring water so that we may wash," Bryna suggested with wry practicality.

"Yes, some water would be nice." Pamela roused herself from her black study. "At least we shall not go to our fates looking like slatterns."

"Très bien," Mubarak agreed, relieved by the attitude of the two women. He hurried to fetch a basin of warm water for them.

Gratefully they scrubbed the worst of the grime from their hands and faces, combed their hair with their fingers, and straightened their wrinkled dresses. As she did so, Bryna was pleased to discover her mother's locket still concealed under her clothes. Her captor had not found it.

At last the door opened and Nejm Al Anwar himself appeared, wearing a dingy white turban and the red robe of the slave trader. Belted around his waist was a Turkish scimitar, its surface dull and tarnished but its edge honed and deadly looking. Bryna scrutinized the Arab with interest as he slouched in the doorway, speaking to someone in the hallway outside. A quiet gasp came from Pamela when he entered, but neither she nor Theresa moved. Drawing a deep breath, the American girl went alone to speak to the gaunt, unkempt man.

"Are you Nejm Al Anwar?" Bryna asked politely in French as she neared him.

"Away, woman, I have no time for you now." A forbidding frown on his face, Nejm looked over his shoulder to see who dared approach him. Ah, the American was awake. Stepping into the room, he walked around his latest purchase, his black eyes raking her from the tips of her bare toes to the crown of her dark head.

"Where are your shoes?" he demanded curtly.

"I . . . I have none," she stammered, taken by surprise.

Gasim Al Auf, Allah blacken his face, was not satisfied to overcharge me, Nejm seethed. He also stole the slave's shoes. The trader scowled at Bryna as if it were her fault.

"Please," she entreated, "I must speak with you."

"Silence!" Nejm roared, continuing his inspection. She was taller than he had thought, and by Allah, she had blue eyes, marking her as one who could cast spells. And what was worse, he realized those blue eyes held no real fear of him.

The infidel woman proved this shortcoming by

addressing him firmly, "You must listen to me, monsieur. I am not a slave."

"You are my slave," he countered scornfully, turning to leave.

"*Non,* wait." The girl plucked at his sleeve to prevent his departure, oblivious to the collective gasp that went up from the women, Arab and European, behind her.

Enraged, the man whirled, his expression ugly, his sword drawn. "It would be wise, kaffir, to remember slaves can be killed by their masters for disobedience."

"I am not a slave," Bryna repeated stubbornly, refusing to retreat. "My name is Bryna O'Toole. My father is Blaine O'Toole—"

Nejm slashed the air in front of her face viciously with his sword to silence her. Then, placing the point under her chin, he pricked her skin lightly and cursed, "*Wallahi,* deceiver, you most worthless of women, I do not care if your father is the Aga Kizlar to the *kadin* of the sultan himself. I tell you, you are my slave and you will obey me."

Her chest heaving with fury, Bryna forced herself to stand still as a drop of blood trickled down her neck and spread in a tiny stain on the collar of her dress.

"Dispute me and I will cut out your tongue," the Arab threatened ominously. "Many men prefer silence in their women.

"That is better." He lowered the sword and stepped back. "Come, you may be spared a trip to the souk. A buyer has come." He beckoned Pamela and Theresa, who had watched the scene, horrified, from across the room. They came at once, weaving their way resignedly past the stunned and silent Arab women.

"Now follow me," Nejm ordered. "Keep your heads bowed and show much respect, for this man is a marriage broker of Baghdad. He is a great man, a hajji who has made pilgrimages to both Mecca and Medina, those most holy of cities."

"Do not argue," Theresa murmured in warning behind Bryna. "I do not believe he would cut out your tongue, but I have heard the bastinado is painful indeed, a form of torture. They beat the soles of the feet with a rod, sometimes crippling the victim. You do not wish to be punished in such a manner."

Swallowing defiant words, Bryna led the other women down the narrow corridor behind the slave trader. The rebellion quelled, Nejm strutted importantly at the head of the procession, resembling nothing so much as a bantam rooster, trailed by three disheveled, unwilling hens.

He stepped into the *majlis,* or reception room, and motioned the women to follow. They hesitated in the shadowy hallway and peered through the open door. Behind them, Mubarak spoke quietly and insistently in French, herding them into the room before taking his position in the doorway.

Although far from luxurious, the *majlis* was the most comfortable room in Nejm's house. A few worn carpets decorated the floor, and cheap, colorful cushions were tossed onto low, threadbare divans. Through the open grillwork over the windows, a solitary mimosa, flowering in the courtyard, could be seen. Ceramic pots filled with water were positioned in the corners of the room to cool it.

On the divan at the far end of the room sat the roundest man Bryna had ever seen. He lounged, sipping coffee, eating gazelle's horn pastries and sweating profusely in the heat. A sleepy-eyed black boy stood behind him, lethargically wielding a huge ostrich feather fan. When the man spoke sharply over his shoulder, the lad immediately put more energy into his fanning, but his effort diminished as soon as his master turned his attention elsewhere.

"*As salaam 'alaykum,* Hajji Suleiman Ibn Hussein," Nejm greeted his visitor respectfully.

"*Wa 'alaykum as salaam,* Nejm Al Anwar." The fat man's voice was sweet and surprisingly reedy for one so large.

"Welcome a hundred times," Nejm intoned. "May Allah give you a happy day."

"May your day be blessed and prosperous, though not too prosperous at my expense." Suleiman wheezed at his own joke. He looked to where the women stood and asked, "They speak French?"

"Yes."

"Come forward, my lovelies," he instructed them kindly in French. As the women stepped forward, the potential buyer inspected the two dark-haired girls who stood nearest him. They were beautiful indeed, but even though their heads were bowed decorously, he saw too much pride in their manners.

Through the screen of her lowered eyelashes, Bryna regarded the corpulent man with equal interest. Suleiman Ibn Hussein was obviously a man of great wealth; his very bulk bespoke a life of plenty. Under his scarlet tarboosh with its meticulously wrapped white turban, his face, flushed from the heat, showed signs of indulgence. His eyes were almost lost in folds of fat, and over his triple chin his beard was combed to a neat point.

"Permit me to introduce myself," Suleiman said. "I am Hajji Suleiman Ibn Hussein of Baghdad. My old friend Nejm Al Anwar, this most courteous of men—May Allah watch over him!—has arranged for this private display today, knowing how I despise crowded auction houses. They tend to be so uncivilized in the Mahgreb." He smiled appreciatively as the procurer positioned himself behind his buyer to whisper bits of helpful information into his ear.

"Come closer now where I can see you. And you, frightened little hare, come out of hiding," the obese man gently urged Pamela. "I know you are there behind the others."

Reluctantly, the blond-haired girl slipped between Bryna and Theresa and stepped into the light.

"Mashallah," Suleiman breathed when he saw the dainty British girl with her pale skin, honey-colored hair, and brown eyes. She was a houri, a woman such as those who await true believers in

Paradise. The dark beauty of the others dimmed to his Eastern eyes as Pamela presented herself, her head bowed sorrowfully.

"You have done well this time, Nejm," Suleiman purred in Arabic, stroking his beard thoughtfully. "I will take this pale-haired one. It is unfortunate, however, you have only one blonde and no red-heads."

"Unfortunate indeed. But the other two, Hajji, are they not also fair?" Nejm cajoled. "The one has the glow of fire in her hair if you look closely."

Almost as an afterthought, the buyer glanced at the other girls again. They resembled each other slightly. He toyed with the idea of selling them as a pair. Both women had dark hair and both looked aristocratic, but there the similarities ended. The Spaniard was dainty, with olive skin and tousled curly locks. The American was tall, but she was graceful. Her skin was fair and the pink of the dress she wore lent its color to her cheeks. Her hair was dark, but in the light there were indeed glints of red. It was too bad about her eyes, he mused, but perhaps somewhere he could find a buyer who was not superstitious.

"The dark ones are strong and healthy," Nejm pressed. "They will bear many sons and bring a fine bride price."

"I do not know." Suleiman sighed expressively, reaching for a sweet. "In Arabia are many dark-haired women."

"But none so fair," the slave trader argued.

"I suppose," the fat man replied doubtfully.

"But at least Arabian women are obedient daughters of Islam. These two—"

"Will hear and obey your every order, my lord," Nejm finished his sentence eagerly. "They, too, will be Moslem as soon as they have made their *shahada,* their professions of faith."

"I do not know," Suleiman repeated dubiously, watching the slave trader's tense reaction out of the corner of one hooded eye. "Have they any blemishes, beyond the unfortunate color of that one's eyes?" He nodded toward Bryna, noting that her blue eyes watched their exchange with intelligence.

"None, *sidi,* they are perfect," Nejm assured him, although he had not inspected their bodies.

"They are virgins?"

"Of course." The trader assumed an air of injured dignity. "Do you wish them to disrobe?"

Suleiman waved his hand in negligent refusal. White women were at a premium and greatly desired in the harems of Arabia. As quickly as he reached Jidda, he could easily sell any of these, sight unseen.

"Then you wish to buy them?" Nejm asked eagerly, but his potential purchaser remained noncommittal. The slave trader coaxed and bargained and finally, in frustration, threatened to withdraw his offer to sell any of the women. But even as he herded them toward the door, waving his arms behind them and shouting, Suleiman seemed unmoved.

"Wait," the Turk called as if he had made a sudden decision. "Perhaps I could take the Spaniard off your hands, if that is the only way you will let me buy the blonde."

"No, Hajji, all three or none," Nejm insisted boldly, thoroughly enjoying the haggling.

"Than you must send them all back to Mubarak." Suleiman sighed. His sides quaked gleefully under his caftan as he watched the other man's face fall.

"Oh, Suleiman, Beloved of Allah, I fear he has relieved you of your wits if you will pass up such delicate blossoms of womanhood," the trader lamented, gesturing extravagantly toward the women.

"He has not deprived me of my wits completely, for I will not buy any women without bargaining first, Nejm. Let us speak of their worth. But I warn you, if I must take all three to have the one, I expect a good price from you."

"Wallahi," Nejm cried as if affronted, "I have never been anything but fair to you."

"What do you suppose they are saying?" Pamela found the courage to whisper to Bryna.

"I think they are striking a bargain," Bryna answered, drawing herself up, "and they are much mistaken if they think I am going to stand by quietly and be sold."

"Remember the bastinado," Theresa muttered in her ear.

"*Oui*, remember the bastinado," Mubarak advised from behind the women. Stepping into the room unobtrusively, he grasped Bryna's arm so tightly that she nearly cried out in pain. Holding her in place, he whispered urgently, "I do this for your own protection, mademoiselle, for I tell you, you will regret it if you shame my master."

"Silence, women!" Nejm bellowed. "Mubarak, take them back to the harem." Rubbing his hands in anticipation of the second round of dickering, the trader returned to his customer.

CHAPTER

✧✧✧✧✧ **5** ✧✧✧✧✧

"BALEK! MAKE WAY!" SULEIMAN'S LITTLE SLAVE shouted. Holding the stirrup of his master's donkey, he trotted alongside, urging the crowd out of their path. The party made slow progress as the massive Turk swayed from side to side on his donkey, his ample girth overhanging either side of the tiny saddle, threatening in many spots to brush the walls along the narrow streets.

Behind him, Bryna, Pamela, and Theresa followed on foot, sweltering in stiff black haiks and yashmaks. They were flanked by Suleiman's guards, four armed Nubian eunuchs, and marched through the streets at a brisk clip.

Bryna tried to keep up, the men's sandals Mubarak had finally located to fit her flapping in the dust. Hoping for a miracle, she looked around desperately, her vision impaired by the heavy veil she wore. If only she could spy her father's face in the crowd, she would call out to him, she could escape.

Soon they passed through a gate into streets that became wider and less congested. The air even seemed cleaner. Slowly they descended toward the shimmering blue brilliance of the ocean, which they could see in the distance beyond the sunbaked brick buildings. Glancing over her shoulder, Bryna thought she could see Blaine's home perched on the cliff above them.

Suleiman's company stopped before a large whitewashed compound. The marriage broker dismounted with an exercised wheeze and led the way into a pleasant courtyard, its lush growth encircled by colorful tiled walls. In each of the four corners of the enclosure, small fountains tinkled musically, and in the center another shot a stream of water into the air, where glistening droplets caught the sun like tiny prisms. The main house, built around the courtyard, was spacious and open, permitting a sea breeze even in the walled courtyard.

Breathing heavily, Suleiman collapsed on a stone bench. "Turki," he gasped, motioning for the black boy to fan him. As the three white women in their uncomfortable costumes and the Nubian guards stood by in the sun, the boy applied himself energetically to his task.

When he had recovered sufficiently, the fat man clapped his hands and an aging black eunuch appeared. Dignified and efficient, the slave bowed to his master and presented him with a cup of water.

Between greedy swallows, Suleiman said, "This is Jamil, head of my household in Tangier. He will see to your needs. All you must do is ask. Listen to him well, for he has much to teach you.

"Jamil, take them to the baths right away."

"Yes, *sidi.* Follow me," Jamil instructed the women in French. He led his charges past a luxurious *majlis,* through an exquisitely crafted iron gate to a breezeway leading to the building that served as harem. They did not stop at any of the closed doors lining the corridor. Instead the eunuch led them straight through the building into the baths.

Several female Arab bath attendants met them at the door. They laughed and chattered as they helped the newcomers remove their clothing, their voices dying to awed whispers when Pamela's fair hair and skin were revealed.

"My master has done well today." Jamil's forbidding face softened approvingly. "Skin so fair I have never seen."

At a nod from him, three servants came forward and took charge of the new women. The girl assigned to Bryna was a striking Berber with a warm smile and intricate tattoos along her dusky arms.

When she learned her caretaker spoke neither French nor English, Bryna said little. She suffered herself to be stripped and led to the baths. She did not fuss and try to hide her body as the European women did, but she refused to surrender her locket. Using sign language, the Berber girl made it clear the necklace would be returned after the bath. Too weary to argue, Bryna gave it to her, oddly pleased when the other girl admired it. The only possession left to her, it kept the Creole girl from feeling as if she had slipped into a nightmare where she would be forever lost.

The bath was over none too soon for Bryna. Wrapped in a towel, she was laid on a bench and her thick hair spread out to dry. Skillfully the Berber girl massaged Bryna's back and neck, relieving knots of tension and strain, then left her to nap. After nearly an hour Bryna was awakened and given a cup of cool water to drink and some clothes.

The gauzy caftan Jamil had selected for her was the same blue as her eyes and richly embroidered with golden threads. With the Berber girl's assistance, Bryna slipped it over her head. It slid into place, skimming her hips with a sensuous hiss of silk on skin.

Her dresser smiled approvingly and gestured for her to sit on the bench. Shyly she fastened the golden locket around her neck. Then she brushed the American girl's hair to a glossy sheen and braided it with a golden ribbon in one simple plait down her back. Skillfully she shaded Bryna's eyelids with a blue powder and lined them with kohl. She applied rouge lightly to her cheeks and, as a final touch, painted her lips a brilliant carmine.

The slave stepped back and regarded her creation with obvious satisfaction. She slid a pair of decorated *babouche* slippers on Bryna's feet. The backless shoes were made of fine scarlet Moroccan leather and fit perfectly.

Her job complete, she led Bryna to a tall mirror that hung nearby. Bryna stared at her reflection incredulously. Her costume made her look exotic and seductive, but her cheeks reddened with a contradictory blush. The plunging neckline of her gossamer dress left little to the imagination. Involuntarily her fingers plucked at it, drawing the edges together for modesty's sake. Secretly amused by her reaction, the Berber girl bowed and departed, leaving her to locate her companions in separate corners of the room.

"What do you suppose happens next?" Pamela asked no one in particular. Refreshed from her bath, the English girl seemed calmer now. Dressed in a pink-and-silver caftan similar to Bryna's, she looked soft and almost relaxed.

Theresa glanced at her distractedly but did not answer as she paced the length of the narrow room. Conversation was forgotten when three servants appeared with their lunch. The women were seated cross-legged on the floor and served *khli,* a pickled chopped beef with rice; a colorful sweet pepper salad; flat bread; fruit; and a smooth, cool concoction Jamil called *most.* They ate, carefully hiding their left hands in the folds of their robes.

They had barely finished when Jamil presented each girl with a small filmy square of fabric.

"Follow me, mademoiselle," he instructed Pamela.

Unwillingly the English girl rose, throwing a helpless look toward her companions as she was led away.

"Cover yourselves," the eunuch instructed over his shoulder. "You are about to meet a man who is neither a kinsman nor a eunuch. You must be properly veiled."

On the opposite side of the baths from the harem, Jamil opened a door that led into a small chamber. "Remove your shoes, please, before entering," he told Pamela. "That, too, is our custom."

When she had obeyed, he set her slippers inside the door and gestured for her to enter. Then the door closed. Bryna and Theresa glanced at each other nervously but remained in their seats, their gazes fastened on the door.

After a time it opened, and Jamil beckoned Theresa.

"No," the Spanish girl muttered. "I will not go with him into that room."

"Theresa," Bryna said softly, "I do not believe he intends to harm you. And remember what you told me about punishment."

"*Sí*," Theresa agreed woodenly, and went to where the eunuch waited. He ushered her into the room, the door closed, and Bryna was left alone.

After a few moments an angry screech and the tinkling of broken glass came from the inner chamber. The wait seemed interminable before Jamil returned and signaled for Bryna, his temper obviously frayed.

"By the Prophet, I have never seen such behavior," he informed the American girl through thin lips. "God destroy your house if you do likewise. No, do not remove your shoes or you will cut your feet." He flung the door open and waited for her to pass.

Filled with dread, Bryna entered a sparsely furnished room, where she was greeted by a flustered old man. He greeted her, sidestepping the servants busily sweeping up shards of glass.

"*Bonjour,* mademoiselle, I am Halef, the hakim—the personal physician—to Hajji Suleiman Ibn Hussein. Allah praise him as a good and generous master. I mean you no injury, so please have the goodness not to behave as the others."

"What happened?" Bryna surveyed the room uncomprehendingly.

"The Inglayzi woman wept piteously. The Spaniard threw a pot at me. Just because I was ordered to make sure the new women are healthy. It is ordinarily so simple." He gestured feebly toward the divan. Bryna's eyes widened as she surmised his intent.

"I will allow you to examine me," she agreed brashly, determined to have the upper hand, "but only if the others leave the room."

"Everyone?" Halef's face registered shock at the idea. This woman had a most disconcerting way of meeting his gaze. There was perhaps fear, but no submission, in her blue eyes. "All of them cannot leave."

"All of them," Bryna repeated firmly.

"That is most unorthodox," the old man wavered, evaluating her demand, remembering the others. "You promise to cooperate?"

"*Oui.*"

"You will not make trouble for me later?"

"*Non.*"

"Then I suppose it would be permissible."

"I do not like it, Hakim," Jamil spoke up suddenly. "I should be here in case you need me."

"Stand outside the door, Jamil. I will call if I need you."

"But to be left alone in the harem . . ." the eunuch protested. Even though they spoke French, he looked around uneasily for fear they might be overheard by the servants.

"Calm yourself, my friend. She has given her word. Granted, it is the word of a kaffir, but she will honor it.

"You must, you know," he told Bryna seriously, "for Suleiman would be greatly displeased if he found out. But I will do as you ask." The doctor chased the servants from the room and dismissed the eunuch firmly.

The physical examination to which Bryna submitted was mercifully brief, but humiliating. She was relieved to join the others in the private apartment they were to share. Red-eyed from weeping, Pamela met her at the door.

"Are you all right, Bryna?" she asked frantically.

"Yes, and you?"

"I'm all right, but I do not know about Theresa." She looked with concern toward the saffron-clad girl, who paced the room like a caged animal. Her bare feet slapping softly against the tile, she muttered ceaselessly in Spanish.

"I do not know what they did to her," the British girl said anxiously, "but it must have been terrible. She has not said a word to me since Jamil brought her here."

"Nothing was done to her that was not done to you or to the American. The Spaniard will recover soon," Jamil spoke dryly from the doorway, "as you did.

"Now it is time for kef," he continued as slaves circulated, refilling the jars of water in each corner that cooled the room. "Sleep, then after evening prayers, my master will send for each of you individually. You need not veil yourselves, for he wishes to acquaint himself with each of you. No one will see you here but eunuchs. Pray remember to enter Hajji Suleiman's presence with humility, as befits a woman of the East."

Their attention on the servant, Bryna and Pamela missed the look of utter horror that flitted across the Spanish girl's face.

Despite her nervousness and Theresa's dire muttering, Bryna lay down on one of the divans and managed to sleep. Exhausted by tension, she awakened when the cry of the muezzin—*"Allahu akbar"*—drifted in on the twilight breeze.

She opened her eyes to see Pamela sitting tensely on the divan across from her, while Theresa still prowled the room, her path bringing her to pass back and forth between the two couches.

"I suppose Suleiman will send for us soon," the blond girl whispered, obviously frightened.

"Don't worry." Bryna tried to smile reassuringly, but it was a weak attempt. "If we were going to be harmed, it would have happened before now."

"I guess," Pamela agreed with a marked lack of conviction. "Although the examination was far from comfortable."

90

"True, but Halef did not harm you intentionally." Bryna nodded toward Theresa. "Did she sleep at all?"

"I don't think so. I napped for a while, but when I awoke she was still pacing. It's eerie, Bryna. When you speak to her, she does not seem to hear."

"*Bon soir,* young ladies." Jamil threw open the door. "I bring dinner and then you, most fair"— he pointed at Pamela —"will be the first to go to our master. Allah grant him joy."

"Why must I always be first?" Pamela found the inner strength to protest.

"Because you are a rare treasure, foolish woman. Few have I ever seen to compare to you. Eat, for I will come for you soon."

Bryna and Pamela tried to interest Theresa in food, but they received only a contemptuous stare in response. After they had eaten, Jamil returned to take Pamela to Suleiman, and Bryna was left with Theresa in the room, silent now except for the other girl's muttering.

Nearly an hour passed before Pamela returned. The tiny English girl bolted into the room as soon as the door was opened and threw herself down on the divan, weeping bitterly. Bryna went immediately to her side. When she looked up, she saw Jamil lead Theresa gently toward the door. With a sound akin to a snarl, the Spanish girl wrenched her arm free and walked in front of the slave, her shoulders stiff and her head held high.

"Pamela." Filled with dread, Bryna touched the other girl's shoulder. "What happened?"

"It was horrible," Pamela sobbed. "Suleiman sat on his divan and looked at me and asked questions."

"Did he hurt you?"

"No."

"He did not touch you?"

"No, but I cannot abide disrobing in front of all those people," Pamela wailed.

"All what people?" Bryna asked in a choked voice.

"The people in the *majlis*—Suleiman and the guards and the servants. They all looked at me when I was n-n-naked."

Brought up in a convent, Bryna could hardly conceive of such treatment, but she did not dwell on it. Instead she asked insistently again, "You were not harmed?"

"No, no one touched me. Suleiman does seem kind, for a Turk." The English girl sniffled. "It was just being unclothed in that room full of men, even if most of them are not really men, you know. It is hideous what they do, even to little boys like Turki."

"I know," Bryna murmured, turning her mind now to the interview to come. She tried to calm her inner turmoil, to steel herself. At least she knew what to expect and she must get through it without losing her temper or showing fear. She must talk to Suleiman reasonably.

It was not long before Jamil returned for Bryna, but when he came he was flanked by two of Suleiman's Nubian guards, and Theresa was not with them. The old eunuch's dark face was grim.

"Where is Theresa?" Pamela asked shrilly, rising on her elbows. "What have you done to her?"

"Ask rather what she has done to herself, the poor mad one, to break the laws of Allah," Jamil replied solemnly. "While standing before my master, she seized the knife from the belt of one of the guards and drove it into her own heart without warning."

"Oh, no." Pamela burrowed her head in the pillows. Her voice muffled, she asked, "Is she dead?"

"*Insh'allah . . .* it was the will of God."

While Bryna knelt beside Pamela and endeavored to console her, the weeping girl raised her tearstained face and cried wildly, "Poor Theresa, she only did what we would like to do."

"Do not think you can follow your friend to *Nasrani* heaven," Jamil interjected sourly. "These guards are here to prevent that."

"I would not kill myself," the blond girl confessed sadly. "I haven't the courage."

"It takes more courage to live, Pamela," Bryna told her fiercely. "I will live and so must you." Holding herself erect, the American girl followed the servant from the room, leaving the two guards to watch over the sobbing Pamela.

Silently Bryna followed Jamil through the breezeway, trying not to think of what was to come.

The old eunuch did not look back. Though he could not ordinarily tolerate infidels, he was impressed with this strong, dark-haired girl.

When the pair drew even with the corridor

leading to the stables, an agonized scream rent the still night air.

"What was that?" Bryna gasped.

"Only the incompetent guard being punished by bastinado."

"Isn't that a severe punishment?"

"His carelessness cost my master a sizable investment," Jamil explained. "Do not waste compassion on him. The *sidi* allows him to live, which is more than he deserves."

Bryna decided it was best to keep her feeling of revulsion to herself. Without another word she followed the eunuch to the doorway to the *majlis*.

Removing her shoes, she ducked her head and went inside. It nettled her to bow her head docilely when approaching a man, but if she displeased Suleiman now, she might never have the chance to tell her story.

Bryna's meek entrance was wasted. The marriage broker stood to one side of the room, washing his hands in a bowl of water. He scrubbed vigorously at his hands and forearms, as a part of Moslem ritual, regretting it had been necessary to touch a corpse and thus become unclean.

While she waited for him to finish his ablutions, the Creole girl lifted her head to survey the room. The evening breeze stirred the tapestry wall hangings to either side of her. But no evidence remained of what had occurred mere moments ago. Except for an oddly bare space on the floor where a rug had been, the room was orderly and serene by the light of the oil lamps.

She ducked her head quickly as Suleiman waddled to the dais on which his divan was placed. He positioned himself on it without looking at her, staring off into space for a moment before speaking. When he broke the silence, his reedy voice was sad.

"I could not make the Spaniard see that I wished her no harm. But as Allah is my witness, I did not. Do you understand?" He glanced down at her for the first time since she'd entered the room and was taken aback. Lit from behind by the torches that shone through the door from the passageway outside, the girl's curvaceous figure was clearly silhouetted beneath the flimsy gauze of her caftan. He had bought a treasure without even knowing it. "I will not harm you," he said lamely.

"I know." Her low voice floated to him.

"Bien," Suleiman pronounced, seemingly heartened by her fearless response. Though she stood with her head properly bowed, there was nothing humble in her proud, erect bearing. "Now look at me and we will talk."

Bryna complied, and the man gazed upon her appreciatively. She was prettier than he had thought. In the lamplight, her face was pale and lovely beneath sleek, glossy hair. The skin would be soft to the touch . . .

"What are you called?" he asked gruffly, forcing his mind back to business.

"My name is Bryna O'Toole." She was ready to present her case when the man spoke.

"Do you know how a woman is named in the Arab world?"

She shook her head.

"We call her by her given name, followed by the word *bint*, which means 'daughter of,' followed by her father's name. So your name is Bryna bint . . . ?" His eyebrows lifted questioningly so they nearly disappeared under his turban.

"Bryna bint Blaine."

"Good, good." Suleiman smiled benevolently. "Now Bryna bint Blaine, you are American?"

"Oui."

"I know little of America," the marriage broker mused, "except that your sultan, Andrew Al Jackson, sent your sailors to rid our seas of the Barbary pirates. How difficult it is now to find white women for purchase. That is why I have only the three, er, two of you."

Suddenly he became very businesslike. "My hakim says that you are in excellent health. *Alhamdillah!* And that you are a virgin. May Allah be thanked a thousand times. I will find you a good husband."

Bryna felt a hot wave of color rising in her face. "If you will only let me speak . . . please, sir," she blurted.

"Sidi," he corrected pleasantly.

"Sidi, a husband has already been selected for me." She knew it was a lie, but she tried to speak in terms the Turk would understand.

"He is not a husband until you are married."

"But you must permit me to go home. I am not a slave. My father is Blaine O'Toole—O'Toole Effendi." She paused, looking for a flicker of recognition in the

96

fat man's eyes, but there was none. "He . . . he is a merchant here in Tangier."

"I do not know him. He trades in women?"

"No, in spices."

"Ah, that is why. We are not in the same business." He waved his pudgy hand as if the subject were closed.

"My father will pay a ransom for me," the girl insisted.

"Even if he were a king among merchants, I do not think he could pay enough ransom, Bryna bint Blaine," Suleiman disagreed. "You will fetch a great bride price.

"But there is no time for such negotiations. I have been away from Baghdad too long already. I consulted a seer and the signs are propitious. He agrees winter is the best time to depart, for in only a matter of months, the heat will be killing in the desert."

"But—"

"Enough, young lady," the broker interrupted, but his voice was not unkind. "We leave tomorrow to join a large merchant's caravan in Fez. From there we journey to Arabia, where many wealthy men seek white-skinned houris for their harems. Understand, Bryna bint Blaine, *Insh'allah*. Whatever shall be, shall be as Allah wills it."

She stared up at him dully, her face blanched of all color. Powerless, she was beyond even anger.

"It is your kismet," Suleiman explained weakly. "It would be wrong to resist fate. You do see that, don't you?"

Bryna could not answer. Her words caught on the lump in her throat as tears threatened to spill down her painted face.

"There is one other thing you must do before you return to your apartments." The marriage broker spoke slowly as if to a child. "You must undress. I must see what I have purchased."

Faced with the prospect of disrobing before the men in the room, Bryna could feel the composure she had managed to maintain slipping away. Her eyes widened and she shook her head in desperate refusal.

"Surely you knew what to expect." Suleiman sighed, his patience beginning to wear thin. "Did not the golden-haired one tell you what happened here?"

"*Oui,*" she whispered hoarsely.

"Then she must have also told you that I did not harm her. Obey me now or Jamil will remove your clothing for you."

Hearing the eunuch stir in the doorway behind her, Bryna obeyed reluctantly. She pulled the caftan over her head, shivering when the warm night air reached her body, and stood tense and poised as if she would run away. She could not bear to meet Suleiman's eyes, but she could feel his gaze upon her and struggled with the urge to cover herself with the garment she still held crumpled in her hand.

The marriage broker drew a quick breath. "*Mashallah,* you are lovely."

The long dark braid intertwined with ribbon rested on one creamy shoulder. A thin golden chain encircled her slender neck, and from it dangled a small locket that nestled at the base of her throat, glittering in the lamplight with each throb of her pulse. The girl's legs were long. Her breasts were not large, but they were well formed, jutting above her narrow waist, and the gentle flare of her hips was enticing.

"Turn around," Suleiman requested calmly.

The mortified girl revolved slowly.

"*Mashallah,* indeed," he murmured. "You may dress."

Gratefully Bryna whipped the caftan over her head and tugged it rapidly over her body. When she was dressed Suleiman pronounced appraisingly, "Surely the *jinn* gave you blue eyes and a face that is fair. Just as surely they gave you a body to confound and delight men. Have no fear, Bryna bint Blaine, you will have a mighty sheik for your husband. One with wealth and power, I assure you. Your sons will be lions of the desert.

"Go now," he said, abruptly concluding the interview. "Jamil will escort you to your room."

Gratefully Bryna departed, unaware of the ache of longing she had created in Suleiman's loins where the other two women had not. The girl was desirable, but he would never taste her pleasures, he told himself sensibly. Hajji Suleiman Ibn Hussein was the best seller of harem slaves in the Ottoman empire, and women—even this one—were merchandise and nothing more.

Pamela was waiting when Bryna returned to the harem.

"From now on, speak to me in English whenever possible," Bryna instructed before the other girl could speak. "That way we may speak more freely, since the guards are not likely to understand it."

"Yes, let us not make it any easier for them than we must." Pamela nodded in approval, then asked anxiously, "Are you all right?"

"Insulted, but not injured," Bryna replied, tensing all her muscles in order to control the shaking that had begun when she'd left Suleiman.

"I know, you poor dear," the English girl murmured. "Why don't you cry? It will make you feel ever so much better."

"No." Bryna shook her head stubbornly. "I will not waste the tears."

"How can you be so brave?" Pamela asked, about to cry herself. "I'm so terribly frightened."

"I am afraid, too," Bryna admitted, "but we will find a way out of this. But sleep now. We leave for Arabia in the morning."

"Oh, no," the other girl wailed. Throwing herself facedown on her couch, she cried herself to sleep.

On her divan, Bryna lay stiffly, thinking of her father and of Derek. Did either of them search for her? Could they hope to find a rare white woman in a Moslem country? She tried to hope, until at last she sank into an exhausted, dreamless sleep.

The moon played hide-and-seek behind the clouds as Blaine O'Toole wearily urged his horse up the steep street toward his house. It had been a long day and he was eager for his bed.

Suddenly he reined his Arabian stallion to a halt. The back of his neck prickled with an unexpected sense of foreboding. Something was wrong. The lamps at either corner of the compound were always lit after sunset and left to burn through the night. Tonight they were dark.

His saddle creaked in the stillness as the big man shifted uneasily and scanned the front of the house through narrowed blue eyes. Was he seeing things, or was the gate standing open? Though there were no windows along the street, there was not even a glimmer of light from inside as the gate swung to and fro on the soft breeze. Then a metallic glint and a flutter in the moonlight caught his attention.

Dismounting, Blaine drew the small pistol he carried in his pocket and went to investigate cautiously, ready for ambush the moment he approached. But no one leapt out from the courtyard. Absently he reached out and fingered the piece of pink fabric flapping on the gate. The material was a soft cotton, and it looked as if it came from a woman's dress—the dress Bryna had worn when she saw him off that morning, he realized suddenly.

Swearing under his breath, Blaine yanked on the knife that held it in place. The fabric drifted to the dust at his feet as he examined the dagger bleakly. It was native in design, with the fine Toledo blade so common along the coast of North Africa.

The handle was wrapped in soft Fez leather. Turning the weapon over in his hand, he read the Arabic lettering tooled into the leather on the other side. It read "Al Auf"—"the Bad."

Gasim Al Auf, that bloody pirate! Blaine thought he had destroyed him at their last meeting. Obviously Gasim lived, but he would not live long if he had harmed Bryna.

"Bryna!" her father bellowed in alarm. "Are you all right? Where are you?" There was no further need for stealth. Al Auf was not in the house if he had left this blatant sign of his visit. Blaine threw the gate open with a clatter and rushed into the courtyard. His gaze roved the light and shadow, but there was no one to be seen. At first the only sound was the play of water in the fountain; then a groan came to him from the kitchen on the other side of the courtyard, where Hannah sat on the brick floor, cursing in five dialects of Arabic and rubbing her head. But she had seen nothing, neither her assailant nor the mistress.

Racing into the dark house, Blaine checked the deserted rooms downstairs first. In the dining room he noticed the door to the terrace was open. There he nearly tripped over a figure, sprawled on the cold tiles. Yusef . . . still unconscious. Where was Bryna?

Blaine took the stairs three at a time, dreading what he would find. He heard a moan as he opened the door to Bryna's bedchamber. Fatima stirred on the bed, where she had fallen when she was struck, but there was no sign of his daughter.

With grim efficiency he revived the servants and herded them into the library. Addled and nursing blinding headaches, they recounted the visit of the mistress's Inglayzi friend during the afternoon, but after that none could recall anything out of the ordinary, not even a noise.

"I would have protected her with my life, effendi," the old houseman maintained stoutly, "if I had but known she needed protection. Say the word and we will track the villain to the ends of the earth."

"No, Yusef." Blaine sighed. "First the police must be notified. But tomorrow . . . " He did not finish his sentence.

The servants were silent. They knew, as Blaine did, that the police could do little to find a kidnapped girl. The young mistress had probably already been spirited away to the Casbah, the Arab quarter, where it would be nearly impossible for anyone to find her.

But he had to try, her anguished father told himself. He had to find her. He could not let her down. Tomorrow he would haunt the souks, the center of all information in Tangier, searching for the clue that would lead him to Gasim Al Auf . . . and to Bryna.

"What is going on here?" Blaine strode into the midst of a dispute in his own courtyard. Tired and aggravated from a week of combing Tangier for clues of his daughter's whereabouts, he did not think an hour's rest was too much to ask. "What the hell is this bedlam?" he roared, his Irish brogue thickening in his irritation.

Both men ceased their shouting at once and turned to face the wrathful, red-faced man.

"O'Toole Effendi," Yusef answered respectfully in French, "I tried to tell the Inglayzi that the mistress is not at home—"

"I demand to see Bryna," Derek Ashburn interrupted hotly in English. He shouldered past the old servant to present himself to the master of the house.

"I do not know who you are to make demands," Blaine replied with deceptive mildness, "but my daughter is not here, Mr. . . . " He paused and regarded the elegant young man questioningly.

"Ashburn. Lieutenant Ashburn." Derek snapped to attention. "I am pleased to meet you, Colonel O'Toole."

" 'Tis Mr. O'Toole these days."

"Bryna told me a great deal about you."

"I doubt that," the big Irishman disagreed, but he shook the proffered hand. "She did not even know me until two weeks ago."

"Is she in, sir? I have tried every day for the past week to see her, and this old blackguard would not allow me in the front door. Acts as if he doesn't understand a word of English." Derek scowled at the old servant. "And I've forgotten all the French my tutor ever taught me."

"Yusef speaks little English, but he follows orders well enough. I am sorry, young man. There is no time for niceties. Instead of entertaining visitors, we must prepare for an expedition. I fear you have come at a bad time." Blaine gestured at the piles of provisions stacked around the courtyard. "I am going to search for my daughter."

"To search . . . ?" Derek seemed genuinely baffled before he glared at Blaine belligerently. "I say, what is going on? What has happened to Bryna?"

"She was kidnapped from this house last week," the girl's father replied simply, making no effort to soften the blow.

The color drained from Derek's handsome face. "Last week? And you are just now going to look for her?"

"I have only just learned where she might be." Blaine frowned, resentful of the younger man's implication. "Finding a missing woman in Moslem North Africa is not a simple matter, Lieutenant Ashburn. But I assure you I will find her and I will bring her back. Good day." He nodded toward the gate in dismissal and turned to walk back toward to the house.

The British soldier held his ground stubbornly. "I am going with you."

"No, lad," Blaine said over his shoulder. "This is family business."

"I am going with you," the young man repeated firmly. "I have every right . . . as Bryna's fiancé."

"Her what?" the Irishman thundered, whirling on him.

Poised for confrontation, Derek did not flinch. "Her fiancé. Didn't she tell you we are to be married?"

105

"She did not," Blaine bellowed, his face turning even redder with restrained wrath.

"She must not have had time. I only just proposed," the Englishman explained confidently. "We . . . we love each other, you see, sir. And I will not rest until she is safe again."

"Lieutenant Ashburn," Blaine said, combing his fingers through his hair wearily. How could Bryna have hooked up with a soldier? That was the worst choice of a husband she could make.

"Derek, sir," he prompted.

"Derek, you do not know what you are getting yourself into," Blaine informed him with ill-concealed impatience.

"I don't care. I will not rest until we have Bryna back."

"You may care when I tell you who her abductor is."

"I do not think so. Who do these people think they are to kidnap the daughter of a British subject?" Derek countered arrogantly.

"Bryna was taken by Gasim Al Auf," Blaine went on, ignoring the young soldier's comment. "That's Gasim the Bad, one of the vilest pirates ever to ply the Barbary Coast. He withstood even the efforts of the American navy to rout him.

"Now he's come to Tangier to seek revenge on me. I killed his only son in battle when his cutthroats tried to take one of my ships, so he's taken my only daughter. A tooth for a tooth, the Arabs believe, and an eye for an eye. I'm fortunate he did not kill Bryna outright." He sighed. "I don't know what Al Auf plans for her, but I know I must get her back quickly, before he harms her."

"We will, sir, we will," Derek pledged earnestly.

Blaine gauged the young Englishman with shrewd eyes. Something about Derek's story did not ring true, but whatever his reasons, the lad obviously wanted to go along. There would be time to sort out the details later, and in the meantime he could use a good man in a fight where he was going.

"Very well," Bryna's father conceded. "My informant tells me Gasim went to Tripoli three days ago. My arrangements are made. Make yours today and be ready to leave at dawn, if you're going with me."

CHAPTER

✦✦✦✦ **6** ✦✦✦✦✦

BRYNA SHIFTED, STIFF FROM LONG HOURS IN the cramped litter. Opening the curtains a crack, she surveyed the barren wasteland through which her camel plodded. This was the Fezzan, the heart of North Africa, where each day passed under blazing sun as the one before it.

Christmas and New Year's had come and gone since she had been sold into slavery. Every day, every mile took her farther from the promise she'd had of love and a new life. How often in the past three months, she had listened for the sound of pursuing hoofbeats. By now her father and Derek must know she'd been kidnapped. Blaine had sent for her and said he loved her. Derek had proposed and said he wanted to spend his life with her. Surely one—or both—would come for her. That they might not be able to find her she refused to consider. She remained stubbornly optimistic, refusing to surrender to despair, encouraging Pamela who already looked to her for guidance.

"What shall we do, Bryna?" the English girl asked frequently.

"We'll live one day at a time and look for a way to escape," was Bryna's practical answer. "Whatever comes, we will survive."

She wished she felt as confident as she sounded. Their small caravan crossed hundreds of miles of desert, traveling from well to brackish well. From dawn and into the night, the camels were on the move, their soft feet slapping against the sand. The caravan rode toward the rising sun and its blinding rays shone on white sand, reflecting into the squinting eyes of the travelers. They had made good time, traveling by night a few times to escape detection by raiders, camping during the day, hidden by the dunes, setting a constant watch and sweltering in their tents.

Bryna soon discovered life in the desert was exacting for the hardiest of souls. The travelers endured intense heat and cold, hunger, searing winds that intensified thirst, and sandstorms that left them searching for lost tools and implements when it was over. For weeks on end each person was rationed to a pint of precious water a day, meted out at the end of each day's travel. To extend their supply, sour camel's milk was added to make a mixture called *shanin.* True to Suleiman's prediction, Bryna soon learned to appreciate even that.

Night fell in the Sahara, cold and clear and starlit. The men huddled together around fires of dried camel dung and reveled in the small victory of surviving another day in the hostile environment. Shouting in the desert stillness, they told fantastic stories, greatly embellished and as old as time and the desert, which made them forget the rigors of their journey for a while. They spoke of epic acts performed by them and by heroes long dead.

Bryna and Pamela talked, too, slumping wearily in their tent. Their conversation was not of deeds, but of dreams and memories. Pamela told Bryna of her quiet, comfortable childhood in the ancestral home and of the excitement of her first social season. Bryna recounted her trip to Morocco and spoke of Blaine and Derek.

For both girls, past and future seemed far away. There was only the present, scorching heat and white sands. They scratched dry, parched skin and conjured up images of clean, cool water that did not reek of goatskins or taste of sour milk, of pools in which to bathe. Then they sipped gamy-flavored water from their goatskins once more before retiring. Exhausted, they lay on their pallets and tried to ignore the continual thirst and hunger pangs they now knew so well.

In the emptiness of the desert, Bryna thought of survival and not of escape. Suleiman taught the women some Arabic, for they would find little French spoken in Arabia. She found it difficult but loved the poetry of the formal language.

As her vocabulary increased, the girl brightened with hope each time the palms of an oasis appeared on the horizon. From behind her veil she scrutinized each tiny village, those dusty collections of hovels populated by no more than a few families, a midwife, and an imam to lead them in prayers. Nowhere was there succor for two white women being taken to Arabia against their wills, not from the residents of the oases, not from the provincial representatives of the Ottoman empire, not from the tribal sheiks through whose territories they passed.

At Abu Hamed, Suleiman hired Sudanese guards, three of them boys, to see his party safely across the Nubian Desert to the port of Suakin. After nearly two weeks, the caravan climbed from the desert to the heights. A pleasing breeze swept over the travelers, and the Red Sea stretched out below them, sparkling in the afternoon sun.

Their shadows were long in front of them when they descended to camp on the shore of a small cove. From the mountainside a huddle of mud brick buildings could be seen in the distance to the north. Tomorrow Suleiman's party would sail from Suakin, but tonight they would camp outside the town.

The camel drivers chose an even, sandy patch next to a grove of palm trees and set up the tents. As usual the women were herded into their tent while the men celebrated outside. Even Suleiman's Nubian guards joined in the lightheartedness, conversing happily with the guides, who were from a village near their home.

Now everyone could relax. The women, safe in their tent, had been no problem on the journey. Food and water were plentiful, and Suakin was nearby if they needed more. One of the pack camels was slaughtered, and the men cast lots for the delicacy of the raw, salted liver. Tonight they would feast.

Bryna watched through the tent flap while the men ate, then smoked after dinner. They were cheerful and noisy, and bursts of laughter could be heard while the women ate dinner in their tent. The men stayed up quite late, talking and telling stories from their inexhaustible supply. Even Suleiman contributed, choosing from the stories of Scheherazade, directing the conversation away from the subject of women and houris, for he was ever mindful of the treasures in the tent behind him.

Even when the slave trader, tired and sated, retired to his bed, Bryna continued her vigil. She watched guides, slaves, and camel drivers roll up in their cloaks and lie down beside the dying campfire. The Nubian assigned to guard the women's tent snored lightly, leaning against a tree, his musket held loosely between his knees. The only sign of activity in the sleeping camp came when two of the Sudanese boys, free from their elders' watchful eyes, crept to the beach for a moonlight swim.

When no one in the camp had stirred for a long time, Bryna picked up a small water skin and opened the tent flap. She glanced up at the full moon and wished the night were not so bright.

She slipped out of the tent with no clear plan of action. She had discussed escape with Pamela many times, but the English girl maintained it was too dangerous, that she could never survive such an attempt. At last, Bryna had privately concurred.

She regretted leaving Pamela, but she knew it was the only way to save both of them. The English had only just begun to make their presence felt in Egypt. If Bryna could reach them in Cairo, she could secure asylum for herself and rescue for her friend.

Staying close to the tents, she stole to the edge of the dark camp. She ran silently across a moonlit clearing toward a thicket of palms that stretched almost to the beach. Among the trees she dropped to the sand and listened, her heart pounding, but she heard no sounds of pursuit.

She made her way toward the water, halting in the shadows when she reached the cove. The coast-line, washed with gentle waves, stretched north for nearly a mile to another stand of trees that ran down to the waterline. A rocky promontory pre-scribed its southern boundary.

A short distance from the grove of trees that hid her, the two Sudanese boys, stripped to their loincloths, frolicked in the surf. Their voices car-ried clearly on the night breeze. She was glad of the warning, but if they were not quiet, they would wake the camp. Then their swim—and her escape—would be ruined.

She spied their clothes where they had left them just a few feet from her hiding place. Rapidly she gauged the older of the two boys as he thrust himself upright in the water. He was about her size, she judged, elated as a plan came to her.

Creeping to the edge of the grove, she used a long stick to drag his clothing to her. Quickly she doffed her djellaba, keeping only her sturdy leather sandals, and donned his clothes. His aba was scratchy and smelled of sweat, smoke, and camel dung, but it would serve as a disguise.

Bryna took care to wrap the turban cloth tightly around her head. She had learned that the larger the turban, the more prominent the wearer, and she had no wish to draw attention to herself.

Before she left, she gathered her own clothes. When the boy discovered his were missing, he would set off an alarm. The entire camp would search, and if they found her garments in the sand, they would know at once she was gone. She must give herself as much of a head start as possible.

Wadding her clothes into a compact ball and shoving it under her arm, she slung the water skin over her shoulder and ventured out into the moonlight. She would walk first to the south, she had decided, leaving footprints in the sand to mislead her pursuers. Then she would take to the water and double-back toward the north and town.

Drawing a nervous breath, Bryna strode across the beach at an angle to the swimmers. She was almost past before they saw her and called softly, thinking she was the friend they had left in camp. She was grateful when the moon disappeared for a moment behind a wisp of cloud. In the darkness perhaps the boys would not be able to distinguish the face under the turban.

Conspiratorially she gestured to silence them and shook her head at their invitation, pointing toward the rocky promontory. She hoped she looked like a lad who was out to explore.

Apparently they decided that was just what she

was. They did not continue to call but threw curious glances over their shoulders as she sauntered along the beach. In close-knit tribal life, solitude was not a concept easily understood. Bryna could feel their eyes upon her as she stopped here and there unconcernedly to pick up seashells.

Losing interest in her, they continued their water sport. When Bryna reached the promontory, she continued her charade, bending frequently to examine small pools in the rocks. Finding a large crevice, she hid her clothing and continued to ramble. At last she rounded the point and was blocked from the swimmers' view by a huge boulder.

Instantly she ripped the turban from her head and wrapped the long, lightweight cloth around her waist, securing the water skin against her body. Bryna had never swum in an ocean before, but she was a strong swimmer. She only hoped she could drift silently past the boys. After diving into the chilly water, she paddled out about a hundred yards, then turned northward with swift sure strokes.

She drew even with the Sudanese boys as they played. They were not aware of her presence as she knifed underwater silently. She surfaced a good distance beyond them, gasping for air, blinking saltwater from her eyes, then resumed the smooth, even strokes that would carry her to the north end of the beach and the grove of trees that slanted out to sea.

She dog-paddled until she found her footing, then waded ashore at the far end of the cove, crouching so no more than her head was visible on the surface. When she was quite close to the shore, she ducked under a wave and let it carry her into the stand of trees. Sand and shells cut her hands when she thrust them out in front of her to cushion the impact as she collided with a tree trunk.

Stunned and waterlogged, she sprawled in the sand and watched the wave that had carried her recede. Then, scrambling to her feet, she plunged into the shadow, where she poised, listening. No alarm had yet been raised. She paused long enough to unwind the long strip of fabric from around her waist and wring it out. Hastily she wrapped the limp, wet turban around her head again.

Feeling her way through darkness and tangled undergrowth, she emerged on the other side of the thicket, out of sight of the camp and almost at the water's edge.

Bryna sprinted along the beach at the waterline so the waves obliterated her footprints. As she raced toward the town, her only thought was to pass through the deserted streets without observation. If she could find a hiding place, she would stay there until she was sure Suleiman had sailed.

An hour later she had concealed herself among some fallen trees in a tiny copse on the opposite side of Suakin from the camp. Her heart still pounding and her breath burning in her chest, she burrowed under prickly brown foliage. She had escaped, but what should she do next?

With her slender figure and the turban to hide her hair, she might be able to travel disguised as a stepped on the heel of her sandal. Its straps broken, the flapping shoe caused Bryna to trip and fall into an open square where the traffic of several streets converged. She rolled to escape more clutching hands, her maneuver taking her to the feet of one of Suleiman's Sudanese guides. Her blue eyes widened in horror when she recognized him.

Although he had never seen her without her veil, the man knew without a doubt that this was the woman he sought. What a beauty she was under the dirt that smeared her face! No wonder Suleiman had delayed his departure in hopes of finding her.

A grin splitting his thin face, the guard reached for the tumbling girl. His hand grasped the cord that held her water skin in place against her body. Bryna tore from his grip and left him juggling the obscenely wobbling skin. She disappeared as quickly as she had appeared, dodging into the swarm of people entering the square from one of the side streets.

With a curse the man followed, but by the time he had forced his way through the crowd, she was nowhere to be seen. Had he looked closely, he might have recognized her, for immediately after seeing him, Bryna had ducked into a doorway, kicked off her remaining sandal, and with shaking hands rearranged her turban. Then, putting a half-witted smile on her face, she'd padded out barefoot to join the stream of passersby.

She followed the flow of traffic to the waterfront, where huge sambuks were being loaded by

boy. But what of her blue eyes? And how would she communicate? She spoke very little Arabic, but, dressed as a Sudanese tribesman in the Sudan, she would be expected to speak the language. She could pretend to be mute, but she must also feign deafness, she mused, for she could see no way to avoid conversation unless she pretended to be a half-wit. The superstitious Arabs would go out of their way to avoid a demented person. Wearily the girl wrestled with the problem until she fell into an uneasy sleep.

It was very hot and flies were buzzing around her face when Bryna awoke. Her stomach rumbled, but she determinedly put hunger from her mind. Instead she drank some tepid water from her water skin, grimacing at its bitter taste. Throughout the sweltering day, she remained in her cramped hiding place. Once she heard voices and peered out through withered palm fronds to observe Suleiman's guides, searching for her.

The insects that shared her sanctuary crawled all over her body, causing her to itch in a dozen places. Her stomach still complained of hunger and cramps crept up her weary legs, but Bryna lay still and gritted her teeth. When the searchers left, she saw no one else. She supposed Suleiman had given up and sailed, but she stayed in her hiding place the rest of the day.

On the second morning after her escape, Bryna drank the last of her water, nearly gagging on the dregs that had settled at the bottom of the skin. When she heard the faint cry of the muezzin from the mosque in town, she rose stiffly and made her way into Suakin. By the time she arrived, most of the town would be at midday prayers and she could pass through the streets relatively unnoticed. While others rested, she would explore the waterfront to find a vessel upon which she could stow away. But first she must find food and water.

The girl walked cautiously through empty streets to the well in the middle of the town. She drank greedily and filled her water skin before setting out for the market.

Suakin was an international port. Even during prayers the souks were full of non-Moslems. Bartering and arguing loudly, merchants and shoppers paid no attention to the gangly youth wandering in their midst. She ambled toward the food stalls, drawn by the aroma of cooking food. Her mouth watered, but she had no money and nothing to trade but the locket around her neck. She fingered it speculatively, but she could not bear to part with the last remnant of her past.

Hunger warred with conscience, winning in the end. Bryna inched toward a fruit stand and looked around furtively. The vendor argued loudly with another man in a corner of the stall. Ascertaining that no one was watching, she laid her hand casually on a display of glossy oranges, arranged in a pyramid. When she moved her hand, the pinnacle of the pyramid was gone. Glancing around innocently, she started to pocket it when her eyes met the incensed stare of the merchant. Her heart sank. She had been seen.

He shouted and lunged toward her. Br[y]na [did] not understand what he said, but his inte[ntion was] clear. Immediately she bolted from the fru[it stand,] the irate man on her heels. Her dismay at dr[opping] the orange lessened when her pursuer st[opped] long enough to pick up his purloined mercha[ndise.] Perhaps he would give up the chase. But his te[mper] had not cooled, and he ran after her, shouting [at the] top of his lungs.

As she sped through the streets, the pan[icked] girl spied a large building where many men co[ngre]gated just outside the doors. She darted int[o the] crowd, hoping to lose her pursuer. She had al[most] worked her way through the sea of humanity [when] she glanced back and ran headlong into a s[trong] back.

Bryna's turban was displaced in the colli[sion] and her hair tumbled from beneath it, cascad[ing to] her shoulders. The glossy tresses and her deli[cate,] chiseled features marked her as undeniably f[emale.] The shocked men, coming from the Friday s[ervice] at the mosque, reacted angrily at the sigh[t of an] unveiled woman masquerading as a boy.

Rough hands held her, pulling at her [clothes,] revealing curves beneath the coarse fabr[ic. She] fought to free herself. Behind her, Bryna [heard] shouts of the vendor coming closer as h[e made] his way through the throng. Desperately s[he hit] and kicked, landing a few well-aimed b[lows. With] an agonized yelp, her captor loosened h[is hold and] she broke free.

As she darted away, someone in [the crowd] fr[...]

sweating porters. At the outskirts of town, she found a beached dhow at the water's edge. Shoving with all her might, Bryna set the little boat afloat. Holding on and swimming beside it, she propelled it beyond the breakers, hoisting herself aboard as soon as she was able. She ignored the faint, angry shouts from shore and set sail for open sea.

All the next day, Bryna made little progress toward the coast of Egypt. There was no wind, and the currents carried the dhow steadily eastward. Knowing she had little hope of survival unless she was rescued by another vessel, she watched the horizon for signs of another ship while the blistering sun and the lack of food and water took its toll on her.

On the second morning, when she sighted a large boat sailing in her direction, she used her last ounce of strength to signal it. As the sambuk drew near, the girl collapsed into an exhausted heap on the bottom of the dhow.

Bryna was not aware when the larger boat drew even with her craft. She did not hear the captain bawling orders to the crew, did not see the passengers lining the rail, did not realize when a brawny seaman was let down with a rope to lift her to the waiting hands of her rescuers.

Outstretched on the *sasch*-wood deck, Bryna felt a shadow fall across her face, then a cup was put to her lips. Eagerly she gripped it with shaking hands and drank.

"By Allah, Bryna bint Blaine, if you do not wish to make yourself sick, do not drink so fast."

It could not be!

Opening her eyes with extreme effort, she saw the imposing silhouette looming over her, blocking out the sun. The features on the shadowy visage became distinct as Suleiman leaned toward her, his round face smug.

"Non," she whispered.

"Oui, Mademoiselle. Praise be to Allah, you have found us when we could not find you."

The pleasant, reedy voice of the marriage broker was the last sound the distraught girl heard as she surrendered to welcome unconsciousness.

CHAPTER

✧✧✧✧✧ **7** ✧✧✧✧✧

"DID YOU HEAR WHAT I SAID, MY LOVE? I WANT to marry you. I intend to ask your father for your hand." Bryna stirred fitfully, unwilling to relinquish her dream of Derek. His handsome face had been so earnest when he proposed to her. But she awakened.

Ill and dispirited, Bryna lay in a cramped cabin aboard the sambuk. Her eyes closed tightly, she listened to the confusion and clamor of voices from just outside the door to the cabin. Typical of Red Sea vessels, the boat was packed to bursting. Groups of people clustered on deck, even cooking and sleeping there. For a price, Suleiman had managed to secure two berths in the overcrowded women's cabin for Bryna and Pamela.

"*Haj-al sala,* come to prayer. Devotion is better than sleep," called the imam. The din died down, and soon Bryna heard male voices as they prayed in unison.

The sound was as constant at sea as it had been in the desert. Heaving a deep sigh, Bryna opened her eyes and saw Pamela leaning over her.

"Good morning," the English girl greeted her coolly. "How do you feel?"

"Fine, *merci*. Just disappointed." Bryna sipped thankfully from a cup Pamela offered.

"Well, I was half out of my mind with worry," Pamela declared reprovingly. "You gave us such a fright, you know. Whatever were you thinking, putting out alone to sea in a tiny boat? When you were rescued, Suleiman said it was a wonder you were not taken by Yanbo pirates. Then who knows what your fate might have been?"

"Who knows now?" the American girl asked flatly. "What kind of punishment does Suleiman have in mind for me? Do you know?"

"He says the experience was punishment enough. He says now that you know there is no escape, you will be a better slave."

"There must be a way," Bryna muttered mostly to herself.

"Oh, you will not escape again and leave me behind, will you? Promise me you won't. I do not want to be alone in this godforsaken part of the world." Pamela laid her head down on the bunk beside Bryna and began to weep bitterly.

"No, I will not leave you behind the next time." Filled with remorse, Bryna stroked the other girl's head. "When we escape, we will go together," she assured her, knowing she had just given up any hope of flight.

"Thank you." Lifting her tearstained face, Pamela smiled wanly at Bryna. "I must find you some food. I imagine you are starving. I know I am."

Speedily she went to speak to Turki, who was posted just outside the cabin door, leaving Bryna to her despair.

A few days later the sambuk moored at Jidda, the main military depot of the Ottoman empire in Arabia. It was difficult to see from the single porthole of their tiny cabin, so the women had only a vague impression of sun-washed walls, rugged fortifications, and batteries, all backed by purple mountains, the Hijaz, in the distance.

They waited for Suleiman as their cabin-mates departed one by one, summoned by their men. At last the slave trader appeared. It was the first time Bryna had seen him since the morning of the rescue. He said nothing of it, but his limpid eyes were reproachful.

"Prepare yourselves to go ashore, my doves." He gestured extravagantly. "It is a lovely spring day, and we will walk the short distance to our lodgings."

Resignedly Bryna and Pamela pulled their *burqus* into place and followed him onto deck. Far from a lovely day, the heat of the *Tihama*, the coastal plain, shrouded them like a wet, steaming blanket. Suleiman's party descended the gangplank into a sea of shouting, sweating humanity. Bryna even forgot her rancor temporarily as her fascinated eyes tried to take in every detail. She had never seen so many people at one time.

As the burial place of Eve, the mother of all, Jidda was considered a holy place. Today the city was flooded with thousands of pilgrims. Suleiman's party had arrived at the end of the month of *Dhul Qa'da*, when travelers from throughout the world gathered to prepare for hajj, the journey to Mecca and Medina, the holiest cities of Islam. For centuries the chief industry of Jidda had been the landing, moving, and shelter of pilgrims. The expense of hajj was great, and Jidda was a wealthy city.

In the teeming throng at the waterfront, the girl saw for the first time the green turbans of the descendants of the Prophet. Here beggars, left destitute from earlier hajjs, shouted loudly to newcomers for baksheesh. Well-dressed young Arabs loudly boasted of their skill as *delils*, or guides, to the holy cities. Porters, their faces marked with three scars on each cheek, which showed they had been born in Jidda or Mecca, led Egyptians, Moors, and Syrians through the crowd. Desert Bedu wandered by, and swarthy Turkish and Egyptian soldiers shouldered their way arrogantly through the horde, ignoring the scowls of the Arabs they jostled.

Anxious to escape the crush, Suleiman made swift arrangements for his baggage to be taken to his lodgings, then he led his entourage single file away from the docks. The huge bazaar ran the length of the city wall, parallel to the waterfront. On the other side of the souk, the group passed into broad streets, wider than most in the Arab world. Jidda was a graceful old city, its affluence obvious to those who passed through it.

Suleiman's small procession came finally to a residential section, a disorganized jumble of four-

and five-story houses lining streets and alleyways. The houses were lovely, white-walled structures with lattice-screened balconies, arched doors, and gates into private gardens. Unlike the ones in most Eastern cities, the homes in Jidda were graced by huge, bowed windows that faced onto the sunny street. The facade of each house was a work of art, its windows and doors framed by exquisitely carved casings.

The slave trader stopped in front of the large house with rich teak doors where he often lodged on visits to Jidda. He lifted the brass-ring knocker and dropped it. Instantly a servant appeared, and the visitors were admitted to a pleasant courtyard.

The man of the house was not at home, so his veiled wife greeted Suleiman shyly and showed his party to a comfortable apartment that filled one wing of the sizable house. Suleiman established the women there and, after resting, went to a coffee-house to make his presence known in the city.

Hajji Suleiman Ibn Hussein was famous throughout Arabia for his lavish but discreet private sales. They were to be anticipated in a land where such events were often the chief method of marking time. Suleiman invited only the elite and sold only the rarest and most exquisite. This sale, though small, would be one of his finest, he decided.

Bryna and Pamela were blissfully ignorant of the marriage broker's plans. Relieved the worst of their grueling journey was behind them, the exhausted girls spent their days enjoying the comforts of a real house and tried not to think of the future.

It seemed to Bryna that she would never again get enough water—to drink, to bathe in, to cool herself. She hoped never to see another desert. As for Pamela, she was content to eat heartily of the tasty offerings presented by the landlord's wife. She did not even voice her constant hope for rescue.

After the women had rested for several days, Suleiman brought them each a set of new clothes and a shy maid to assist them.

"We are to have guests, and you must look your best," he explained lamely in the face of Bryna's accusing stare.

The girl took one look at the diaphanous trousers with their embroidered bands at the waist and ankles, at the short blouse, delicate sandals, and sheer, flowing *ghata,* or head covering, and knew that these were garments for the harem. She seethed, cursing herself as much as Suleiman. She and Pamela were about to meet their fate—their kismet, as the slave trader had put it—and they had done little more in the past few days than eat, sleep, and bathe, recuperating from the effects of the desert.

Her mind began to work rapidly. If they could escape the house, they could vanish into the mass of pilgrims. If she could secure a yashmak and a haik for Pamela so no one could see her fair skin . . . If she could steal a boy's clothing for herself again . . . If they could find a boat captain who spoke French . . . If they could reach Cairo . . .

As if he were reading her mind, Suleiman cautioned, "Do not think you can flee, Bryna bint Blaine. My guards watch all doors of the household. You will not escape again. They will not again be so careless as they were at the Red Sea."

That evening the maid helped the women dress. Pamela was clad in ethereal blue with silver embroidery. Bryna's clothing was rose, its embroidery peppered with silvery crystal beads.

In the harem the women could hear when the guests began to arrive for the sale. Bryna paced, the beads on her costume clicking with each step. Her nerves were taut and tightened more with each sound of male laughter floating in from the *majlis* as the men were made comfortable and Turki served refreshments.

"What will happen to us, Bryna?" Pamela asked, nervously popping a grape into her mouth. "Do you think Suleiman will sell us together? I cannot believe he would separate us. He actually seems rather fond of us, in his way . . . " Her prattle trailed off when Suleiman, clad in his finest Turkish attire, summoned them.

He ordered them to affix their filmy veils and follow him to the hall, where he positioned them in front of a grill through which they could see the *majlis* without being seen themselves.

"Some of the most important men in Arabia are here tonight," Suleiman boasted to his charges. "Many important sheiks seek wives. There is Abu Ali Al Rashid, and Ibn Hasan, and look!" The slave trader's fat face reddened apoplectically. "There is

Nassar bin Hamza, the nephew of Sheik Sharif Al Selim, one of the richest men in all Arabia. The Selims are sayyids, descendants of the Prophet himself. *Alhamdillah!* What a wondrous gathering is this!"

Peeping through the grill, Bryna shuddered when she saw the young man Suleiman indicated. He was a soft, pudgy fellow wearing a rich aba and a silk kaffiyeh. The aghal that held his head covering in place was wrapped with golden cord.

At first glance Nassar bin Hamza's round face might be considered handsome in an effeminate way, but if one looked closely, his countenance was cruel and repellent. His murky brown eyes were narrow, his nose hooked slightly. The mouth above the pointed beard was small, mean, and thin-lipped.

"Come, my doves, it is time to greet our guests." Suleiman grasped each woman by an elbow and led them to the door of the *majlis.* When they appeared, all conversation in the room stopped and the potential buyers looked at them expectantly.

Bryna never remembered clearly the details of that dreadful night. Dimly she was aware that Suleiman welcomed his guests while gripping the women's arms painfully in his nervousness. She did not remember walking to the small platform at the front of the *majlis.* Somehow she was there and all eyes were focused upon her with the penetrating, hawklike stares of the rugged men.

Drawing on her limited Arabic, Bryna tried but could not understand all that was said as Suleiman described each veiled woman in detail, praising them as superior candidates for marriage. He answered numerous questions, producing documents to prove they were virgins. At last he drew the women forward and removed their veils.

"Mashallah," came the collective murmur. There was no other sound in the room as all eyes were drawn to Pamela's fair coloring.

Before Suleiman could say another word, Nassar spoke lazily from his divan. "You may as well set your price for the one with hair of gold, Suleiman. I must have her. I will better the offer of any man in the house."

For an instant an expression of annoyance flashed across Suleiman's face, replaced just as quickly by an obsequious smile. He had planned to sell Bryna first to allow the anticipation to build for the sale of the blonde. *Insh'allah,* Nassar bin Hamza was a man who knew how to get what he wanted, even if it took away the joy of bidding for it.

"You wish to buy her outright? Do I hear any objections?" The slave trader's gaze swept the assembly, but as he had imagined, no one protested. A few men grumbled under their breath, but no one could afford to outbid the powerful house of Al Selim, neither monetarily nor politically. The fair one was beyond their grasp. So be it.

"Very well, bin Hamza," Suleiman agreed reluctantly. Gently he pushed Pamela behind him, where she could no longer distract the bidders. Eager to escape the probing eyes, she did not question him. And her Arabic was still so poor, the girl did not realize she had been sold.

"What am I offered for this one?" Suleiman called, gesturing to Bryna.

Bidding was brisk and lively, until finally the American girl was sold to Sheik Al Rashid as a gift to his youngest son. The stern-faced old man rose and claimed his purchase, taking Bryna by the arm to lead her from the platform.

Comprehension dawned in Pamela's brown eyes. Emitting a frightened screech, she clung desperately to her friend. Small Turki attached himself to Pamela, wrapping his arms around her waist to pull her from Bryna, but the wailing girl would not relinquish her hold. Suleiman looked on helplessly as the four ranged like stairsteps across the dais, with the tall Bedouin at the head and Turki as the bottom. In his corner, Nassar laughed aloud as the incensed desert chieftain looked to the marriage broker for assistance.

"Pamela bint Harold," Suleiman scolded the weeping girl in French, "release Bryna bint Blaine at once. She must go where Allah decrees. And you must not displease your new master."

"I must go with Bryna." The English girl sobbed piteously. "Bryna, don't let him take you away. You promised."

Impatiently the sheik pulled Pamela from his newly acquired slave and thrust her toward Suleiman. The force of his movement threw Pamela and Turki off balance, and they careened backward into Suleiman. All three tumbled onto the divan at the far side of the dais.

Nassar roared, bent double with laughter. He

rose and stepped toward the platform, wiping tears of mirth from his cheeks. "A moment, Abu Ali," he said, detaining the sheik. "It would seem my fair Inglayzi does not wish to be parted from the tall one. Let me purchase her from you at a profit, then all will be happy."

"How much profit?" Abu Ali asked suspiciously.

"One hundred riyals?" Nassar suggested with hardly a thought of his dwindling inheritance.

"By the Prophet, my son Ali would receive great joy from this woman," the older man argued. "Look at her. She is a houri who will bear many sons. This is a woman of great value."

"All right, I will give two hundred riyals for her." Nassar glanced in Bryna's direction and shrugged carelessly.

"A man can always get gold. A Bedu would rather have camels," Abu Ali suggested craftily. "The riding camels of Al Selim are the best in Arabia."

"Very well, I have three riding camels and ten pack camels with me in Jidda. I will give you the riding camels and you may choose two from among the others."

"Six," Abu Ali countered.

"Four and no more."

"For the sake of your uncle, I will take five pack camels."

"Four and no more," Nassar repeated.

The desert chieftain considered a moment. "Take her," he grunted. He released Bryna abruptly, amazed at the other man's extravagance. "A man can get a wife another time, but seven Al Selim camels ... "

Nassar took Bryna's arm and pushed her to the divan, where Pamela lay weeping, her tousled blond head buried in satin pillows.

"Hush, Pamela," she whispered with a wry smile, "we are going to be together. I think he just traded some camels for me."

Seemingly watching the disgruntled would-be bidders depart, Nassar was gratified to note out of the corner of his eye that the blonde ceased her wailing and mopped away her tears at a word from the other woman. The dark-haired one might be useful, and she was not unpleasant to look upon. He cared nothing for superstition. Even with her blue eyes, she was valuable. Perhaps the loss of his uncle's camels had not been in vain.

Suleiman waddled over to join Nassar, and soon the two men were haggling over a price for Pamela. They finally settled on an amount that provided a healthy profit to the marriage broker.

The fat slave trader summoned Turki, who appeared carrying two bundles that contained all the clothing Suleiman had bought for the women since their purchase in Tangier.

"Farewell, my doves," the marriage broker said almost sadly. "Take these things with my blessings and the blessing of Allah. May he protect you on your journey."

"Come," Nassar ordered arrogantly in French, the language with which Suleiman had communicated with them. "Do not linger. I am your *sidi* now." He was their master, he thought with a thrill of pleasure, and without a command of the language these women would be completely dependent upon him. He liked that idea. He would instruct his slaves not to speak to the women at all on the way home. Let them ask him if they needed something.

As the girls departed, escorted by Nassar's small army of servants, Bryna glanced back at Suleiman. His sorrow at their parting was already forgotten. He sat cross-legged on the platform of the deserted *majlis,* gleefully counting his money. She had just been sold for a third time, she thought bleakly, and she liked it no better than before. How were her father or Derek ever to find her?

Nassar's good mood deteriorated rapidly as his party approached the home of his host, an old family friend. He began to pout, ordering his servants about curtly. He wanted to enjoy his new possessions, but he knew he could not tonight. Once they arrived at the villa, the girls would be whisked away to the harem with the other females of the household. Then he would be expected to sit up until all hours of the night, discussing the Koran and the Hadith, the traditions of the Prophet. Being a descendant of Muhammad was indeed burdensome at times.

Insh'allah . . . for tonight, Nassar thought petulantly. But tomorrow they would leave for Taif, his family's summer home. Then he would do as he pleased. No one would dare stop him. His lips twisted into a smile of lecherous anticipation.

Immediately after prayers the next morning, Nassar went to the market to buy horses for the journey. His party left Jidda soon after the midday call to devotions. They mounted and rode away over the protests of his host, who had wished to impress Sharif Al Selim through his nephew. The young man would not even consider lengthening his visit, so under the blazing noonday sun, when most people were at rest, his train of horses and pack camels left the city through the exquisite Bab al Mecca.

They passed under battlements atop the gate that loomed black against the faded sky. Swatting at legions of mosquitoes that bedeviled them, they rode through a cluster of straw huts that made up a settlement just outside the walls. Then, free of the city, they galloped across the Tihama plains toward the Hijaz mountains.

Passing through miles of rocky desert, Nassar reflected on the behavior of the tall woman. He had been chagrined to discover this morning that she spoke faltering Arabic. Unwilling to leave Pamela out of any conversation, he had commanded the American to speak to him in French so the Inglayzi could also understand.

Bryna had been obedient to his orders so far, but he could see in her blue eyes how she longed to rebel. If only she would, he smiled lazily. It was sometimes amusing to tame a wild creature. He knew how lovemaking would be with her, passionate, even violent. But after he had taken her, he would return to his first love, the golden-haired Pamela.

The young Arab's loins ached at the very thought of her cool blond beauty. He did not speak to the objects of his fantasies as they rode behind him, but he glanced back continually at the English girl's cloaked figure, his imagination working as he devoured her with hungry eyes.

As the party ascended into the mountains, the humid, stifling air of the Tihama was left behind and the breeze was cool and juniper-scented. Eagles wheeled lazily in the cloudless blue sky above their aeries, and in the mountain passes baboons shrieked down at the travelers as the line of graceful horses picked their way along the rocky paths, descending into the lovely valley where Taif nestled far below.

Higher up, another rider shared the vista. Sharif Al Selim reined his mare to a halt and stopped to enjoy the view. Down the trail behind him, the chieftain could hear his kinsmen and retainers laughing and talking among themselves as they ambled through a copse of wild olive trees. They were less concerned with flushing game from the bushes than with enjoying each other's company.

Despite the easy camaraderie he was missing, Sharif was pleased to have a moment of solitude. He sighed deeply and turned unfocused eyes on a green mountainside in the distance. When would the ill fortune that seemed to pursue him tire of the chase?

It had been a day much like this just last month when even more bad news had reached him. As the sheik had returned from the hunt and neared his house, the mourning cry had reached his ears. Shrill and piercing, it rose from the women's quarters, lingering on the wind, and it could only mean death. Throwing himself from his saddle, he was greeted in the courtyard with the news that Zayid, his impetuous nephew, was dead, another victim of his father's murderers.

Later Sharif had walked alone in the hills behind his villa, trying to ease his own pain while the keening wail seemed to echo from the rocks. It rose not only from his own home, but from the houses of his people. His sorrow was not his alone; it was shared by the tribe, for one day the young man would have succeeded Sharif as sheik. Now the only one left besides the small children was Nassar.

As Allah willed, Sharif reflected, but his mouth tightened nonetheless at the thought. In the year since his father's death, Nassar had squandered most of his inheritance. No doubt now he would spend Zayid's share of the legacy just as rapidly.

There was nothing wrong with the young man that some schooling in Bedouin ways would not have corrected, Sharif mused, but it was too late now. The inevitable hardening that came when the sons of nobility lived with the Bedu was intended for boys. Nassar had been soft and sickly all his life, and his mother had convinced Hamza not to expose him to the deprivations of the desert. Nassar had stayed safely at home.

Sharif knew, however, that the young man's weak appearance concealed a will of iron when it came to having his own way. Nassar also had a notoriously bad temper. It was legendary among the servants, although Sharif had never actually seen him mistreat a slave.

Now, since Zayid's death, Nassar was *ibn 'amm*, the son of her uncle and the mate, according to Arab custom, for Sharif's daughter, `Abla. The thought pained the chieftain. Although he was not close to his daughter, he would not wish her cousin on anyone. Thank God she was young yet, he thought darkly. Perhaps by the time she was old enough to wed, his nephew would have mellowed with age.

Absently the man's gaze swept the panorama before him, narrowing when he saw the small caravan descending to the valley floor below.

Even from this distance Sharif recognized the horseman who slouched along in the lead. It was Nassar. But why was he coming back to Taif so soon? He had been sent to Mecca two weeks ago for dual purposes. He was to participate in hajj for the first time, earning the title of Hajji, as was fitting for a sayyid. After *Eed al Adha*, the feast celebrating the end of pilgrimage, he was to remain in the holy city long enough to purchase a load of wheat and barley brought by caravan from Syria. *Eed al Adha* would not occur for nearly two weeks, yet here he was. Even more puzzling was the identity of the women he brought with him.

Sharif wheeled his horse and doubled back on the trail. A short distance down the mountainside, he met his surprised entourage.

"Where do you go so quickly, Sharif?" one of the men called.

"To the villa," the sheik responded, reining his horse near Sa'id, his cousin and most trusted friend. Quietly he told him what he had seen.

"Do you wish me to accompany you?" Sa'id asked immediately.

"No, take the others on the hunt," Sharif requested. "Enjoy yourselves. It is said that a man forgets his birth and suffers in death. He must not neglect the life in between.

"Good hunting," he bade the others, and urged his horse toward home—and the harem, for that was where he would find his nephew.

CHAPTER

✦✦✦✦ **8** ✦✦✦✦

THE SHRILL, WELCOMING TRILL OF THE WOMEN greeted Nassar and his retinue as they approached the pastel-hued villa. The young man spurred his horse mercilessly and galloped toward the two waiting figures, swathed in concealing black cloaks and masklike *burqus.*

"*As salaam 'alaykum.* Welcome home, my son," Fatmah, the shorter and stouter of the two, called as he dismounted.

"Peace to you, ya Umm," he greeted his mother. "And to you, Latifeh," he said to his aunt. "It is good to be home."

"Tonight we will roast a goat to celebrate," Fatmah announced, "but for now, let us receive you in the harem, where a cool drink will refresh you."

Nassar tossed the reins of his horse to a waiting servant and commanded Bryna and Pamela to follow him, ignoring the questioning glances his mother and aunt shot at him.

The girls trailed behind him through an exquisite courtyard, more beautiful than they had ever seen. The elegant stone house was built in a U

141

shape around the courtyard. An airy *majlis* formed much of the base of the U, with a kitchen at the back. The lower floor of the left wing housed storerooms; a private chamber for the sheik's trusted servant, Abu Ahmad; and a dormitory for the male servants. Upstairs were apartments for the male members of the family. Nassar's overlooked the courtyard; and a spacious apartment, facing the gardens at the back of the house, belonged to Sharif.

The right wing was connected to the *majlis* by a breezeway. A formidable door barred the entrance to the harem, where the household's women and children lived. Women servants slept in a dormitory near the front of the house, while Sharif's small family, Fatmah, Latifeh, and `Abla, occupied the back section, an enormous suite of apartments that opened onto a pleasant walled garden.

The procession had no sooner reached the women's quarters than Nassar's mother and aunt ripped the *burqus* from their faces and pounced on the young man with questions.

"Who are these women?" they demanded in unison, turning hostile eyes on the newcomers, who hesitated in the doorway.

"Slaves," Nassar answered noncommittally, sprawling on a pillow.

"We do not need more serving girls," the sensible Latifeh protested, offering him a cool drink.

"Then it is just as well that I purchased them as wives," the young man answered, smiling at her smugly.

"Wives?" Fatmah shrieked. The portly woman sank down beside her son and clutched at his sleeve. "What of your betrothed?"

"What of her?" Nassar shook free of her grasp. "I am not even sure I should marry her since Zayid's death. After all, now I have to marry `Abla."

"It is true that `Abla is your *bint 'amm,* the daughter of your father's brother, and obligated to marry you, but you have been pledged to Farida since childhood," his mother argued reasonably.

"Yes, you must honor that vow," Latifeh confirmed.

"Very well, I will marry both of them," Nassar agreed indifferently, "but I will also marry these two."

"Not until you have done your duty by Farida," Fatmah scolded.

"I want these now, *Umm,*" he cajoled his mother. "You will not mind if I have them, will you?"

"I have told you my feelings. If you are to wed them, it must wait until after you have married Farida," she answered firmly.

"Then I will take these as concubines," Nassar countered just as firmly.

"Nassar!" Fatmah gasped. Leaning back on her pillow, she fanned herself with a palm leaf fan. "What can you be thinking?"

"Yes, Nassar, you cannot—"

"I may not be a scholar, but do not tell me I am forbidden by the Prophet to take them, Latifeh." He scowled at his aunt, who was nearly as learned in Islamic law as a man. "If I took this issue before the

ulema, that holy court would back me up. I intend
to have these women . . . now."

"Why now?" his mother pleaded.

"I will show you why!" Jumping to his feet, he
strode to Pamela and ripped the burka and *ghata*
from her head. The shocked girl retreated in confusion, her eyes wide as her blond hair tumbled to
her shoulders. Nassar seized her arm tightly and
thrust her to stand before the older women.

"Let them look at you," he snapped.

"Allah protect me from the devil!" Fatmah
wailed. "You have brought a kaffir into our home."

"You cannot keep her," Latifeh argued despite
Nassar's warning. "You would become unclean
every time you touched her."

"Then I will wash until she makes her *shahada*.
Mind your business, woman," he snarled.

"What about this one?" Latifeh pressed, unde-
terred. She pointed at Bryna, who was poised at the
door.

"Come here and take off your veil," Nassar
ordered his unwilling slave.

"Allah will turn his face from us, so great will be
his displeasure," Fatmah moaned when Bryna stood
bareheaded before them, her chest heaving in
restrained anger. "Another kaffir, and this one has
the blue eyes of a bewitcher."

"What will we do with foreign women in the
harem? How can we even speak to them? I doubt
they understand the tongue of the prophet," the
ever-practical Latifeh said with a disdainful snort.

"You speak a little of the language of

Frankistan." Nassar shrugged carelessly. "I prefer they speak the language of the Franks, anyway."

"I do not know enough to make the infidels understand my commands," Fatmah complained to her son, who ignored her.

"I do not think you have to worry about that with this one," Latifeh murmured, watching the American girl closely. "I think she understands what we are saying.

"What is your name, girl?" she asked Bryna directly in Arabic.

Bryna looked at the woman and replied evenly, "Bryna bint Blaine Al O'Toole."

"My lady," Fatmah corrected stridently. "Tell her she must address us with respect."

"Tell her yourself." Latifeh frowned at her. "By Allah, I do not know how she could help but hear you when you screech in her ear." Turning to her nephew, she said, "This Bryna bint Blaine is not stupid, but her accent is hard to understand and she is as tall as a man. Why did you buy her?"

"To keep the golden-haired houri happy."

"You have surely been possessed by a jinni, Nassar," she responded disapprovingly. "What will people say when they find you have taken not one, but two infidel wives?"

"I will be the envy of all men when their wives and sisters tell them how beautiful my Inglayzis are. They will speak of my prowess around the campfires."

"Do not do this, my son," Fatmah begged. "You will bring shame upon our family."

"Shame! Do not speak to me of shame," Nassar screamed, suddenly galvanized into action. He lashed out, stomping around the room in a fit of temper, driving his fist into columns and kicking at the pillows and dishes on the floor.

While he ranted, Bryna prudently removed herself to a window overlooking the harem garden. Shrugging off her black cloak in the heat, she perched on the broad sill and tried to follow his tirade.

"Has Sharif done anything to lessen our shame since the death of my father?" Nassar demanded hotly. "He did not avenge our name with a *ghazzi* on the dogs who raided us."

"It was not fitting," Latifeh defended their new husband. "Theirs was a tribe of low standing. It would blacken our face to war with them."

"Yet he allowed Zayid to seek revenge," he jeered.

"Yes, he allowed Zayid to go." Fatmah sighed. "I do not think he could have stopped him."

"And all my beloved brother did was to get himself killed," the flabby young man scoffed, uncaring that his mother still mourned his older brother. "Now the raiders have disappeared into the sands, and still there is no blood for blood, no retribution.

"So do not speak to me of shame, old women. Has your precious Sharif sired any sons—or even tried? He did his duty and married you, but has he taken a woman to bear him children? Has he even ceased to be celibate? A man is his sons, and Sharif is no one. The father of a daughter. I ask you, where is the honor in that?"

"Where is the honor in what, Nassar?" a deep, rich voice inquired quietly from the doorway, and Sharif stepped into the room.

From her seat on the windowsill, Bryna inspected the new arrival with interest. This would be Nassar's uncle, the powerful Sheik Sharif Al Selim. That he was a leader of men was evident in his very bearing. His easy confidence demanded respect. Tall for an Arab and well proportioned, he stood erect with legs slightly spread. One strong, brown hand caressed the hilt of the sword that swung at his side. The man's back was to the window, and over his shoulder Bryna caught glimpses of a handsome, craggy face, bronzed by the sun.

From what she could see of him, Bryna decided Sharif Al Selim looked as if he were in his mid-thirties. Even though his neatly trimmed black beard was peppered lightly with silvery white hairs, he hardly looked old enough to be the revered leader of the respected tribe. Beneath his snowy kaffiyeh, his headdress, the sheik's eyes were an unexpected slate color. Their gaze was disturbingly direct and penetrating.

Sharif's loose-fitting white *thobe* and russet aba did not disguise the muscular figure beneath. A saffron sash encircled his lean midriff. Tucked into the sash was a jeweled silver dagger and a brace of pistols.

The moment of his entrance seemed frozen in time as Sharif took in the tableau. Nassar halted his frantic pacing and gazed at his uncle defiantly, while Sharif's wives stared at him openmouthed, consternation written on their lined faces. And in the midst of the chaos, a pale blond beauty stood, still swathed in her cloak. Her head was bowed and tears seeped from her tightly shut eyes.

"Silence," Sharif roared when Nassar and both of his wives began to talk at once. "Now," he addressed his nephew in a more moderate tone, "where did this woman come from?"

"Jidda," the younger man mumbled sullenly.

"Jidda? You were supposed to be in Mecca for hajj."

"I will go on hajj next year. This year I heard I could get a better price on Egyptian grain in Jidda, so I went," Nassar lied. He had gone to Jidda for pleasure, wanting to see that port city while it bustled with pilgrims. He had planned to be back in Mecca by the time hajj began, but he had lingered overlong. Then, hearing of Suleiman's private sale, he had decided to stay on, putting the inevitable confrontation with Sharif from his mind.

It was worth it, even if his uncle was furious, Nassar thought, gazing possessively at Pamela.

"I saw you from the mountains as you returned, and you did not bring grain with you," Sharif interrupted his gloating. "And now that I think of it, you had only six pack animals and no riding camels. Where are the others?"

"I traded them," Nassar responded sulkily. "I will pay you for them."

"You traded my camels?" Sharif repeated in a deceptively mild voice. "What, in the name of Allah, did you trade seven good camels for?"

"That one." Nassar nodded toward the window behind the man. The sheik glanced over his shoulder. His body stiffened involuntarily, then he turned slowly to face the girl. Sharif was glad no one else could see his face as he beheld her sitting there, wearing a rose-colored harem costume in the manner of the Turks. Her face was shadowed as the sun streaming through the window behind her created a warm halo around her glossy hair. His gray eyes widened incredulously. Something about her reminded him of Noorah. How serene and docile she looked, how young, like his dainty, lovely Noorah.

But the resemblance disappeared when the girl rose and her face was clearly seen. She was lovely, though she was tall, almost as tall as he. And her eyes were blue and fearless as she met his scrutiny proudly. If she were a man, she would be a warrior, he thought, but as a woman she was disturbingly beautiful.

For a long moment Bryna faced him warily. At last Sharif shook his head as if waking from a dream and turned to his nephew. "What do you plan to do with these women?"

"I plan to marry them."

"Both of them?"

"Yes, and Farida and `Abla as well," Nassar retorted belligerently before his uncle could continue.

"I see . . . four wives," Sharif mused. "Well, it is not forbidden to have four wives if you treat them equally. But usually wives come only one at a time."

149

"Then I may have them? All of them?" Nassar asked eagerly, disregarding the caution in his uncle's voice.

"Do not rush me," Sharif exhorted, pacing the length of the room. "This decision requires thought."

It was time his nephew settled down, Sharif reasoned as he walked. Nassar was a born trouble-maker. Perhaps four wives would keep him busy. Still, these two were infidels . . .

Reaching the end of the room, he pivoted and his gaze fell distractedly upon Bryna. Annoyed by his own inattention, the man riveted his eyes to the tiled floor and continued to pace, trying to sort his thoughts. But with every step he was aware of her quiet presence. He passed her twice more, and Sharif's mind was made up, whether he liked it or not.

"Let us speak first of your *bint 'amm* and your intended," he commanded suddenly. "Because `Abla is still young, we need not concern ourselves with that marriage at present, but you must marry Farida as soon as we return to Riyadh. When the foreign women submit to Islam, you may marry them, but in meantime they must remain untouched."

"But, Uncle, I want the fair one now," Nassar whined. "She is mine, and I want her as my concubine."

"No."

"It is not forbidden."

"No, but we are descendants of the Prophet,

and it is not meet. All four women will be wives, according to the Koran, and all must be treated equally. Do you pledge this?"

"Yes," Nassar said with a pout.

"Then hear me, my ladies," Sharif instructed Fatmah and Latifeh as he strode toward the door. "Teach them what they must know to be wives of a Selim and good daughters of Allah, and find something decent for them to wear." He paused at the threshold. "Come, Nassar, leave the harem to the women," he ordered.

Sullenly the young man followed, throwing resentful looks at his uncle's back. Sharif could order him to leave them alone, Nassar thought wrathfully, but they were his slaves and he would do what he wanted with them. The sheik would not always be around to make sure his command was carried out.

The sun set early in the mountains. Soon after his evening meal, Sharif stepped out on his balcony to watch the moon rise over the eastern slopes. Later he would join his kinsmen on the roof before it grew too cool, and there they would say their evening prayers and pass a few hours in talk. But now he needed to be alone with his thoughts. Baffled by his response to the girl Nassar had brought into their home, the sheik sought refuge in solitude for the second time that day.

A movement in the harem garden below caught his eye, and as if summoned, she stepped into view, dressed in a pale blue *thobe,* the loose dress of the Arabs, with a snowy *ghata* covering her dark hair. The paths between the flower beds were dimly lit by lamplight from the house that seeped into the darkness through the open doors. Unaware of his observation, she strolled, stopping to pluck a scarlet rose. Closing her eyes, she inhaled the rose's fragrance, and although he had glimpsed her face only once, Sharif could almost see the sooty fringe of lashes against her ivory skin.

Entranced, he watched as she walked to the tinkling fountain in the far corner of the courtyard. Sitting down, she released the flower to float in the water. In the faint light, it was a spot of bright color.

Bryna watched pensively as it drifted. Suddenly she lifted her face and looked to where Sharif stood on the shadowed balcony. He did not move, certain she could not see him in the darkness, but all at once the moon burst into full light over the mountain and her eyes found his across the courtyard. Unaccountably the man's heart raced, and he felt a stir best forgotten.

He fought to control his long dormant emotions, and before clouds enshrouded the moon again, his handsome face rearranged itself into a fierce scowl. He glowered at the girl, then, arrogantly, he settled his sword at his hip and stalked back into his room.

Bryna sighed when he whirled and disappeared from view. She needed a friend, and she had seen an odd glint of recognition in his gray eyes that afternoon in the harem. But now he seemed hostile, as if he disliked her very presence in the garden. She fought back ire, forcing herself to realize it was directed not at the man, but at the situation over which she had no control.

One thing was certain, she thought, turning her mind to the problems at hand, the women in the harem had no intention of showing any warmth or kindness toward their unwelcome charges. Fatmah, the elder wife, had assigned each of the newcomers a bedroom at opposite ends of the harem, as if she feared what would happen if the foreigners were allowed to stay together. Bryna and Pamela were given food by curious servant girls and shown to the bath, then allowed to nap during the afternoon.

They had been awakened for the evening meal and instructed to join Fatmah and Latifeh as they sat in the common room, chattering away in Arabic. Bryna had squirmed on her pillow in the stuffy harem while Pamela sat beside her dully, not caring that she was obviously the subject of the conversation. At last Bryna could stand it no longer. She rose, nodding amiably toward the older women, and motioned toward the garden, her request to go outside clear. Fatmah glared at her, but Latifeh, the younger woman, gestured in dismissal. Bryna did not wait to find out if Fatmah agreed but departed swiftly.

Outside, Bryna walked dispiritedly, trying to formulate a plan. When she had a better mastery of Arabic, she would explain to the sheik that she was a free woman, that she wished to go home. She hoped he would consider the wrong that had been done when she was sold into slavery. She prayed her hope was not misplaced, for Sharif Al Selim seemed different from any man she had met in the Arab world. She had understood enough of what had been said that afternoon to know that when he had rendered his decision, he had spoken wisely and justly.

Then she had discovered him watching her from his jasmine-covered balcony, his expression unreadable. When he frowned as if she had offended him and went into the house, she felt as if she might never have the chance to appeal to him for her release.

Bryna's contemplation was interrupted when a small projectile plopped into the fountain and splashed water on her. A muffled giggle came from the branches of the fig tree overhead. Looking up, she spotted a pair of pale dancing eyes peering at her through the thick foliage.

"Bon soir," Bryna called. "What are you doing up there?"

As a reply, she received a fig in her lap and more giggles. The branches swayed as the child attempted to conceal herself more completely.

"Won't you come down?" Bryna coaxed softly. After a moment an impish face revealed itself and studied the girl on the ground speculatively.

There was more rustling of leaves as the urchin eased herself off the limb and hung by her hands for a few seconds before making the short drop to the ground. The little girl adjusted her rumpled clothes and shyly presented herself to Bryna.

She was an exquisite child about six or seven years old. Curious and solemn, she approached warily. Her gray eyes, set in a delicate face smudged with dirt and tree sap, seemed too old for the rest of her. But that impression fled when she smiled, revealing the gap left by the recent loss of baby teeth.

The little girl was barefoot. Her clothes, in poor repair, hung on her thin body. Her thick black hair, a riotous mass of ringlets, was matted and tangled around gold hoops that hung from her ears.

"Do you speak French?" Bryna asked, smiling down at her.

"Not very well," the child responded haltingly.

"What is your name?"

"`Abla bint Sharif Al Selim."

So she was not the child of a slave, but the daughter of the house, Bryna realized with a start. She should have recognized those amazing gray eyes. But why was the child so ragged and unkempt? Bryna did not question her but introduced herself instead. "I am Bryna . . . Bryna bint Blaine."

"I know, Fatmah told me when I returned with the herds. You were in the bath. Are you really an infidel?" she asked excitedly. "I have never seen one before."

"I am"— Bryna searched for the word — "Nasrani, from America."

"Oh." `Abla was unimpressed. Suddenly her lips curved in a conspiratorial smile. "Did you like the way I hid in the tree?"

"You hid very well." Bryna laughed. "I didn't see you until you dropped the fig into the fountain."

"I know. My father did not see me at all. He never does."

The way the child spoke made Bryna want to put her arms around her, but she refrained. If she had learned one thing during her months in Islamic North Africa, it was the Moslem's aversion to contact with infidels.

"How is it you speak French, `Abla? I may call you `Abla, may I not?"

"Oui," The girl edged closer. "My *grandpère* spoke the Frankish language to me. He was my mother's father, and he said she would have liked for me to learn it."

"Your mother?"

"Noorah. She died when I was born," the child explained seriously. "It must be confusing for a foreigner, but I do not have a mother. Fatmah and Latifeh are my father's wives. He married them last year when my uncles were killed. He had to take the widows of his brothers, you know. It is our custom."

`Abla fidgeted, bored with adult conversation. "Can we go in and see the other infidel? I heard the servants whispering in the kitchen, and they say she has hair the color of the white sands and almost as glistening."

"All right." Bryna smiled. Brushing the bruised fig from her lap, she rose. "I will introduce you to Pamela."

"Pamela? What a funny name."

"Pamela bint Harold," Bryna amended.

"It is still a funny name." `Abla giggled. "Yours is too, but I think you are very nice for a kaffir." Slipping her hand unexpectedly into Bryna's, the little girl skipped as they returned to the harem.

"About time he showed up," Blaine muttered, peering out of the window of the rented room he had shared with Derek on the outskirts of Tripoli for the past week. "I was beginning to think our information, as expensive as it was, might be wrong."

Derek joined the big man at the window and looked out at the dusty street. Trailed by a glum servant riding a donkey, Gasim Al Auf rode along on an unkempt horse, on his way to visit his latest paramour, a dancing girl from a waterfront cafe.

"I still do not see why we couldn't have just gone to the village when we first got here, instead of waiting for him to come into town," Derek complained.

Blaine looked at the young man with ill-concealed annoyance, doubting again whether he had ever seen any action beyond the parade ground. "'Tis hard to see how you got to be a lieutenant, lad, if you spent your time storming the castle. First, all of Al Auf's family and most of his men live in that village. We would not have had a chance. Second, we didn't know at first whether he might be keeping Bryna there. I will not have her harmed."

"Nor will I," Derek snapped, before adding stiffly, "You are right, of course, Colonel, as always.

I bow to your superior experience in battle."

Blaine considered reminding the young upstart that he was no longer a colonel, but since it had done no good so far, he simply suggested, "Why don't we save the hostility, Ashburn? We're going to need it for the fight that is sure to come."

They returned their attention to the scene across the street. Gasim dismounted and went inside. The servant led both mounts around the corner to a stable yard behind the house.

Blaine and Derek left their house by the back way and looped around. They found the servant drowsing in the shade of a skimpy acacia tree. He did not even look up when the horse, tied to the drinking trough, nickered softly at the sight of the two strangers. Silently they stole into the stable and watched the house.

They did not have long to wait. Gasim soon emerged from the back door, straightening his clothes. Calling harshly to the servant, he walked toward his horse.

If Gasim Al Auf was surprised when the two men materialized from the shadowy stable, swords drawn, he did not show it.

"Ah, O'Toole Effendi," he greeted his enemy in Arabic. "I knew we would meet again someday." He unsheathed his own sword. Seemingly reluctant, the servant did the same.

Without warning, Gasim gave a bloodcurdling yell and charged at Blaine. But the big man was ready, and steel rang against steel.

Brandishing his sword lazily, Derek advanced

on the servant at once, drawling, "It's rather a poor idea, y'know, to interfere in a private quarrel."

To his surprise, the little man answered in heavily accented English, "I agree it is unwise, but what can I do? Even slaves have honor." With a look of resignation, he faced Derek.

"I've come for my daughter, Al Auf," Blaine stated evenly, meeting every slash of Gasim's blade.

"You have come all this way for an unworthy woman?"

"You knew I would."

"I thought better of you, especially since you must know I have sold her by now."

Blaine stepped up his attack in response, causing Gasim to fall back against the rump of his horse, which shied uneasily behind him. The Irishman was not even breathing hard when he resumed the conversation, "I imagined you would sell her, but I'll have the name of the buyer from you before you die."

"I will never tell you," Gasim snarled.

The two old enemies fought savagely, unaware that the other battle being waged in the stable yard was over. Derek had disarmed the servant, though not as easily as he had expected, and now he stood with his blade against the little man's throat. Neither moved as they watched Blaine press the pirate against the tree and disarm him.

With an enraged roar, Gasim drew his dagger, a match to the one he had left in the gate in Tangier. Using the tree behind him to launch himself, he lunged wildly at Blaine. But his foot caught in a root and he lost his footing, falling heavily at his opponent's feet.

In fairness, Blaine waited for the pirate to rise, but he did not stir. Warily the Irishmen knelt beside him and rolled his limp form onto its back. Blood stained the sand beneath Gasim, and the ornate hilt of the dagger protruded from his chest.

The Arab's eyes opened heavily. "You will never know, O'Toole." His laughter ended with a last rattling breath.

Blaine's face was bleak when he looked up at Derek. "Dead," he muttered.

From the house, the death wail rose and the woman ran to throw herself across Gasim's body.

"Perhaps this one can tell us what we wish to know before we kill him," Derek suggested, shoving the skinny servant toward Blaine.

The Arab's gaze slid around to the young man's angry face. He did not believe they intended to kill him. They behaved in the strangest ways, these Inglayzis.

"Please, *sidi*, for you are my master . . . " He approached the big man beseechingly. "My name is Mustafa bin Abdul. Taken from an Egyptian ship, I became the slave of Al Auf, God blacken his face. Now I am yours, O victorious one."

"All I want is some information, Mustafa," Blaine answered.

"I live to serve." He scowled down at the weeping woman and shouted, "Silence, worthless one! My *sidi* wishes to speak with me."

"What did Al Auf do with my daughter?"

"That wicked one sold her to the slave trader,

Nejm Al Anwar."

"I suspected as much," Blaine muttered, "but I could get no answers in the souks."

Suddenly Mustafa saw a chance to ingratiate himself to his new master and perhaps to make a profit.

"In your wisdom, you know the reason, O'Toole Effendi," the slave volunteered quickly. "The shop-keepers would tell you nothing because you are an infidel. Had your humble servant been with you, you would have learned that she is at Nejm's no longer."

"Where is she?"

"I heard before we left Tangier that she had been sold again."

"To whom?"

"I cannot recall. Alas, the gates of memory are locked to your poor servant."

"Would a key of silver unlock them?" Blaine asked knowingly.

"Much better would be a key of gold, master."

"I thought as much." He tossed a gold coin into the dust at the man's feet.

"This is highway robbery," Derek objected when Mustafa picked up the coin and bit it. "I could have killed him. He's lucky to get away with his life."

"Let him speak." Blaine held up a silencing hand.

Mustafa pocketed his money with a smug expression and said, "Now I remember, *sidi*. I heard she had been sold to Hajji Suleiman Ibn Hussein, a marriage broker of great repute."

"Do you know where he is now?"

With a defiant glance at Derek, the servant wordlessly extended a grimy hand. When another coin joined the first, he said helpfully, "No doubt the hajji joined a caravan to the east. But to pursue him across the desert would be foolhardy, *sidi*. Would it not be better to send a message to his home in Baghdad? There is a man here who sends messages by pigeon . . . for a price, of course."

"Of course," Blaine agreed gravely. "And you could introduce me to him . . . for a price." He was silent for a moment as he sorted through the options. "If you take me to this man, Mustafa, you may have your freedom."

"I say . . . " Derek sputtered.

"May Allah bless you a thousand times!" the surprised Mustafa cried. In giving him his freedom, Blaine had gained a slave for life. "May your herds increase, my master. May you—"

"Enough, Mustafa. Take us to this man you know."

CHAPTER

"IT IS TRUE, BRYNA BINT BLAINE, YOU HAD NO mother either?" `Abla's gray eyes widened at the discovery. "Just like me?"

"My mother did not die when I was born," Bryna replied, laying her needlework in her lap in favor of talking to the child. "But she died when I was very young. I barely remember her."

"I do not remember mine at all," `Abla said sorrowfully. "Sometimes I wonder about her. My aunts say she was beautiful and kind . . . like you."

Bryna smiled down at the little girl sitting beside her. "She must have been special indeed to have such a special daughter. I am sure she would have been proud of you."

"Do you really think so?" `Abla asked breathlessly. "Even though I am clumsy and in the way and my clothes are never neat?"

Bryna laughed aloud. "That sounds exactly like a description of me when I was your age."

"And were you sometimes lonely, too?" `Abla asked, suddenly serious again.

From across the main room of the harem,

163

Latifeh, Sharif's second wife, watched Bryna and
`Abla while they talked, their dark heads close.
Curious, on the pretext of inspecting the garment
upon which Bryna worked, she ambled over to
where they sat.

"It is beautiful, isn't it, Aunt Latifeh?" `Abla
asked as the woman examined the elaborate
embroidery.

"It is good," Latifeh admitted. She addressed
the American girl in a pidgin mixture of French and
Arabic. "Who taught you this?"

"No one," Bryna answered shyly. Though she
liked her more than Fatmah, she did not know
Latifeh well. She did not yet know that this serious
woman would be her instructor in the teachings of
the Prophet.

"You knew how to do this before?"

"No, I admired the border on your *thobe,* so I
thought I would try it."

"Mashallah, you have done well." Summoning
her best French, Latifeh asked carefully, "Do you
know what is called this pattern?"

Bryna shook her head.

"'The Tent of the Pasha.'" The woman's hennaed
finger traced the colorful stitches. "Such needlework is difficult."

"Did you know, my aunt," `Abla interjected, eager
to share the bond between her new friend and herself, "that Bryna grew up in a huge harem, bigger than
ours, perhaps even bigger than the emir's?"

"It was not a harem," Bryna corrected gently. "It
was an orphanage."

"What is this . . . orphanage?" Latifeh sat down, her eyes alight at the thought of adding new knowledge to her vast store.

"It is where children who have no mother or father are kept," Bryna explained falteringly.

"They have no *amm*—no uncle—to protect them?"

"No one."

"I suppose it could happen," the Arab woman granted dubiously. "But no one in their tribe takes them in?"

"In America, we—"

"Latifeh!" A disapproving screech interrupted the conversation and Fatmah descended upon them, her fat body quivering with indignation. "Have you nothing better to do than gossip with kaffir slaves?"

`Abla darted from harm's way, out a side door, as the woman rose, shamefaced. Ordinarily the harem authority on etiquette and custom, Latifeh had momentarily forgotten Bryna's station in life.

"*Ya hú*, O worthless one," Fatmah shouted at the foreign girl in Arabic, and waved her arms threateningly, "fetch me a sherbet from the kitchen and be quick."

Fuming with silent anger, Bryna went to do as she was bade. When she returned moments later, Latifeh was deep in discussion with Fatmah.

" . . . have never seen her smile before," Bryna overhead the younger wife say. "When she is with the infidel, it is as if she is a different girl."

"I tell you it is not good," Fatmah argued. "The

proverb says, 'A child's heart is like a precious jewel without inscription—'"

"I know," Latifeh cut in. "'It is therefore ready to absorb whatever is engraved upon it.' But I tell you there has been no one to engrave upon `Abla's heart. Our husband hardly acknowledges her existence, and neither you nor I have taken the time to teach her. What harm can this friendship do?"

"Much, I fear. Quiet, now," Fatmah cautioned, seeing that Bryna had returned. "So there you are, daughter of Satan." She accepted the dish with ill grace. "It took you long enough."

Bryna did not reply, but again she understood she was not welcome in the women's quarters, for many reasons.

Little attention was paid to her or to Pamela, however, as frantic preparations began for the feast of Eed al Adha. In the bustle of activity, the foreign women were busy from dawn to dusk, dragging wearily to their beds at night. Because they ranked lowest in the harem, they were given the most menial of tasks.

For Bryna, this meant grinding grain for the innumerable loaves of flat bread that would be consumed during the feast. A huge mortar and pestle were placed under a carob tree near the kitchen, and she was positioned there, facing the house, with huge bags of grain. Her task was mindless work, and at first she felt an impotent anger at her situation as she ground the grain and sifted the husks from the fine meal all day, pausing only for meals and a short kef in the afternoon.

With so much time to think, memories of other times returned, but Bryna would not allow herself to dwell on them. They were too painful. To keep her mind busy while she worked, she watched the comings and goings of the household, listening to passing conversations while she mentally reviewed the Arabic `Abla was teaching her. In exchange for French lessons, the little girl had undertaken Bryna's education with glee and surprising ability.

On the day before the feast, while Bryna labored, Pamela appeared in the kitchen door, seeking a breeze to cool her. At Nassar's insistence she was kept inside, where the sun would not darken her skin or coarsen her hair. She had been sent to assist in the baking.

After glancing cautiously over her shoulder into the kitchen, she hurried to where Bryna sat beneath the tree. "Won't you be glad when this day is over and we can have a bath?" she asked in greeting.

"Very glad," Bryna answered, imagining a long soak in warm water to relieve the ache in her shoulders and back from bending over the mortar.

Pamela leaned against the tree trunk and ran her fingers through her sweat-soaked hair beneath her *ghata*. "I have never been so hot in my life."

"Not even in the desert?" Bryna teased, continuing to work.

"Not even then," the English girl confirmed. She stared up the hill at the servants who dug pits in the ground at the side of the house, a distance from the men's wing. Behind them, Fatmah and Latifeh toiled in the heat to pitch a large tent. "I understand that the pits are for cooking, but what are they doing?"

"Building a tent large enough to hold all the male guests. That's their job as the sheik's wives. It seems everyone has a task," Bryna added, nodding toward `Abla, who followed the women, beating tent pegs into the hard ground with a small stone hammer.

"We certainly have our tasks in the kitchen." Sighing, Pamela stirred and faced back toward the house. When no one seemed to be looking for her, she settled back against the tree again. "We've been cooking for days, and I am heartily sick of the smell of goat and sour milk."

Bryna nodded sympathetically, but before she could speak the cook appeared in the door to the kitchen and scowled at Pamela.

"I am coming," the blond-haired girl called to him in French. "I knew he would come looking for me," she muttered to Bryna. "He is turning into such a tyrant."

"I thought you liked him."

"He is a lamb, but if he makes me say *La ilaha-illa-llah, wa Muhammad rasuli-ilah* one more time, I think I shall scream."

"There is no God but Allah and Muhammad is the messenger of Allah," Bryna translated. "He wants you to be a good Moslem."

"What are we going to do, Bryna?" Pamela asked intensely. "I cannot give up Christianity for Islam, can you?"

"No," the American girl admitted soberly. "I know we must face it eventually, for Nassar has made it clear I must become a Moslem or be sold into a bordello."

"Then we will become Moslems," Pamela said insistently. "I do not believe he would sell me, but I could not bear to be separated from you."

"Do not give up hope, *chère*," Bryna encouraged. "Perhaps we will find a way to escape before we must make the *shahada*."

"Escape?" Pamela repeated skeptically, then she sighed. "Well, I suppose we must continue to hope, but I fear we must learn to say as the Arabs do—*Insh'allah*. It is the will of God."

With that, she turned and went back into the house, leaving Bryna to her grinding and her disturbed thoughts.

Finished with her work, `Abla bounded down the hill to join her friend in the shade. *"Alhamdillah,"* she said, unconsciously mimicking her aunts as she dropped to sit on the ground, "this feast is going to be such fun."

Bryna shoved back a lock of dark hair that strayed from beneath her *ghata* and stared wryly at the little girl. Her light veil stuck to her moist face, she could feel the sweat trickling down her spine, and every muscle was sore.

But `Abla looked at her innocently, her face alight with anticipation, and asked, "Do you have Eed al Adha in your country?"

"No," Bryna grunted, pushing down hard with the pestle to break the hulls.

"Then you don't know yet, do you? About all the things you've been missing?"

169

"No, why don't you tell me about it while I work?" Bryna suggested. "That way you can practice your French."

"Très bien." `Abla began earnestly, "Tomorrow morning, very early, the sheep will be driven here and my father will select those without blemish for the feast. We'll cook many sheep because all our relatives will be here. Well, most of them.

"After they're cooked, my father will give food to the poor, because he is the most important man in our village, in the entire world, I think. Then we will feast. The men will go into the tent, and the women and children will go to the harem. When dinner is over, there will be music and singing and dancing. And we will have stories in the women's quarters."

"Is the entertainment your favorite part of the day?" Bryna asked.

"Oh, no, I like the food."

"You and Pamela." The American girl chuckled.

"The Inglayzi does eat a lot," `Abla agreed gravely, "but she is bigger than me. Though she is not as fat as Fatmah," she added with innocent candor. "Do you think Pamela will get fat, too? I think Nassar would like it. He likes his mother."

Bryna did not answer, but `Abla did not notice. Her mind now on food, the child suggested, "Can we go in now and find something to eat?"

"All right," her friend agreed. "I am hungry and I haven't taken a rest all morning."

The pair walked toward the house, Bryna's flour-dusty hand resting on `Abla's shoulder.

Naturally, the child's arm wrapped around her waist. Together they disappeared into the kitchen.

On the hillside behind the house, Sharif reined his mare to an impatient, prancing halt and watched his daughter with Bryna. Even though the woman was veiled, he had no doubt of her identity. He was right to have allowed her to stay, he mused. Already it seemed as if she belonged here. Perhaps more good than he had anticipated could come from the presence of Bryna bint Blaine in his household. Even `Abla seemed happy.

Pondering what he had seen, the man turned his horse slowly down the trail toward the villa.

That evening the women of the harem lounged around a low table in the common room of the women's quarters. Their preparations for the feast were finished. Tomorrow relatives would arrive. Fatmah and Latifeh talked volubly, reminiscing about Eed al Adha celebrations of the past.

Bryna sat across the table, quietly embroidering. `Abla sprawled on the floor beside her, watching her needle flash with every stitch. Only Pamela was missing. The English girl had disappeared into the walled garden after dinner, welcoming the cool evening after her day in the stifling kitchen.

Suddenly the outer door of the harem opened and Sharif strode imperiously into the women's quarters. `Abla jumped to her feet with a cry of happiness, and Fatmah and Latifeh immediately flew to greet their husband. Bryna knew no veil was needed before family members beyond the sheer *ghata* she wore on her head, but she was uncertain what she should do. Putting aside her needlework, she rose respectfully.

"*As salaam 'alaykum,* my lord," Sharif's wives said in unison.

"*Wa 'alaykum as salaam.*" The man frowned slightly as `Abla danced in mute elation around him, but he did not correct her. Taking care not to trip over the excited child, he sat down on a pile of cushions in the center of the room. Placing a hand on each knee, he regarded the women benevolently. "Sit, sit, all of you."

Though somewhat puzzled by his rare visit, his wives sank down obediently on either side of him. Fatmah signaled nervously, summoning a servant to bring coffee. Noiselessly Bryna sat down across the table. Only `Abla continued to stand, lingering indecisively behind her father for a moment before she returned to Bryna's side.

With a smile for the little girl, Bryna took her work into her lap so `Abla could sit beside her. Sharif's eyebrows lifted quizzically when his daughter curled up next to her friend, flashing him a smile of pure contentment.

While sipping his coffee, Sharif conversed politely with Fatmah and Latifeh. He seemed to have forgotten anyone else was present as he inquired after his wives' health and discussed the arrangements for Eed al Adha, heartily approving their plans. Baffled expressions on their lined faces, the Arab women responded carefully to every question.

After a while the conversation lagged and

Sharif glanced at Bryna. She sat, with her head bent over her work, her dark hair screening her face from his view as effectively as a veil. He wished he could see her again closely, to see if her resemblance to Noorah was real or imagined.

"What is it you do, Bryna bint Blaine?" he asked in slow, careful Arabic.

"She is embroidering a belt, *Abu,*" `Abla answered enthusiastically for the American girl before she could speak. "It is 'the Eye of the Camel' pattern. She just learned how to do it. Would you like to see?"

Glancing at Bryna for permission, the child did not notice the wary look that passed between her aunts. She scrambled to her feet and took the unfinished strip of fabric from Bryna. Oblivious of Fatmah's forbidding frown, she carried it to her father and stood beside him while he inspected it.

"Is it not beautiful?" `Abla asked softly, her small face as proud as if it were her own handiwork.

Bemused by the usually silent child's behavior, he nodded.

Whirling, `Abla flashed Bryna a gap-toothed smile and chortled in Arabic, "He likes it! That means you must give it to him."

Bryna stiffened, feeling the almost tangible dislike in the narrowed eyes Fatmah turned on her. As she hesitated, Latifeh, sitting on Sharif's other side, nodded her reluctant agreement to what `Abla had said.

Bryna met Sharif's gray eyes, feeling a disquieting flutter of attraction as she did so. "If it pleases," she said carefully in Arabic, "it will be yours."

Sharif accepted graciously. When he returned the strip of fabric to `Abla, he continued to look at Bryna. She did not resemble Noorah exactly, he decided, but still there was something pleasing about her. No, more than pleasing. *Mashallah,* this woman had spirit, and she was beautiful to his eyes. Suddenly conscious of the silence as his wives watched him, he tore his attention from her and returned it to his daughter.

The little girl was unaware of the tension in the room as she squirmed in front of her father, eager for his notice. "I have been teaching Bryna bint Blaine to speak our language, Abu," she lisped. "She learns quickly. Fatmah wonders if Bryna is *ins* or jinni, but I do not think Allah created her from a smokeless fire like the jinn, do you? I think she is ins, a person just like us."

"Hush, little one," Sharif said not unkindly, "tonight you make as much noise as *el-Bil,* all the camels of the tribe. Go and sit now."

When the little girl had returned to Bryna's side, Sharif clapped his hands. Three maids entered with smiles on their faces as they bore stacks of folded clothing for Fatmah, Latifeh, and `Abla, each female of the sheik's harem. The surprised cries of delight drew Pamela from the garden. Silently the English girl entered and sat on a cushion beside Bryna.

His gaze drawn by Pamela's movement, Sharif frowned distractedly toward the women across the table. Turning to his wives, he spoke in rapid Arabic.

"My father asks if Nassar has bought clothing for you and Pamela bint Harold so you will not shame us when our relatives come for Eed al Adha," `Abla whispered. "My aunts say yes. He will bring the garments tonight."

Nodding briskly at the news, Sharif missed the brief flare of anger in Bryna's eyes. Shame him indeed, she thought resentfully. It was Nassar who shamed him when he brought Pamela and her here as slaves.

"Then all is in readiness for tomorrow," the sheik pronounced. With that, he departed as confidently as he had come, leaving Fatmah and Latifeh to stare resentfully at the newcomers.

Eed al Adha dawned cool and crisp in the mountains. The sun, while still low in the eastern sky, was a weak portent of relentless heat in which the celebrants would swelter throughout the day.

Shivering in the dim light, Bryna and Pamela donned the clothing Nassar had given them. He had chosen carefully for his women. The colors were becoming, the fabrics rich and opulent, and the veils sheer and daring. The young man wanted to be certain that everyone would talk of his wives-to-be for weeks to come.

Pamela was clad in blue and lavender. Bryna wore a brilliant blue that matched her eyes. Over her *thobe*, she wore an aba woven with blue, black,

175

and red stripes, the stripes shot with gold threads.

The foreign women met in the common room to admire each other's exotic costumes. They were soon joined by Fatmah and Latifeh. The jingle of the Arab women's jewelry could be heard long before they appeared. Dozens of golden bracelets clanked on their fleshy arms as they moved, chains of coins were affixed to their veils and draped over their foreheads, and lavish earrings dangled at their ears. Despite their adornment, the older women, swathed in ostentatious dark-colored robes, resembled a pair of plump ravens beside two enchanting nightingales.

Fatmah began at once to issue officious instructions in her pidgin French. As elder wife, the responsibility for this holiday feast was hers, and she would not have it ruined because of a stupid blunder by the infidels. She had suggested locking the foreign women in their rooms, but Nassar would not hear of it. To her surprise, neither would Sharif. *Insh'allah*, she must do what she could to make sure everything progressed smoothly.

Adding to her distraction was `Abla, who pirouetted around the room, clad in the new clothes her father had furnished. The little girl was thrilled with his gift of a red *thobe*. Like Bryna's, her dress was exquisitely embroidered at the neck and the sleeves. Her hair was clean and glossy, pulled back neatly into two fat braids that bounced against her thin back with every springing step she took. Bryna had spent hours the night before brushing the tangles from `Abla's unruly mop and this morning, convincing the unwilling little girl to join her and

Pamela in the bath.

Many of Fatmah's objections to the friendship between the tall American and Sharif's daughter melted away in spite of herself when she saw `Abla dressed for the feast. The child would never be the beauty Noorah was, there was too much of her father in her, but the improvement in her appearance was astounding.

At midmorning the Selim relatives began to arrive at the villa. The men greeted each other loudly and lounged about the tent beside the house while their wives and children were shown to the women's quarters. Careful of her finery, `Abla joined her cousins playing in the courtyard.

Since most of the servants labored in the kitchen, Bryna and Pamela, observed balefully by Fatmah and Latifeh, served refreshments. The older women had drilled them for days, and now the foreigners proved to be excellent hostesses, making the guests feel comfortable and welcome. The sisters, cousins, aunts, and nieces of the Selim clan also watched the infidels but found no fault with their behavior. Nassar's new slaves were demure, subservient, and remembered always to serve with the right hand. The dark one even smiled a little and attempted a few clumsy words of Arabic.

At last the Arab women gave up their scrutiny and started a dozen conversations, chatting among themselves, catching up on news of family and friends. They were not unkind to the white women, they simply ignored them, no longer interested in monitoring their every move.

But there was one whose sharp eyes still followed Bryna as the girl moved through the room, listening, trying to understand. Alima realized uneasily that this Bryna bint Blaine was one to be reckoned with. Her manner, while gracious and gentle, still revealed great pride and strength. She was more fit to be the wife of a sheik than of slothful Nassar, the old woman decided. True, she had blue eyes and she was an infidel, but . . .

Irritably Alima Al Selim put the thought away from her. The foreign woman belonged to Nassar, and it was an old woman's foolishness to dream of what could not be.

After a while Sharif's servant, Abu Ahmad, tapped on the door to the harem and told the women that the distribution of meat to the poor was about to begin. Chattering and donning their *burqus,* the women poured from the apartments. Fatmah caught Bryna's arm before she could follow and handed her a pair of black cloaks and stiff *burqus.*

"You must not wear these outside," she insisted, tugging on the sheer veil the girl held in her hand. "Cover yourself like the rest of us. We are going out to where the men congregate, and some of them will not be family. I will not have anyone say my son is to wed immoral women who do not have the decency to veil properly before strangers."

Understanding the gist of her tirade, Bryna reluctantly accepted the garments and handed a cloak and *burqu* to Pamela.

"What's wrong with this veil?" the English girl protested, ignoring Fatmah's irate glare. "It's much cooler."

"Just because Nassar gave it to you does not mean you should wear it," Bryna said determinedly, plucking the sheer length of fabric from Pamela's hand. "It is too revealing to be worn in public."

"But—"

"Listen to me, Pamela," Bryna cautioned when the other girl opened her mouth to argue. "I just heard the women speaking of a woman who was put to death by her husband because he thought another man looked at her. Nassar may think he wants others to admire you, but if he became jealous—"

"Don't say it." Pamela shuddered, donning the *burqu* at once.

Then they joined the others in front of the house, where the poor of Taif waited. Involuntarily Bryna's eyes sought and found the head of the household. Sheik Al Selim was known for his generosity as well as his wealth. He did not lack in grace, either, for he greeted each almsman as though he were an honored guest.

She could not help but think he was magnificent, dressed in a snow-white *thobe* and an aba of gray woven with gold. His white headdress billowed in the wind, secured by a gold-wrapped *aghal.* A sash of purple belted around Sharif's trim waist held a pair of jeweled daggers and his ever-present sword in place.

Quickly Bryna ducked her head when Nassar,

bored with the proceedings, allowed his eyes to drift toward the bevy of women.

The young man frowned when he saw his two slaves standing beside by his mother, unmistakable by her bulk. Fatmah had made them wear cloaks and burqus. The effect of the clothing he had chosen was ruined, he realized.

Beside him, Sharif carved steaming sheep carcasses to distribute to the poor. The sheik's gray eyes drifted continually toward the women clustered outside the door to the courtyard, the children ranged in front of them. There she was, he thought, his knife slowing its carving motion. The tall one at the back was Bryna, he decided, oddly pleased with the discovery. When her blue eyes met his fleetingly before she looked away, Sharif was disconcerted by a sudden rush of feeling. He jabbed at the slab of meat in front of him and sawed at it viciously.

He was disturbed by the effect the girl had on him, not just today, but every time he saw her. Only yesterday, returning from his ride, he had directed his mount to where she sat beneath the tree, grinding meal. He had stared down at her, but when she had turned her face toward him, her eyes questioning over her veil, he could not frame a simple phrase. He could not find the words even to tell her he was glad of her friendship with his daughter.

`Abla was like a wild creature, Sharif brooded. After Noorah's death in childbirth, his grief had been so intense, he had not been able to bear even to look at his daughter. He had shunned her, leaving her to Noorah's father, who had loved the child dearly. But the old man had died when ˋAbla was only four, and then she had had no one.

With no women in the harem, Sharif had assigned her care to the household servants. Although ˋAbla's presence was a physical reminder of his wife's death, he had wished when he brought Fatmah and Latifeh into his home last year that they would take ˋAbla under their wings. But his hopes were in vain. Fatmah was engrossed in Nassar, and Latifeh was mostly uninterested in the girl. Once again there was no one for ˋAbla—until Bryna bint Blaine.

He had wanted to tell this to the foreign woman yesterday, but he had stumbled, tongue-tied, like a green boy. So the mighty sheik had scowled down at her, spurring his mare fiercely in his haste to escape her expressive gaze. Târiq had sensed his anger and reared, lunging away.

Determinedly putting the memory from his mind, Sharif glanced around the assembly. ˋAbla stood in front of the women, a spot of bright red against their black cloaks. Her little face was clean and her hair was combed and braided. She reminded him of her mother, but for some unexplained reason the pain he usually felt at the thought had lessened.

He smiled at her as he bent over the joint he was carving. Catching his eye, the little girl grinned her gap-toothed smile in return. Unusually happy, Sharif cut a large portion of meat and gave it to the next person in the long line that wended by him.

❖ ❖ ❖

A moody frown on his aristocratic face, Derek carelessly laid out another game of solitaire on the crude wooden table. Once the cards were dealt, he did not play but slumped back on his chair to brood over the inactivity. It could drive a man mad.

Tripoli was worse by far than any of the backwater posts he had known so well during his military career, the Englishman thought bitterly. Having resigned his commission, he had hoped for more adventure than he had seen in the army. But for more than two months he and Blaine had waited here in the heat and the flies and the dust, first for the arrival of Gasim, then for a message from Suleiman Ibn Hussein. And they had nothing to show for it but an irritating little Arab slave who worked daily to convert his infidel masters to Islam.

Heaving a lethargic sigh, Derek sat up and began to play, if only to pass the time.

"It's here!" Blaine burst into the room, waving a small paper excitedly. "The message from Baghdad has finally arrived."

Derek was on his feet at once, the cards in his hand forgotten. "Where is she?"

" 'Tis as we feared," the big Irishman answered soberly. "Ibn Hussein sold her in Arabia."

"The bastard." Derek watched the other man pace the room.

"Aye, Bryna is with the Selims, one of the most powerful families in the entire country. We're going to have a hell of a time getting her back."

"But we will get her back," the young man insisted quietly.

"Sit down, Ashburn," Blaine requested. He took the seat across the table and spoke urgently. "You and I must talk, for there's something I must know. I do not like to think of it, but you do realize that it is possible Bryna is now a slave in some fat emir's harem?"

Derek's face paled at the blunt question, but he gazed steadfastly at the older man. "I realize it. I just hope it is not so."

"No more than I," Blaine said passionately. "But what I am trying to say is that my love is a father's love. It will not change because of what has happened. Bryna is still my daughter."

"I still plan to marry her," Derek declared evenly.

"Are you sure, lad? Because you are not compelled to go with me to Arabia."

"Not compelled to save the woman I intend to make my wife?" the young man asked coldly. "Whatever has happened to Bryna is not her doing. I will go with you to rescue her."

"So you do care for her." Bryna's father nodded in satisfaction.

"Of course I do." Derek's frown deepened. "Do you think I would have come all this way if I didn't?"

"I'm not sure what I think, Ashburn." Blaine leaned back in his chair, shaking his head. "You're a hard one to figure."

"Well, there is one thing of which you can be sure, Colonel," Derek retorted. "An army of Arabs can't keep me from Bryna.

" 'Tis a good thing," Blaine muttered, "for it may be an army of Arabs we're facing before this is over."

CHAPTER

✧✧✧✧✧ **10** ✧✧✧✧✧

SLOWLY LIFE SETTLED INTO A SUMMER ROU-
tine at the Selim villa. Latifeh began the religious
instruction of the foreign women. In many ways the
teaching of Muhammad did not differ markedly
from those of the Christian church, but the convent-educated Bryna still dreaded the day she
would be asked to make her *shahada*.

The days were busy, full of housework and broken occasionally by visits from Alima or another
female relative. Bryna and Pamela were assigned
various responsibilities, simple household chores.
In the desert it would be different, harder. Pamela
sometimes complained, but Bryna was pleased to
be occupied with other tasks besides the mindless
grinding she had done before the feast. Still, when
the opportunity presented itself, she worked in the
cool shade under the carob tree, where she had
spent so much time before Eed al Adha.

One day, near kef, as she shelled nuts there,
Bryna heard a piteous whimpering coming from the
mountain behind the house. She stopped what she
was doing and listened. The whining continued. It

sounded like an animal in pain.

Jumping to her feet, she ran toward the sound. In a clearing surrounded by boulders, she found Sharif's saluki, little more than a puppy, with one front paw wedged tightly in a fissure between two huge rocks. The dog tugged frantically at the trapped paw, bloodying the brown fur on his leg and yelping all the more when he saw the girl.

Bryna comforted the animal and gauged his situation. He had apparently stepped in the hollow between some jagged rocks, cut his foot, and become stuck. In his frenzy to escape, the dog had created a small avalanche, dislodging several large loose stones nearby, which slid into the fissure and trapped the paw even more firmly.

While the grateful saluki tried to lick her face, Bryna carefully began to remove the small pile of rocks mounded around his leg, hoping to free it without causing further injury. She was so intent on her rescue, she did not realize Sharif had arrived until he halted Târiq beside her and dismounted. Although Arabs usually valued dogs little, they were generally attached to their graceful salukis, and the sheik's face was concerned as he knelt beside Bryna.

"How badly is he injured?" Sharif asked in slow, careful Arabic so the girl could understand.

"I cannot tell." She did not look up, continuing to lift stones from the fissure. "I think he hurt himself more trying to escape."

"Let me help." Sharif bent to the task, murmuring to the dog as he worked.

Behind the screen of her lowered lashes, Bryna's eyes flickered between the man's intent face and his strong brown hands as he lifted the rocks away.

The closer the puppy was to release, the louder he whined and yipped and the more he twisted and tugged.

"Hold him so he cannot run, Bryna bint Blaine," Sharif instructed. His gaze swept her face to see if she had understood.

The girl nodded and obligingly shifted her position, placing her arms around the dog's body while Sharif freed the trapped paw. The man frowned in concentration, trying to ignore the fragrance of sandalwood that wafted to him from her hair. She held the puppy gently, though her arms tightened around him when he was freed. Although the little saluki was in pain, he now wriggled happily, trying to reach his owner, who had risen once the rescue was complete.

The dog's joyful gyrations threw Bryna off balance when she attempted to stand with the saluki in her arms. Sharif grasped both her arms, steadying her as he pulled her to her feet. When Bryna's eyes met Sharif's over her burqu, his grip tightened and everything around them seemed to recede—the forest, the heat of the sun, even the dog squirming between them.

Sharif recovered himself first. Suddenly aware that he still held Bryna's arms, he released her. Nodding down at the saluki, he said gruffly, "Here, let me take the dog. I know he is heavy."

Awed by the rush of attraction she felt for the sheik, Bryna did not trust herself to speak. She transferred her burden, disconcerted that the act necessarily brought her even closer to the man. She all but shoved the puppy into Sharif's waiting arms, and retreated a step before bending to examine the dog's injury.

"I . . . I must look at the cut," she said, gratefully averting her face. "He's getting blood all over your *thobe.*"

"No matter." Sharif glanced carelessly at the once snow white garment before returning his gaze to Bryna. All he could see was the top of her head as she inspected the puppy's paw. "How bad is it?"

"It must be cleaned and sewn," she answered hesitantly, searching for the right words. Taking off her sash, she wrapped it expertly around the wound, then petted the puppy, which had ceased its struggling and lay, whimpering, in Sharif's arms. Her hand on the animal's nose, she said falteringly, "Hot and dry."

"Come, we will take him to Abu Ahmad to be doctored. Stay close behind me." Sharif turned and started down the mountain with only a quick glance to make sure she followed. At a low whistle from her master, Târiq trailed behind them.

As the couple neared the house, they were met by Abu Ahmad, who was making his way slowly up the mountain, having heard the dog's yelps. The servant's eyes widened when he saw Sharif, his clothing spattered with blood. "My sheik," he stammered, "are you—"

"It is not my blood, Abu Ahmad, but the saluki's. I would ask you to treat his injured paw while I take Bryna bint Blaine back to the harem." Passing the injured dog to his servant, Sharif stepped back to reveal the girl standing behind him.

Abu Ahmad's eyes bulged as he regarded her with alarm.

"Is there anyone else around?" Sharif asked.

"They are resting—at kef—as all of us should be." The old man glared at Bryna almost accusingly.

"Alhamdillah," Sharif breathed with relief. Turning, he explained carefully, "You have performed a service for me today, Bryna bint Blaine, but no one must know you wandered from the house alone, nor that I found you on the mountainside. Abu Ahmad will say nothing." He glanced toward the old man for agreement and received it. "Nassar, your *sidi*, would be very angry if he knew—angry enough to beat you or even to sell you—because you were alone with another man. It is his right, and there is little I could do to protect you. Do you understand?"

Bryna nodded, angry and a little frightened as she realized the possible consequences of her impulsive, kind action. It was unfair. Scorching words rose to her lips, but she swallowed them, unwilling to offend Sharif. She knew he protected her at risk to his reputation if anyone ever discovered their meeting on the mountain.

"Go, then," he ordered gently. "We will not speak of this to others."

Safe in her room, Bryna wept, knowing she had

missed an opportunity to plead her case to the sheik.

For days afterward she was tense, fearing that someone had noticed her absence that afternoon, but she relaxed finally when no one spoke of it. Certainly Fatmah's behavior toward her had not changed. Once Bryna and Pamela had learned their household tasks, the old woman supervised only sporadically, coming in at odd moments to criticize.

During one of the hottest days of summer, Bryna and Pamela refilled the huge pots set in the corner of the harem's main room to cool it. It was a job usually left to servants, but the servants were slaughtering and drying meat for the impending journey to the family home in Riyadh.

Her face flushed with heat, Pamela suddenly put down the jug she carried with a decisive thud and sat on a bench. "Let's rest for a moment, Bryna," she urged. "We have been at this all morning, and my back hurts."

Setting down her own jug, Bryna looked at her friend closely, The English girl's eyes were dull and darkly circled, and her blond hair was lank and drab. Bryna fetched her a drink of water and asked solicitously, "Are you ill, Pamela?"

"Thank you." The girl accepted the gourd and drank deeply. "No, it is just the heat, and I am so tired. 'Pamela, do this. Pamela, do that,'" she mimicked, "as if I were a servant. Well, I am not," she said crossly, "and I am not accustomed to such work. I don't know how you do it, Bryna." She sighed. "You talk about your terrible temper, but I haven't seen it once since we got here."

"I haven't had time to lose it," Bryna replied lightly. "My time has been taken up trying to adapt to this strange country."

"It is all rather confusing," Pamela agreed. "Why, I—"

"What do you think you are doing, daughters of Satan? Did I not tell you to fill the jars?" Fatmah's strident voice cut across the conversation, causing both women to start with surprise.

"We were just resting for a moment," Pamela said defensively.

Fatmah's hand shot out, her fingers lacing in the English girl's blond hair. She yanked, nearly dragging her from the bench. "I will tell you when you may rest," she shouted. "Now get up!"

"Release her," Bryna's voice rang out strongly.

Shocked and stunned that the American would speak to her in such a tone, Fatmah obeyed without thinking. Then she turned on Bryna with narrowed eyes and a raised fist.

"Just because you give us our orders does not mean you may abuse us," Bryna interjected hotly. She did not threaten Sharif's elder wife, but placed herself between Fatmah and the weeping Pamela, glaring down at the squat Arab woman.

"Slaves can be beaten," Fatmah insisted.

"Not by you," Bryna countered evenly.

"You think you can escape punishment because you are Nassar's property?" Fatmah sneered. "Wallahi, I am his mother and I can beat you."

"Call for help, then, for you will not beat me

without a fight." Bryna held her ground. "And not without a hearing by Sheik Al Selim."

"Stop, Bryna." Pamela choked on her tears. "Don't you see you are putting yourself in danger for nothing?" Jumping to her feet, the English girl ran, sobbing, to her room.

To Bryna's amazement, Fatmah watched Pamela's retreat disapprovingly, but she did not pursue her. Shaking her head, the woman stared contemptuously at Bryna and muttered, "You are mad, both of you. One day I will sell you to the *yazidi*, the devil worshipers." Then she went into her own room and closed the door.

Bryna went to Pamela's door and tapped lightly, entering the room when there was no answer. Lying facedown on her divan, the English girl did not look up.

"Pamela, are you all right?" Bryna asked anxiously.

"No, I am not all right." The agitated girl rolled over and glared at her friend. "I hate it here, and I simply cannot bear the thought of spending the rest of my life in Nassar's harem."

"I do not care for that idea, either. But we will find a way out, *chère*," Bryna promised.

"Stop saying that." Pamela's voice was harsh.

Surprised by her friend's intensity, Bryna sat down on the edge of the bed and laid a hand against her forehead.

Pamela pulled away and rolled so she faced the wall. "Do not worry. I do not have a fever," she said tonelessly now that her anger had passed.

"What's wrong, then?"

"It's the heat. I suffer terribly from it, you know. Just leave me. I'll soon be better."

"Are you sure?"

"Of course. I just need to rest," Pamela said with a gallant and insincere smile.

Acquiescing to her wishes, Bryna departed, feeling unsettled. She knew something was wrong, something more than heat. She didn't know that Nassar went to Pamela's room each night when the harem was asleep. At first he had wooed and coaxed the English girl, until at last he'd lost his temper and threatened to sell Bryna into a brothel if Pamela did not submit. Frightened by the possible loss of her friend, the girl had not realized Nassar had no intention of selling Bryna. He was attracted to the tall, dark girl and would one day go to her bed, but it was Pamela for whom he burned.

When the blond girl wavered, the determined Arab had forced himself on her, smothering her cries in a pillow. Bryna had not heard her protests at the other end of the harem. `Abla and Latifeh had slept through them. Fatmah had turned a deaf ear.

Nassar continued to visit Pamela's room, repeating his threat, growing bolder each time. She would tell no one, he knew. His secret was safe.

Safe, at least, until he was discovered. `Abla had risen early to look for truffles with her female cousins when Nassar emerged from Pamela's room, adjusting his robes. His busy hands stilled when he saw the little girl, looking past him to where Pamela lay crumpled and weeping on the bed. `Abla glared at him, then wordlessly brushed past him to tend to the English girl.

Nassar hastened from the women's quarters. By the time he reached his apartment, he knew he could not marry his cousin. He had seen hatred in her eyes, and no wife could look at a husband so. Men were superior to women in all ways.

There was a problem, however. As Sharif's only child, `Abla would inherit his property. Unless she did not live, Nassar mused; then he would be sole heir. Another decision was rapidly reached. `Abla had to go.

He did not put his plan into action until Sharif went to Mecca on business a few weeks later. Thinking `Abla was with the herds, Nassar visited his mother and aunt and explained that the family had a dire problem.

A young boy from the village had seen `Abla in the souk and had been captivated by her beauty, he started calmly. He realized she was young, but she was old enough to know she should not entice a man. This temptation was an unpardonable sin on her part. If the young people ever found themselves alone together, they would not be able to control themselves and would dishonor the house of Selim, he ranted, working himself into a righteous frenzy. Steps must be taken immediately to keep the family name from being ruined, so he, Nassar, would act in Sharif's absence, doing what must be done. He would kill `Abla as `*urf,* the law of custom, demanded to preserve what was left of family honor and avoid inevitable shame.

From the garden, the little girl eavesdropped long enough to hear her aunts regretfully agree with Nassar. Her eyes wide with fear, she rushed to find the one person who would help her.

Bryna was washing clothes in the fountain in the sunny courtyard, beating the wet linen against a smooth stone. When she heard `Abla's frightened wail, she ran at once to find out what was wrong.

`Abla threw herself into her friend's arms and related in a jumble of French and Arabic what she had heard. Although she did not understand all of it, Bryna knew Nassar intended to harm the child.

She must get `Abla away from Nassar until the sheik returned, Bryna decided. Surely he would not allow such a thing to happen to his daughter, even if he had ignored her for most of her young life.

"If I have tempted a man, I deserve to die. But I know of no such person." `Abla wept on her shoulder.

"Do not even say such a thing," Bryna interrupted kindly. "Listen to me. Do you remember the big boulder we found when we hiked in the mountains?"

"The one shaped like a sleeping camel?"

"*Oui.* Go there and stay. I will join you soon with food and water and blankets."

"What will we do then?"

"We will find a cave and hide until your father comes home."

"Like the Prophet when he fasted and received his revelations?" Fear forgotten, `Abla's gray eyes shone at the prospect of an adventure.

"Yes, like the Prophet." Bryna laughed in spite of the gravity of the situation. "But I would rather not fast, so I will get some food. Now go and don't turn back for anything. I'll bring everything we need."

After the girl had scampered away, Bryna stole quietly to her quarters and packed clothing and blankets for each of them in woolen saddlebags. Then, careful not to alert the others, she crept to the kitchen during kef and gathered food and water for several days. Lugging the bags and water skins up the mountainside, she found `Abla, and together they searched for a hiding place.

At last they found a small cave with a natural chimney where they could have a small fire at night. The entrance was obscured by a tree and invisible to the casual observer. There they set up a crude camp and waited. `Abla was still child enough to forget the reason they were there and exult in the adventure.

The first evening the fugitives heard the servants calling them, but they stayed where they were. The next day more people, including townspeople, searched in hopes of the reward Nassar offered.

Three cold nights passed before Bryna decided to risk returning to the house. Warning `Abla to stay hidden, she donned a black burnoose, drawing its hood over her head to hide her face. Then she crept to the villa in search of Sharif.

As she approached the sleeping house, she was met by the sheik's saluki. The dog whined and squirmed with joy when he recognized her. She scratched behind his ear affectionately, and he let her pass.

Inside the back door of the villa, the girl hesitated, her heart pounding. It was forbidden for her to do what she was about to do, but she could not turn back. She still seethed with fury at Nassar, and she would not let `Abla down.

Purposefully Bryna stole up the stairs to the men's wing. She had never been inside before, but she had often seen Sharif on his balcony in the evenings. Surely she could find his apartment. Pausing in the long hallway upstairs, she deliberated an instant. Which door was his? To choose the wrong one could mean punishment, even death. Drawing a steadying breath, she rapped lightly on one, praying it was his.

In his quarters, Sharif was about to retire. He had just returned from his journey, and no one but Abu Ahmad knew of his presence yet. Tomorrow would be soon enough to see his relatives and receive their welcomes.

After a meal of cold meat, he had dismissed his servant and settled into a tub of steaming water, hoping to work the cramps out of his muscles. He was not as young as he once was, he thought regretfully as he stepped from the tub. Before he bent to dry, he flexed his weary shoulders in an effort to relieve the strain of hours of riding.

Sharif paused in his stretch, listening, uncertain if he had heard a knock. But it came again, soft but insistent.

"Min? Who is it?" Hurriedly drawing on a robe, he strode to the door and threw it open.

By the flickering light of the oil lamp in the hall, Bryna saw Sharif in the doorway. His robe, loosely wrapped, exposed a smooth, hairless chest, its surface dissected by a ridged scar from a past battle. Lower, it clung to his damp body, revealing muscular legs. He was not wearing his kaffiyeh, and for the first time she saw his long, jet-black hair.

For a moment the girl was silent, stunned by a sudden rush of feeling. Sharif was magnificent—virile and handsome. She was shocked to realize that the stirrings of desire she had felt for Derek paled in comparison with what she felt for this man she barely knew.

Sharif's handsome, angular face was disbelieving when he beheld the apparition at his door. "Noorah," he breathed, and swept the black-cloaked wraith into his arms at once, holding her close.

The specter was flesh and blood, warm and sweet. Perhaps it was his imagination, but for a moment her body, molded to the hard length of his, seemed yielding, even willing, for his caress.

Then she drew a shuddering breath and gently loosened his hold on her. "No, my sheik, it is Bryna bint Blaine," she said in a tremulous voice.

He released the girl abruptly and shoved her from him. Pulling his robe tightly about him, he stepped back without a word and permitted her to enter the room. When he had closed the door, he crossed to a peg on the wall and wrapped a sash very deliberately around his waist. Then he put on his headdress, taking great pains to arrange the folds. When he had regained self-control, he set his *aghal* in place and turned to the woman. She was obviously shaken, but no more disturbed than he.

"I told you Nassar could kill you for being alone with a man. Why have you come to the men's quarters? Are you mad, woman?" he asked harshly.

"It is `Abla," was her simple reply.

"`Abla?" His puzzlement brought another scowl to his face. "What about her?"

"Please, follow me," she murmured in her faltering Arabic.

He caught her arm roughly as she turned to lead him from the room. "I will not follow until you explain."

This time the girl jerked away, rubbing her arm where his fingers had grasped it as if she were burned. Her hood fell back to reveal blue eyes that searched his fierce expression uncomprehendingly. Unveiled, Bryna's face roused feelings in him nearly forgotten and almost too hard to resist. Against his will, he reached out to touch her cheek.

"Please, *sidi*," she implored raggedly, retreating a step, "you must follow me."

Sharif scowled darkly and dropped his hand at once. He opened the door and looked in both directions to be sure the hallway was clear. Then he gestured brusquely for her to lead.

The only sound as Bryna led the man through the hall was the rustle of her voluminous clothing. Although nothing could be seen of her body through it, the sway of the fabric as she walked was faintly provocative, and Sharif felt an unwelcome swell of desire.

Gliding through the moonlight in front of him, his silent guide led him into the mountains to a place where a tree grew against the stone face of the cliff. Turning, she pressed herself against the rock and sidled behind the tree to disappear into the small cave he had not seen before. He followed her lead and found himself standing in a small cavern.

Before his eyes could accustom themselves to the darkness, a small form launched itself at him and wrapped spindly arms around his waist.

"Abu," `Abla greeted him tearfully.

Sharif disengaged the arms and held his daughter away so he could look at her. "`Abla, what is the meaning of this?" he asked, his voice gruff with surprise.

When the little girl explained what had occurred during his absence, a look of cold fury crossed Sharif's face. Even if there was a young man—which he doubted—Nassar should have waited to give the order for `Abla's execution. His nephew was her ibn *'amm*, but a daughter was a father's responsibility. The choice of her life or death was in his hands.

With a quick glance at Bryna, Sharif gripped his daughter by the shoulders and delivered his decision. `Abla gazed up at him trustfully as he spoke, calmly, deliberately, and slowly enough that the foreign woman could understand.

"It is not necessary that you die, `Abla. Nassar's

worries about your virtue are groundless at this time. You are still very young for such things"— he paused with a smile —"and before Bryna bint Blaine came, your face was too dirty to judge its beauty.

"Soon you must veil yourself and behave as a lady, but for now I command you to cover yourself when you go to the souk. If you follow the example of the Prophet's wives, it will please your cousin, will always preserve your honor, and you will be known as a devout young woman."

When Sharif finished speaking, he clasped `Abla's small hand in his big one and turned to Bryna. "It seems you have performed another service for me and mine, Bryna bint Blaine," he said softly. "Thanks between the Arabs is not customary, but I thank you tonight for my daughter's life."

Bryna's breath caught in her throat at the glow in Sharif's gray eyes. "No thanks are necessary, my lord." She hesitated, considering the wisdom of making a plea for freedom, but she did not want him to think she had done what she had for reward. For some reason his approval was suddenly important to her.

"Come, then," Sharif ordered kindly, "let us go home . . . together."

Outside, `Abla grasped Bryna's hand with her free one. Together the three walked back to the house, hand in hand, as the moon set behind the mountains on the other side of the valley.

The next morning Nassar hurried to the harem to see if anyone had heard anything of Bryna and

`Abla. Women knew things a man did not. The corpulent young man was drawn up short when he saw the faithful Abu Ahmad guarding the door to the women's quarters.

"Let me pass," Nassar ordered importantly.

"I am sorry, bin Hamza," the old man replied politely, "but I cannot. My master wishes to see you first in his quarters."

"Sharif has returned?"

"Last night."

Nassar could see no use in arguing, so he pivoted on his heel and marched directly to his uncle's quarters.

"There you are, Nassar." Sharif was so angry that he wasted no time with pleasantries. "I wish to talk to you about `Abla."

The younger man's face blanched, but he covered his nervousness by saying, "We have looked everywhere for her, *ya amm,* but she is nowhere to be found. I fear she may have been kidnapped by my wretched slave, Bryna bint Blaine, for she has run away."

"`Abla was not kidnapped by Bryna bint Blaine or anyone else!" Sharif roared. "Your cousin has been in hiding for fear of her life."

"What . . . what are you talking about?" Nassar stammered, stalling for time while his mind worked.

"I am talking about your plan to kill her. If you wish to renounce your claim on `Abla, you may do so," Sharif informed the young man coldly, "but you have no right to kill her. That is a father's prerogative."

"But she would shame the family," Nassar offered beseechingly. "When I tell you, you will understand why I decided to kill her."

The sheik cut him off with an impatient gesture. "Show me the young man. Bring him to the *majlis* and let the elders hear him."

Nassar stared into Sharif's eyes, dark with fury and hardened to two points of steel, and knew he was defeated. "That is hardly necessary, Uncle, if you, as sheik, have decided your daughter is not to be punished." The young Arab's voice was insinuating. He would not surrender graciously.

"I have seen no reason to punish `Abla. I have told her to veil herself in public to spare you further embarrassment."

"Very well," Nassar acquiesced grudgingly, preparing to leave. "Is there anything else?"

"No. Yes!" the sheik said vehemently. "Bryna bint Blaine is not to be punished, either."

"Runaway slaves must be chastised," Nassar insisted petulantly.

"She has returned to the harem . . . to her *sidi*." Sharif spoke the word distastefully, but Nassar did not notice.

"That is my point exactly. I am her master."

"You have yet to repay me for my camels," his uncle reminded him dryly.

"But I will. Bryna is mine to do with as I please."

"Never forget, Nassar, the duty of a sheik is to guard the weak. As your lord and protector of this family, I tell you, have thou a care of this woman as of mine own eye. Though she is a woman and a

203

slave, I will be watching, and if I see you abuse her, I will offer Bryna bint Blaine sanctuary as surely as if she were born Bedu. She is under my protection. Do not harm her or I will demand blood for blood."

The order chafed, but Nassar obeyed, for he knew Sharif would follow through on his threat.

Although they were incensed by the runaways' behavior, Fatmah and Latifeh also respected the sheik's wishes, and gradually life in the harem began to return to normal. Everything was as it had been before, except for Bryna and Pamela's friendship.

The English girl's brown eyes were accusing when Bryna returned. For days she refused to speak to her friend, keeping to her room, bathing at a different time. Bryna might have been angry, but it was obvious Pamela was ill. She no longer greeted mealtime with delight, and, uncharacteristically, she often sent food away untasted.

"Please," Bryna pleaded one evening when she met Pamela in the outer chamber of the harem, "I must talk to you."

The other girl regarded her with hostility, but then she nodded and allowed herself to be led out into the garden, where they could speak privately. She sat on a bench and gazed up unresponsively at Bryna.

"Pamela, tell me why you are avoiding me. I thought we were friends."

"I am a better friend than you know," the English girl snapped, "yet you left me again after you promised you would not."

"I promised I would not escape without you and I did not. I was gone for a few days, but I came back. When we escape, it will be together."

"We will not escape. I know that now," Pamela answered dully. "And there will be no rescue."

"Do not give up. There is always hope."

"For you, perhaps—your father or Derek may find you yet—but not for me."

"I know you are not well," Bryna pressed gently. "I've heard you retching in the morning when I pass your room. Is there anything I can do for you?"

"There is nothing anyone can do for me." Pamela rose suddenly and drew her aba tightly around herself. "We are lost, Bryna, lost forever in a savage world," she said. Then she marched back into the house, leaving Bryna with her thoughts.

From his balcony, Sharif watched them. Bryna's unveiled face was alive with tenderness and compassion, while the Inglayzi seemed pale and sad. When the blonde stood, he saw the reason for her sorrow in her thickening waist.

So Nassar had taken the fair one in spite of his promise. Had he also lain with Bryna bint Blaine?

Sharif's hands tightened on the rail of his balcony until his knuckles were white. For an instant he experienced feelings utterly foreign to him. The sheik realized he would like nothing more than to thrash his nephew with his bare hands, but in doing so he himself would lose face.

Drawing a deep breath, Sharif forced himself to think as the head of his family. It was not fitting that either of the infidel concubines be made a wife before Nassar's intended. Sharif would order Nassar to leave Bryna bint Blaine alone and hope that the damage done when his nephew lay with the Inglayzi was not irreparable.

The troublemakers in his tribe already questioned the wisdom of allowing the white women to stay. Sa'id had warned Sharif that the hotheaded Mautlauq muttered against him, though not yet in *majlis.* Whether Mautlauq felt strongly about the infidels was not the question, Sharif realized. The Ottomans sought to sow dissension among the tribes by offering wealth and position to lesser sheiks. For many reasons, the sheik could not allow Nassar's marriages to become an issue.

As soon as summer's heat was over, he must take his family back to Riyadh, where Nassar would marry Farida. This year the Selims would not linger in the mountains. Sharif would send a messenger to Farida's father immediately, asking him to make the necessary arrangements.

But the sheik was not the only one to take note of Pamela's changing body. Fatmah watched with pursed lips as the girl wandered through the harem like a wraith. It was not right that the white concubine should bear Nassar's first son, his mother thought resentfully. Farida should be first. The old woman knew what she must do. Summoning a midwife from the town, she obtained an herbal powder that, when administered to the unsuspecting Pamela over time, would eliminate the problem.

CHAPTER

✦✦✦✦✦ **11** ✦✦✦✦✦

IN THE TIME OF TWO DOGS, THE HOTTEST PART
of summer, assessors came to Taif to collect *zakat*,
the holy tax. Sharif's kinsmen met their obligation
with near melancholy, for it meant their stay in the
relative cool of the mountains would soon be over.
As the days shortened, the men rose from their
beds at three o'clock each morning and went onto
the roof to search the skies for Suhail, the star that
signaled the end of summer.

When it appeared in the night sky, Sharif
ordered his family to prepare to return to Riyadh.
Water skins that had been chewed by rats were
hauled from the storerooms and repaired.
Provisions were assembled and packed. Suitable
gifts were selected for the sheiks through whose
territory they would travel.

On the morning of their departure, Sharif
inspected his *smala*, his caravan of family and
retainers, which ranged along the road in front of
his villa. His men stood by their riding camels at the
head of the line. Behind them, the women, some
with small children, waited beside their camels,

which were lashed from tail to nose. Following the women was a train of pack animals laden with the household items of the entire tribe. Herds of camels, sheep, and goats, tended by herdsmen and the children who were old enough to walk, followed. Down the road Salubas, itinerant craftsmen who attached themselves to Bedu tribes, waited, mounted on asses, ready to trail behind the Selims in the dust.

At the head of the procession, the sheik swung gracefully into his beautiful Njed saddle. Attached to his camel by a long lead rope, Târiq pranced, seemingly eager to be off.

As the camels roared and spit in protest, servants assisted Bryna, Pamela, and several other women into their doubled-poled saddles. Fatmah and Latifeh were loaded into litters made of light wood and shaded by cotton canopies that swung between camels.

From his position, Sharif signaled the men who rode before him with the banners of his tribe, and the caravan lurched forward. Fortunately he was too far away to hear the disapproving murmurs among the women when they noticed he wore the sash given to him by the infidel woman.

Bryna heard and flushed with anger at their snide comments, but she did not care as she watched the sheik riding erect and proud, wearing her gift. She did not even care that Fatmah glowered at her from her litter.

The sheik rode through Taif's narrow streets on the way out of town, looking neither left nor right.

When he drew even with Alima's home, he turned to gesture in farewell. His aunt's black cloak and veil stirred in the morning breeze as she stood on her balcony. Clasping her *tespi*, sliding the prayer beads in her fingers, the old woman watched sadly until the caravan had disappeared down the dusty road.

As the party traversed the black gravelly plain, its slanting descent to the desert interspersed with boulders, Sharif told himself he would allow his *smala* and its herds to move slowly until they were accustomed to the heat and the rocky terrain. In this way he justified the snail's pace to himself, but in truth he relished life in the desert. After a long summer amid the elegant surroundings in Taif, he enjoyed the simpler ways of the tent dweller.

They rode for hours, the men perched on their knees in Bedu fashion on the backs of their camels, singing and talking loudly among themselves. The women were mostly silent, fanning themselves and observing the monotonous, colorless vista as they swayed from side to side on the backs of their camels.

Bryna was quiet, too, but her silence masked elation. She was cheered that customs were less restrictive in the desert and she was not forced to wear a stifling *burqu*. She felt the wind stir her *ghata*, lifting her hair from her shoulders, and relished her lightweight clothing and cool square of veil.

At midday the travelers dismounted at one of the many *qibla*, horseshoe configurations of rock made to point the way toward Mecca, and prepared for worship. The men of the tribe washed while water was still plentiful and spread their prayer rugs, while the women withdrew discreetly to one side.

Bryna knew Pamela's secret now. When the morning sickness did not pass and the English girl grew steadily sicker, Bryna became tender and protective, trying to help her hide her changing body under the voluminous robes. Bryna had known travel would be difficult for her friend, but she was alarmed by her faltering step and the pinched whiteness of her face. Casting a cautious glance toward the worshipers, she steadied Pamela's arm and whispered, "Are you all right?"

The girl turned dazed eyes toward Bryna. "Oh, fine," she murmured unconvincingly. "Just a bit hungry, you know."

Urgently Bryna looked around for Fatmah or Latifeh, but before she could find them, the men began to pray, reciting the Fatiha, the first sura of the Koran. Bryna had heard it so often in her months among the Moslems, she could say it herself.

When prayers were finished and the men gathered under a tree, Bryna left Pamela in the sparse shade of a juniper bush and went in search of Sharif's wives. She found them sitting in the shadow of a huge boulder, surrounded by chattering women. Taking them aside, she explained Pamela's weakened condition.

"If the Inglayzi is hungry, has she not enough

sense to eat?" Fatmah asked rudely. "She does little but eat and grow fat anyway." Irritated at having her kef interrupted, she marched toward Pamela's couched camel, trailed by Bryna and Latifeh. Yanking down a small sack that hung on the saddle frame, she shoved it into Bryna's hands.

When she opened it, the American girl found bread and a soft sheet of dried apricot paste, called "mare's skin." Mixed with water, the paste could be spread on the bread and eaten while on the move.

"See, even you are not so stupid that you cannot open a bag to get what is within," the Arab woman snapped.

"No one told us . . . " Bryna tried to explain. Seeing Latifeh shake her head, she stopped, knowing her defense would do no good.

"Thou fool, can you kaffirs do nothing for yourselves? Must I also show you how to drink from a goatskin?" Fatmah raged.

"That won't be necessary," Bryna answered in measured tone, restraining her anger with difficulty.

Sharif's elder wife glared at the American for a long moment. Let this witch defy her again and learn the consequences, she fumed to herself. Fatmah was in no mood for argument after swinging in a litter for hours, sweltering the heat. But the girl said nothing, biting her tongue until the woman turned to leave.

"My lady," she ventured then, "I have noticed some of the women leaving their camels to walk for a while. May I?"

"Please do." The old woman smiled nastily and stomped off to rejoin her friends in the shade.

Latifeh stayed behind, her annoyance tempered by practicality. "It would not be a good idea to walk, Bryna bint Blaine," she advised, speaking French as much as possible so there could be no misunderstanding. "There will be much work when we set up camp, and you are not accustomed to it. You should spare yourself at first."

Suddenly remembering herself, she admonished, "If you are too tired to set up Nassar's tent, no one else will do it for you. I know I will not. Then my nephew will beat you."

The Creole girl was glad she had heeded Latifeh's word when the caravan stopped for the night. Instructing the foreign women to watch, Fatmah, Latifeh, and `Abla pitched Sharif's huge tent. It was the duty of the women of the family, even though the sheik had many servants. They spread the black-goat hair panels on the ground in the center of the camp and secured the edges with ropes before raising the poles underneath. They worked together smoothly, the entire process taking less than five minutes.

Then Fatmah directed Bryna and Pamela to a sandy spot in the gravelly terrain where Ali, Nassar's lone herdsman, waited, ready to unload the household goods from the back of a pack camel. Bone-weary and sore, the foreign women were now expected to set up their master's desert home.

When they set clumsily to work, Ali withdrew a

short distance away to unload. Trying to ignore the stares she felt on every side, Bryna spread the tent material on the ground as Fatmah and Latifeh had. When the side wires were in place, she strained to raise the *am'dan,* or center pole, alone, refusing to allow her sick friend to undertake such heavy work. As Bryna struggled to tighten the flapping fabric over the pole, Pamela wielded a stone hammer awkwardly, pounding the pegs for the waist wires into the soft sand.

The women of the camp were noticeably silent as they loitered over their chores, watching the kaffirs' efforts with sidelong glances. They sniggered among themselves and laughed aloud when the wind caught the goat-hair panel and pulled the cords from the ground, destroying the foreigners' handiwork.

As Bryna and Pamela surveyed the wreckage, the Arab women returned to their work with sly smiles. Even Ali hid a smile behind his hand. Only `Abla came to stand beside her friend as Bryna fought back tears of frustration.

"It was not your fault it did not stand," `Abla said sympathetically, her loyalties torn. Finally, unwilling to speak ill of her father's wives, she pointed to a spot not ten feet away and recommended brightly, "Try pitching the tent there. Where you built before, the sand is soft and the pegs will never hold."

With a grateful smile, Bryna followed her suggestion. `Abla helped Pamela with the pegs, ignoring the frowns of her father's wives, and soon

Nassar's tent was pitched and anchored sturdily.

Open on one side to admit a breeze, the tent consisted of two chambers, a *majlis* and a women's quarters. Only Sharif's tent was larger. As sheik, he must have a *majlis* large enough to hold all the men of the tribe.

Once Nassar's *majlis* had been organized, bags of grain and other supplies were dragged into the curtained women's quarters to serve as pillows. Pamela lay down "for just a moment" with a grateful sigh. In the cooking area, `Abla hovered helpfully at Bryna's elbow, explaining the duties of a Bedu housewife. The American girl listened as she picked through the copper cooking utensils that cluttered the space. Together she and `Abla explored the contents of the saddlebags Ali had unloaded.

"What's this?" Bryna asked curiously, pulling out a wooden box.

The little girl took it and opened the hinged lid. "Oh, it's empty," she said disappointedly. "You are supposed to keep things in it like household medicines or anything Nassar gives you to put in it. But come now." She summoned Bryna as she scampered from the tent. "I must show you how to keep the water skins cool."

Outside the tent, `Abla showed her a bed of neatly piled brush upon which the skins were laid so air could circulate around them. They were shaded by a small canopy of goat-hair anchored on four short sticks.

"Gathering brush is my job in my father's household," the little girl explained. "My father had one of our servants gather yours because Nassar has no servants or children. He ordered them to bring firewood as well. He does not say so, but I think he is grateful to you for helping me," she added shyly.

"`Abla." Latifeh beckoned. "Do you not have chores of your own to do?"

"I must go now," the child called over her shoulder. "It is time to cook dinner, but don't forget to build Nassar's fire."

Taking an armload of brush to the *majlis,* Bryna found the young Arab sprawled on the saddlebags that served as his pillows. His mare, tethered to the center pole of the tent, whinnied softly when the girl entered.

"So there you are," he greeted her arrogantly as he drank from a bowl, burying his nose in white foam. When he looked up, drops of camel's milk dripped from his lips to speckle his black beard. "Where is Pamela bint Harold?"

"She is lying down."

"It is not right for her to sleep just before sunset. It is unhealthy," he said, but his protest seemed halfhearted. He eyed Bryna with new interest. His uncle had forbidden him to use her, but surely there was a way. "Why does she rest?" he asked carelessly.

"She is not feeling well," Bryna replied, trying to ignore the man's lecherous gaze on her. Stooping, she dropped the kindling beside the fire pit.

"Then she should rest," the young Arab conceded magnanimously. "Perhaps you should both rest, for we reach the sands tomorrow. I will tell Ali to bring some *halîb,* some camel's milk, to strengthen the golden-haired houri. I think the desert will be hard on my fragile flower, but not so hard on you. You are strong, eh, my tall beauty? You will bear me many sons." Lazily he reached out and caught her hand.

"Not if I can help it," Bryna said through gritted teeth as she tried to wrench free.

"You are my slave and do what I command," Nassar ordered, scowling. "And I command you to sit beside me."

"I thought it was time to cook dinner," she argued desperately.

"I said, sit." Nassar's grip tightened on Bryna's hand until she thought her fingers would break. With a mutinous glare at him, she knelt on a cushion as far from Nassar as his grasp would allow.

"Closer," the young Arab demanded, yanking her toward him. Suddenly changing his tack, he said cajolingly, "You are to be one of my wives, Bryna bint Blaine. We should get to know each other better, I think."

"The way you got to know Pamela?" she snapped.

"If you like." He slid an arm around her and attempted to pull her near.

"I do not like," Bryna announced, shrugging his arm from her rigid shoulders. "I will keep your house, Nassar bin Hamza, but I will not be your concubine."

"You . . . you are my slave," he sputtered in amazement. No woman had ever spoken to him in such a way.

"Yes, but on our first day in Taif the sheik forbade you to touch either Pamela or me until we have made our *shahadas.* You took her contrary to his orders, and soon everyone will know what you have done. What will happen, I wonder, if you present such solid evidence of your disobedience again?"

For an instant Nassar saw the infidel woman through a red haze. Then he released her arm and threw himself back against the cushions, demanding, "What have you cooked for my dinner, worthless one? I want to eat."

"I have not had time to cook anything yet," she explained with exaggerated patience as if speaking to a spoiled child.

"By the beard of the Prophet, do not speak to me thus. You anger me, woman." Nassar scrambled to his feet. "I warn you, Bryna bint Blaine, from this day on, I will expect my dinner on time. I will not punish you today, for I am pleased with the *beit sha'r,* the house of hair, you and my Inglayzi have built for me. But next time . . . " He let his voice trail off menacingly.

As he stomped off in the direction of Sharif's tent, he yelled over his shoulder, "Thou cursed of your two parents, tonight I will eat with my uncle."

Kicking at the firewood in a fit of Irish temper, Bryna did not notice Pamela peeping out from the women's quarters until she spoke.

"Is he gone?" the English girl asked wearily.

"He's gone." Bryna stroked the velvety nose of Nassar's horse. "Do not be frightened, *chère*," she comforted the high-strung animal. "I'm angry with your master, not with you."

"Must you make friends with it?" Pamela asked peevishly. "I do not know why these people insist on bringing filthy animals right into the tent."

"Next to his camels, she is Nassar's most treasured possession, and I am becoming rather fond of her, too." Bryna scratched the mare's forehead affectionately. "Her very presence in this tent proves something to the Arabs."

"What is that?"

"That I am not a bewitcher. They believe evil cannot enter where a purebred horse is kept. Yet here I am."

"I suppose," Pamela agreed apathetically. "Let's do go to sleep, Bryna. Nassar said we could rest, and tonight I am so tired, I don't even want to eat."

"I'll be there soon. `Abla told me the goats must be milked when they are brought into camp in the evening."

"Then I will help." Pamela started to rise heavily.

"No, you rest. I will milk and then I will join you."

So exhausted were the girls that they did not even awaken when the women of the tribe trilled a greeting to a visitor that night. The *rabia*, or guide, for this portion of the journey had arrived. Sharif's party would be accompanied by a different *rabia* in each territory through which they passed. Each guide would carry the banner of the local sheik, which advised that Sharif's *smala* was under his protection while they were in his region.

Sharif's wives hurried to prepare a meal for the *rabia*. They complained about the absence of the foreign women, but Nassar told them flatly that his women were not available to help.

When Bryna rose just after dawn, she was already lagging behind on the day. Throughout the waking camp, coffee was being made on fires rekindled from the last night's embers. Because there had been no fire at Nassar's tent, Bryna had to build one before she could start to cook. Pamela's inept assistance was more a hindrance than a help.

Nassar came to breakfast in a sour mood. While he waited, he sipped coffee impatiently and unleashed a tirade upon Bryna's head. She watched with relief when he left at last, leading his mare, to join the other men beside the line of couched, waiting camels.

As she hurried to wash the breakfast pots, Bryna watched Sharif's tent out of the corner of her eyes. `Abla had told her yesterday that when Fatmah and Latifeh began to take it down, all the other families would hurry to do likewise for it meant *ráhla,* time to move. If the sheik's tent remained an hour past sunrise, the caravan would camp for another day.

When she was about to give up, Sharif's wives appeared and began to fold his tents. The foreign women found the dismantling of the tent much easier than the construction. They had everything packed when Ali came with their riding camels in tow.

"So at last you rise from your beds," Fatmah hissed from her litter when they joined the other women. "You left us to cook for the *rabia* last night while you and the pale-haired woman slumbered like babes in your tent. God blacken your faces."

"We did not even know the *rabia* had arrived," Bryna explained.

"Hah!" Fatmah snorted. "How could we leave this morning without a guide?"

"Yes, hah!" Latifeh echoed indignantly.

Then the Arab women closed the curtains of their litters, thwarting any reply.

Sharif's *smala* traveled swiftly through the morning, turning southward until the plain gave way to desert. The blazing sun beat down on them, the heat rising from the reddish sand to create mirages of water spread out like lakes before them.

Although Bryna suffered in the heat, she could not understand the behavior of the Bedu. The hotter it became, the more they bundled up, claiming it built up a layer of cool air between their skin and their outer clothing. In desperation she tried their method, but she found the dampness repugnant.

She was drooping listlessly on the back of her plodding camel, wishing for a breeze, when Sharif rode the length of the straggling *smala,* pausing an instant near the women. He did not stop or even slow his camel, but his gray eyes flicked over the girl. Sensing she was being scrutinized, she straightened and turned to see who watched her. When her gaze found his, the man scowled and urged his camel on at a gallop.

For no reason, tears pricked the backs of Bryna's eyelids as she watched him ride away, his white kaffiyeh fluttering behind him. Would she ever understand this hard, unyielding man? she wondered miserably. Since the night she had visited his room, something had changed between them. It seemed as if he could not forgive her for going there, even though she had done nothing wrong. Now every time he looked at her his expression became grimmer and more forbidding than before.

Yet she had seen his face suffused with tenderness, had witnessed his kindness to `Abla. He had even touched her own face with surprising gentleness. What had turned that gentleness to harshness?

Resuming his place at the head of his *smala*, Sharif gave the order to stop for the night. He answered the questions posed to him, but he did not join in the conversation of the men gathered around his campfire. In fact, the sheik did not even hear them as his mind returned to his last meeting with his aunt.

He had found Alima in her harem garden, tending her potted fruit trees. Each one was a dwarf, rare and unusual in Arabia, and the old woman fussed over them as if they were her children.

"So you have come to bid me farewell, my

lord," she said when the man was settled on a bench with a cup of *rubb Rumman*.

"We leave at dawn," Sharif confirmed.

"I will miss you, nephew." She smiled sadly. "Whose conversation offers me as much enjoyment and stimulation as yours?"

"You could come with us," he offered softly.

"And share a harem with Fatmah and Latifeh? I think not," his aunt snorted uncharitably. "Just knowing they are married to my favorite nephew is curse enough. I do not wish to see them every day. No, thank you, I will stay in Taif, in my own home."

Knowing the subject was closed, the sheik did not argue.

"How fares the blue-eyed American, Sharif?" Alima asked, seemingly absorbed in pinching the buds on a tiny lemon tree.

Sharif tensed, immediately on guard. He knew his aunt too well to suppose the question was casual.

"Well enough." He shrugged indifferently. "She is learning our customs and a little of our language. And `Abla seems to like her. Why do you ask?"

"Because I, too, like her. I have watched her a great deal over the past few months, and there is much to like. This girl is fair, my sheik, and she will make a fine wife—"

"For my nephew," he finished for her flatly.

Alima frowned at him in annoyance. "She will be wasted on Nassar."

"What are you saying, Aunt?"

"I am saying," she explained patiently, "that you should buy Bryna bint Blaine from Nassar."

"What!" the man exploded, springing to his feet.

"Your nephew wants the blond houri, not the other. Well, perhaps he wants her, but only because he is greedy for women. He is even greedier for money. I tell you, he would sell this Bryna for a price, and she would be good for you, Sharif. I know it."

"Because you had Hirfa read the sands again?"

"I knew it before," Alima replied defensively, but she held her ground in front of him.

"Do not tell me you are beginning to believe the nonsense that old woman tells you."

"You are changing the subject, my lord," Sharif's aunt said calmly. "We were speaking of Bryna. Tell the truth. Do you not find this woman pleasing?"

"She is foreign," he countered almost desperately.

"Your mother was foreign to our ways," Alima reminded him calmly.

"I have two wives already." Crossing his arms on his chest, he stared stubbornly at a spot over the woman's shoulder, refusing to meet her eyes.

"There is room for another."

"Not this one."

"You find her beautiful," Alima accused gently.

"Disturbingly so," the sheik admitted, "but it makes no difference." Weary of argument, he sank down on the bench and turned troubled eyes on his aunt. "Hear me now, Alima, for I will not say this again. What you suggest cannot be. Bryna bint Blaine belongs to my nephew—as his intended wife."

"He has not married her yet," Alima argued.

"Upon my orders."

"So you will not even offer to buy her?"

"No," Sharif said harshly, "it would not be right."

"You will not seek the will of your heart." The old woman sighed in resignation. "Marry her to Nassar quickly, Sharif, and settle them in their own home. You cannot keep her with your harem. Lo, she may be as fair as the moon, but she will be as unattainable to you. It is not a good thing to have your heart's desire at hand, my nephew, and still unreachable."

In his camp in the desert, Sharif forced himself to turn his attention to the matters at hand. But when he lay down to sleep that night, his aunt's words still rang in his ears.

CHAPTER

✧✧✧✧ **12** ✧✧✧✧

TIRED OF RIDING AND OF FEELING FATMAH'S baleful stare upon her, Bryna dismounted and walked to the fringes of the *smala,* where she was joined by Taman bint Sa'id. Seeing the older girls walking together, ʾAbla soon came to dog their steps, nearly treading on their heels in her efforts to stay close.

In the beginning ʾAbla had been their translator, but now they spoke mostly in Arabic, falling back on French only when Bryna did not know the proper word. The child listened to the conversation approvingly, smiling in encouragement when the American girl faltered or mispronounced a word. She was proud of her student, for Bryna was learning quickly.

She was pleased, too, with the friendship between her cousin, Taman, and Bryna. Although Taman was older, ʾAbla had always thought her a silly female, always fussing with clothes and casting sidelong glances at the young men. But now she did not seem so bad. Perhaps she should not tease Taman so much, ʾAbla mused.

Quickly she abandoned that generous thought. Taman was so easy to tease. It had been funny at first, watching her cousin posturing, trying to imitate the behavior of the other women toward the kaffir. The Arab girl had struggled to maintain an air of superiority, trying hard not to like the foreigner. But in the end, Bryna's friendliness and Taman's kind nature had overcome all the obstacles to friendship.

"Wait, look," Taman murmured, slowing so `Abla nearly collided with her.

Bryna looked at them questioningly as the Arab girls turned to watch a handsome young man who reined his camel to a halt, his gaze fixed on the ground.

"Watch him," `Abla whispered excitedly. "Daoud bin Hatim is the best hunter of hares in the whole tribe."

Suddenly the young Arab threw himself from the back of his camel and approached a hole in the sand stealthily. Falling onto his stomach on the ground, he thrust his hand in the hole and withdrew a kicking hare by its ears. He held it up for the approval of his companions, who observed from nearby, and smiled at their cries of *"Mashallah."*

Then, drawing his knife, he cut the animal's throat expertly and hung it by the feet from the frame of a pack saddle, high above the ground.

"How did he know there was a hare in the hole?" Bryna asked curiously.

"Because there were tracks going into it, but none coming out. Daoud's eyes are sharp indeed"— Taman sighed admiringly —"and so dark and beautiful."

"His eyes are so dark and so beautiful," `Abla mimicked, retreating rapidly when the older girl wheeled on her. "And so often they are turned toward you, my cousin."

"`Abla bint Sharif, I warn you," Taman threatened in a low voice, "do not embarrass me."

"Daoud already knows you like him," the child said, giggling as she scuttled just out of reach of the blushing girl.

Suddenly `Abla lost interest in her game. Pointing toward a group of children congregated around a small tree jutting from the sand, she cried, "Look, a jinni tree!" She raced off at once to inspect the tiny scrub plant decorated with bits of fabric and shiny scraps of metal as an offering to the spirits.

Bryna glanced at Taman sympathetically, knowing how she hated to be teased. The youngest child of Sharif's cousin Sa'id, the girl had been named Taman, which meant "That's the lot." With five daughters and only two sons, her parents had finally wearied of disappointment, and after Taman there were no more children.

Bryna had become fond of the Arab girl in the past few weeks. As they became acquainted, they found they had something in common, a love of herbs and healing. Soon Taman was identifying desert plants for Bryna while they walked and describing their uses. She also introduced the foreigner to *thaluk*, a salad plant, and *thunma*, a wild tuber that tasted rather like potato. Together they hunted for wild leeks and sorrel to give some variety to their monotonous desert fare.

Now Taman's pleasant face was dark with wrath toward her small cousin. "Do not mind what `Abla says, Taman," Bryna advised softly. "She is just a child. Everyone knows Daoud is going to offer for you. The only question is when."

The Arab girl smiled diffidently at her friend and revealed, "He needs only a few more camels. He will ask my father for me as soon as he can meet my bride price."

Seeing her young cousin returning, Taman rapidly changed the subject. "I think by afternoon prayers, we should reach the well, *Bir* al Nafud. I will be glad to have clean water to drink again."

"Me too," `Abla cried, falling into step behind them. "I am tired of drinking *shanin*. Won't you be glad to reach the well, Bryna?"

"I look forward to being in a place for more than one night," the American girl replied fervently. "Pamela needs to rest. We will stay there a few days, won't we?"

"Insh'allah." Taman shrugged. "But probably, for the grazing is good there."

Suddenly sand flew as a blur of brown fur raced in a tight circle around the girls. Squirming with bliss at finding Bryna, Sharif's saluki barked joyously and bounded along beside her, his paw now completely healed.

"By Allah, what was that?" Taman laughed, shaking sand from her aba. Then she turned to Bryna in mock exasperation. "Does every beast in camp follow you?

If it is not the sheik's hunting dog, it is Nassar's mare."

"I like animals," the other girl answered simply.

"I know and still I—"

"Allah protect me from the devil," `Abla squealed from behind them as if she were frightened. Only her mischievous grin gave her away as she squeezed between the two older girls and pointed at a huge camp dog headed their direction. "*Ya ummi,* save me! Here comes the big black dog again."

The little girl's dramatic display of nervousness set the little saluki off again. Yipping shrilly, he left Bryna's side to tear back and forth along the length of the caravan.

"Surely you do not believe the big dog is possessed by demons just because he is black," Bryna chided the child over the din.

"Fatmah says—" `Abla began.

"Fatmah says I could be a bewitcher because I have blue eyes," Bryna interjected, "but you do not believe that."

"It makes one wonder, though," Taman said with a chuckle, "when you make friends with such a fearsome beast as this one."

The huge black dog loped toward them, his pink tongue lolling out of his mouth. Matted and flea-ridden, his coat was thick and shaggy. The veteran of many battles, his nose was crisscrossed with scars, and most of one ear was missing. But when he saw Bryna, his bushy tail wagged happily.

She gave him a friendly scratch behind the ears. This dog belonged to no one and to everyone, and his function was to guard the camp from strangers. He bared sharp, pointed teeth, and his deep bark sounded the alarm when anyone approached day or night.

Because the Bedu did not name even their salukis, Bryna privately dubbed the big dog Smemi, after `Abla's favorite story of a little boy who could hear everything, even the dew fall. She alone seemed to have no fear of the big dog. Although Taman and `Abla no longer ran, they eyed him distrustfully as they walked.

Ahead of the procession, the saluki ran now for the sheer joy of exertion. As he zoomed past them, the men paused in their talk to watch. Then they resumed their good-natured argument where they had left off, debating who bred the better camel, the Al Rashid or the Al Murrad.

Only Sharif and Nassar turned in their saddles to watch as the graceful saluki looped back on the desert floor to circle three female figures lagging at the back of the train. Both men recognized Bryna's tall form at once.

Nassar glowered in her direction, sulky at seeing her afoot. "Wallahi, why do I bother to furnish that one with a camel?" he asked peevishly of no one in particular. "She hardly ever rides with the women. Bryna bint Blaine is to be one of my wives, yet she trails behind us like a serving girl."

Sharif said nothing, but his gaze rested on her for a long moment. Then, cursing under his breath, he turned to the limitless horizon.

True to Taman's prediction, the *smala* reached

Bir al Nafud, just before afternoon prayers. It was a barren spot in the desert with only a few stunted bushes to give evidence of the presence of water nearby. The well itself was nothing more than a hole in the ground. The tribe waited while the water was tested. Finding it clean, the sheik signaled for the camels, the Bedouin's first concern, to be watered.

The clamor was deafening as camels spit and roared and herdsmen shouted. Once the herd was watered, a semblance of order returned and the men turned their attention to their horses. The children drove the flocks of sheep and goats to the troughs, and the women set about building the tents. The moon was high overhead by the time silence settled over the camp.

It was still dark when Bryna awakened. Through the night the temperature had dropped, and now the girl was glad for her blankets of Aleppo wool. Burrowing deeper, she tried to sleep again but found herself listening to the noises of the dormant camp. The Bedu said camels never slept, and from outside she heard the soft rasp of sand as a camel shifted its position. On a pallet beside her, Pamela stirred and whimpered in her sleep. Just on the other side of the cloth wall of the tent, Nassar snored sonorously, and somewhere in the distance, a baby cried.

It must be near dawn, Bryna thought groggily, but no birds sang to herald the new day. In the sleeping desert there was no sound but the wind.

The girl lay still, relishing the comfort of her

bed for a few minutes longer. As soon as there was enough light to distinguish a white hair from a black one, the call to prayers would sound and her day would begin.

While the Arabs prayed, the men out in the open, the women in their tents, Bryna enjoyed the only time she had to herself all day. She was grateful that in the desert she and Pamela slept separately from the other women. In those early morning hours she left the English girl to sleep and wrestled with her feelings in privacy, trying not to give in to despair, trying to prepare herself for another day. She forced herself to hope, refusing to consider what would happen if rescue never came.

Bryna had taken naturally to the duties of the *umm al'-ayyal*, the mother of the family. Now, as prayers ended, she rose and awakened Pamela. While the English girl rekindled the cooking fire, Bryna ground the beans for the morning coffee.

Outside the tent it was relatively calm while the servants called together their flocks and counted the sheep to see how many remained after the night. It was not necessary to count the goats, but the sheep did not cry out when attacked.

During the lull, Bryna made coffee and breakfast for Nassar. Pamela, looking ill at the smell of food, sat with him in his *majlis,* as he demanded every morning. Bryna joined them while Nassar ate. The flabby young man complained about her cooking, but he always ate.

Once Nassar had loosed his mare to graze unfettered around the camp during the day and gone to his uncle's *majlis,* his women ate their own hurried breakfast.

Leaving Pamela to scour the breakfast pots with sand, Bryna picked up a leather bucket and set out for the well. Nassar's mare nickered softly and followed, nudging the girl's back insistently with her soft nose. She tarried a moment to feed the horse a dried fig. Stroking its powerful, muscled neck, she whispered in its ear, "Someday I will jump on your back, little mare, and we will ride away and we will never come back."

But even as she said it, Bryna knew it was not true. She could not leave Pamela. Besides, where could she go? There was no sign of a town anywhere, and in fact they had not even seen another human being outside of their *smala* for nearly two weeks. How could she hope to survive and to keep the pregnant English girl alive in the desert?

When Bryna returned to Nassar's tent a short time later, Ali was hanging a heavy goatskin, bulging with camel's milk, from the tripod. Pamela sat down in the shade to swing it rhythmically until the contents had turned into *leben,* or yogurt. Although the job was tedious, it was easy work for the pregnant girl.

Bryna and Pamela talked while they worked. This morning the American girl treated the water skins with butter to keep them from sweating. When she finished she dragged the bedding out of the tent to sun. Then she settled in the shade to grind the grain for bread for dinner.

From Sharif's *majlis,* the voices of the men reached her as they discussed matters of tribal business. They considered it men's work, she realized, but she listened, recognizing Sharif's voice, deep and even and reasonable.

After kef, when the camp began slowly to stir again, Taman appeared to invite Bryna to go herb gathering. Quietly so they would not disturb anyone, the girls prepared to leave camp.

"Bryna, where are you going?" Pamela's voice came shrilly from the shadowy interior of the tent. Her blond hair tousled from sleep, she rushed out to catch her friend. "Why are you stealing away like this?"

"I am not stealing away, Pamela," Bryna said patiently. "I'm going to gather herbs with Taman."

Although she did not understand the words, Taman frowned at Bryna's solicitous attitude toward the Inglayzi. She did not understand her tenderness toward Pamela, for they were not even kinswomen.

"I thought you were still asleep," Bryna was explaining. "Would you like to come? We are not going far."

"No, I'll be fine here," Pamela said with a sigh, her fears allayed. "Nassar is going hunting with his friends this afternoon, so I will have some peace. But you will be back soon, won't you? Before tea?"

"Of course."

"I'm glad. I could not bear to go and drink Fatmah's vile, nasty tea alone."

Perplexed, Bryna assured the English girl she would return on time. While they were still in Taif, Fatmah had instituted the custom of tea, and now she insisted that she saw no reason to discontinue a civilized practice just because they were in the desert. She insisted Nassar's slaves present themselves for tea every day. Bryna was not fond of those calls on Fatmah and Latifeh, but Pamela hated them.

Bryna did not waste her time trying to tell the English girl that the tea the Arab woman served was potent and sweet but hardly vile. She did not remind her that no matter how unpleasant Fatmah was, teatime was always the most peaceful time of day. Each day the foreign women trudged to Sharif's tent to visit his wives. And each day Pamela seemed to sink deeper into dependency and despair.

While Bryna and Taman wandered, picking herbs where they could find them, Bryna brooded, worrying over her friend. Despite Pamela's thickening waist, her face had became drawn and gaunt. And there were shadows around her dull brown eyes. All this traveling was torturous for the delicate girl, and the strain was beginning to show itself emotionally as well as physically.

"You think of the Inglayzi," the Arab girl said almost accusingly when the other girl passed a *thaluk* bush without even seeing it.

"Yes." Bryna sighed. "I cannot help worrying about her."

"Why do you worry? Is it not enough you do her work for her?"

"Only the heavy chores, the ones she is not strong enough to do."

"To live among the people of the tents, one must have strength," Taman said bluntly. "Before I met you, I thought all infidel women were weak and helpless, but you are not. You should have been born a Bedu, Bryna bint Blaine, for here you belong. All things are as Allah wills and cannot be changed. Your life is with us now."

Bryna did not trust her voice to protest, so she nodded miserably. Perhaps it was true, but in trying to reassure her, Taman had voiced her worst fears. She might never escape.

Dispiritedly the girl returned to camp, to endless chores, to Pamela's wan face, to Fatmah's interminable tea. At Sharif's tent that afternoon, she listened politely to the unceasing dialogue between his wives. Fatmah coughed and wheezed and complained of a chest cold. Nights in the desert were too much for an old woman to endure, she grumbled. It would be good to reach Riyadh.

On the other side of the curtain that divided the *majlis* from the women's quarters, Sharif could hear the rise and fall of female voices. Recognizing Bryna's, he listened attentively. He had often heard the girl talking to the blond infidel in their unintelligible Inglayzi tongue and wished he could understand. But today she was speaking Arabic. Although she occasionally stumbled over the words, she was improving, he thought with satisfaction.

Suddenly a shadow crossed his face and the sheik rose abruptly and strode out of the tent. Târiq appeared at once in response to his beckoning whistle. Sharif threw himself on the mare's back and rode into the desert, his kaffiyeh streaming behind him.

What was wrong with him? he asked himself fiercely. It was not right for him to have such interest in his nephew's intended. He did not know this woman, yet she was never far from his thoughts. Had he been bewitched by her blue eyes after all?

Sharif halted his horse at the crest of a dune and looked out over the arid landscape. His back to the sun, he cast a long shadow across the sand. Bryna bint Blaine was beautiful and desirable, but she was not a bewitcher, he admitted to himself. He was attracted to her as a man is sometimes attracted to a woman, nothing more.

But she must never know. He had admitted it to Alima, but no one else must ever know or even suspect, the man realized grimly. Though her behavior had been chaste, Nassar could easily kill her to protect his *wejh,* his face. Sharif Al Selim was a man of honor. He would stay away from Bryna bint Blaine, he decided, for her own good and for his.

As he returned, Sharif paused on a rise overlooking the camp. Children played in front of the tents, and he could smell dinner cooking on a hundred different fires. The songs of the camel men could be heard as they returned from grazing, leading their herds, summoning strays. Sharif relished the clamorous, comfortable familiarity of his encampment in the desert. It was good and right and Bedouin.

Below, Bryna walked toward the clearing where the goats and sheep crowded together, her milk pail in her hand. Purposefully the sheik averted his eyes and turned Târiq toward his tent.

Unaware of Sharif's observation, the girl picked her way through the flock until she found Nassar's goats. All around her other women had already found their animals and squatted beside them to milk. Several women carried babies in slings on their backs. One child, just old enough to walk, tottered, his dark head barely visible over the backs of the sheep and the goats.

Just as Bryna bent to milk, she was nearly knocked off her feet by Sharif's saluki. He greeted her with a glad bark that caused the goat to prance skittishly to one side. As the dog prepared to launch itself enthusiastically at her again, she interrupted her milking long enough to squirt a warm stream of milk into the dog's face. She chuckled aloud as the saluki backed away with a surprised yelp.

The girl's smile faded when the flock shifted restively and the thunder of hooves reached her ears. Rising slowly, Bryna stared at a cloud of dust a short distance away in the desert. The young hunters were returning, racing at breakneck speed toward the camp, their salukis coursing gracefully at their sides. One of the Arab women shouted a warning to the others and began to fight her way among the frightened, milling animals toward the tents.

Surely they will stop, Bryna thought. But they bore down on the flock with reckless glee, close enough now for her to see Sâlih, Taman's elder brother, in the lead.

As the hoofbeats grew louder, the herd animals sidled nervously, their eyes wild with fear. A goat kicked over Bryna's milk bucket, spilling the contents into the sand, and a ram butted hard against her hip as the flock split in panic, surging against the sides of the clearing. Over their terrified bleating, Bryna heard the wails of a child.

"Walid!" one of the women shouted. "Where is my son?" Pressed by the herd against a tent, she tried in vain to push her way free, her fearful eyes scanning the panicked flock.

Through the dust, Bryna spied the top of the child's head in the midst of the flock and struggled toward him. She had to reach him in time, she thought determinedly. If he was not trampled by the sheep and goats, he would surely be run down by the horses in matter of moments. Reaching the boy, she snatched him up just as the horses pounded down upon them. With a desperate cry, she tossed the sobbing child through the air to his mother's outstretched arms. But, hemmed in by the terrified flock, Bryna could not escape.

Suddenly Smemi appeared from between the tents. Planting himself between Bryna and the racers, the big dog growled and snarled, causing the lead horse to rear. Sharif's saluki was at his side at once, yipping and snapping at the horse's legs. With a curse, Sâlih managed to hold on, but he could not control his mount. The mare reared and bucked, her sharp hooves slashing the air, threatening to crush Bryna. As she attempted to retreat, the girl was dimly aware of the angry shouts from the other riders as they were forced to rein in violently.

From behind her, a strong arm coiled around her waist and swept her onto the back of a horse and out of danger.

"First the dog would protect you, then the master," a familiar voice said in her ear as the white mare picked her way daintily through the chaos.

"Sheik Al Selim," Bryna whispered shakily. She did not have to turn around to know who held her so firmly against his solid, muscled chest. Acutely aware of his nearness, the girl shifted uneasily, trying to increase the space between them.

"No," the sheik shouted suddenly over his shoulder. Gripping Bryna tightly, he wheeled his horse. She gasped in alarm as she saw Sâlih, his gun drawn to shoot the black dog, frown up at his chief in angry askance.

"Leave him," Sharif ordered. "The animal did nothing more than protect the woman."

Leaving the dust and the frenzied animals behind them, they rode slowly to Nassar's tent. Halting in front of it, the man seemed lost in thought. He did not dismount or move to release her. Bryna sat bolt upright, stiff and very still, uncertain what to do. If the powerful arm locked around her waist would relax, she thought, she would slide to the ground and run away—from the man and from the emotions she was experiencing. But his grip did not loosen, and she pushed the absurd idea from her thoughts.

"My sheik," she ventured at last in careful Arabic, "I must thank you."

"I told you before, one Aribi does not thank

another," he answered tersely.

"But I am not Arab, and I am grateful to you. You saved my life." Twisting, she turned earnestly to her rescuer for the first time. Her words were forgotten when she found their faces very close, so that her light veil brushed his beard. They stared wordlessly, each mesmerized by the other's nearness, seemingly captured in time, though only an instant passed. Bryna's breath caught in her throat at the fleeting look of longing in Sharif's gray eyes.

But suddenly the eyes narrowed impatiently. The sheik thrust her away from him and set her on the ground with a jolt. "Do not thank me, woman," he growled. "Thank Allah that today was not your day to die."

As he rode away, Sharif cursed under his breath at the misery he had seen in Bryna's blue eyes before it was replaced by dislike for him. He did not know which hurt more.

Just before dawn, a bronzed, bearded man stood alone on the bow of a sambuk and searched the horizon for the first sight of land. Lost in thought, he was unaware that his brows were knit fiercely over his blue eyes, the wrinkles of his forehead disappearing under his turban. His striped djellaba billowed behind him on the salt-scented breeze as the little ship plowed through choppy waters toward the rocky Arabian coast.

"Good morning, sir," a voice said quietly behind him, careful not to be overheard by the people who slept on the deck.

"Good morning, Ashburn," Blaine answered without turning.

"It took a moment to be sure it was you." The young man chuckled softly, moving to stand beside him on the bow. "You are beginning to look the Algerian you claim to be. It certainly seems to agree with you more than it does with me. Sun and sand and wind, thirst, then sun and sand and more wind. I have never seen such an inhospitable place as the Sinai, nor do I hope to again."

" 'Twas only the beginning. Ernst said Arabia is mostly desert."

"Ah, yes, Ernst, the desert expert." Derek sighed, his frown revealing his annoyance for their guide.

"I didn't hear you complaining when he talked us past three different sets of Arab tribesmen." Blaine returned the frown. "Or when he got us through that scrape in Tur and onto this boat."

"I suppose he has earned his pay so far," Derek admitted grudgingly, "but he is a bothersome fellow. He and Mustafa are as thick as thieves."

Ernst was bothersome, perhaps, but indispensable, Blaine thought. And it was a good thing he and Mustafa got on so well. They made an outstanding pair of guides. Ernst's knowledge of the Arabian peninsula was as useful as Mustafa's sword arm. Staring out at the predawn sky, the man remembered the past fortnight since they had received Ibn Hussein's message.

When Blaine and Derek had learned they must

go to Arabia, Mustafa had found Ernst Mann, an impoverished Swiss scholar who spoke five languages as well as several Arab dialects, to be their guide. With his surprisingly dark coloring and encyclopedic memory, the slight, middle-aged man passed easily as an Arab.

Having lived for years in North Africa, Ernst had heard of O'Toole Effendi, so he answered their summons with interest. Yes, he had been to Arabia briefly several years ago and lived to tell about it. Now it was his ardent desire to return and perhaps even to visit Mecca and Medina. But to undertake such an expedition required funds, funds he would never amass working as a scribe in the souk at Tripoli.

He readily agreed to guide the men, and he took charge of planning and provisioning for the journey with brisk efficiency. At last he turned his attention to their disguises.

"It would be best," Ernst mused thoughtfully, "for you to pose as French-speaking Algerians. You do speak French?"

"*Oui*," Blaine said at once.

"Yes . . . I mean, *oui* . . . I mean, not very well," Derek stammered, reddening. "Damn it, man, haven't you another idea? I was never much on French lessons. I learned enough to get by, and I've forgotten it all now."

"Then you will remember," Ernst replied, unperturbed. "You have until we reach Tur on the Red Sea. Until then we speak nothing but French. Agreed?"

Taking Blaine's nod as their mutual assent, he launched into his plan, speaking rapid French. "We will buy camels here for the journey across the desert, if this is agreeable to you, O'Toole Effendi." Receiving another nod, he continued, "We do not want to be slowed by too much burden, so Mustafa will buy only enough food for the crossing. We should be able to sell the camels easily when we reach Tur. There, too, we can catch a boat for Jidda."

At first Derek had looked confounded as he tried to follow the conversation, but his expression soon turned to utter loathing. Though he said admirably little through the next few weeks, his expression had not changed on the grueling journey across the desert. Blaine knew every time he looked at him that the Englishman detested speaking French, deplored the heat and the sand, and resented Ernst, but most of all he hated camels.

Blaine felt some sympathy for the young man as they rode for miles each day. The camel was not an easy beast to like. The Irishman also understood, being something of a dreamer himself, that Derek had imagined he was some sort of knight, out to save a damsel in distress. He had not counted on charging to Bryna's rescue on the swaying back of a camel, and as a result his morale was at low ebb.

In Tur matters had improved for the tiny expedition. Derek showed he could and would pass as an Algerian. They had sold their camels, the young soldier bidding farewell to his with no regret. Blaine had paid dearly, but the four men had gotten the only cabin on this crowded sambuk. Soon they would be in Arabia; they were getting closer to Bryna all the time.

The sun was rising when Derek shifted restlessly behind Blaine. "I know you probably do not wish to go in, Colonel," he said almost apologetically, "but we must. People already think it odd we prefer to pray in our cabin. We must not be caught on deck by the dawn."

"When I talked to him last night, Ernst said we'd arrive in Jidda by noon." Blaine spoke more to himself than to his companion as they walked toward their cabin. "By midafternoon we should be fitted with camels and equipment, then we'll be off."

"So soon?" The soldier nearly groaned at the thought of interminable days on the back of a camel.

"Jidda is not as sacred to the Moslems as Mecca or Medina, but it is still a holy city," the other man explained. "It is dangerous for us to linger there."

"*Très bien*, but let us at least have a cup of coffee to fortify ourselves first," Derek said heading toward the sound of the coffee grinder.

CHAPTER

◇◇◇◇◇ **13** ◇◇◇◇◇

THE COOKING FIRE WAS LITTLE MORE THAN embers when Bryna placed a little pot on it to heat.

"Nassar has left and I'm about to go," Pamela announced from the opening of the tent. "You are coming, aren't you?"

"Of course," Bryna mumbled as she carefully measured out the contents of a small glass vial. The unsteadiness that had kept her at home last night after her near accident seemed a remote memory.

"I've never been around anyone who made medicines before. Is that for Fatmah?" Pamela asked curiously, watching Bryna with interest.

"It is."

"I am sure she deserves it." The English girl sniffed, her nose wrinkling in distaste at the pungent odor emanating from the pot. "But whatever is it for?"

"The rattle in her chest. Haven't you heard it?"

"She never stops talking long enough," Pamela answered with uncharacteristic sarcasm. "Why do you bother with that old harridan?"

"Because she is sick and needs this medicine," Bryna answered absently.

Pamela sighed and pulled her burnoose tight around her bulky body. "Well, I really am leaving now. You will join me soon, won't you?"

"Soon," came the muttered answer.

Pamela smiled wryly at her preoccupied friend, but she did not linger. In the desert, women were allowed to join the men for coffee if they sat to the back and were quiet. The pregnant girl generally felt better in the evening than she felt during the day, so she was eager now to join the others.

Bryna was hardly aware she had gone. She relished her solitude, humming while she ground cinnamon, cloves, and red peppers for Fatmah's spice poultice. Putting her face near the steaming pot, she inhaled, then jerked away instantly and fanned herself. Even without spirits it was going to work, she thought with satisfaction, blinking back tears that sprang to her eyes. Just a little longer to simmer. She sat down beside the fire and stirred the thick mixture, her mind going back to the afternoon.

Nassar had been away and Pamela napped in the women's quarters while Bryna sat in the *majlis* with her embroidery, hoping for a breeze. Unexpectedly Umm Walid, the mother of the boy whose life Bryna had saved the day before, presented herself in front of Nassar's tent. Although she was accompanied by a small delegation of women and children, they remained a distance from the tent as she approached.

Relieved to find the foreign woman alone, Umm Walid, with a bashful, snaggletoothed smile, accepted Bryna's invitation to sit down. Then, putting aside the bundle she carried, she politely sipped a cup of *leben*.

When she was ready to reveal the purpose of her visit, the Arab woman reached for her bundle and untied it, spilling out its contents before Bryna without fanfare. The awed girl stared at the vials of rare herbs, the skeins of glossy thread, and a gold chain with a tiny pair of tweezers attached to it. Umm Walid explained, speaking slowly so the foreign woman would understand. She was offering these things, she said, in gratitude for her son's life.

"But . . . " Feeling the eyes of the waiting women upon her, Bryna swallowed her modest reply and responded in the proper Arab manner.

"*Mashallah,* how glad I am to have these spices," she exclaimed. Picking up a skein of thread, she admired it, holding it so the other women could see. "Just look at the color, as crimson as the sunset."

"*Mashallah,*" the audience murmured appreciatively, stepping closer.

Umm Walid smiled proudly. "See, this is how you wear the chain," she instructed, turning helpfully so Bryna could see the back of her head. "The tweezers can be used to pull thorns from your feet. And the key to your housewife's box should be worn there, too. Nassar bin Hamza did give you one, didn't he?" She seemed skeptical.

"*Aywá,* oh, yes," Bryna assured her. Retrieving the unused wooden case, she displayed it so everyone could see. Then she opened it and placed her treasures inside. When the box was locked, Umm Walid affixed the key to the chain and arranged it on Bryna's *ghata* so it bumped gently against the nape of her neck.

"Now you are indeed *umm-al'-ayyal*, Bryna bint Blaine," the Arab woman declared. "*Allah-isalmak*, God give you peace." Then she strode from the tent, pausing only long enough to retrieve her son from one of the women.

"*Allah-isalmak*," they repeated shyly. Then they followed Umm Walid.

Bryna coughed from the fumes as she stirred the thick liquid. It was done. Taking great care not to spill a drop, she poured it into a small crock and covered it with a square of fabric. She would give the poultice to Fatmah and the instructions to Latifeh.

She should hurry, she realized suddenly, for it was late. Feeling the chill in the air for the first time, she went inside for her burnoose, emerging after a moment to draw a deep, gratifying breath. The sky was velvet black and lit faintly by a thin crescent moon. The heavens were sprinkled with stars that seemed to glitter in the crisp night air.

"Quick, Bryna, come and see," `Abla hailed her as she walked to the sheik's tent. "*Alhamdillah!* You will never guess! Another of Daoud bin Hatim's nagas had her baby right here!"

"Another?" Bryna allowed `Abla to lead her to where the children clustered near the camels.

"Soon Taman will be a maid no longer," the child predicted, grinning despite the glint of warning in the other girl's eyes.

With the children, Bryna watched in wonder. The calf, only hours old, wobbled on feet much too large for its body. Already decked with the blue beads believed by the Bedouins to increase the milk of a nursing mother, the naga also observed as her calf took a few tottering steps. The little animal's head bobbed up and down as if too heavy to be held by the long spindly neck. It bawled plaintively and stumbled toward the children. Reaching out to steady it, Bryna was surprised to find how downy its fur was. Unable to resist, she crooned softly and petted its fuzzy back.

"Wallahi, take away your hand, woman," a male voice commanded arrogantly. "And do not touch it again. You will cause the camel's growth to be stunted, then it will be of little value."

Bryna searched for the source of the reprimand and saw Abu Hatim, Daoud's grandfather, as he passed in the darkness on his way to Sharif's tent. The white-bearded old man halted momentarily to glower at her, his lined brown face a testimony of a lifetime spent in the desert. Small and spare, he carried himself with the dignity and confidence of a tribal elder whose voice was respected in the council. And he obviously expected obedience from her.

Set in his ways, the old Bedu disapproved of Nassar's foreign women. While still in Taif, he had said so, but after much debate the *majlis* had allowed the infidels to stay. Grudgingly Abu Hatim admitted they had broken no laws or caused any trouble. Still he stayed clear, watching the blue-eyed kaffir distrustfully.

"You children," he scolded the youngsters, "go now. The hour grows late."

They scattered at once, leaving Bryna to face Abu Hatim alone.

"I meant no harm," she apologized in hesitant Arabic.

"I suppose none was done," he answered gruffly. "But mind what I say. Do not touch the calf again." With that remonstrance, he set off without even a glance back to see that she obeyed.

It was said, among the Bedouin, that the chief's tent can always be told by the pile of coffee grounds outside the tent. In that case, Sheik Al Selim must be the most generous leader in Arabia, Bryna thought as she followed Abu Hatim to the campfire that burned in front of Sharif's tent.

Bryna stood at the fringes for a moment, watching as the people settled in for the *qasidah,* recitations of poetry. Coffee had been served, and the members of the tribe were ranged around the crackling fire in order of their importance.

By the fire's glow, she could see the elders assembled in the shelter of the tent with their sheik. They sat in a large arc that formed the top of the sprawling circle. Near the tent on either side were the men of lesser importance, with the male servants at the bottom of the circle. Behind them sat the women.

Bryna observed as Abu Hatim took a seat at the edge of the circle. He was much too polite to make someone else move. But Sharif spied the latecomer and greeted him, "Step thou hither, Abu Hatim." And the sheik himself shifted to make a place for the venerable old man.

While much attention was being directed to the position of Abu Hatim, the girl slipped into the crowd of women and sat down beside Pamela. Sa'id stood at the top of the circle, ready to speak, when Bryna became uncomfortably aware of muffled cries behind her and a great deal of movement among the women.

She tried to ignore Sa'id's frown of annoyance as Smemi materialized from the darkness. The black dog waded into the tight knot of women, snuffling loudly and thrashing those seated nearby with his wagging tail. When he located Bryna, he nuzzled her face with a rough wet nose, then lay down blissfully at her side. Curving his big body around her, he provided warmth and a welcome place to rest her back.

Although he scarcely looked in her direction, Sharif was very aware of Bryna's presence across the campfire. He had not seen her since he had held her in his arms yesterday, safe from danger. Last night he had searched for her face among the women, almost fearful of what his reaction would be if he found it. Now she was here, and it was with great effort that he turned his attention to Sa'id's poem of an ancient Bedu warrior.

The sheik appeared to be enthralled by the account of heroic actions as he stared into the fire, but his thoughts were on Bryna. Occasionally his gaze drifted upward and he watched the girl covertly over the flickering flames. She listened to the qasidah with as much rapt attention as he himself was trying to exhibit. Guiltily Sharif realized that the end of the poem was near and he had heard almost none of it.

"*Mashallah,*" he pronounced nonetheless when Sa'id finished, "it is said, 'The beauty of man lies in the eloquence of his tongue.'"

"*Mashallah,*" the others said. After the recitations came the music. Although many Moslems were opposed to music making, Sharif allowed the *rubabah,* a one-stringed guitar, and small drum called the *tabl* to be brought out.

He listened distractedly, willing the evening to be over. But he welcomed the end of the night's activities no more fervently than Bryna as she, too, tried to put away the disturbing memory of yesterday's embrace.

"He is frowning at you again," Taman remarked casually as the girls walked the next afternoon.

Bryna did not have to look up to know she spoke of Sharif. "I know." She sighed. "I think he hates me."

"No," Taman disagreed, "his face is always dark this time of year. This is the month his wife died. It is not good to think too much of the dead, but I believe our sheik still mourns for Noorah."

Bryna walked on without replying. She supposed the information the Arab girl offered should make her feel better, but it did not.

As they neared the well beside which the *smala* would camp, Bryna noticed huge pillars of stone jutting up from the sand some distance away. Glad to find a new topic of conversation, she asked, "Look, what is that?"

"Another ruined town without a name." Taman shrugged carelessly. "There are many buried in the sands." Her mind now diverted from the subject of Sharif, she asked Bryna, "Are you going out with us to gather locusts?"

"I suppose. Nassar claims they are his favorite food and says Pamela will cook breakfast in the morning while I gather some."

"He must be fond of them to eat what the Inglayzi cooks." Taman grimaced distastefully. "Then I will see you an hour before dawn while the locusts are still sluggish from the cold."

In the predawn darkness the Selim women searched for locusts, which rested, fat and sated, on fretted leaves. Shivering from the cold, Bryna gathered the insects rapidly until her basket was full.

When she looked up from her labors for the first time, she realized she had become separated from the main body of women and was now only a short distance from the ruins she had noticed yesterday. The walls, painted rose and gold by the sunrise, seemed to beckon her, promising a rare moment of privacy. She was not expected back at the tent for some time, so, trailed by Smemi, she started toward the deserted town, set on a closer look.

Bryna left her basket under a scrawny palmetto and stepped through a gap in what had once been the walls of the town. Smemi whined apprehensively at the sound of the wind whistling through the stones. The girl was slightly unsettled by the eerie sound, but she was far too interested in the ruins to turn back.

She stood in a tiny chamber with no ceiling, its walls collapsed on two sides. Its only door was blocked with rubble, but she could see, over the crumbled wall on either side of it, another chamber with three of its walls still standing. Scrambling over the obstruction, she examined a faded, ancient mural.

Shielded from the wind, Bryna was comfortable. She unfastened her heavy burnoose and removed her light veil. Later it would be hot; later she must don her veil and return to her duties; but for now she was free to wander.

One room linked with another, and at last Bryna turned a corner and found herself in a chamber that was almost completely intact. His claws clicking against the stone floor, Smemi made a quick circuit around the room, then halted near the opposite door, whining again uneasily. The girl also felt a stir of nervousness. This chamber had been occupied recently. The ashes in the fire pit in the center of the room were fresh, and the aroma of cooked meat still seemed to hang in the air. Glancing toward the corner, she saw a pile of saddlebags stacked neatly and covered with a rug.

Smemi growled, low and menacingly, as a faint sound reached their ears. His teeth were bared as he strained to determine its source. It sounded like footsteps.

Bryna's heart skipped a beat. She had been

foolish to come here alone. Taman had said this was the season of raiders, and she had walked into a possible hiding place for the thieves with only the big black dog for protection.

As if reading her thoughts, Smemi snarled and placed himself in the doorway between Bryna and whoever approached.

The girl nearly cried out in relief when Sharif's voice reached her. "Bryna bint Blaine, are you there? Are you all right?

"My lord? Yes, I am fine."

"Then tell your fierce protector I am a friend." Sharif appeared in the doorway, his sword drawn, his handsome face distressed. But his concern gave way to wonder when he saw the unveiled girl kneeling beside the big black dog. Washed by pale light that spilled in through the only window, Bryna's hair glowed with a red fire and her face, tilted up toward him, was fairer even than he had remembered.

"Mashallah," the sheik breathed involuntarily, his steely gaze locking with Bryna's blue one. "Thou art beautiful."

"And thou," Bryna answered instinctively, without thought. Although she was unaware she had done so, she rose and held out a hand as if reaching for him. She was conscious only of her heart pounding as Sharif stepped nearer.

His sword held at his side, the man crushed her to him in a powerful one-armed embrace, murmuring, his voice thick with relief, against her hair, "Praise be to Allah, that I have found you unharmed. A party of raiders has been using this ruin. I was mad with worry when I realized you were here."

Bryna stood very still, trying to sort through the sensations she was feeling. She felt secure and protected in Sharif's embrace, but there was more to it—it was as if her entire being reacted to his nearness. Her knees felt weak. Her breasts pressed against him seemed to swell with longing, and the lower part of her body was swept with a delightful warmth. She did not understand the feelings, did not care to understand them. She only hoped Sharif was feeling the same emotions.

Wanting nothing more than to be even closer to him, to breathe his scent, to feel the warmth of his lean, hard body, Bryna pressed nearer and wrapped her arms around his waist.

Sharif's arm tightened on her shoulders spasmodically, then, drawing a ragged breath, he said in a choked voice, "No, no, this is wrong." Reluctantly he released the girl and stepped back from her embrace, his heart breaking when she would not meet his eyes.

Bryna stood with her head bowed, unwilling to look at him for fear she would cry. Not for shame or fear, she realized, but for frustration and longing.

"Come," Sharif ordered gruffly, guiding Bryna out into the blinding sunlight, "we must leave here. The raiders' party is too small to attack our *smala*, but they would delight to prey on three people alone."

"Three people?" Her voice was taut with unshed tears.

Sharif looked at the girl beside him. She seemed as shaken as he felt himself. Desire coursed through him with each pounding beat of his heart, but he forced himself to speak calmly, "Sa'id and I rode out to investigate the ruins. When we had finished, I saw the footprints of a woman and a dog in the sand, so we decided to search. Who else could it have been but you?

"Veil yourself now," he ordered, then shouted, "Sa'id! I found her."

A muffled shout answered them, and soon they were joined by the sheik's second in command. While Bryna retrieved her basket, Sharif looked closely at Sa'id, relieved to see he did not seem suspicious to find the girl alone with him.

"We will walk back to camp," Sharif announced, relieved to realize it would be impossible to balance both Bryna and her basket on his mare. He did not think he could be near her again without making her his own.

"It is not meet that the men should walk with a slave," Sa'id protested.

"I am sheik and I desire to walk. But you should ride, my old friend. I will see you back at camp."

"If you walk, I walk. Where you go, I go, my lord." Sa'id snorted, letting his chief know his opinion of walking and of playing chaperon to a slave.

Sharif and Bryna started across the sands toward the camp visible in the distance. Behind them, Sa'id led the horses and muttered ominously each time Smemi approached, his tail wagging.

For a time, they walked in silence. At last Bryna

worked up her courage to glance at Sharif. To her chagrin, she found he was watching her.

"Your Arabic is improving," he said casually, trying to regain his composure.

"'Abla has been helping me." Her response was a whisper on the wind.

The silence stretched out between them until they had neared the camp.

"My lord Al Selim . . ." Bryna began urgently. Then, hearing Sa'id curse as he stumbled in the sand, she fell silent. She could not ask for her freedom. She could not even speak openly to Sharif in front of the other man. "I . . . I am sorry I caused you such trouble this morning."

"It was no trouble," the sheik assured her politely. "But please do not wander so far away again. The big dog is no protection against evil men." Nor against foolish ones, he thought to himself bitterly.

They stopped suddenly at the fringes of the camp, and Sharif asked, "My nephew . . . is he good to you?"

Bryna's blue eyes met his for an instant. But before he could read what they held, she lowered them and replied, "He has not harmed me."

"That is not what I asked you, Bryna bint Blaine," Sharif said sharply, "but I suppose I must take it as an answer. I have no claim upon you."

With that he turned and strode away, leaving Sa'id to follow.

The next morning the *smala* resumed its slow

progression toward Riyadh. Once again every day passed for the travelers as the day before. At last the red sands gave way to white, grazing became harder to find, and the distance between wells became greater. After a while both water and food were rationed.

What was wrong with her? Bryna wondered, shifting uncomfortably on her fidgeting camel while the men inspected some tracks, their voices loud in the desert stillness. They examined each set of tracks they came across and knew at once how many men had passed, what kinds of camels they rode, and, in some cases, who the other travelers had been.

While she waited, heat shimmered up from the sand, causing Bryna's skin to feel as if it were stretched as tight as a tent wire across her cheekbones. Her eyes burned and watered from the glare of the sun. And she felt she would scream when Sharif's men galloped across the sand to milk any roaming naga they saw.

When would they rest? she wondered irritably. She was tired and it was becoming more and more difficult to curb her temper. It was good Fatmah was no longer so antagonistic toward her. Since she had used Bryna's poultice, the old woman was almost civil.

Then there was Pamela. The English girl hardly seemed interested in food now, a great change for her. Deprivation meant little to the Bedouins. For weeks at a time they might live on a handful of dates and some camel's milk, but it was no diet for a pregnant woman.

"Bryna, look over there—wild thyme." Taman's voice interrupted her brooding. The Arab girl pointed to a scrawny plant that grew nearby in the shade of a palmetto. "I think there might be more. Shall we pick some?"

Bryna sprang from the back of her camel and landed on her feet in the sand beside the other girl before the question was finished. Laughingly Taman steadied her eager friend and they set off to harvest the herb. Delighted to find even more than they had expected, they worked their way along the camel train, stopping near the herds at the rear.

When the caravan lurched to a start, Bryna and Taman hurried toward the head of the procession. There was little danger they would be left behind, but they hoped to escape the dust stirred up by the herds.

A terrified bellow stopped them. Whirling, the girls watched as a camel sank in the sand not more than fifty yards from them.

"A *shott*—sinking sand!" Taman's voice was filled with dread as she backed up a step, mistrusting the ground beneath her feet. "And it's one of Daoud's nagas."

The camel flailed and roared in vain as she sank up to her belly in the sand. Her calf, only two or three months old, poised at the far edge of the *shott*, bawling piteously, then it followed its mother, sinking at once up to the knees.

"No," Bryna cried, sprinting around the *shott* to where the calf now struggled. She could do nothing for the mother. The naga's roars were weakening as she sank rapidly, with only her hump and her head visible above the shifting sand. But there was still time to save the calf, the girl thought stubbornly.

As she approached the far side of the *shott*, she slowed her step. Along the edge the ground gave way in inches, crumbling into the quicksand. It seemed for an instant as if she were standing on a shore and the camels were swimming in a pool of loose sand.

"Do not get too close," Taman shouted across the *shott*. "The sand will give way under you." She waved her arms to attract the other girl's attention, but she came no closer.

Bryna retreated for a moment and called across to her friend, "If I can reach it, I can hold its head up."

Before Taman could argue, she went as close to the edge as she dared and lay down on her stomach. Stretching her arm as far as she could, she reached for the baby camel. But the distance between the animal and her grasping fingers seemed to increase with every panic-stricken move it made.

With a mighty lurch and one last agonized bellow, the naga disappeared completely under the sand, leaving no sign of her fierce fight for life. Now the only sound was the pitiful cry of the struggling calf.

"Go for help," Bryna shouted to Taman. She strained, her breath rasping from exertion, stretching until every muscle burned and ached, but she could not reach the calf. It continued to sink, its eyes rolling toward the girl in horror.

If she could just reach it . . . Gingerly she eased

forward.

Suddenly a pair of strong hands encircled Bryna's ankles and she was jerked backward. Her head slammed against the ground and her upper body made a long, deep furrow in the sand as she was dragged from the edge of the *shott*. Spitting sand and kicking blindly, she fought, arching her body to strain toward the camel calf, now sunk in the sand up to its head.

"By the beard of the Prophet! Are you mad, woman?" a voice snarled above her. "It is no use. The calf is gone."

Pushing herself up on her elbows, Bryna stared bleakly at the smooth surface of the *shott*.

Standing astraddle her, Sharif bent and gripped one of her arms painfully, turning her to look at him. His fear had turned to wrath, and the face she saw looming above her was furious.

"Answer me, Bryna," he ordered, dragging her roughly to her feet. "Have you gone mad? If I had not come, you would have joined the camels in the sinking sands."

"I . . . I just wanted to save the calf." Swaying on her feet, she stared up at the man dazedly.

Despite his wrath, Sharif longed to cradle Bryna in his arms and comfort her. But he did not allow his desire to show in his eyes this time. He had known since that morning at the ruins that Alima had been right. Having this girl at hand, yet unattainable, was not a good thing. It would drive him mad.

Disturbed by the very feel of her and anxious to

be away, he released her arm and snapped, "Death comes quickly in the desert, Bryna bint Blaine. This day it nearly found you . . . again." Then he pushed her toward Taman who stood weeping nearby.

"Nassar, Sa'id," Sharif shouted when his men approached, drawn by the excitement. "Send your women back to their camels and see they stay there."

Before the men could rebuke them, Bryna dusted the sand from her clothing and led Taman toward the riding camels. The numbness she felt was wearing off, and in its place was impotent rage. Irrationally she wanted to wail and shriek at the brutality of the desert and the Bedouin life until her anger was spent. She wanted to fling herself at Sharif, screaming her sorrow, sorrow for tenderness turned to harshness. Instead she walked away with as much dignity as she could muster. She would not cry in front of him.

"I was afraid you would be sucked into the sands." Taman was sobbing. "Why did you do such a foolish thing?"

"I thought I could pull the calf out of the *shott*. I could not let it die without trying to save it." Bryna's voice shook with emotion.

"Lo! we are Allah's and lo! unto him we are returning," the Arab girl quoted with a whimper. "Do you think camels are worth dying for? Not even Daoud's are worth it, not even if he could never meet my bride price."

For the next few days, the very air around the Selim camp seemed to crackle with tension.

Lightning was frequently spotted in the distance, but no sign of rain appeared on the horizon. Sharif's face was severe as he pressed his *smala* toward their next destination, the family well, *Bir* al Selim.

Although she took great care to avoid him, Bryna too felt the strain. She was absent from the communal campfire until she learned of Nassar's boast that he had banned her from attending as a punishment for her foolishness at the *shott*. Obstinately she returned the next evening. When her gaze met the sheik's across the fire, she knew she should have stayed away. How could she have ever thought she saw a flicker of desire in those hostile gray eyes?

Noticing how Sharif's moody eyes rested on her friend, Taman mused, "I have never seen our sheik so angry for so long."

"Things have not been the same since the *shott*," Bryna said despairingly after a moment. She had never discussed Sharif with anyone, not even Taman.

"It is true he was furious when you put yourself into such danger. But, no, something more disturbs him," the Arab girl insisted.

Bryna did not answer, but she asked herself again: Had she ruined everything by responding to her body's urging? She had done nothing more than embrace him. Had Sharif found her caress so distasteful? She was miserable at the thought, but she said nothing more to her friend.

"Do not worry. Perhaps in time he will forget

his wrath," Taman counseled wisely, "and all will be well, unless he is displeased that you do the Inglayzi's work." Then, veering easily from her favorite complaint before Bryna could protest, she teased, "Or perhaps he hasn't forgiven you for curing Fatmah's sore throat."

Bryna smiled in spite of herself, for even at this distance they could hear the incessant drone of the old woman's voice.

The Selims crested the hill above their well just before sunset. Even through the dusk, Sharif could tell something was wrong. He urged his camel to a gallop, and his men followed him down to the deserted clearing. It was evident at once from the stench that their well had been fouled. The water, polluted and undrinkable, might not be fit for use for years to come.

Intruders had camped there for several days, and now Sharif's best trackers knelt where the camels had hobbled. By examining the tracks, they quickly ascertained who had dared despoil their well and how long ago they had left.

The women set up camp in dismal silence while the men discussed *ghazzi.* In Sharif's *majlis* the elders resolved to raid the intruders' camp in retribution for this crime against their tribe.

"Let us ride now while they are not expecting us," Nassar urged heatedly. "We can burn the dogs' camp to the ground."

"We must abide by the rules of *ghazzi*," Sharif enjoined.

"We must avenge our honor," Nassar argued,

becoming bold when he saw nods of agreement from several hot-blooded young men.

"There would be no honor if we attacked after midnight or burned the cooking tent of our enemy," his uncle said firmly.

"That is true," Sa'id seconded. "Their women and children must eat. We have no quarrel with them. We fight men."

"Blood for blood," Nassar insisted.

"No blood has been shed here," Sharif answered with weary patience. "We will take their camels as the price for their insult."

"Many camels," Abu Hatim interjected unexpectedly. "The signs are propitious."

"We go tomorrow," Sharif spoke decisively, "not tonight. But before another day has passed, we will have our revenge. Let the warriors be ready to leave at dawn."

"Allahu akbar," Daoud cried fervently as the men rose. "It is as it should be. I against my brother, I and my brothers against my cousin, but tomorrow it will be I and my cousins against the world."

"Allahu akbar," Nassar echoed with a dangerous gleam in his eyes. "Tomorrow we will have revenge."

The entire tribe worked well into the night. There was no coffee or qasidah, only ominous quiet, broken occasionally by industrious sounds coming from the Salubas' encampment nearby. The craftsmen sharpened swords and knives and spears, while the Selim men checked and tended their harnesses and cleaned their guns for the impending battle. At each tent subdued women and children prepared provisions for their warriors' rapid desert crossing.

The men slept and Bryna was preparing to retire when Latifeh approached Nassar's tent.

"Have you seen `Abla, Bryna bint Blaine?" the older woman asked. Her muted voice was heavy with weariness and exasperation.

"No, my lady."

"No one has seen her. I called her three times and she did not answer. I cannot awaken the entire camp," Latifeh muttered with a frown that did not bode well for the little girl.

"Shall I go and look for her?" Bryna asked worriedly.

"Yes, find her and bring her back," the Arab woman answered, her sigh revealing concern for her stepdaughter. "But do take care. There are sometimes jackals waiting in the darkness."

Bryna was relieved to find that the desert, lit by the moon, was nearly as light as day. Still, she remembered Latifeh's warning and hastened her step, calling `Abla's name in a low, urgent voice.

"Bryna?" `Abla's tousled head appeared over the top of a large dune. In an instant she had scaled it and slid down the other side to stand beside her friend. "What are you doing here?"

"A better question might be what are *you* doing here?" Bryna tilted the child's chin and looked down kindly at her tearstained face. "What's wrong, `Abla? Why did you run away from camp?"

"I didn't run away," she said sniffling. "I just

didn't want Abu to see me cry."

"Why are you crying, little one?"

Sympathy was more than the little girl could bear. Suddenly she clasped her arms around Bryna's waist and began to cry. The American girl sat down in the sand, drawing `Abla beside her. The child buried her face in Bryna's lap, her narrow shoulders heaving with sobs. Gently Bryna stroked her head and let her cry.

When `Abla's weeping had subsided, she suggested gently, "Why don't you tell me about it?"

`Abla sat up and looked at the other girl through gray eyes that were much too mature for her age. "Tomorrow is the day my mother died," she explained gravely. "Even though my father can hardly bear to look at me sometimes because of it, he is my father. Now he is going to fight and I am afraid I will have no one."

Tears sprang to Bryna's eyes as she remembered so clearly the feeling of being unwanted and alone. "Oh, `Abla, I know exactly how you feel. But you must know that your father loves you."

"He does?"

"Of course he does," Bryna assured her. "It just hurts him to remember your mother. My own father had the same problem for many years. But I know now that he loves me."

"Then why did he sell you?" `Abla asked in bafflement.

"He did not sell me." Bryna tried to keep the indignation out of her voice. `Abla was young and did not understand any world but her own. "I was kidnapped," she explained, "taken from my father's home."

"Was his camp not guarded?"

"Yes," Bryna answered, puzzled as to how she might explain.

"Then he rides in *ghazzi* like my father," the child concluded. Then she asked sadly, "Your *abu* will come for you someday, won't he, Bryna?"

"Perhaps . . . if he can find me." The American girl sighed.

"I hope he cannot, not ever," `Abla replied with childish candor. "If you went away, I would miss you almost as much as I would miss my father."

"I am not going anywhere yet, so do not borrow trouble," Bryna responded crisply, reminding herself suddenly of Sister Françoise. Hôtel Ste. Anne seemed a lifetime ago, she thought sadly.

Rising, Bryna held out her hand to `Abla. "Remember this, *chère,* everyone says your father is a great warrior. Nothing is going to happen to him."

`Abla looped her arm loosely around her friend's waist, and they walked slowly back to camp.

It was not until Bryna awakened just before dawn that she realized it was `Abla's birthday. Poor child, she thought as she stirred on her pallet, she thinks of it as the day her mother died. As daylight began to give muted color and form to her surroundings, Bryna's eyes fell upon the reds and blues of the unfinished *ghata* she was embroidering. The colors were perfect for `Abla. It might not be Bedouin custom, but the little girl was going to have a birthday gift, belated though it might be.

That pleasant thought had to be put away immediately as the last preparations for *ghazzi* were made. After dawn prayers the men rode away, heavily armed and dressed in black robes, the lower halves of their faces veiled. Following them to the edge of camp, the women let down their hair and trilled loudly to ensure victory in battle. Then the women, children, and old men returned to their silent tents.

Household chores filled the morning, but by afternoon the camp had settled into uneasy waiting. Occasionally quarrelsome female voices shattered the hush as the wait became onerous. Nerves were on edge in every tent. When Fatmah, strained from waiting, screeched at Bryna over an imagined transgression, the American girl stalked from the tent, her temper barely under control.

Back in Nassar's *majlis,* Bryna, nearly unnerved by the oppressive silence, worked mechanically on `Abla's *ghata.* She wondered if she should go again to look for the little girl who had not been seen since morning. Before she could do so, she heard `Abla's piping voice.

"They are coming! They are coming! With many camels!"

The women rushed out to welcome the returning warriors. Driving the herd before them, the men rode into camp, tired and dusty, but triumphant. Badly needed skins of water and food hung over their saddles. Herdsmen ran to meet the victors, their elation balanced by the hard work that lay ahead of them.

The men dismounted in front of their tents

without a word of greeting to their wives. But their happiness showed on their faces and could wait until they were alone with their women. All but Nassar were beaming.

He stormed past Bryna and Pamela and threw himself down on the pillows in his *majlis.* Nothing had gone as he wished. His flabby body ached from the swift ride across the desert. And his pride hurt because it had been Sa'id who had led the second group when Sharif split the band for attack. Then, to add insult to injury, the sheik had prevented him from killing one of their foes.

"Camels, not blood," Sharif had roared at his nephew over the din as the men thundered through the enemy camp.

Ya Amm Sharif, you will not always be chief, the young man thought petulantly. When he became sheik, the name Selim would be feared by all Aribi.

The young Arab pouted in his tent while outside, the present leader of the tribe announced gladly, "Tonight there is water for coffee. We will speak of the *ghazzi* over the campfire. Tomorrow we will feast. We will dance the *ardha* and celebrate!"

When Bryna rose at dawn, the delicious aroma of roasting meat filled the desert air. The servants were already gathered around a pit, arguing about the best way to cook camel.

There was a festive mood in the camp even before the races and the shooting contests took place. At about midday the men went to Sharif's *majlis,* where they were served from several great dishes of meat over rice, captured from their enemy.

When everyone had finished eating, the women formed a large circle, and in the middle the men danced, their swords flashing in the sunlight. Among the jubilant dancers, Sharif whirled gracefully, his robes and kaffiyeh swinging in the desert breeze. When his searching eyes found Bryna, he smiled unexpectedly, happiness transforming his rugged face at the very sight of her.

The girl smiled tentatively in return, but as always with Sharif, she felt a tempest of unexpected desire. Afraid everyone would read her emotions on her face, she was almost glad when a tug on her aba distracted her.

`Abla was beside her, her little face alight with happiness.

"Is today not a glorious day, Bryna?" she asked blissfully.

Lifting her gaze, Bryna saw that Sharif still watched from the corner of his eye. Though he did not look at them directly, his smile broadened even more when he saw his daughter with Bryna.

The feelings Sharif Al Selim roused in her could only cause trouble, Bryna thought fleetingly. She belonged to Nassar, and Sharif was forbidden to her.

But then, inexplicably filled with joy, she thrust the thought from her. She put her arm around `Abla and smiled radiantly at the little girl's father.

"Indeed, *chère*," Bryna whispered, "it is the most glorious day I have known for a very long time."

CHAPTER

✦✦✦✦✦ **14** ✦✦✦✦✦

AFTER THE VICTORY CELEBRATION AT *BIR* AL
Selim, the *smala* resumed its seemingly endless
journey. Despite the supplies Sharif's men had
taken on their raid, food and water were still
rationed. Every drop of water was precious, for
now they had even more camels than before. There
was not even enough for coffee, but the Bedu had
no fear. With their sheik's careful planning, they
would soon reach the next well, where they would
rest.

The tribe seemed reasonably content as they
rode through the arid, unchanging landscape. Even
Sharif smiled now and then when one of his men
would offer casually to trade one of the camels that
had been his share of the booty. The others would
take up their part of the game with enthusiasm, discussing the finer points of various camels. They
bargained affably for hours without the least intention of trading.

Listening to their voices as they floated back
from the front of the caravan, Bryna smiled, too,
knowing the game was a way to pass the time on

the long march. Each negotiation invariably ended with the phrase *Yafteh Allah,* which meant "Allah opens the door of daily bread," a way of saying the traders were not really likely to do business.

As they traveled, she was pleased to note improvements in Pamela's health, despite the lacks in a desert diet. Even though the English girl was still pale and wan, her lackluster stare brightened now that she and Bryna were no longer summoned to tea by Fatmah. By the time they reached the well, Pamela had recovered her appetite and was more like her old self.

Sharif's *smala* had been camped beside the well for a few days when Smemi's bugling bark heralded the approach of visitors. The men rode on horseback, which meant they had come from a short distance away. The women were hastily sent to the tents, and Sharif greeted the callers as they entered the camp.

"What is the news?" he called cordially.

"The news is good, praise Allah," they responded genially. "What is the news with you?"

"None but good."

When they dismounted, Sharif invited the callers to his tent for coffee. The visitors joined the sheik and his men in the *majlis,* where they were offered bread and salt as honored guests. In turn they invited Sharif's camp to join them for a wedding feast that night. The sheik accepted but warned that only his family and the family of his nephew would be there. He could not leave the camp unguarded.

Learning they were to visit another camp that night, Bryna worked quickly to complete the *ghata* she was making for `Abla. The white fabric was intricately worked in bright blue and red thread with glints of silver running through them. Yes, she thought, her little friend was going to be pleased.

But Bryna did not know how pleased until she saw the joy in `Abla's gray eyes.

"Oh, Bryna, it is so beautiful! Are you sure it is for me?"

"Yes . . . and this." She held out a small square of the same gauzy fabric. "Since your father said you must veil yourself soon, I thought it would be nice if the veil matched the *ghata*."

"I have never had anything so beautiful!" Immediately the child threw the embroidered *ghata* over her tousled ringlets and ran to show Fatmah and Latifeh. Then, taking her friend's hand, she skipped along beside her to Nassar's tent, where the young man lounged idly in his open *majlis*.

"See what I got, Nassar!" `Abla pirouetted around her cousin.

"Where did you get it?" He glanced at her without much interest.

"Bryna gave it to me," the little girl chattered happily.

"You gave it to her?" He looked at Bryna questioningly. Then, catching the edge of the headdress, the man tugged it from `Abla's head and examined it. "Why?" he asked, glaring critically his American slave.

"It was a birthday gift," Bryna retorted. Without thinking, she snatched the *ghata* from Nassar's hands and returned it to `Abla.

When Nassar sat up, his dark eyes narrowed dangerously, Bryna knew she had gone too far. Feeling one of his tantrums coming, she turned to the child. "You'd better go and put that away for now, if you want it to look nice for tonight."

"Oh, that's right," `Abla crowed with delight. "I can wear it to the wedding. I will look so beautiful. You'll see, Bryna," she called over her shoulder, running off toward Sharif's tent.

After a moment of ominous silence, Nassar got to his feet slowly. "Why did you embarrass me in front of my *bint 'amm*, woman? And why did you give that *ghata* to her? It is much too fine for a child."

"It was a gift," Bryna answered, displaying more calm than she felt, for she knew she had never borne the full brunt of Nassar's temper. By defying him openly, she had given him a reason to punish her.

"Tell `Abla you want the *ghata* back," he ordered, advancing a step toward her. "It will look much better on Pamela."

"I will not." The girl's voice was low but determined. She held her ground, refusing to retreat.

"Wallahi, you defy me?" Nassar bellowed. "Do not make me beat you. It is too hot."

"I made it for `Abla," Bryna maintained staunchly. "I will make another for Pamela, if you like."

"You are my slave," he snapped furiously. "I give you the food you eat, the clothes you wear, and the threads you use to embroider. The fruit of your labors are mine, just as you are mine."

Bryna struggled to contain her own temper. "You may give me food and clothing," she said, "but you did not give me the threads for that *ghata*. Umm Walid gave them to me. I worked on it only after my chores were done. That *ghata* was mine to do with as I pleased."

"Perhaps it is not too hot for a beating after all. Then I will prove to you who your master is." Gripping her arm tightly, Nassar pulled the resisting girl toward him, finding suddenly that he liked the idea of punishing her. It aroused him to think of humbling her at last. His breath was hot on Bryna's face as he ripped off her veil and kissed her with wet lips and probing tongue. It had been too long since he had had a woman. The prostitutes in the Saluba camp offered only momentary satisfaction.

"Nassar . . . " Pamela's voice floated from the women's quarters, where she had been listening.

"What?" he roared. His mind on taming Bryna, he was annoyed by the interruption.

"If you are truly going to have Bryna make a *ghata* for me, may I have a pink one?" Coming into the *majlis*, the English girl put a hand on Nassar's arm and smiled up at him enticingly.

The moment the Arab's grip loosened on her, Bryna retreated. She scrubbed at her mouth with the back of her hand as if she could remove even the memory of his sodden kiss. Nassar did not see. He stared down at Pamela, all thought of the dark-haired girl forgotten. How often he had longed for his blond houri to look at him so. He sank down on the pillows, pulling Pamela with him.

"Pink, with golden threads," she wheedled prettily, throwing quick warning glances toward her friend. "She will do it if you ask. Please, *sidi*."

"Make a *ghata* for Pamela, Bryna bint Blaine, of pink silk," he ordered arrogantly. "And have it finished by the time we reach Riyadh." Lying back, he pulled Pamela down so her head rested on his shoulder. A reluctant houri, the English girl gazed at her friend with beseeching brown eyes. If Bryna protested, this diversion, so distasteful to her, would be for nothing.

"I . . . I would be happy to, but I have no pink silk," Bryna said hesitantly.

"Then buy some. We come to a town soon." Nassar tossed several copper *tawilahs* at Bryna's feet. When she had picked up the coins, he gestured for her to leave.

Bryna ducked out of the open tent and into the blinding sunlight. Sharif stood nearby, his face stark with anger. He had witnessed the entire scene, she realized, and would probably speak to Nassar about allowing such shows of temper from his slaves. She walked away quickly, feeling sick, knowing his narrowed gray eyes were upon her.

Bryna kept to herself at the wedding and for days afterward. Tension filled the air each time she caught sight of Sharif, for his gray eyes seemed to smolder with contained anger. She was relieved when the *smala* moved on and the sheik turned his mind to other things.

Sharif was also grateful, for he wanted nothing more than to forget the sight of Nassar forcing his kisses on the unwilling girl. It was not his affair, he kept reminding himself. But he watched over her nevertheless, failing to understand why she avoided him, refusing to meet his eyes.

After several days of travel, Fatmah visited Bryna. Once she had received the respectful hospitality due her, the old woman said reluctantly, as one *umm al'-ayyal* to another, "Bryna bint Blaine, I have come to tell you it is my husband's wish that Nassar and his women accompany us to *Kasr* al Haroun tomorrow."

"*Kasr* al Haroun?"

"A small town where we will buy food and visit the merchant Faud al Haroun, an old friend of my husband's family." Fatmah added darkly, "You can see it is important that neither you nor Pamela bint Harold do anything to dishonor our name. You represent the household of a great sheik. Take care to behave properly." Then old woman rose to her feet with painful dignity.

Despite her dislike for Fatmah, Bryna said sympathetically, "I see your legs are paining you, my lady. Will you take some ointment I have made?"

The woman accepted her offering with a grudging smile. Before she limped to her tent, she turned to Bryna gravely. "For your own good, remember what I have told you. I cannot say for sure what my lord Sharif would do, but if you dishonor my son, I know he will kill you."

As the *smala* neared a well the next day, Sharif's family veered off from the others and rode toward *Kasr* al Haroun. Bryna sat sedately in a camel litter, yet she was excited at the very prospect of a trip to a town. She clung desperately to the idea of escape. Where there were people, she might find help, she thought hopefully, but her plans were shattered by her first sight of the dusty settlement in the distance, its squat buildings barely discernible on the horizon.

This was hardly worth wearing a *burqu*, the girl thought uncharitably, for the town looked no better when they approached it through parched, terraced fields. At the outskirts were a large well and several camel-powered mills for grinding meal.

In single file the Selim camels passed through the narrow streets. First Sharif, then Nassar, then Sharif's women, followed by Bryna and Pamela. Abu Ahmad, Sharif's servant, brought up the rear with the pack camels.

They passed through the souk, where men sat on rugs in shady stalls, smoking and talking. After the calm of the desert, the noise was deafening as merchants hawked their wares and bargained loudly. Bryna was relieved when they turned onto a quiet residential street.

When the small caravan neared the largest house on the street, Sharif gave the signal to stop. Before their camels were couched, Faud Al Haroun waddled out to meet them.

"*As salaam 'alaykum.* Welcome to my home, Lord Selim," Faud greeted his honored guest with a

congenial smile. Wearing the white turban and
robes of a town Arab, he was about sixty years old,
nearly as round as Suleiman had been, and even
shorter. His arms spread wide as he strode toward
Sharif, the old man presented an imposing picture.

"*Wa 'alaykum as salaam,* noble Faud Al
Haroun." The sheik met his father's old friend and
embraced him.

Turning to look at Sharif's entourage, Faud
asked cordially, "Is that Nassar bin Hamza I see?
Dismount, young man, and peace be unto you."

"And unto you be peace," answered Nassar.
"And to you, Ibrahim bin Faud," he greeted a young
man who joined them.

Faud's son returned the greeting politely but
without much relish, placing his forehead against
Nassar's while they clapped palms. Then the men
strolled toward the house, leaving the women to be
helped from their camels by Abu Ahmad and Faud's
servants.

As Bryna waited for assistance, she looked curiously at the two black-veiled females who waited
just inside the courtyard. Latifeh had told her that
Faud was a recent widower. These must be his
daughters, Oma and Waqi, who would serve as his
hostesses.

Faud's daughters said little as they led their visitors through the comfortable house to the harem.
But when they removed their *burqus,* their faces
were friendly. Waqi, the younger, was only a few
years older than `Abla. Oma, her sister, was four-
teen and already accomplished at her housewifely

duties. The girls welcomed Fatmah and Latifeh warmly and exclaimed over how much `Abla had grown since their last visit. To the foreigners, they said nothing, though their dark eyes drifted to them curiously.

Sharif's wives exchanged uncomfortable glances, uncertain how to introduce the infidel women. In the desert it had almost been possible to forgive their strangeness. But in town, among friends, the Arab women searched for explanations, their embarrassment for Nassar's impetuousness returning.

`Abla suffered no such chagrin. Taking Bryna's hand, she led her forward and announced in a piping voice. "Oma, Waqi, I want you to meet my friend, Bryna bint Blaine."

"As salaam 'alaykum," Bryna said graciously.

"Wa 'alaykum as salaam," the girls responded in unison, their expressions showing pleasure at being greeted in their own language.

"Bryna is one of my cousin's intended," `Abla explained importantly, "and this is another, Pamela bint Harold."

Pamela smiled wearily and allowed the Arab girls to touch her blond hair shyly.

Remembering their duties as hostesses, Oma and Waqi invited their guests to remove their cloaks and sit down. If they were surprised when they saw Pamela's pregnant bulk, they said nothing. While their guests enjoyed a light repast, they chatted, drawing Bryna and Pamela into the conversation.

After making sure the older women were not

too tired, their hostesses suggested diffidently that the women might enjoy a trip to the women's *hammam*, or public bath, and perhaps a stop in the souk afterward.

At the bath, as Bryna rounded the corner to her assigned changing booth, she swerved to avoid running into a black-clad Arab woman who walked toward her.

"A thousand pardons," she murmured, stepping back. At exactly the same instant, the other woman did the same. Bryna started forward again, and the Arab woman did likewise. With shock, Bryna stopped and stared. She was seeing her own image in a mirror. Her blue eyes blurred with tears, the girl stepped into the changing room and looked at her reflection sadly.

This was Bryna bint Blaine, she thought bitterly, who looked like nothing more than a Bedu woman. Her feet were dusty and her brown hands rough from hard work. Through the holes in her *burqu*, her eyes, though blue, were lined with the kohl the Arab women used to lessen the glare of the desert sun.

Almost reluctantly, she removed her *burqu* and stared at herself disbelievingly. She had been a girl when she'd arrived in Tangier, but the face she saw today was no longer childish. Her mouth was the same and her nose still slightly upturned, but her face was thin from deprivation and tanned to a light golden color from days in the desert. The last time she had seen him, Derek had said she was beautiful. Would he think so now? The girl he had loved had ceased to exist many months ago. In her place was a determined young woman.

Almost unwillingly Bryna continued her inspection, revolving slowly before the mirror. Under her *ghata* her hair was very long, hanging in a windblown mass past her trim waist. She undressed, discovering her naked body was lithe and slender, although her breasts looked fuller than they had. Everything about her seemed changed. The locket she wore at her neck was the only reminder of the girl she had been.

Despondently she joined the other women in the steaming baths, but her downcast mood could not last as `Abla splashed ecstatically in a tile-lined pool, clowning and chattering with Faud's daughters. Pamela soaked contentedly, looking more fit than she had for weeks. Even Fatmah and Latifeh smiled.

While the women lingered in the baths, the men emerged from their *hammam* nearby. Ibrahim and Nassar went at once to tour the coffeehouses of the town, while Faud and Sharif set off for one of the merchant's warehouses, trailed by Abu Ahmad.

"Come, let me show you something," Faud said, stopping at a squat building with several high, shuttered windows. Unlocking the door, he peered into the shadowy interior. "*Bismallah,* in the name of God," he muttered, and entered cautiously, motioning for the other man to follow.

Heat rolled from the dark building in waves. Gingerly Sharif stepped inside, pausing to allow his eyes to adjust to the gloom. His nose flared at the offensive mix of smells that assailed him: coffee and spices, pungent dyes and spoiled food, unwashed flesh and urine—or worse. He stiffened at a muffled curse from the darkness.

"What is this, Faud?" the sheik demanded, his hand resting on the hilt of his sword.

"Nothing. I tripped over a coil of rope that my assistant, God destroy his house, did not put away. Come, this way." In the dim light Faud could be seen, beckoning from beside a wall constructed of bags of rice.

Glancing in silent warning at Abu Ahmad, who poised in the doorway, Sharif followed the merchant warily. The sheik was not a suspicious man, but he was a careful one.

As he walked toward Faud, the fat merchant picked up a sturdy-looking pole. Sharif's hand tightened on the handle of his sword.

"Have to get one of these windows open," Faud puffed, struggling to reach one of the tiny shutters near the roof.

When it opened to admit some light and a faint cleansing breeze, he nodded and said, "This is what I wanted you to see."

Stepping around the stack of rice bags, Sharif discovered a giant of a white man, chained to the wall. Sitting with his back against the clay wall, he did not even look up when the Arabs entered his makeshift prison. His clothes were in tatters and matted brown hair hung to his shoulders, but even in chains there was a certain pride in his bearing.

"Who is this?" Sharif asked.

"A slave." Faud shrugged. "I was told he is an armorer. I do not need such a servant, but I thought you might find him useful."

"Where did you learn your craft?" Sharif asked the man. The slave did not even look his direction.

"He is a mute," Faud said quickly, "and he understands only the Frankish tongue, something I did not know when I bought him. *Insh'allah.* You speak the language of the Franks, do you not?"

"It has been a long time," the sheik muttered. His gray eyes swept the filthy cell with disgust. "Why is he chained, under such conditions?"

"Thus I bought him from a slave trader who traveled through here some weeks ago. I might have removed them," Faud revealed reluctantly, "but he fought to escape like one possessed. Allah protect me from the devil! He nearly killed two of my servants. It was all we could do to get him in here. Do you blame me for locking him away?"

"How much do you want for him?"

Surprised by the sheik's interest, Faud named a price that was very reasonable.

Before he would agree, Sharif addressed the slave in halting French, rusty after years of disuse, "Your *sidi* tells me you are a mute. This is true?"

For the first time the big man looked up. His expression was unreadable, but his dark eyes were intelligent. Slowly he nodded.

"You are an armorer?"

Again he nodded.

"Are you a good one?"

A faint smile flitted across his dirty face and he nodded again.

"Your *sidi* tells me also that you are locked in here

because you hurt two men in an effort to escape."

A rebellious glimmer showed in the slave's eyes, and he turned away moodily.

"Hear me, infidel," Sharif commanded. "I am the Sheik Sharif Al Selim. I can take you from this room and make you a part of my household. But I will not, unless I have your word you will not try to escape. Will you give it?"

The hulking slave regarded Sharif assessingly. The sheik looked to be a fair, even a compassionate, man, but not one to cross. Deliberately the Frenchman stood and thrust his shackled hands toward him.

"I will take him," Sharif told Faud in Arabic. "Unlock his chains."

Faud complied, muttering a prayer under his breath as he eyed the giant distrustfully. From the other side of the rice bags came the sound of a sword being unsheathed. Abu Ahmad stood by in readiness.

When the shackles fell away, the big man rubbed his wrists to restore the circulation. Then he dropped to one knee before Sharif.

"What is he called?" Sharif asked Faud.

"I do not know, my sheik. We call him Kedar."

"Kedar—'the Powerful.' Good." He spoke to the slave in French. "Kedar, I accept your *bay'ah,* your oath of allegiance. Your loyalty will prove you, not bowing. Stand up now, man."

Kedar obeyed with a look of respect in his dark eyes.

"Abu Ahmad, I know you are there," Sharif

called to his old servant in a faintly accusing voice.

"Yes, my lord." The old man appeared around the stacks of merchandise, his sword still in hand.

"Take Kedar to the baths and find a place for him to sleep among the servants. He has given his word he will not run away," he reassured the old man before he could protest.

"Go with Abu Ahmad," he instructed his new slave in French.

Reluctantly the old servant sheathed his sword and led the hulking Frenchman into the light of day.

Allahu akbar, God is great! Faud thought. Today had been a most satisfying day. Before he retired, he summoned Oma to his private garden. Only by asking his daughters could he learn anything of Sharif's household.

Oma appeared at once, as if she had been awaiting his call, thoughtfully bringing with her a pot of coffee and another helping of the pudding he had enjoyed so much at dinner.

"Are you enjoying your visit with Sharif's harem? Are his women well? And those of Nassar?" The man couched his questions carefully.

"Yes, *Abu,*" she said in answer to all three questions at once. "But I wish to speak to you of Nassar's slave."

"The pale-haired houri?" he asked eagerly, remembering Nassar's gloating.

"No, the Inglayzi is heavy with child."

"Oho!" Faud's eyebrows rose. Nassar had not mentioned that. "What of the other?"

"She is yet a maiden, I am sure of it. And even

289

though her eyes are blue, she is fair indeed."

"Blue?" The man nearly choked on his coffee. "No one told me of this."

"Did you think a Bedu would boast of it?" the girl asked with a wisdom beyond her years. "But, *Abu*, you are an educated man. Surely you do not fear blue eyes?"

"I suppose not," he answered his daughter dubiously. "Her hair is not gold, I take it?"

"No, but it glows with a quiet fire. It is dark, yet red."

"And she is docile and well mannered?"

"Yes, yes!" Oma clapped excitedly, bouncing on her seat as her father began to show more interest. "Latifeh—"

"Latifeh the learned?" he interjected sourly.

"The same. She has been educating the infidels to the teachings of the Prophet. I think this Bryna bint Blaine will make a fine wife, but I do not believe Nassar really wishes to marry her. Fatmah wishes he would not marry either one, but he seems set on having the blond girl."

"Why do you tell me this?"

"Because you should remarry, my father. Both of your wives are dead, and Waqi and I will both be of marriageable age soon. Then who will take care of you? This woman could be the wife of your old age," she argued persuasively. "She could bear you many sons."

He toyed with his coffee cup, a considering look on his fat face. "Waqi feels this way as well?"

"Oh, yes, *Abu*."

"Then I will speak with bin Hamza tomorrow. Perhaps it is as you say, perhaps he will sell her."

"Perhaps, *Abu. Insh'allah.*"

Insh'allah, he thought. But Nassar was a greedy young man who always seemed to be in need of money, and he, Faud, was one of limited means.

But as he bowed down for prayers the next morning, the merchant had an inspiration. Why not give the troublesome French slave to Sharif in exchange for a good word to his nephew? Everyone would benefit. Sharif would have his armorer at no cost, Nassar would be richer in money if not in women, and Faud would have his young wife. *Alhamdillah.* It could work!

So the old man said nothing when the young men departed for a day's hawking, waiting until he could make his proposal to Sharif in privacy.

"The American girl is not for sale," Sharif declared, to Faud's amazement.

"But I thought she belonged to Nassar," he stammered apologetically.

"He bought her, but he traded my camels for her and he has yet to repay me." Sharif felt a bewildering sense of outrage. What was wrong with him? Faud had not offended merely by offering to buy Nassar's slave.

"If she is yours legally, I will buy her from you."

The sheik shook his head doggedly.

"Be reasonable, Sharif," Faud urged. "For the sake of Musallim, your father, I will make it worth your while. I will give you the armorer plus the price of the camels."

"You would pay for seven Al Selim camels?" The sheik's voice was deceptively mild.

"Seven?" The merchant gulped. Al Selim camels were among the most valuable in Arabia. But he remembered what Oma had said about the girl. "Yes, I will pay the price."

For a moment Sharif saw his old friend's face through a red haze, and his fists clenched and unclenched as he fought for control. At last he sighed deeply. "I am sorry, Faud. She is not for sale."

Faud's fat face darkened momentarily, then he shrugged. "As Allah wills it. A mere woman must never interfere in a friendship."

Sharif did not answer. When his small caravan departed to rejoin his *smala* that afternoon, he left a purse in payment for the Frenchman. It contained what Faud had asked, plus a few extra gold pieces.

"Allah keep you on your journey, Sheik Al Selim," the merchant called as they rode away. He hefted the purse in his hand and smiled with satisfaction. "And may your shadow never be less."

"Water," the sick man croaked, "water."

"Praise be to Allah, the Englishman is not going to die!" Mustafa exclaimed.

"I wasn't going to let him die," Blaine muttered.

"Surely you are a great hakim, O'Toole Effendi," the little slave agreed, hovering just behind him.

"Let's just say between Ernst and me, we've had a bit of experience with these fevers," the Irishman grunted.

"But, *sidi,* I saw with my own eyes your skill," the Egyptian flattered with natural ease.

Blaine frowned and ordered, "Just fill that cup with water and hand it here."

When Mustafa had obeyed, he held the cup to Derek's cracked, dry lips. "Easy, lad, easy," he cautioned, allowing him only small sips so he would not choke.

After seeing that his patient rested comfortably, Blaine drew the Arab servant away from the bedside and instructed him quietly, "Find Ernst and tell him Derek has regained consciousness. We must make ready to leave."

"What you say is true, *sidi.*" The servant expelled a breath in relief. "It is dangerous to stay longer. I will tell him at once."

The big man stood at the window and stared down unseeingly at the throngs clogging the street of Jidda. His party had barely touched solid ground when Derek collapsed with a fever. Mustafa had located a cheap inn, where no one would ask too many questions. There Derek had thrashed deliriously in a narrow bed and insisted he must find Bryna. He had been wrong . . . so wrong, he groaned. He must go to her at once. It was all the others could do to keep him in bed.

Now the worst was over, but so much time had passed. And each day it seemed as if Bryna was farther away.

Not since Catherine's death had he been so torn by duty, Blaine brooded. If only the young

Englishman had not been so ill, he could have gone. But he could not leave him in Jidda to die. Whatever Bryna's relationship with him, whatever his own feelings about him, he reflected, Derek had stood by him in the fight with Gasim and had withstood the hardships of desert and sea.

Let no one say Blaine O'Toole had not returned the favor, he told himself. He had stood by the lad through his illness.

"Colonel . . . " The invalid's voice reached him weakly.

"Ashburn, you're awake." Blaine strode toward the bed.

"How long?" Derek asked, swallowing painfully.

"Two weeks."

"When do we leave?"

"In three days, if you can."

"I can." He sat up, the exertion bringing a cough.

"It's going to be hard on you, m'boy, until you have your strength back, but we cannot tarry here."

"I will make it," the young man countered stubbornly.

Blaine sat on the chair beside the bed. Leaning forward, his elbows propped on his knees, he said bluntly, " 'Tis only fair to warn you, Derek, Ernst and I have talked about it. If you cannot keep up, we will leave you and Mustafa in the first village we come to."

"I hate to undo any plans the two of you may have made, but I am going with you to find Bryna."

"Still determined, eh?" The big man rose and

grinned at him. The lad had more backbone than he had realized at first.

"More determined than ever, thank you," Derek retorted with surprising vigor. "Besides, we would not want to separate that happy couple, the Arab and the Arabist. I am ready to leave when you are, but for now, send Mustafa up with some food, will you? I could eat a—"

"A camel?" Blaine suggested, chuckling to himself as Derek's pillow sailed past his head and bounced soundlessly off the door.

CHAPTER

✦✦✦✦✦ **15** ✦✦✦✦✦

"DAOUD, SÂLIH, LOOK TO THE WEST AND TELL me what you see," Sharif called to the two young men one day as the *smala* marched.

"It is raining!" Daoud answered with a jubilant whoop.

"Look, rain on the horizon!" Sâlih shouted to the others, gesticulating wildly.

A shout rose up from behind them as all eyes turned to look at the gray-streaked sky.

"We are near an oasis," the sheik mused, "but rainwater is always welcome."

"Alhamdillah!" shouted the others.

"Tell me," Sharif addressed the young men with a smile, "you have the fleetest horses in camp. Do you think you could reach the rain before it stops?"

"Insh'allah," the young men answered. But they leapt gladly from their camels to their horses. With exhilarated shouts they galloped away, balancing jars in front of them, the hooves of their horses flinging sand onto the cheering onlookers.

The *smala* watched until the men and their horses were small dots in the distance, then Sharif gave the order to move on to the oasis. The caravan had been traveling for several days. Progress was slow, but the travelers' mood was light as they neared their destination.

For the past few days Sharif had lessened his vigilance, for Nassar spent every free moment with Pamela now. Free of the sheik's constant glower, Bryna also relaxed. She walked, sometimes with Taman, sometimes alone, enjoying the relative freedom of the desert. Occasionally she nodded her encouragement to Kedar, the new slave Sharif had bought in *Kasr* Al Haroun.

Wearing a thobe that was much too short for him, the big man balanced precariously at first on the back of a swaying pack camel, looking nearly panic-stricken. But as he became more comfortable, he rode along in silence, returning the smile when Bryna looked in his direction. They had never even spoken, but the girl felt as if she had found a friend.

But Bryna was not completely carefree today. She worried about Pamela and her unborn child. The English girl was ailing again. She had seemed so much improved when they had visited the town four days ago. And three nights ago at dinner, she had had her usual ravenous appetite. Bryna had watched, amazed, as the petite blonde ate an entire loaf of bread, then asked for dessert.

"Eating for two, you know," she joked for the first time in months.

But yesterday and the day before, Pamela had lost everything she had eaten. It hardly seemed right, now that they no longer had to worry about near starvation, that she was ill.

Bryna was not the only one who fretted on this fine day. Swinging in her litter, Fatmah brooded. This morning the Inglayzi had scarcely been able to rise from her bed. All day she had swayed on her camel, looking as if she wished she could die. What if she did die? It would be Fatmah's fault. The bitter potion she had administered secretly in Pamela's tea was not meant to kill her, only to rid her of the child. The woman reviewed her actions of the past three days, regretting that she had doubled the dosage to make up for the days when there had not been enough water for tea.

During the afternoon, Daoud and Sâlih returned to the *smala*. Their clothes were dry after their ride across the desert, but the jars they carried were filled with rainwater. They were greeted with exuberant cries as they rejoined the caravan, headed toward the oasis that loomed before them.

Bryna stared at the parklike refuge with wondering eyes. It was the most beautiful oasis she had ever seen. A luxuriant carpet of tribulus covered the desert floor nearby. Succulents bloomed among them in multicolored profusion, their perfume filling the air. A sandy clearing offered a perfect campsite in the shade of a veritable forest of acacias and fig trees. Three small pools of clear water that adjoined each other were screened from view by a border of huge *safs*, or palmettos. Jutting from the lush green vegetation were tall, swaying date palms, silhouetted against the cloudless sky.

As the herdsmen watered the camels at the pool nearest the campsite, Bryna searched for Pamela. She found her, still perched on the back of her couched camel. Her face was pale and there was a vacant look in her shadowed eyes.

"What is it, Pamela?" Bryna asked worriedly.

"I don't know. I just don't feel well today." The answer seemed to take all the girl's strength.

"Let me help you." The American girl extended a hand in assistance. Pamela leaned toward her as if she would take it, then suddenly she pitched from her saddle, landing facedown in the sand. A dark stain of blood covered the back of her *thobe* from her waist nearly to the hem.

"Pamela!" Bryna cried, kneeling by her side as the women hurried to see what was wrong.

"So sorry," the English girl whispered. "Just a bit dizzy." Then her eyes closed and her head lolled to one side.

"Is the Inglayzi dead?" Fatmah breathed in horror.

"She has fainted."

"Stay with her, Bryna," Taman urged, unexpectedly sympathetic. "Abla and I will set up Nassar's tent as soon as we have built our own." She looked in silent askance at Sharif's elder wife, receiving a nod of assent.

Pamela lay near death for two days as her body cramped and strained to rid itself of the child she carried. Bryna never left her side, feeding her, bathing her with cool water, until at last Fatmah's potion completed its deadly work and Pamela miscarried what would have been Nassar's first son.

The young Arab lurked outside the women's quarters, terrified that his houri might die. When Pamela began to show slow signs of improvement, he was still so fearful for her health that he petitioned Sharif to stay at their latest campsite long enough for Inglayzi to recover.

Sharif needed no persuasion. There was time before the rainy season started, and he wished to rest the camels for the last arduous leg of their long trek. Besides, he did not want to see the foreign woman die.

He was still in no hurry to move when Pamela recovered enough to rise shakily from her bed. The Selims continued to camp at the oasis.

The weakened girl insisted she be allowed to work immediately. She knew what her friend had done for her before, but she had been too sick to care. Now, she declared pluckily, she would pull her own weight in Nassar's household.

When no argument would change her mind, Bryna sent her to gather figs from a tree where the women and children congregated. It was easy work, and the convalescing girl could sit in the shade for a while without fear of recrimination, for all the women took their time at the pleasant task. Bryna set about the monotonous work of preparing *leben*. Weary and drained from nursing Pamela, she swung the skin back and forth, glad to think of nothing in particular.

As sounds of the camp swirled around her, Bryna nearly missed the one sound that stood out in sharp contrast with the others. From somewhere nearby, a voice was speaking French. She raced around the tent to discover Sharif, standing with his back to her as he inspected a rifle, hefting it appraisingly in his hand. Kedar, the hulking silent slave, could be seen departing.

Was it the new slave who spoke French? Or could it have been the sheik? She had only heard him speak Arabic. He seemed so completely Arab, she had not even considered that he would speak another language. She hesitated uncertainly, overwhelmed by the possibility.

"What do you want?" Sharif asked when he turned to find the girl standing behind him. Her blue eyes, wide above her veil, were fixed on him almost beseechingly. As much as he might wish to hear what she had to say, he could not be seen alone with her behind the tents. "Speak, woman, and be about your work," he ordered.

Drawing a steadying breath, she responded in French, "I seek the man I heard speaking French." Her face was alight with hope.

"I—I thought Americans spoke English," he stammered.

"In Louisiana, where I come from, we speak French as much as English."

Sharif digested that information with a look of wonder. Stepping nearer, he gazed down at her as if he had found an unexpected treasure. "Why did you not tell me?"

"I did not know you spoke French. Why did you not tell me?" she asked, her voice vibrant with joy. Her eyes sparkled as she tilted her head to look up at him.

Sharif's smiling demeanor sobered as he remembered himself. "This is not fitting, Bryna bint Blaine. We cannot linger behind the tent. Go back to your work. We will speak another time."

"But—" she protested, bewildered by his sudden change in attitude.

"*Rûhh*, go," he ordered harshly. "Your sheik commands you."

Disappointed and angry, Bryna obeyed. Settling in front of the tripod, she told herself fiercely that she did not care if the mighty sheik did not want to talk to a lowly slave. *Dieu*, how she detested the arrogance of all Arab men, especially Sharif. In her mind she summoned his every scowling expression, but those memories were crowded out by recollections of a smile that was almost boyish. Even her memories of Sharif Al Selim kept her off balance, she thought wrathfully. With a vigor born of frustration, she gave the goatskin a mighty push.

Bryna's tempest of unwanted emotion was mild compared with Sharif's vexation. He was delighted at the thought of talking with the girl. Returning to his tent, he reviewed their brief conversation. It had revealed that she was educated and well-spoken, and he longed to know more about her, to hear her story from her own lips.

But he must not. For her good as well as his, he must not seek out this woman, he reminded himself savagely. But as the day wore on, he found he could not get her out of his mind.

"You sent for me, ya amm," Nassar said, answering Sharif's summons the next day.

"Sit, nephew, and hear my idea." After sending for coffee, the sheik asked, "You have visited the town that lies to the north?"

"A few times." In no mood for a lecture, the young Arab regarded his uncle warily.

"I have been thinking that after many months in the desert, there is news a man can receive only in the coffeehouses, and our women would like to visit the souk and sell their handiwork."

"You are taking the *smala* into town?"

"No, after our visit to *Kasr* Al Haroun, the smell of civilization still hangs upon my robes. We will be in Riyadh soon enough and I will miss the desert. I thought perhaps you would like to take them in the morning and lead them home after sunset prayers," Sharif suggested. "It would be good experience for you to have such a responsibility. What do you think?"

"You would let me lead them, and not Sa'id?" the young man asked excitedly.

Sharif nodded. "But there is one stipulation if the people are to go."

"What is that?" Nassar asked suspiciously. He had known it was too good to be true.

"The common slaves must stay behind and someone must stay with each tent. Those who have servants enough to dismiss from the herds may leave a servant. Those who do not must leave a family member." The plan made good sense, but Sharif felt duplicitous because he knew Nassar could not dismiss Ali from the herds. Since he must leave someone with the tent, he had no doubt

Nassar would take Pamela and leave Bryna.

The party departed merrily the next morning and Bryna was indeed left behind, but she did not seem to mind. Sharif was constantly aware of her as she hurried to finish her tasks so she might have a rare afternoon of leisure. He watched wistfully as she disappeared toward the pools with a bundle of laundry, but he did not follow. He must not be alone with her, for he feared what might happen. Instead he waited. There would be time to talk to her later.

After midday prayers, Sharif found her seated under a tree in the middle of the camp. As she leaned over her embroidery, her hair fell in damp, heavy strands under her *ghata.* She had washed more than the clothes this morning, he thought with a smile.

Positioning himself on the opposite side of the tree, he leaned against the trunk and began to mend his saddle. He worked silently for a time, his mind distracted from his task for each breeze carried on it the clean, sweet fragrance of her hair. In the middle of the deserted camp, while the others slept through the heat of the day, the couple began to talk quietly.

Bryna's heart pounded in anticipation. The opportunity she'd awaited had arrived. She would soon appeal to the sheik for her freedom. But time spent among the Arabs had taught her well: business must be broached slowly, once the courtesies and proprieties had been observed. Only after a leisurely conversation would it be proper for her to present her petition. As they talked, Sharif was pleased to discover that although the American girl seemed nervous with him at first, she was as intelligent as he had thought and quick-witted, too. To his amazement, Sharif found himself telling her things he had long ago forgotten—childish adventures, the story of his life.

So enthralled was Bryna with his tale that she forgot for a moment the urgency of her request.

The sheik was the son of Musallim, a Selim chieftain and Zeineb, an Ottoman princess, the old man's third wife. The marriage had been arranged as a political alliance, but the aged sheik doted upon his young bride. She was fond of him as well and bore him a son, Sharif.

Then, in quick succession, two daughters were stillborn and another son died in infancy. Always delicate, the princess went into a decline. Frantic to please her, the sheik promised that she could visit her homeland when she recovered. This gave her renewed purpose, and within six months Zeineb had recovered sufficiently to return to her father's court for a visit. She departed, accompanied by Abu Ahmad, one of the sheik's most trusted retainers, and Sharif, now aged four.

At home in the Ottoman court, the princess was reasonably happy, although she missed her husband. Unexpectedly word came that Musallim was dead and had been replaced by his brother, Malek. The new sheik had married off Musallim's widows and offered now to marry the princess himself when she returned to Arabia. Although she had been fortunate in her first marriage, she could not bear the thought of marrying another man, not even her brother-in-law. Diplomatically she declined. She tried to send Abu Ahmad back to Arabia with the message, but he stubbornly refused. His duty was to protect the princess and her son, and he would do so in Arabia or in Ottoman Turkey.

Zeineb settled into a small palace and dedicated herself to the rearing of her son, teaching him music, poetry, and literature. But when he was eight years old, the frail woman died. The young Sharif had no clear memories of his homeland, but it beckoned him. His grandfather, the sultan, forbade him to go, making him a virtual prisoner in his palace. The old potentate did not want the boy to return to Arabia. After all, he had only half brothers and sisters there; in Turkey he had his grandfather and a chance of succession to the throne.

Once again Abu Ahmad was dismissed to return home, and once again he refused. The sultan was only mildly annoyed. The lad could use a man to teach him manly arts, he thought, while he taught Sharif politics and power. Over the next four years the boy learned not only of diplomacy and government, but of corruption and court intrigues. He learned of the empire within the empire, built and overseen by powerful eunuchs.

When at last the sultan sickened, Sharif made plans for flight. He feared that when the old man died, even though he was low in the line of succession, he might be murdered by fearful uncles or cousins. As the deathwatch progressed, the faithful Abu Ahmad gathered provisions and purchased fast camels. The moment the death keening began, they fled. By the time the covert poisonings and overt manipulations began, the boy was well on his way to Arabia.

Abu Ahmad had trained his young charge in many athletic feats and had taught him to fight in the Arabian style, but nomadic life was difficult for a soft boy brought up in the courts of the Sultan. Yet Sharif found his inner strength in the vast emptiness of the desert. Daily he grew taller and tougher and more agile.

The awkward, introverted stripling arrived at Malek's home in Riyadh and was welcomed. At first it was Alima, his aunt, who made his life bearable, but slowly he adapted to life in Arabia. Sharif was schooled with his cousins, the sheik's sons. Another cousin, Sa'id, became his best friend. They fenced, rode, and flew their falcons together. They studied the Koran, arguing late into the night. And they were friends to this day.

At fourteen Sharif was sent to a Bedouin tribe in the desert. At sixteen he returned to Riyadh a man. Soon he was heard in the *majlis* and earned the trust of Malek, whom he served for nine years.

When Malek died suddenly, Sharif did not know what was said privately among the tribal elders. He did not know they admired his reputation as a fearless warrior, his even temper, and his well-thought-out opinions. He knew only that when the council met, he found himself, to his amazement, sheik of his tribe at the age of twenty-five.

For nearly twelve years now he had led the Selims, good people who flourished despite the zealots, the Wahabis, who'd settled in their territory. They had enjoyed peace and prosperity, Sharif said with a smile. They were truly blessed by Allah.

When it became necessary for him to take a wife, the young sheik selected a daughter of a powerful chieftain in Medina. Once again an arranged marriage blossomed into love, and Noorah became the light of his life. Sadly they had been married only a year when she died giving birth to `Abla. The hakim did all he could, but Noorah died and `Abla lived. Poor little `Abla.

Sharif could not tell Bryna about the numb emptiness he had felt all these years. He'd performed his duties automatically, living for the welfare and honor of his tribe and his family. When his half brothers died, he had married their widows, as was right. He did what he must, feeling nothing but sadness—until now.

All these thoughts of honor . . . Suddenly the sheik hated himself for what he was doing. He despised himself for arranging this meeting in his nephew's absence. And he had been the one who had sent him away. Filled with self-loathing, Sharif jumped to his feet and stalked off, leaving Bryna alone under the tree, hurt by his sudden shift of mood and despondent over the opportunity she'd missed.

In the days that followed, Sharif struggled with his growing obsession with Bryna. Wrestling with his feelings, he hunted, sending his saluki coursing after gazelle day after day as he galloped behind. He stayed active, as if exertion would keep him from giving in to his weakness.

"Wallahi, I wish Sharif would sleep away his *zahlán*, his melancholy, whatever causes it," Sa'id griped wearily after a long day's chase. "To do so would be better—for all of us."

But the sheik would not, could not. Tired and restless, he lay awake at night, longing for the girl as her name echoed in his head. Truly it was best that men and women were kept apart, he reflected, fighting the ache to touch her, to lie with her, to be with her until the end of time. He must avoid her, or who knew what the consequences would be?

It had been a year since Bryna's capture, and her burdens had never seemed so heavy to her. In need of solitude one afternoon, she walked alone in the lush oasis, settling beside the isolated pool farthest from camp. There in a copse at the water's edge, she sat down despondently, hidden from prying eyes.

While the caravan had moved through the desert, she had almost forgotten what lay at the end of the journey. Now she remembered with stunning clarity that when they reached Riyadh, she would be forced to marry Nassar. And she had wasted her only chance for freedom, she thought, surrendering to depression.

Gazing at her reflection in the water, the girl

felt the same disquieting emotion she had felt in the *hammam*. The face that stared back at her from the pool belonged to an Arab woman, draped and covered, perhaps doomed never to know freedom again. Deliberately she removed her *ghata* and veil and turned her face to the pale, dappled sunlight that filtered through the trees. For a long moment she savored the feel of the rising wind, rustling the leaves around her, stirring her unbound hair, until she heard for the first time a distant roll of thunder.

It was going to rain, she realized with a start. She should get back to the camp. But when she picked up the crumpled pile of fabric that was her veil, she could not bring herself to put it on. It was the uniform of a prisoner.

She was alone in a strange land. The more she knew about this wild country, the more she knew escape was improbable for her alone and impossible if she took Pamela, she thought bitterly. After months of wandering in the desert, she did not hold much hope that her father or Derek would ever find her. And how she hated the idea of having Nassar as a husband.

If she had not been kidnapped, she and Derek might have been married by now. They might have gone to England, and she would have had a normal life, the family and the sense of belonging she had always wanted.

Why was she torturing herself with what might have been? Bryna asked herself as she stubbornly tried to visualize Derek's face, without success. Perhaps it had been too long since she'd seen him.

Or perhaps the memory of his hazel eyes had been supplanted by the presence of a pair of piercing gray ones.

Heaving a mighty sigh, she wondered again why Sharif had stalked away from her in anger the last time they had talked. She reviewed their conversation for the hundredth time, trying to decide whether she had said something that offended him. He had been so gentle one moment, so forbidding the next. Even as his smoldering gaze had followed her the past few days, she had not been able to forget the tenderness of his caresses. She had never known such a man, difficult and mercurial and remarkable.

And now she did not even have the comfort of his friendship. She might never feel his touch again, might never touch him, but she could not bear the possibility that he hated her. Her loneliness seemed suddenly too much to endure. She began to cry softly, unable to hold back the tears.

Sharif also sought privacy. When he spied the first ominous black cloud, he knew every man in camp would seek shelter in his tent from the rain. He needed a moment of quiet before they came.

As he walked beside the secluded pool, the sheik caught sight of Bryna sitting on the other side. She was alone, and he could not resist giving in to the desire to gaze upon her unveiled face once more. Shielded by the trees, he made his way toward her, stopping when he realized she wept.

His heart nearly broke at the sound of her deep, hopeless sobs. Heedless of the impropriety of being alone with her, the man went to her.

"Why do you weep?" he asked softly in French.

The girl started violently but relaxed when she saw it was Sharif. "You frightened me. I did not hear you approach, my lord," she said, dashing the tears from her eyes.

"I asked, why do you cry?" he repeated.

"Because I am lonely, because I am in a foreign place, because I may never go home again," she answered, feeling oddly defiant.

"Arabia is your home now," the man insisted gently but firmly. Taking her hand, he pulled her to her feet. His searching gray eyes drank in Bryna's beauty as the wind whipped her dark hair. Belatedly realizing he still held her hand, he released it.

"You may find it strange here now, but you will learn to love it," he assured her, struggling to keep his voice light. "Here you will marry and have children and grow old and fat and contented. And it will not be such a bad life, eh?"

Surely that was not a description of life with Nassar, Bryna thought bleakly. She looked up at the man sadly and whispered, "I am a freeborn woman, my lord. I have a home and I want to go back to it."

Pain wrenched the sheik at the thought of Bryna's leaving, and he interrupted harshly, "Enough. Do not say more." Placing his hands on her shoulders, he caught her gaze and held it. "Do not speak of your past, Bryna," he commanded in a gentler tone. "You will only make yourself sad."

"But, Sheik Al Selim—"

"When you marry," Sharif went on with effort, "you will be a slave no more."

"No, I will be Nassar's wife," she murmured dejectedly, thinking one was as bad as the other.

"Yes, his wife." The sheik's voice was harsh as he tried to control his emotions. "Have you not learned enough of our ways to understand *'Insh'allah'*?"

"As Allah wills. I know," she whispered shakily.

All at once Sharif's hands tightened and he drew her against his hard, muscular body. Gazing lovingly into her eyes, he murmured her name and lowered his mouth to hers, claiming it tenderly.

Bryna's emotions were at war. She had wanted this to happen, she realized, although Nassar would kill her if he knew. She had longed for Sharif's touch, but this could not be. She must not allow herself to feel anything. The pain would be too great, for she could never truly have Sharif.

But, against her will, her body responded hungrily to his caresses. When his lips found the pulse in the sensitive spot below her ear, she forgot her qualms and molded herself against him. His mouth returned to hers, demanding this time, as his tongue darted between her parted lips, exploring, exciting, inciting. Liquid heat flowed through her veins, and she returned his kiss with ardor.

Shaken by their passion, they stood locked in an embrace, the rising wind whipping their robes about them.

"*Bismallah,* what have I done?" the sheik groaned suddenly, finding the strength at last to thrust Bryna from him. "I have told myself again and again that what I feel for you is wrong. Can it be Allah's will that I love you as I do?"

"Sharif," she whispered, her expression as miserable as his.

"No! What is written cannot be unwritten. Veil yourself now and return to the tent of your *sidi,* your future husband," he forced himself to say. "We must not be alone together again."

Trembling, Bryna picked up her veil and tied it into place with numbed fingers. Avoiding the man's tormented gray eyes, she turned without a word and stumbled down the path to the camp.

While Sharif watched her depart, the sky opened above him and rain began to pour. His despairing face was lit by the jagged bolt of lightning that rent the dark sky, and the rain mixed with the first tears he had shed since Noorah's death.

CHAPTER

✧✧✧✧✧ **16** ✧✧✧✧✧

THE AIR WAS CLEAN, AND GLISTENING RAIN-
drops still hung from the trees when Sharif
announced his intention to go falconing the next
morning. He had to get away from the camp, to put
thoughts of Bryna away from him for a while.

"Wallahi, tonight we will eat bustard," his
retainers exclaimed excitedly to each other as they
mounted their horses and rode into the desert.

Late in the afternoon two camel riders
approached the Selim camp, wearing the robes of a
tribe far to the west. Because the men were away, it
was the duty of the sheik's wives to greet the guests
and make them comfortable. Fatmah and Latifeh
followed the codes of Bedouin hospitality scrupu-
lously.

Anyone seeking hospitality in a Bedu camp was
an honored guest for three days. It was the custom
that the first day was for greeting, the second day
for eating, and the third for talking. After that time
the host might ask tactfully if he could help the visitors prepare for the continuation of their journey.

The hunters arrived just before sunset, quiet

and subdued after the strenuous exercise. Sharif immediately noticed the two strange camels hobbled near the others, and he stiffened. The last time he had seen them, they wore the small saddles of southern tribes. Now they wore the double-poled saddles of this region, but he recognized them: they belonged to the raiders who had killed his brothers. Dismounting, the sheik inspected the brand on the flank of each animal. There could be no doubt.

He strode to his tent, and there his suspicions were confirmed. Last year's marauders, now dressed as tribesmen of the West, lolled insolently in his *majlis* against his woolen saddlebags, rudely refusing to rise to return his greeting.

A long moment passed as the men appraised each other. It was obvious the way Sharif's jaw worked that he knew them, and under other circumstances he would have killed them on sight. But Fatmah and Latifeh had not known. They had behaved as proper Arab wives, and now these murderers were his guests. He was bound to honor that commitment.

Sharif's dilemma made the visitors bold. They greeted the great sheik like an old friend, making themselves comfortable, taking the best meat at dinner, drinking more than their share of coffee, and monopolizing the conversation, traits most uncharacteristic to the Bedouins. Sharif knew they were disliked by everyone in camp, but he could not ask them to leave before the prescribed three days were up.

Late in the third day, when the visitors should

have been thinking of departure, they pushed the limits of hospitality too far. As they lounged in Sharif's *majlis*, watching Bryna and Pamela at work around Nassar's tent, they asked if they might use them since they were only infidel slaves. Nassar searched for an appropriate answer. It was the practice in some southern tribes, but slaves or no, these women were to be his wives and the young man had no wish to share them.

To his amazement, before he could reply, Sharif erupted in anger, driving the visitors from his tent. "*Hayâtak,* by thy life! You despoil our hospitality," he roared. "Sons of camels, thou basest of Arabs who ever hammered a tent peg, get out!"

"We are your guests," one of them whined. "Your food still fills our bellies."

"Yes, wallahi, and while it does, I will not kill you. But the moment you rid yourselves of it, your lives are in peril. Flee, dogs, or die."

Muttering to each other, they grabbed their belongings and departed, riding into the desert with many looks backward. The last sight of them from the camp was when they halted atop a dune. One of them looked back at the tents and lifted his clenched fist as he cursed the inhabitants, "God destroy your house and all who dwell in it!"

In the sheik's tent the men looked at each other uneasily, but no one spoke. Secretly Nassar was elated that Sharif had solved his problem for him, but what his uncle had done was shameful. Perhaps he was temporarily possessed by an evil spirit, Sa'id suggested, expressing a willingness to treat his deranged friend with a hot iron to rid him of the curse. When Sharif declined, they watched their leader closely for the rest of the afternoon, relieved that although he brooded, he did nothing else out of the ordinary.

The next night whoops filled the air and raiders rode into camp. Against the rules of *ghazzi*, they attacked after midnight and fired the tents before making away with the camels.

Bryna and Pamela rose from their pallets to the barking of dogs and confused shouts, to ringing steel and sporadic gunfire. They rushed to the curtain that divided the women's quarters from the main section of the tent. Through the open front they saw figures milling around the camp.

Fire provided illumination, and in its glow Bryna saw three raiders dismount swiftly and run toward their tent. She smelled smoke, and suddenly the goat-hair fabric over their heads blazed in the night air. The women ducked to escape the inferno, wrapping their veils around their heads.

Bryna ripped at the curtain between the sections of the tent, and the girls stumbled through the rent. In the *majlis*, Nassar freed his mare, unfastening the iron ring that linked her to the tent pole. Then, drawing his sword, he faltered, looking bewildered against the backdrop of flames.

"Come," he shouted, suddenly in control of the situation when he saw Pamela's panic-stricken face.

Just outside the tent, Bryna saw `Abla dart out of the way of one of the raiders' grasp. Tossing a small water skin to the girl, she shouted, "Run,

`Abla, run!" The child staggered when she caught the skin but quickly scurried into the darkness.

Bryna's interference turned the raiders' attention to Nassar's tent. The soft young Arab brandished his sword awkwardly and tried to shield Pamela with his body. One of the attackers aimed his lance at Nassar and took a menacing step forward, his arm tensed to hurl the weapon. Suddenly Fatmah appeared from nowhere and threw herself in front of Nassar. When the raider released his spear, the old woman was impaled first. The shaft went through her body and pierced Nassar. For one horrible instant Bryna could not tell whether it had also wounded Pamela. Mother and son slumped to the ground while the horrified English girl looked on. With a triumphant shout, the marauder claimed her.

Another Bedu, not much more than a boy, advanced menacingly on Bryna. Suddenly Smemi raced toward her attacker, snarling and snapping. The raider halted, obviously terrified of the shaggy beast. But Smemi's fearsome growl ended in an agonized yelp when a spear pierced the back of his neck. With an anguished cry, Bryna knelt and cradled the dog's big head in her lap, his blood pouring onto her *thobe*. With a salute to his rescuer, the boy seized her and dragged her through the camp toward the camels.

Both Bryna and Pamela fought their attackers, kicking and biting. Bryna's captor struck her, bringing the taste of blood to her mouth. Her head reeling, she was vaguely aware that men fought for their lives all around her. She could hear the moans of the wounded, and some of Sharif's men sprawled dead on the ground. With an exultant shout, another raider joined his comrades, hauling Latifeh's protesting figure behind him.

"Bryna!" She heard her name faintly through the screams and the crackle of the fire.

Unmindful of the consequences, she tore at her captor's viselike grip and strained to see over her shoulder. In the fray behind her, Sharif fought wildly to reach her. When the raider yanked the girl toward his camel, she tried to wrench away. He clouted her again on the side of the head. The last thing she saw in a blur of pain was Sharif as he fell, wounded.

The three women were hauled roughly onto the camels in front of their captors. Bryna was thrown over the saddle so hard that she gasped for air, feeling as if her body were bruised to its very core. Through a red haze of pain, she recognized the two Bedu who had abused their hospitality only a few days before.

With a shout, the rest of the raiding party bolted to their camels and, driving the Selim herd before them, galloped out of camp. Bryna was jarred in front of the gangly Bedu boy until they had traveled nearly ten miles. Then the party halted for a brief rest. Latifeh scolded loudly while trying to hide her face from her abductors. She had not even had time to snatch up a veil during the attack. The women were shoved from the camels and their wrists bound, the ropes tied to the camels' saddles.

The raiders lingered for a few minutes, congratulating each other, so secure were they in their victory. Then most of the men remounted and headed west across the desert, singing victory songs as they rode. The three who had taken the women remounted and urged their camels forward, dragging their captives behind them.

Bryna felt as if her arms would be torn from her shoulders each time the camel jostled. None of the women wore shoes, and soon their feet were cut and bleeding from the sharp, cutting edges of the sand. Latifeh's face was a mask of suffering, and Pamela looked as if she were unconscious on her feet. Only the will to survive kept Bryna going.

When the sun rose, the men did not stop for prayers but forged deeper into the Rub al Khali, the Empty Quarter. A desert within a desert, it covered thousands of miles of inland Arabia. There was little water, less life, and no hope. As the day wore on and the blazing sun beat down on them, the men, displeased with the slow pace, gestured for the women to be taken back on the camels. Wearily they obeyed; there was no hope of escape.

The party passed through mile after mile of glistening white sand, rippled by the heated wind that blew it against them. In the stark emptiness, dead plants poked through dunes, giving the land a wasted, barren look. Tying their kaffiyehs around their faces, the men took their prisoners across the singing sands, where every step murmured with a harmonic effect.

As evening fell and Bryna thought she would die

of thirst, they stopped. The sun had created mirages all afternoon, but no water was found. The men had drunk from their skins, but they had given none to the women. Now they offered no more than a grudging swallow. After securing the women, the men unsaddled the camels and set up a skimpy camp with no tents, only a three-stone fireplace. They untied Latifeh and demanded she cook for them.

While the old woman bent stiffly to her task, the men came to where the girls sat, still bound. Pamela's captor ripped the headdress from her head, and his beady eyes lit at the sight of her fair hair. When Latifeh saw what they were doing, she railed at them, interjecting her ample body between them and the girls. With a curse, one of the raiders slapped her and shoved her out of the way. The Arab woman fell heavily, her head hitting one of the stones of the fireplace. She did not move again. Unconcerned, the men returned to their inspection, forgetting their hunger.

They untied Pamela and stood her in their midst, pushing her from one to the other until she cried and pleaded. At last her abductor dragged the girl behind a nearby dune while the other two waited their turn. Bryna could hear Pamela's cries and moans of protest and pain. When the first one had finished, he strode cockily back into camp and motioned for the next one to go. The second disappeared behind the dune, and Bryna heard more of the pitiful wailing. The youngest was last. He watched while the first man cleansed his hands with sand after touching the kaffir.

Calmly rolling Latifeh's body aside with a stick, the man lit the campfire and set about baking bread. The adolescent paced, made more eager by the cries he heard. When he could stand it no longer, he turned to Bryna as if he would drag her from the camp.

She had only one chance, the girl realized. Placing all her hope in the superstitious Bedu nature, she narrowed her blue eyes and summoned an ominous, malicious look. "Know you not what a bewitcher can do?" she muttered in Arabic. "Touch me and I will call upon you every *ghul,* every monster of the desert."

The boy recoiled in horror, hurrying to the older man to report her threat.

"What is this you say, woman?" the man demanded. Wiping the flour from his hands onto his aba, he came to stand before her. Smiling craftily, Bryna began to croon a nonsensical Creole song from her childhood.

"What is she saying?" the boy asked fearfully.

"Return my friend to me," she demanded in Arabic, turning wild eyes on them.

"She is mad." The raiders retreated rapidly, kicking over the cooking pot in their haste.

Bryna continued to sing, her voice increasing in volume as she rose to her knees.

"Farouk," they called to their comrade, "bring back the white woman before the witch curses us all."

There was a muffled curse from behind the sand dune, and Farouk appeared to lay Pamela's limp, naked body beside the fire.

Crawling on all fours to the unconscious girl, Bryna covered her friend with her aba, then crawled to Latifeh's side. The dead woman's eyes seemed to stare at darkening sky. Returning to Pamela, Bryna cushioned her head in her lap and watched as the men withdrew a safe distance to argue among themselves.

At last the raiders lay down to sleep. They were exhausted, and tomorrow was soon enough to decide what to do about the women. Wearily they stretched out, lying on their stomachs to prevent hunger pangs. Bryna kept watch, until at last her own fatigue overcame her.

She awakened at dawn to the prayers of the Moslem men, every muscle in her body aching. Opening her eyes, she saw the vapor of her breath in the still air. She could feel the ebbing heat of the fire. It had dried half of her dew-wet dress, while the other side was cold and clammy against her skin.

The men resumed their argument. What were they to do now? They had had the blond-haired woman, and the other was mad. They could hardly kill one possessed by a spirit, but why haul her all over the Empty Quarter?

They could sell the pale one in Oman, one of them suggested, but his plan was discarded. She would never make it across the Rub al Khali. It would be better to leave the women here, they reasoned, and go to get their share of the camels. They could refill their water skins at a small oasis back a short distance, then they would ride like the wind to join the others.

Unexpectedly the boy objected. "The women will die in the desert."

"What does it matter?" one of the men asked. "We will not have killed them. Whether they live or die is the will of Allah. Leave them."

Hearing the soft pads of the camels as the raiders rode away, Bryna sat up. In the morning dimness a red stain could be seen, spreading slowly beneath Pamela's body. Poor Pamela, never fully recovered from her illness—how was she to survive such ill treatment? Bryna wondered, tears swimming in her eyes.

Tenderly she stroked the English girl's cheek, finding the skin hot to the touch. One of her eyes was black and swollen, and blood smeared over her cracked lips. Bryna looked around desperately. The men had not left even a small water skin.

Rising shakily to her feet, she smoothed her wadded, bloodstained *thobe* and assessed the situation. They had no food, no shelter, no water, and no hint of where the nearest well or oasis might be, if indeed they could reach one without camels. The first step was to stay alive.

Pamela moaned and opened her eyes. "Bryna," she whimpered weakly, "I hurt so badly."

Bryna made the injured girl as comfortable as possible. Then, going to retrieve Pamela's dress, she searched for any sign of hidden water beneath the sand. A withered shrub sent up one pitiful gray-green branch.

After dressing her fevered friend, she returned to the spot to dig for hours until she hit a small pocket of murky water. She dipped her headdress in it and took it, dripping, to wet Pamela's lips. The injured girl's eyes flickered open. They were glazed with pain.

"Is there more?" she rasped.

"Just what I found in digging. Suck on this and get what water you can out of it." Bryna put the corner of the headdress into Pamela's mouth and watched as she drew a little liquid from the damp material.

"Save some for yourself," the injured girl whispered through parched lips.

Bryna performed the same motions for herself, greedy for the moisture but knowing it was not enough to keep them alive in the blazing heat to come.

She gazed over at the ruins of the campfire. The pot that had held the beginnings of last night's dinner lay upended in the sand, its unsavory-looking contents swarming with ants.

"Inedible," she muttered.

"Don't worry, Bryna," Pamela said hoarsely, "even I am not hungry yet."

Bryna smiled in spite of their dire situation, causing her split lip to bleed again.

"Where is Latifeh?"

"She is dead. I will bury her, then we must decide what to do for ourselves."

"Very well." The English girl sighed wearily and closed her eyes.

Bryna dug a shallow grave in the sand and dragged the woman's body to it, carefully positioning it so her battered feet pointed toward Mecca. Generously she wrapped her own aba around Latifeh's dead face. Then she covered the grave.

In the fine sands of the desert, Bryna found no rocks to place over the grave to keep the animals away. She had done the best she could. Still feeling that she should do something to honor the woman who had been killed defending her, she knelt beside the grave and recited one of Latifeh's favorite verses from the Koran.

Bryna returned to Pamela. The sun was beginning to beat down on them unmercifully. In a high dune nearby, she hollowed out a space in the shady side and half carried, half dragged Pamela to it.

The injured girl bit her lip to keep from crying out in pain. "What are we to do, Bryna?"

"We will wait here for rescue."

"Do you think there is anyone left to search for us?"

"Of course," Bryna replied as confidently as she could. She had seen Nassar die and Sharif fall to a blow that must have killed him.

"You should try to go back alone, Bryna. It is your only chance. If you find help, you can send them back for me."

Bryna considered Pamela's suggestion for only a moment. Her chances in the open desert were not much better than here. If they stayed in one place, perhaps the tracks they had left would lead searchers to them. But, most of all, she could not leave Pamela to die alone. Her promise, the one she had chafed under, came back to haunt her. She could not leave her friend.

"Let's stay here until you feel better, then we will both go back," she suggested gently. "We can follow the direction of the tracks the camels left as we came."

"But . . . " Pamela did not have the strength to argue. Easing down to sit beside her, Bryna rested the girl's head on her shoulder. Then they waited.

For rescue or for death? the girl wondered. How long could they last in the desert? Even if Sharif lived, would he come for them?

As the sun progressed around the dune, Bryna moved Pamela's limp body to keep it shaded. The injured girl awakened once to murmur, her tongue thick with thirst, "You have been awfully good to me, Bryna. I want you to know I shall never forget you."

"Don't talk. Save your strength," the American girl encouraged.

She slumped in the sand beside Pamela and tried to pray, but instead the Fatiha droned through her mind. How could they hope to survive? Their throats were parched already, and the heat, now nearly unbearable, would only get worse throughout the afternoon. But tonight would be cold, and there was nothing to use as a shelter, Bryna noticed almost indifferently. At last she, too, fainted, her battered body seeking relief in unconsciousness.

CHAPTER

✦✦✦✦✦ **17** ✦✦✦✦✦

SHARIF SAT ON A LOW STOOL IN THE MIDST OF the ruined camp and allowed Kedar to tend his injuries. The big slave's hands were surprisingly gentle as he treated the gash on the sheik's shoulder with gunpowder and stitched it closed.

The sheik scarcely noticed. Raw pain that had nothing to do with his wound showed in his gray eyes. The dogs who had raided his camp must die. His wife Fatmah and his nephew Nassar were among the dead lying in the sand. He had watched as Sa'id fell. And the marauders had taken Bryna and Latifeh and the fair-haired girl.

He must find the raiders and reclaim what was his. No matter what their tribal standing, this time there would be *ghazzi*. The Selims could not be attacked twice and expected to stand for it. But before a council could be called, the sheik must attend to his people. They must have the essentials for survival.

With a nod of thanks to the big mute, Sharif drew on his robe over the bandages. Summoning the frightened Salubas from their hiding places, he assigned them to a burial detail. The women of his tribe he set to repairing the damaged water skins and refilling them for the journey to Riyadh. The children were dispatched to search the smoldering tents for undamaged foodstuffs. With relief he watched `Abla scramble off with the others. Praise be to Allah, his daughter was safe, he thought gratefully.

Hearing a weak whimper, Sharif found Smemi lying in a pool of blood. Whining with pain, the big dog strained to lift his head a few inches from the ground and look around as if he were searching for something. Or someone, Sharif brooded. But the effort was too much, and Smemi's head dropped heavily. The dog's eyes rested on Sharif almost pleadingly as the man knelt in the dust beside him. There was nothing he could do, the sheik realized, except relieve the animal's suffering. With a bleak look in his eyes, he stood and aimed his pistol at Bryna's fallen protector.

"Bismallah," he whispered sadly, and pulled the trigger. The dog's mighty body jerked once and was still. "Your job is over now. I will find her for you."

While everyone scurried to their tasks, the men had gathered under the tree in the middle of the camp for *majlis.* His head still reeled from the blow he had taken during the battle, and Sharif sadly missed the voice of his oldest friend in council, but he forced himself to concentrate on what was said by those who remained. Quickly the decision was reached. The women and children would go on to Riyadh in the company of armed servants and guards. They should reach the city within three days, even afoot.

The men would go to war. They must, they would, have their vengeance. There was no time to dream dreams or to have them interpreted, but the tribesmen cheered when *ghazzi* was declared.

Personal sorrows were put aside for now. There would be time for mourning when they reached the safety of home. Then they would sacrifice a sheep for each of the dead and lament their loss.

Efficiently the tribesmen assembled the necessary equipment and took stock of the old and infirm camels that were left after the raid. Overtaking the raiders would be difficult on such sorry beasts, but overtake them they would, or the Selims would follow them to their very tents. More cheers were heard and the trilling of the women when Sharif, clad in the unrelieved black of a Bedu warrior, led his men out to follow the tracks of the raiders.

The pursuers slowed at the edge of the Empty Quarter, but they continued determinedly, following the trail. A large raiding party had passed here during the night, they read easily in the tracks. Three of the camels had carried the women as well as their riders.

They continued to ride for several hours before coming to the place where the marauders had split. The tracks told them that most of the raiders had headed off to the west, herding the camels in front of them. The three riders who had abducted the women had put them off the camels there and forced them to walk.

The Selim band set off to follow the camel herd. Sharif went alone to reclaim the women of his household. Some of his men wanted to go with him, stopping just short of mentioning his recent wound, but the proud sheik refused their aid. The missing women were his responsibility, and he would get them back. The raiding party was to retrieve their camels and to capture the enemies' as well.

As his ancient camel loped across the sands, Sharif gained on the fleeing group as long as the women walked. Trying to ignore the traces of blood on the sand where their feet had been cut, he willed silently that they had continued to walk, slowing the pace. At last the sheik reached a place where the sand showed that the heaviest woman had fallen and been dragged a short distance. Then the smallest had staggered and stumbled. The marauders had stopped there, and the women had been taken back on the camels.

Sharif pressed his own camel as much as he dared. Even though her hump was firm and high, so she was not in need of water or grazing yet, she was old and she tired easily. Finally it became necessary for him to stop for the night to rest her. He would never admit, even to himself, that his own head ached so that it was difficult to see and that the bandage on his shoulder was sticky with fresh blood. Wounds healed quickly in the dry heat of the desert, and Sharif was determined to resume his search in the morning.

No more than an hour after sunrise, he arrived

at a point where the footprints became muddled. Tracks obliterated tracks. Some indistinct imprints left by loaded camels led a little ways to the south before they were covered by windblown sand. Newer clearer prints led to the east, but they showed that the women were no longer being carried on the camels' backs.

Sharif had little choice in the empty desert. Only a face-to-face confrontation with his enemies would reveal what he wanted to know. Where were the women?

Following the tracks, he galloped his camel across the sand toward the rising sun. As he topped a dune, Sharif could see a scrubby oasis below. Dismounting rapidly, he ran for cover, hoping he had not been seen. When no gunfire greeted him, he remained at a distance and led his camel around the oasis to the south, a direction from which the raiders would not expect anyone to appear. Then he hobbled the animal with his *aghal,* tying her mouth with her nose rope to keep her quiet. Stealthily he crept to a concealed place where he could observe the oasis.

The two men dozed under a tall *saf,* obviously sated from a meal. The youngest member of the party, a boy, stood guard, leaning against a palm tree. His eyes were turned westward, watching for pursuers. He, too, drowsed in the heat, lifting a lethargic hand occasionally to brush the flies away from his nodding head.

Grimly Sharif drew his sword, breathed a prayer, and leapt into camp with a bloodcurdling shout. He kicked the leg of one of the sleeping Bedu. The groggy man scowled and lurched to his feet. Instantly the scowl turned to a grimace of fear as the man groped at his side for his sword. Before he could utter a cry, Sharif's sword whistled through the air and caught the man in the neck, nearly severing it. A gurgle was the only sound that broke the stillness. The other man was now awake and on his feet. Drawing his sword with an angry bellow, he charged at Sharif.

Their swords clashed against the sky. Helplessly the adolescent sentinel watched as Sharif efficiently dispatched the man with whom he fought, then whirled on him.

The boy backed up a step as Sharif advanced on him menacingly. The sheik's sword was poised for a powerful blow and his gray eyes were two dangerous points of flint when he asked, "What have you done with the women?"

"The old one d-died," the boy stammered, "but the two younger we left in the desert."

"To die as well?" Sharif roared. "Was it not enough you broke the rules of *ghazzi* and raided my camp by night? Now you kill women?"

"We did not kill them, I swear by Allah."

"Do not defile the name of God with your foul mouth. They are as good as dead, abandoned in the Rub al Khali. Where did you leave them?"

"About two hours' ride to the south. But it was not my doing, I swear . . . " His voice trailed off. "Here, I wish to surrender to you." He offered his sword to Sharif.

Sharif hesitated. What the boy requested was within the rules of *ghazzi*. But he thought of the still bodies lined up on the sand outside his tent—Fatmah, Nassar, Sa'id, even the dog that had trailed Bryna's steps.

"It is too late," he said, and brought the sword down. The boy's head rolled across the sand and landed, its surprised eyes looking up at him.

"Blood for blood," the sheik murmured sadly. "A death for a death."

Unwilling to waste time, Sharif dug a single grave and rolled the bodies into it. After covering it with sand, he washed the taint of the dead from his body, then went to fetch the men's camels.

The beasts were rested and in good condition. By rights the men's possessions were now his. He saddled two sturdy-looking beasts for the women. Then he transferred his own saddle to the back of a strong black camel. After readjusting his clothing to ease the ache of his wound, he wrapped his kaffiyeh tightly around his face. Leaving the rest of the dead men's goods at the oasis, he rode south, leading his camels.

For two hours Sharif rode into the heart of the Empty Quarter, keeping an anxious eye on the horizon. The sky to the east was ominously yellow, a sign of an impending sandstorm, and static electricity charged the air. As the wind whipped at his robes, he leaned into it, praying he could reach the women before the storm's full fury howled around them.

At last he spotted them, two distinct spots in

the desert sands under the odd yellow glare of the noonday sun. His eyes, anxious in his veiled face, swept the vacant campsite. Bryna and Pamela lay on a dune near a mound of sand that was obviously Latifeh's grave. When he called out, Bryna sat up sluggishly.

Leaping to the ground before his mount had fully halted, the Arab hurriedly couched the camels in a tight circle, leaving only enough space for the three humans to lie down. Nostrils closed and third eyelids protecting them against the wind-borne sand, the beasts offered the best protection the humans could hope for against the rapidly approaching sandstorm.

Sharif scooped Pamela into his arms and urged Bryna to follow. Dully she obeyed. He laid the women in the middle of the circle of camels, then he lay between their prone bodies and spread his thick cloak over them just as the fury of the sandstorm exploded around them, blocking out the sun.

The wind howled and cutting pieces of sand beat against Sharif's back. Shielded by the oddly uncomplaining camels, the three people huddled for hours, unable to move. Sharif wished he could give each of the women a drink from the water skin lashed to a saddle nearby, but he could not move against the raging wind. He comforted himself that he had reached them before the storm because surely they would have been killed.

When the wind died, Sharif pushed himself up with effort, displacing the heavy sand that had piled on his back. Beneath him Bryna stirred, blinking sand-crusted eyes. He helped her sit up, bracing her back against the flanks of one of the couched camels. When Pamela did not move, Sharif brushed the sand from her face and examined her. One arm cocked beneath her head and the damaged side of her face buried in the sand, the dead girl looked like a peacefully sleeping child.

Silently Bryna took Pamela's head in her lap while Sharif retrieved the water skin. Absently her hand went to the dead girl's hair and stroked it. The movement stopped when Sharif brought water to her. He allowed her to sip, stopping her when she became too greedy. Bryna's grasping hands followed the bag as he drew it away from her mouth.

He tilted Bryna's chin so she looked at him. No glimmer of recognition lit her stunned eyes. "You must eat something if you are also to drink," he told her kindly, handing her some dates.

She accepted them disinterestedly with her free hand, then the stroking motion began again with the other. She ate the dates, staring vacantly, while Sharif dug a grave for the dead girl.

He wrapped Pamela's small limp body in a blanket and laid it in the grave. To his surprise, Bryna did not protest, even when he began to cover it. She sat motionless, staring off into the distance as if still watching for rescuers to appear on the horizon. Kneeling beside Pamela's grave, the man quoted the Fatiha.

Then Sharif went to his wife's grave and knelt for a moment there as well. When he finished, the sheik washed his hands in the sand and returned to

Bryna. Looking at her closely, he noticed for the first time the blood that stained her *thobe*, and his face blanched. He took her hand and drew her up to stand beside him. Murmuring comfortingly, he lifted her *thobe* to reveal her legs. Blood stained either thigh, but none of it was fresh. Praise Allah, she did not seem to be injured. Swaying on her cut, blood-encrusted feet, she stared with vacant blue eyes at the horizon, unblinking despite the scarlet brilliance of the setting sun.

It was evident the girl could not ride alone on the camel he had saddled for her, but Sharif did not wish to stay in this place of the dead. He would take her to the oasis, where the deaths that had occurred were acts of righteous vengeance, not of evil as in this place. The sheik mounted his camel, lifting Bryna in front of him.

Through her thin dress, her body felt stiff and wooden against his. The girl said nothing, did not cry as they rode through the twilight. Finally she dozed, starting and jerking uneasily against his chest.

When they reached the oasis, Sharif dismounted and hobbled the camels near some sparse grazing. Then he carried the sleeping girl to a spot beside the pool. A wave of cold rage washed over him as he looked down at her, cradled in his strong arms.

Bryna's head fell back limply, revealing a faint pulse under the ugly bruise on her temple. Her parted lips were cracked and swollen and crusted with dark blood. A purple bruise ran across her cheekbone and merged with gray smudges under her closed eyes. Her chest rose and fell unevenly as she breathed, the only sign that she lived.

She was burning with fever, Sharif realized. To immerse her in the pool would bring her fever down immediately, but night, so cold in the desert, was approaching, and she would be chilled in damp clothes. Instead he made a pallet for her and stretched her inert body on it. Then, tenderly, he removed her clothing and bathed her with cooling water.

The first swipes with the cloth removed the crusty layer of sand that had filtered into her clothes during the storm. Bryna lay motionless, unaware of his devoted care. The golden locket at the base of her slender throat glinted in the moonlight. Her smooth alabaster body looked as if it were carved from stone, but her skin, hot to the touch, was also soft. Momentarily Sharif wondered what it would be like to love such a woman, cursing softly as his manhood exhibited a life of its own. He must put those thoughts away if he was to tend her.

Gingerly he sponged her body and covered her with a blanket, then he went to unsaddle the camels. It was the first time in his life he had not tended the animals first.

While he gathered firewood, he heard Bryna cry out in a nightmare, and instantly he was back at her side. Tears seeped from her closed eyes, and her breathing was ragged. He allowed her to cling to him in her delirium until her fright had passed, then he built a small fire, cleansed himself in the pool, and prayed his evening prayers. While he ate, chewing slowly and thoughtfully, he watched her as she slept.

During the night, Bryna's fever broke and her blankets were drenched with perspiration. Sharif fetched his own rug for a new pallet and placed her on it, covering her with fresh blankets to keep her warm. Going to the belongings of the men he had killed in battle, he found another rug and a skimpy blanket and lay down on the ground next to the girl.

Despite his own exhaustion and pain, Sharif slept lightly, awakening at the first hint of dawn. When he awakened Bryna, she looked at him blankly. She still did not seem to recognize him, but at least she showed no fear. She seemed simply to have no will of her own. She was like a child as he dressed her. She cooperated, allowing him to brush the tangles from her hair.

He gave her a drink of water, then a piece of bread and some dates. At first she held the food in lax hands on her lap. Sharif tore off a piece of the bread and put it into her mouth. Mechanically she began to chew. Soon she raised the hand containing a date and ate, but she seemed oblivious of the fact that she ate at all. When she had finished, she patiently allowed herself to be led to the camels and pulled up in front of Sharif again.

They rode northward all day, stopping frequently so Bryna could rest. Today her body was not rigid. She nestled against Sharif's chest and slept without fear.

The next day was much like the first, until they

I believe she will survive," the doctor assured
"She is a strong young woman. But, Sharif, she
never be the same again."

'Was she driven mad?" the sheik asked fearfully.
'I do not believe so. But some things are as bad
madness. She may never have children. Only
h can say."

"I do not care," he said, putting behind him
rs of training. Moslems were taught to desire
dren over all things. "You must help her. I love
"

"That is as I feared," Faisal said gently. "What
you do, Sharif? Marry her, knowing what you
w?"

"Yes, if you do not give me away."

"I will say nothing to anyone, old friend. I am a
ilized man. I understand the heart and its way-
rdness. These Bedu and their superstitions are
metimes enough to make me long to return to
rsia. But are you sure about this?"

A wave of relief washed over Sharif's angular
e. "If you will guard my secret, I will nurse
na. Then, when she is well again, I will win her. I
nt nothing more than her love, Faisal," he said
ply. "She will be my wife."

"As Allah wills it," the other man agreed reluc-
tly. The physician prescribed rest to mend
na's wounded body and mind. Then he gave her
aft to make her sleep, intoning, "Praise be to
h, the Curer, the Healer," as he held the cup to
ips.

'She will awaken when her body is ready," he

reached the edge of the Rub al Khali in the evening
and Sharif began to see familiar landmarks.

During the ride to Riyadh, he worried constantly whether Bryna would ever be well again. What
had her captors done to her? She did not seem to
care whether she lived or died.

The man's arms tightened around her as they
rode. He cared, and because he cared, Bryna would
live. She must. Because, Sharif admitted to himself
at last, he loved her. He loved her as he had never
loved another.

Sharif rode wearily through the fertile irrigated
plain that surrounded Riyadh to the monotonous
drone of water pumps, arriving in the city mere
hours after his men returned from their successful
raid. The Selims had ridden into the sheik's huge
city compound, singing a victory song and driving
their herds, plus a dozen more camels, before
them. Then the warriors had awaited their leader's
arrival as anxiously as the women and children. The
women trilled and the men cheered when Sharif's
camel trotted through the arched gate.

The sheik was touched by their jubilation, but
Bryna, slumped in front of him in the saddle, did
not seem aware of the din that went on around her.
Dismounting, Sharif answered the questions with
which his people bombarded him.

"Where is Latifeh and the Inglayzi?" a man
called to him.

"Dead," he grunted, striding purposefully
toward the women's quarters with Bryna in his
arms. "But do not fear," he called over his shoulder.

"Their deaths have been avenged."

"Praise Allah, blood for blood," the fervent shout went up.

"What did those sons of dogs do to this poor girl?" someone else demanded.

"Yes, was she touched by those swine?"

"No," Sharif shouted, swinging around in the doorway to the harem to face his people. With the girl held protectively in his arms, his bearing was proud, almost challenging. "I reached Bryna bint Blaine before they could harm her. Now she is home where she belongs, and no one will harm her again."

Then the sheik closed the door on the celebration and took his love upstairs to await the hakim.

CHAPTER

✧✧✧✧✧ 18 ✧✧

SHARIF SAT BESIDE BRYNA'S BED W slept, peacefully now, although she ofte restlessly in the throes of a nightmare.

Alhamdillah! how blessed he wa found her alive, the man thought gratefu not know what had occurred in the deser grant that her mind should be untouch evil she had seen. Faisal, his hakim, s think there was hope.

Somberly the sheik remembered interview with his old friend a few days be

"You told the others this girl was not Sharif," Faisal had begun hesitantly, "but .

"But I lied," Sharif stated flatly. "I did whether they had harmed her, but I fea so."

"I cannot tell. She does not seem to treated roughly, but she is not a virgin. so stricken, my friend. It is not unu women who have dwelt in the desert life."

"Will . . . will she be all right?"

told the sheik. "But, as for her mind, I do not know."

Before he departed, the hakim removed the girl's locket and handed it to the sheik. "Keep this for her. It would be a shame if our patient strangled herself with it in her sleep."

Pausing awkwardly at the door, the doctor addressed his friend uncertainly, "Sharif, this girl bears more than a passing resemblance to Noorah . . ."

"You have seen her only when she is sleeping. When she is awake she shows a spirit my gentle Noorah never had. I do not seek another to replace my first wife. I love Bryna for herself."

"You cannot blame me for my concern," Faisal said seriously. "This woman must mean a great deal to you indeed, for you to love her so." Then the hakim left quietly, closing the door behind him.

For me to love her more than honor, Sharif thought grimly, for that was what his old friend had meant. Faisal was right, but how could he explain, even to him, the depth of his love for Bryna?

Following his return to Riyadh, Sharif had gone about his business distractedly. The very night of his arrival, he had ordered two of his favorite camels to be slaughtered in honor of his dead wives and the meat to be given to the poor. He had greeted the friends and relatives who called the next day. He had arranged funerals for his family and visited the father of Farida, Nassar's intended, to offer his sympathy. He had performed his duties as the sheik, dividing the booty of the raid equitably among his tribe. In general the sheik had acted as he always did, but all the time his mind was on the girl sleeping in the harem.

Every possible moment he spent at Bryna's bedside, causing more than a few eyebrows to be raised. Mautlauq muttered to others, spreading the rumor that the sheik was going to be called before the emir himself to account for his actions.

If only she would awaken, Sharif thought now, even dissension among his tribesmen would seem worthwhile. Last rays of daylight slanted into the airy room and washed across the man's outstretched legs while he sat beside her bed, brooding, his chin resting against his chest. Suddenly he sat erect when the girl stirred and blinked her eyes.

She lay very still. Where was she? The room did not seem familiar. How had she gotten here? A perplexed frown furrowed her brow, then she felt another presence in the room. The girl turned a groggy gaze toward a man sitting beside her bed. Under his snowy kaffiyeh, his handsome face was weary but alight with elation.

"Praise Allah," he said exultantly. "*Farha*, my joy." Carefully lifting the girl's head from the pillow with one hand, he held a water cup to her lips with the other. She placed shaky hands around his and drank eagerly, then turned curious eyes to the man who bent over her.

"Where am I?" she whispered hoarsely.

Slowly he laid her back against the pillows and stared down at her disbelievingly. He had not expected her to ask the question in Arabic.

After a moment he answered deliberately in his

own tongue, "You are in my home in Riyadh."

"Riyadh," Bryna repeated. Her dull eyes scanned the ceiling as if she hoped to find an answer there. There was a long silence as she digested the information, trying to collect her thoughts. Then, with effort, she asked him, "Please, effendi, who are you?"

"I am Sharif. Don't you remember me?" he asked, his voice tight with misery.

Her sleepy eyes searched his craggy countenance for a hint of his identity. At last she sighed. "No, I am sorry, I cannot remember. I wish I did. Perhaps it will come back to me later, but for now, would you tell me?"

"I am Sharif Al Selim, the uncle of the man you were to wed. Do you remember that?"

She shook her head.

"Our *smala* was on its way to Riyadh when we were attacked by raiders and Nassar was killed."

"Nassar? The man I was to marry?" she queried hopefully.

"Yes," he responded, feeling a stab of pain. Could it be that she remembered Nassar but had forgotten him?

"He is dead?"

He nodded expressionlessly.

For some unknown reason, she felt no sorrow. Bryna examined the situation as best she could, but she did not understand why she felt nothing, not even a sense of loss.

"Did I love him?"

"I do not know." The man was unwilling to put

thoughts in her head or words in her mouth.

"I do not, either," she whispered. Her eyelids were growing heavy. "Can you tell me one other thing? You called me Farha—is that my name?"

"You are my *farha*, my joy," he murmured, stroking her hand, "as precious and rare as rain in the desert."

But she did not hear him. She was already asleep.

Sharif sat on the bed beside her, holding her hand until the call to prayer at sunset, agonizing over what he should do. It seemed Bryna had no memory before awakening in his home. She did not remember those horrible days in the Rub al Khali. She had forgotten her earlier life in America. She did not even know she had been a slave.

She must never recall those terrible things, he resolved. She would have a new life. She would be happy in Arabia, he vowed. He would make it so.

Resolutely he opened the cupboard beside her narrow divan and thrust his hand inside. He froze guiltily when she stirred in her sleep but did not awaken. Then he withdrew what he sought, the locket she had worn, her only link with the past.

Opening it, he stared down at the tiny portraits it contained—her parents, no doubt. He could see Bryna's gentleness in the woman's serene face and her spirit in the man's. What a marriage it must have been to produce his beloved, a marriage such as they would have one day.

Secreting the locket in the front of his robe, Sharif went to pray and then to find his daughter.

"She doesn't remember anything?" `Abla asked worriedly. "Not even being rescued by you?"

"No, but it is just as well."

The little girl did not agree, for the romance of the situation appealed to her. She put aside her disappointment, however, to ask, "But she was not as she was when you brought her home, was she, as if an evil jinni had stolen her spirit?"

"No, daughter," the sheik responded with a smile.

"But she does not remember me." She nearly wept. "I am her friend. Doesn't she even recall that I taught her to speak our language and she helped me with my French?"

"No, but that, too, is just as well, for all she spoke this afternoon was our tongue. She seems not to remember her old language. With her past forgotten, perhaps she can be happy here with us."

"I hope so." `Abla threw her arms impetuously around her father's neck. "I want her to be so happy that she will not leave us, even if her father does come for her, don't you?"

"Her father seeks her?"

"Perhaps not. Bryna feared he would never find her," `Abla explained earnestly, "and it made her very sad."

"She shall be sad no longer. She has us now."

"I will be good for her, *Abu.* I will not say anything or do anything to remind her of her old life. I love her and want her to stay here. You do, too, don't you?" She looked at the man shrewdly, wise beyond her years.

"Yes, `Abla, very much," he admitted. "But that

must be our secret for a time."

"All right," the girl agreed at once, delighted to share a secret with her adored father. "Now, how can we keep her from remembering?" Immediately she set about hatching a plan.

"We will not keep her from remembering, `Abla," Sharif commanded gently. "But we will not bring up memories, either, good or bad. We will speak only of today and tomorrow, and we will speak only in Arabic. I must warn you, `Abla, she will surely ask questions, and you must not lie to her, for that would be cruel."

"But what if she remembers?"

"Insh'allah."

"Oh, all right." `Abla sighed. Although she did not like the order, she would obey. "But I do have a suggestion." She brightened suddenly.

"Yes?"

"Since Bryna thinks her name is Farha, can we keep calling her that? It is such a lovely name."

"Joy is a good name for her, indeed, daughter. We will call her that. Now run along to bed."

He watched as the child raced out exuberantly, a troubled frown on his face. It was written, "Confound not truth with falsehood, nor knowingly conceal the truth." But Sharif realized he was prepared to do both to keep Bryna by his side.

"Good morning, Farha, peace be unto you," `Abla exclaimed when Bryna awoke. The little girl stood next to the bed, grinning. Her delighted smile was snaggletoothed as new teeth grew to replace the ones she had lost.

"And unto you be peace," Bryna greeted the gray-eyed urchin uncertainly.

"Look, I have brought breakfast for you," the child said, gesturing to a tray on the nearby table. "You do not remember me, do you? *Abu* said you might not. It is all right. I am your friend, `Abla bint Sharif. Can you remember nothing?"

"Nothing. What happened to me?"

"You were injured when raiders attacked our camp in the desert."

"How did I get here?" Bryna asked, sitting up weakly.

"My father brought you. He saved your life." `Abla plumped the pillow efficiently and arranged the rumpled bedclothes.

"Your father? Sharif?" The injured girl groped for the name.

"That's right."

"The sheik," Bryna continued tentatively. An image of Sharif astride a rearing white horse flickered across her mind. "The Sheik Al Selim . . ."

"Yes, yes!" `Abla cried happily. "You remember my father! Do you remember coming home?"

"No . . . Is this my home?" Bryna frowned distractedly, looking around the unfamiliar room. It was pleasant and spacious, but she did not recall it.

"Of course. Never mind, Farha," `Abla comforted her. "You will be better soon. Do you want me to feed you? Your hands are shaking."

"No, thank you. I can feed myself." Bryna stumbled over the words. She did not know which took more effort, spooning the warm liquid to her mouth or concentrating on understanding what the talkative little girl said as she sat beside the bed. At times Bryna's mind wandered, mulling over what she already knew.

Her name was Farha. She had been the intended of Sheik Sharif Al Selim's nephew. But Nassar had been killed and she had been brought here. The little girl—`Abla—said this was her home. But where was her family? Did she have none? Was that why she had been brought to live in Sharif's house? Why was speech so difficult for her? Had she forgotten part of her vocabulary when she lost her memory, or was the language she spoke not her own? Why couldn't she remember?

She pushed the bowl of broth away wearily. Immediately `Abla summoned a serving girl and Bryna's body was sponged with scented water. Then her hair was brushed and braided and she was dressed in a new gown. She tolerated the coddling, knowing there was little she could do about it until she recovered her strength.

"You look better. Do you feel better?" `Abla said enthusiastically.

"Yes," Bryna admitted. "If I trusted my legs to carry me, I would go outside." She gazed toward the window. "It would be good to be outside on a day like today."

"You have only to ask," Sharif informed her indulgently. The sheik stood easily in the doorway, his shoulder against the sill. Below the turban he wore this morning, his bronzed face looked younger than his years and carefree. He laughed lightheartedly from pure happiness when he saw Bryna looking so improved.

"On this first day of your recovery, Farha, your wish is my command," he teased, striding into the room.

"I think I can walk," Bryna protested when he scooped her up from the bed.

"And I think perhaps you are not as strong yet as you think you are," he retorted good-naturedly. With `Abla dancing behind them, he carried Bryna into the warm, sun-dappled harem garden, where he deposited her on a bench in the shade. "How is this?"

"Wonderful," Bryna said delightedly. *"Merci."*

A shadow crossed the sheik's face, but the girl did not even seem to notice the French word that had crept into her conversation. After a breathless instant, he answered courteously in Arabic, "It is my pleasure, Farha. How do you feel this morning?"

He relaxed when she replied shyly in Arabic, "I am much better. I . . . I understand I owe you my life, my sheik. I—"

"Do not speak of your ordeal," he interrupted her. Sitting down beside her, he took her hand in his. "Let us talk of how lovely you are now that you are feeling better and how quickly you will heal under the care of Faisal, my hakim."

"And me," `Abla chimed in. "I am your nurse."

"And you." Sharif chuckled, ruffling the little girl's black hair. "You've been a good nurse, `Abla."

The child said nothing but reddened at her father's unexpected praise.

"Sit here for a while and rest, Farha," Sharif commanded tenderly, preparing to leave. "When you are ready to go inside, `Abla will summon a eunuch. I must go now. Allah grant you a speedy recovery."

Bryna sat with the little girl in the pleasant walled garden throughout the morning. After lunch an elegant-looking man appeared in the doorway to the house.

"Greetings, `Abla," he called to the girl, who ran gladly to meet him. "Good afternoon. May there be upon you nothing but health, if Allah wills, my lady Farha." Faisal frowned worriedly toward the woman on the bench. He had received his instructions from Sharif, but he did not like this, keeping the foreign woman in isolation, giving her a new name to go with a new life.

"Perhaps you do not recognize me," the doctor said smoothly when Bryna stared at him blankly. "Although I was here on the day of your arrival in Riyadh, we have never really met. I am Faisal bin Seif, personal hakim to Sayyid . . . "

Bryna watched the man intently, but in her mind his face was replaced by another, more grizzled visage, and another voice in her head overrode his, saying, "I am Halef, personal hakim to Hajji Suleiman Ibn Hussein."

`Abla cried out in alarm as the girl paled and swayed on her seat, crumbling suddenly in a faint.

Faisal leapt forward immediately to prevent a

fall. With `Abla on his heels, he carried the girl inside and laid her on her bed.

Bryna's eyes fluttered open. "Halef?" she whispered.

"No, Faisal, my lady," the doctor assured her softly, careful because he felt she must be experiencing an unexpected jolt of memory.

She looked up at him sharply. "Who is Hajji Suleiman Ibn Hussein?"

"I do not know, my lady. I have never heard of such a man," the hakim assured her truthfully. "Perhaps he is someone you knew before your, er, accident. Do not strain yourself overmuch. Perhaps it will come back to you someday."

"You can tell me nothing?"

"Nothing." He shook his head sadly.

"Did you know me before yesterday, Hakim?"

"No."

"Is this really my home?" she asked challengingly.

Behind him he heard `Abla's faint gasp of alarm, and he answered carefully, "Sheik Al Selim says that it is, my lady."

"I cannot remember. I know only what others tell me," Bryna said sadly.

"Do not dwell too much upon it, Farha. You are still to ill to think clearly. Now look what I have brought you—al-Birni dates!" Jovially the doctor changed the subject. "Eat them and grow stronger by the day. It is written, 'They causeth sickness to depart and there is no sickness in them.'"

"Mashallah." The invalid smiled, taking the bag

from him and tasting one politely. "'Abla, would you take these to the kitchen?" she requested. "And keep one for yourself."

When the little girl skipped off happily toward the kitchen, Bryna turned to the doctor, her blue eyes clouded with worry. "Will I ever remember, hakim?"

"I do not know," he answered honestly. "But, please, just try to enjoy today. *Insh'allah.* Do not worry about yesterday."

But try as she would, Bryna could not follow Faisal's advice. By day she was plagued with doubts, wisps of vague memory that came at odd moments. At night she was troubled by disturbing dreams, not all of them nightmares.

One dream recurred again and again. In it, a slender, handsome young man, dressed in foreign clothing, held her in his arms. His desire showed in his hazel eyes, and as he bent to kiss her he murmured words she could not hear. She knew he was about to say her name, and she strained to listen, but before he could speak it, she always awoke.

Night after night she lay on her narrow divan and fruitlessly dredged her faulty memory. Who was he, this man who caressed her in her dreams? Had she loved him? When she awoke from the dream, she always felt a devastating sense of loss. But she could not cry.

Others peopled her dreams as well. A big man with dark hair and eyes that were blue like her own. An old woman in a black cloak and a strange black *ghata,* but she wore no *burqu,* no veil, and her skin was so white. Leering Bedu faces sometimes loomed over her, causing her to awaken in a cold sweat. And she saw a girl who was as fair as a houri with golden hair. They were familiar, yet unfamiliar, all of them. Who could they be?

The question would drive her mad if she was not already insane, she thought gloomily. At last, casting about for an answer, Bryna asked the unwilling `Abla about Nassar.

"It is not kind to speak ill of the dead," `Abla said darkly, "but I thank Allah that neither of us has to marry him."

Bryna understood that `Abla had been Nassar's *bint 'amm.* The little girl had known him well. But it was not Nassar's character that concerned Bryna. It was his physical appearance.

"Well, he did not look like our side of the family."

Bryna felt a moment of dread. The man in her dream looked nothing like the Selims.

"Nassar had dark hair and dark eyes, not gray like ours. Actually, to be fair, he was rather handsome, though he was soft and womanish."

Bryna felt a rush of relief. Nassar was not the man in her dream. She knew instinctively that she had never loved him. Had she loved the man in her dreams?

"If you do not mind, I would rather not talk about him anymore, Farha," `Abla was saying politely. "It is not good to think of the dead too much."

"As you wish," Bryna agreed at once, but she was disappointed that she could not question the child more.

The convalescing woman's waking hours were filled with activities with `Abla and Sharif. Other than Faisal, they were her only visitors, but Bryna was content. Only at night did she feel lonely, lost, and confused. She always managed to forget the unsettling dreams for a time when the sheik appeared in the harem. He was a charming companion, solicitous and kind. He told stories, brought from the Ottoman court, of Scheherazade and always managed to win a smile from Bryna. The time they spent together was pleasant, but she sensed the man was constantly on guard, constantly watching her.

She tried in vain to ignore the attraction between them. He seemed to feel something for her as well. It was all so confusing. Had she not been betrothed to his nephew? Why did her heart seem to beat faster when he appeared?

Because, the girl realized with astonishment one day, somehow she knew how it felt to be held against his rugged, muscular body. And sometimes when Sharif bent over her, the corner of his kaffiyeh dipping between them, she had sudden flashes of vision of him without his headdress. His dark hair reached his shoulders, and he was clad only in a robe. She thought she remembered a scar that marked his naked chest. Had she seen him thus? Or was it another half-remembered dream?

Surely she had not dreamed the warm, tender pressure of his mouth against hers. Sometimes, drawn as if she had no will of her own, Bryna would find herself watching him, her gaze coming to rest on his smiling lips. Then intense, unbidden desire would leave her pale and disturbed, fighting to capture an elusive memory.

When this happened, the man had no idea what caused Bryna's turmoil. He knew only that at times his beloved seemed to shrink into herself before his very eyes, leaving him desolate and alone.

After a time she began to show marked improvement, and Sharif was delighted. Color returned to her cheeks, and she protested the pampering she was receiving with a spirit the man remembered and loved. Her eyes did not seem so haunted, and she smiled more easily. How his heart soared when that smile was directed at him.

Sharif was a man in love, but he wrestled daily with his conscience. His feelings for Bryna and his behavior toward her were apart from everything he had ever been taught. Born into royalty and privilege, a leader among his people, he had a strong sense of right and wrong. Since manhood Sharif had always had what he wanted. Now he wanted Bryna, right or wrong. And he was willing to wait until she wanted him in return.

In the meantime he did what he could to make sure she was prepared for marriage. After her recovery, her lessons in Islam resumed. Bryna assumed she had forgotten what she knew and had to relearn it. Sharif hated deception but allowed her to think that was the case. He spent a great deal of time with her, discussing the Koran, delighted to find she was as willing to debate the law as a man.

Still, Bryna felt something was missing. There was more to the blank that was her previous life than Sharif told her. He answered every question carefully. Perhaps he could not tell her more. He maintained that his acquaintance with her had begun less than a year ago. He could not tell her what she wished to know about her past. How would she ever rid herself of the questions and continue with her life? Bryna tried not to surrender to despondency, but over time her confusion changed to depression.

One night while she slept, her dreams took her to a lush green oasis. The wind, cool and laden with the promise of rain, whipped at her clothes and lifted her unbound hair. But she did not feel the chill. She felt only the rising heat of desire as Sharif stood before her.

His gray eyes were intense, mesmerizing, as he leaned toward her, his lips descending slowly to claim hers. His hand caressed her cheek. It was too beautiful to be real, she thought. The thrill of longing as she swayed against his hard, muscular body was enough to wake her from her sound sleep.

Bryna lay on her divan, disoriented and drowsy, listening for the wail of the rising wind. In a half-waking state, she lifted her face for Sharif's kiss. But he was gone.

Her blue eyes opened abruptly. She was alone in her room, and her heart was pounding. Sharif, his kiss, the intense longing she had felt—it had all been a dream. Or had it? Why did she feel so drained, so empty? Why could she not remember?

The distraught girl buried her face in a pillow. Unable to cope with the emptiness she felt, she wept at last.

She did not hear when Sharif entered her room. He looked in on her every night, content to watch her as she slept. But tonight he was dismayed to hear her sobs. He perched on the edge of the divan and placed a gentle hand on her shoulder.

"Farha, why do you weep?"

"I don't know." Her voice was muffled. "Perhaps because I am so confused. I don't know who I am or where I came from or where I belong."

"You belong here," he answered softly.

"Do I?" She rolled so he could see her tearstained face clearly. Her gaze was defiant.

"Of course you do." He pulled her into a seated position, then placed his hands on her shoulders. "Listen to me. Although you do not remember, I told you once before, you must not worry about your old life. It will only make you sad. What will be, will be."

"I do remember, Sharif. *Insh'allah.*" Bryna's eyes widened with recognition at the snippet of familiar conversation, the tender weight of his hands upon her shoulders. She could almost feel the rush of the wind as it had swept them that day at the oasis and again in her dream. "It was real! I remember!"

"You . . . you remember all?" Sharif's voice was fearful.

"Not all. But I remember the oasis. Can it be Allah's will that you love me as you do?" she whispered wonderingly.

"Above all things," he replied, his voice thick with passion and relief. His gray eyes blazed with desire, and with a groan he pulled her to him and sought her lips. Bryna returned his kiss eagerly, thinking of nothing more than the hunger that only Sharif could satisfy.

She murmured urgently and opened her eyes when the man's lips left hers. Standing beside the bed, he removed his kaffiyeh. His long hair looked just as she remembered. Then he removed his clothing and stood naked before her. Ordinarily a modest man, as Muhammad decreed, tonight Sharif gloried in his body. He could tell that Bryna found him pleasing to look upon.

Broad shoulders tapered into a flat torso. An old scar etched his chest, and a new one, pink and puckered, marred his shoulder. His legs were muscular, made powerful by years of riding. She examined him with fascinated eyes, making no protest when he removed her gown.

He stood over her a moment, admiring her body, white in the moonlight. Then he eased her back on the bed and lay down beside her. His strong hands were gentle and questing, his mouth tender yet demanding. Instinctively the girl returned his caresses, offering herself gladly. She felt no shame, but rather wonder at the sensations he aroused in her. Lovingly they joined, soaring together until both shuddered simultaneously in release and Sharif collapsed beside Bryna.

She tenderly brushed his hair back from his

damp forehead. "Why did you not tell me before that you loved me, my lord?"

"Because my love for you was wrong while Nassar lived."

"Is it wrong now that he is dead?"

"It would make no difference." His possessive arms tightened around her. "I would have you for my wife."

"I cannot marry you, Sharif," she refused gently. "Not while I have so many unanswered questions."

"You do not love me?" The powerful sheik felt vulnerable. How could she refuse marriage after what they had just shared? This woman would drive him mad with longing.

"I . . . I do not know. You have been good and kind to me."

"I do not want your thanks," he said harshly, sitting up on the edge of the bed, his back to her.

"No, my lord." She laid her hand on his bare shoulder, feeling his muscles quiver in response to her delicate touch. "I know, you want a wife, a wife who would be honest with her husband. Then I tell you this, I believe I could learn to love you. I know I desire you. And I know that is wrong. Do you think me a terrible person?"

"No, Farha, I desire you, too." His answer seemed to drift to her on the night air. "But I love you, more than you know."

"I care for you, Sharif. It's only that I am still so lost and confused. All I ask is some time before I answer."

"I will give you time, but understand, it is not your gratitude I want. It is your love." Rising stiffly, he turned to gaze down at her. She could not see his shadowed face, but Bryna ached at the pain in his voice.

The man left the room, shaken to the core. What he had just done was against his very upbringing, yet it had been so right. Could it be that forbidden fruit was always sweeter? Forbidden or not, now that he had tasted Bryna's love, Sharif was more determined than ever to have her for his own.

CHAPTER

✦✦✦✦ **19** ✦✦✦✦✦

"THANK GOD YOUR HEALTH IS RETURNING, MY lady. You look fair indeed today," Bryna's maid pronounced, standing on tiptoe to put the final touches on her mistress's coiffure.

"You are kind, Wardha," the girl murmured as the little woman bustled around her, her dark eyes bright with pride. The maid had been with her only short time but already she was devoted to her young mistress.

"And you are modest," Wardha countered. "Look thou hither."

Obediently Bryna turned on her stool to look into the mirror, smiling when she saw her reflection. She felt better than she had for months, and her face reflected the vibrant glow. Her cheeks and lips were naturally pink, and under her sapphire *ghata* her hair was glossy and dark. Lined with kohl, her blue eyes were clear and sparkling.

"Will you wear the golden earrings today?" The maid held them out expectantly.

Fingering Sharif's gift lovingly, Bryna nodded. How good he was to her. There had been many gifts—dresses of fine Halaili silk, attar of roses, oil of absinthium for her hair, a diamond ring to protect her from possession by evil spirits. Although there had been no repeat of that passionate night a month ago, Bryna was secure in his love.

"Mashallah," Wardha exclaimed over her handiwork. "But sit there one moment more." She began to rummage among the vials and jars that held Bryna's cosmetics.

Behind the women a door opened, and a streak of brown fur shot into the room, followed closely by `Abla, her robes flowing out behind her as she ran.

"Allah protect me from the devil," Wardha shrieked in genuine fright. Dropping a jar of powder onto the floor with a clatter, the diminutive maid jumped back, knocking over vials and upsetting a jar of powdered malachite so an that iridescent green cloud hung over the dressing table.

Gasping with surprise, Bryna found her arms suddenly filled with squirming, jubilant saluki. His tail wagging ecstatically, the dog licked her face with joyful affection.

"Oh, no," `Abla groaned, surveying the havoc the dog had created in a matter of seconds, "I didn't know he would do all this. I just thought he would be glad to see you." She hurried to Bryna and tried to pull the dog from her lap.

"And I am glad to see him." Bryna chuckled, maintaining a hold on the wiggling animal as she scratched behind his ears.

"What is all the noise?" Sharif appeared in the

doorway, the curious frown on his handsome face becoming forbidding when he saw the disorder in Bryna's room. "Wallahi, what happened here?"

"It's my fault, *Abu*," `Abla confessed, hanging her head. "Even though you never allow the dog in the house, I brought him into the harem, thinking he could keep Farha company while I am away, visiting Umm Sâlih. It has been so long since she has seen him and I did not want her to be lonely."

"I would not let her be lonely," the man responded to his daughter. His eyes rested lovingly on Bryna, his irritation forgotten.

She was bent over the dog, scratching his belly. The saluki sprawled on his back on the floor, his tongue lolling rapturously and one back leg pumping wildly.

"He knows me." The girl beamed at Sharif. "And he likes me."

"Of course he likes you. Who else had a treat for him every time she saw him? Who nearly ruined him as a hunting dog?" the man teased.

"I did? He is your dog?"

"I am not so sure anymore."

"What is his name?"

"He has no name." He blinked in astonishment at her question.

"Don't you name your dogs here?" A surprised look flitted across the girl's face. She had spoken without thinking. What had she meant by that?

"Judging by the state of this room, I would call him Sheytàn," Sharif answered, keeping his voice deliberately light. "He certainly seems one of life's torments. What would you call him?"

"Rih!" Entranced by the idea of naming the dog, `Abla piped excitedly before Bryna could answer, "Let us call him Rih, the wind, because he runs as fast as the wind."

"Excellent. Rih," Bryna approved. Then she looked up at the man questioningly. "If it is all right, Sharif?"

"I could deny you nothing, Farha," he replied with a smile. "But do not expect him to answer when you call. You would have as much success summoning the wind itself.

"Hurry and help Wardha clean that mess, `Abla, if we are to go to the souk," he urged.

Poised with a broom in her hand, the maid watched with approval as the man led Bryna to the garden to wait. If the sheik did not take her lady as wife, surely she would at least become his favorite concubine, she thought hopefully, bending to her task.

The saluki bounded in circles around them as the couple walked in the garden Bryna had come to love in the past few months. When they sat on the bench, the dog settled himself contentedly at her feet.

"Should you not sit in your *majlis* today, Sharif, instead of going with me to the market?" she asked. "Do not misunderstand me, my lord," she added soothingly when his face clouded. "I love your company more than anyone's, but you do not belong to me alone. Your people need their leader."

"What you say is true. By Allah, you are as wise

as you are beautiful," he said, delighted by the perceptiveness that would make her a good wife to a sheik. "I will sit in the *majlis* this morning and take you to the souk in the afternoon."

"Abla, Wardha, and I could go alone," she suggested daringly.

"Farha . . . " He frowned disapprovingly.

"I have seen other women at the market, accompanied only by a servant."

"Other women have not been stolen from the ones who love them."

"That was in the desert, my sheik. What could happen in the city?"

"I don't know, but let us not tempt fate," he muttered uncharacteristically, and stalked back into the house.

Not long afterward Kedar was working at the edge of the stable yard when he saw Sharif accompany the females of his household to the litters that waited near the back door. The big slave's sharp eyes immediately picked Bryna among the cloaked figures, and when she glanced his direction he beamed and bowed deeply, happy to see the kind lady with his just and fair master.

"That man there . . . do I know him?" she asked Sharif.

"You must have been kind to him. He is not one who forgets such things."

"He looked for a moment as if he would speak to me, but he did not." Her tone was disappointed.

"He cannot speak. He is a mute, Farha."

"But he hears?" At his nod, she asked hopefully,

"Is his name Smemi? I seem to remember that name."

"No, his name is Kedar."

"That is fitting. Was he always with your *smala?*"

"No, I bought him in—"

"In *Kasr* al Haroun," Bryna finished for him with satisfaction, but then her triumphant smile faded. "I remember! Well, I remember the name. Now if only I could recall the place."

"Perhaps you will someday," Sharif said, nearly weak with relief that she had not.

"I know I will," she said seriously. Then she laughed as she nearly tripped over the saluki. "No, Rih, you cannot go. Hold him, Sharif, or he will race us to the market."

Kneeling beside the high-strung, whining dog, Sharif watched until the women's litters disappeared around the corner, escorted by six men at arms. Already he wished he had not allowed Bryna to change his mind.

"Perhaps Sharif loves this woman," Daoud bin Hatim suggested reasonably. He and ten or twelve other men were ranged on the divans of the sheik's *majlis,* awaiting his arrival.

"By Allah, Daoud speaks of love." One of the men snorted. "You have not been married long enough to know the sun does not rise and set in the harem, cousin."

The young man's face reddened, but before he

could retort, his grandfather spoke. "We must remember she belonged to the sheik's nephew and there is no one else to protect her. It is honorable that Sharif has taken the woman into his harem."

"It would be honorable if the infidel had been Nassar's wife, but she was his slave," Mautlauq asserted vehemently. "She is an unmarried woman living in the harem of our chief."

"Perhaps he will take her in marriage," Daoud suggested.

"Perhaps he waits only for her health to return," offered Sâlih.

"Or her memory," said another tribesman.

"More likely she has bewitched him with her blue eyes," Mautlauq grumbled, turning with a start when Sharif spoke from the doorway.

"I will admit I have spent much time recently away from my council, but I assure you I have not been bewitched." The sheik strode into the room and positioned himself in front of his detractor, his arms crossed on his chest.

Mautlauq refused to meet his eyes, but he muttered piously, "It is not mine to say yea or nay if you take the kaffir for a concubine. Only God can determine right or wrong."

"Yet you have judged that is wrong for this woman to dwell in my house, have you not? Would you have me cast her out into the streets?"

"Better that than to blacken our face," the man answered with a challenging note in his voice.

"I tell you there is nothing about the lady Farha that would dishonor our tribe. Have you some proof of wrongdoing?" Sharif's steely gaze caught Mautlauq's and would not release it.

"Is it not enough she is a kaffir?" he mumbled.

"Is this what you think also, Abu Hatim? Or you, Ibn Mahdi?" Sharif's gray eyes swept the bearded faces in the room.

For a long, uncomfortable moment there was silence, then a debate followed, long and loud. Taking the seat of honor, the sheik listened to what each of the elders had to contribute to the discussion, struggling to maintain self-control when Mautlauq derisively described his "fascination" with the foreign woman. If they had been simple Bedu in the desert, he might have killed Mautlauq, but Sharif was the chief of a mighty tribe and would lose face.

At last the sheik rose and began to pace, raising his hand for silence. "I have led you for twelve years, through good times and bad. We have spoken many times in council, and we have always been truthful one with each other. I will be truthful now. As soon as this woman makes her *shahada,* I intend, *Insh'allah,* to make her my wife. Whether you wish to keep me as your chief under these circumstances, only you can say. I leave it to you."

Now that it was necessary to make a choice, the men seemed to feel no more need for debate. One by one they came forward to give their *bay'ah* to Sharif until only Mautlauq was left sitting. Grudgingly he too rose and offered his sword to his sheik, and a cheer rang out in the room. Sharif was still the leader of the Selim tribe.

"My lord"— Daoud leaned to speak confidentially in Sharif's ear as the other men were leaving— "my wife would petition you if you will permit it."

"Bring her tomorrow."

"May your day be prosperous, my lord," the veiled woman greeted him. She offered her hand, wrapped in her cloak, to shake.

"May your day be prosperous and blessed, Taman bint Sa'id," Sharif returned the greeting. "Your husband has said you wish to ask me something."

"Yes, my sheik, may I see Bryna bint Blaine? I have worried so about her."

"You know she has lost her memory?" the man asked cautiously.

"'Abla told me," Taman confirmed. "And she told me Bryna is happy in your home, except . . . "

"Except what?"

"Except perhaps she misses feminine companionship," Taman blurted, trying not to notice his fierce scowl. "I like Bryna and I would like to be her friend still."

Consideringly, Sharif began to pace. Perhaps if Bryna had a friend, a female friend, it would help chase away the sadness that still shadowed her eyes. When they were married, she must again be a part of the tribe, he reasoned. A sheik's wife must not be isolated from the other women.

But Sharif did not want the girl to meet everyone at one time. The very thought terrified him. Who could say which face among many would jog her memory?

Those fleeting glimpses of her past seemed to cause Bryna such pain. He must spare her. Perhaps, beginning with Taman, the Selim relatives could be reintroduced to Bryna slowly. With time, those who still disapproved of the foreigner could be won over. With time, she would adapt and come to accept her new position in life.

"You may see her," he told Taman, "but you must abide by my rules."

"I agree," she said with a nod when he had finished. "Bryna . . . Farha's place is with us. I will say nothing to remind her of her life before she came to us."

"Then I will summon Abu Ahmad to take you to the harem."

Bryna was playing with Rih in the garden when the old servant appeared at the door.

"There is someone to see you, my lady Farha," he announced respectfully. He had tried so hard to dislike her when she first came to the house in Riyadh, but the young mistress had won him over without even trying, as she had won everyone in Sharif's city household.

"Someone to see me?" Bryna rose, mystified. She held the saluki to keep it from jumping on the new arrival when she stepped out into the garden.

"Farha?" the strange woman said tentatively, her pleasant face uncertain.

Bryna nodded hesitantly.

"I see you are still spoiling the sheik's dog," she teased. "Don't you remember me? I am Taman."

"Taman?" Bryna's face looked absorbed and withdrawn as she struggled to remember. Without realizing it, she released the saluki, who ran to sniff at the other woman's feet.

"Taman bint Sa'id?" Bryna asked slowly as the name returned to her.

"That's right," her friend cried excitedly.

"Taman!" She leapt to her feet and ran to hug the other girl. "I remember picking wild thyme with you and—"

"And *thaluk* and *thunma*," the other girl cut in, hoping they would not have to talk about that dreadful day at the *shott.*

"How is your family?"

"My father was killed in the raid on our camp," Taman answered with reluctance.

"Lo! we are Allah's, and lo! unto him we are returning," Bryna said, pleased to have remembered the proper response.

"The rest of my family seem fine when I see them. I am married now," Taman explained almost shyly.

"To Daoud bin Hatim?!" Bryna nearly wept for joy, uncertain whether it was for Taman's happiness or for her as another name came back to her.

"Yes." The bride blushed, as she had so many times in the past at the mention of his name.

"Now things are clearer to me." Bryna sighed. "'Abla goes to visit your mother frequently now because Umm Sâlih is lonely since her last child—you—has gone. I knew her name was familiar. I just could not put it together. When did you marry?"

"Not long after our return to Riyadh, while you were . . . ill."

"I'm much better now," Bryna said easily, "and I am so glad you are here."

Delightedly the young women resumed their friendship. Learning that she had known Taman only a few months before the raid, Bryna asked mostly about their brief association but nothing of her earlier life. Taman answered each question carefully, remembering Sharif's instructions. She was relieved that Bryna did not seem to remember Pamela or how she came to be a part of Sharif's *smala*. Since `Abla had answered her questions regarding Nassar, the American girl seemed to assume she had belonged with the Selims.

After her reunion with Taman, Bryna's life in Riyadh began a new phase. She became more confident, and her growing restlessness was stemmed as she and Taman went to the souk together frequently. No matter how trivial the reason for the shopping trip, they were accompanied by half a dozen of Sharif's guards. But where Bryna had been pliable and docile before, she now chafed under the restriction of so many keepers.

"Do you not understand why the sheik keeps so close a watch on you, Farha?" Taman responded romantically to her friend's complaints. "It is because he loves you."

"How do you know that?" Bryna asked uncomfortably. No one knew of the passion she and Sharif had shared.

"A woman knows these things," Taman replied complacently. "Though he tried not to, he has always loved you."

"If he loves me, he must give me room to breathe," Bryna muttered, never realizing what an un-Arab desire she expressed.

When she petitioned Sharif for greater freedom, he nearly dismissed her request out of hand. But Bryna exhibited a stubbornness that both exasperated and gladdened the man. Oddly, he had found he missed the spark of spirit she had shown so often when he had first known her. At last, to appease his young love, Sharif agreed to assign only the faithful Abu Ahmad to accompany her on her outings. She liked the ancient war-horse, and, accompanied by the grumbling old retainer, she and `Abla and Taman spent many happy hours combing the bazaar for bargains.

The happiness Bryna experienced during that time would always be associated in her later memories with those outings. Riyadh was a beautiful city, its towered walls springing up in fertile fields that extended far into the desert. Within the walls of the capital city, broad streets led to the mosque and el-*Kasr*, the palace of Arabia's ruler. Against the northern walls was the souk, where all manner of merchandise was bought and sold and traded.

But Riyadh was a rigid, joyless place inhabited by zealots. *Muttawwahs,* a kind of religious policeman, roamed the street, bringing those they considered to be wrongdoers before the ulema. Crimes could include infractions such as laughing too loudly or singing. Bryna sometimes shivered when she saw them in the street. They stared at her blue eyes balefully, but none dared accost the woman of the powerful Sheik Al Selim.

Now fully recovered, she took on more and more of the household responsibilities. The burden of the huge home was too much for `Abla's narrow shoulders. Though not officially the mistress of the house, Bryna was fair and efficient in her dealings, and the servants adored her, obeying without fail, calling her Al-Kibirah, "Great Lady of the House."

When she did not understand how a thing should be done, the foreign woman was not too proud to ask the staff. It was through the cook that she learned how the kitchen had been run by Fatmah.

Fatmah. The name brought to mind an unpleasant old woman. She had been one of Sharif's wives and Nassar's mother, Bryna recalled unexpectedly. And there had been another wife, whose name was—she scoured her memory—Latifeh. Yes, the cook encouraged, glad Al-Kibirah was regaining her memory. Perhaps now she would not seem so sad.

What had happened to them? Bryna asked. They were killed by the raiders, was the answer.

Her experience in the Empty Quarter must have been horrible to be so completely blocked from her mind, Bryna brooded that night as she sat alone in the harem, awaiting Sharif. She did not remember the raid; she did not remember her abduction. But she was not sure she wanted to. The flashes of memory she found so disturbing, the wisps of dreams, came less and less since the night Sharif had spent with her.

She now concentrated on the present and on a future with a man who loved her. She only wished she loved him as much in return. Bryna longed to give herself to Sharif body and soul, but something held her back, something she did not understand.

From out in the courtyard, Bryna could hear the sound of the men departing. The sheik had spent the evening on the roof with them, drinking coffee, telling stories, as he was expected to do. But his heart was in the harem, where he would join her for a late supper.

He supposed the men of his tribe would hoot derisively if they knew their chief shed his head-dress and sword each evening and went to eat his meal with the woman. Although the custom was for women to eat only when the men had finished, he enjoyed their quiet suppers together. And while `Abla was away, they had shared many private moments. Wardha retired early each night, leaving the harem to the couple in hopes the sheik would make Bryna his concubine.

Bryna rose when Sharif entered. In the dim light the silver strands that peppered his hair glinted, but his face looked youthful and relaxed. He smiled, the preoccupied expression in his gray eyes softening when he saw the girl waiting for him.

She was dressed in the Turkish style in a rich black brocade robe he had bought for her. A long row of tiny buttons ran from the plunging neckline to her feet. Her skin was burnished to a golden color in the lamplight, and her hair with its dancing auburn lights was unbound, as he liked it.

After dinner they lounged on pillows across from each other, talking softly and intimately. But suddenly the glow of love on Sharif's lean face was replaced by a disbelieving look as a loud snore issued from Wardha's room, then another. Struggling to contain his mirth, he jumped to his feet and held out his hand for Bryna's. They fled into the garden just ahead of the gale of laughter that escaped them.

"Who would have thought such a snore could come from such a tiny woman?" Sharif said, chuckling. "Or from any woman, for that matter? Tell me, my love, do you snore?" he asked teasingly, drawing Bryna into the circle of his arms.

"I don't know. I cannot remember ever having heard a complaint," she returned his jest. Suddenly the laughter left her voice and she reached up to touch Sharif's face, her fingers gently ruffling his carefully trimmed beard. "How handsome you are when you smile, Sharif," she murmured thoughtfully.

"Then I must be the handsomest man in the world when you are near, Farha. When you are with me, the world dances as a bride dances for her groom and I cannot help but smile." The man's tone was light, but his arms tightened around her.

She gazed up at him with speculation in her eyes. "I think you have not always smiled at me. I see you sometimes, in my mind, scowling down at me as if you were furious."

"Not at you, my own," he whispered. "I was

angry, yes, but at myself for loving you when I could not have you."

Unable to meet his intense stare, she looked away. "And now that you have me . . . "

"Do I have you?" he asked soberly.

"I am here, my lord," she answered, raising her face to his.

She met his kiss with passion to match his own, murmuring in protest when his lips left hers to blaze a fiery trail down her slender neck and nestle at the base of her throat. Deftly his fingers worked the buttons of her robe and he slid the rich fabric from her smooth white shoulders.

Dipping his head, he sought her breast, soft and warm and sweet. Bryna's fingers laced through his long hair as she arched against him, gasping at the sensations his touch aroused in her.

With a sudden groan that seemed to come from his very soul, Sharif gripped her arms tightly and pushed her away.

"I vowed I would not take you again until you were my wife to love and honor," he said. His eyes were tortured as he gazed down at her shocked face. "Farha, you must marry me. I cannot bear it if you will not."

All at once, as Bryna stared up at him, Sharif's gray eyes were overshadowed by a pair of hazel ones. In her faulty memory another voice said earnestly, "You must forgive me, you see. I cannot bear it if you will not."

Bryna's face blanched and she swayed in Sharif's grip.

"Farha, what is wrong? . . . " The sheik's concerned voice reached her from far away.

"Nothing . . . nothing, my lord," she answered, trying to remember what he had been saying before this distressing bit of memory.

The man swept her into his arms and carried her inside. Tenderly he laid her on her bed. "Are you ill, beloved? Shall I send for Faisal?"

"No, Sharif, I would just like to rest," she murmured. Turning on her side, she curled up like a frightened child.

He sat with her, holding her hand, stroking her hair until she fell asleep. Freeing his hand carefully so he would not wake her, Sharif kissed her on the forehead and left.

It was only after he had returned to his own room that he realized Bryna had not given him an answer to his urgent proposal.

CHAPTER

✧✧✧✧✧ **20** ✧✧✧✧✧

BRYNA TASTED BLOOD AS THE BEDU CLUBBED her with his doubled fist. Dark, leering faces loomed above her in sharp contrast with the pale desert sky. Breaking away, she tried to run, but the sand was too deep. It sucked at her feet, pulling her down. She was weary, so weary. At last she stopped struggling and sank, the liquid sand lapping at her waist. Suddenly a man, dressed in black and veiled for battle, raced around the edge of the *shott*, plunging in after her to sink at once up to his neck. Only when he turned desperate gray eyes toward her did she realize who he was.

"Sharif!" Bryna's cry of agonized discovery rent the night air as she fought to reach him in her dream. Her bedclothes knotted and twisted, her nightdress drenched with sweat, she sat bolt upright in bed and screamed, "Sharif, no!"

"My lady, are you all right?" Wardha hovered over her mistress in the predawn darkness. `Abla stood beside the tiny maid, her gray eyes wide with alarm.

"I am going to get my father," the little girl announced firmly.

"No." Bryna's opposition was just as firm.

"But you called for him in your sleep. He would want to come."

"Yes, the master would want to know," Wardha seconded.

"How do you know what the sheik would want? I will not have you disturb him because of a silly dream." Bryna managed a weak smile.

"It was the third nightmare this week," `Abla said accusingly.

"Perhaps I should not eat dinner just before bed. Now, do not worry, and go back to bed, both of you."

Having had this conversation twice before, neither Wardha nor `Abla attempted to argue. With unwilling glances over their shoulders, they did as Bryna asked.

She lay back on her bed, looking out her window at the lightening sky. Though drained and weary from her dream, she did not try to sleep. She rolled to her side and nearly hugged the bed to relieve the roiling and pitching in her stomach. She was pregnant, she knew, but she was waiting until she was certain to tell Sharif.

She knew her news would please him. After all, a man wanted a son above all things. Perhaps it would lessen the gap between them. She did not understand why, but the sheik had not returned to the harem since last week, when she had nearly fainted in his arms. Once she had waited for him, filled with pleasant anticipation; now she strolled alone each evening in the tiny walled garden, feeling as if she were an inmate in a lush, sweet-scented prison.

Giving up at last on rest, Bryna rose, brushed her hair, and donned a robe. With a sour glance at the light veil that lay on her dressing table, she stole to the kitchen in search of a piece of bread to calm her stomach. She was not likely to meet any servants at this hour, she thought, and she was tired of feeling like a prisoner.

In the kitchen she gathered a loaf of bread, a small crock of butter, and a pitcher of water. Taking them with her, she climbed the back stairs to the roof.

The night was cool and the clay of the rooftop felt cold under her bare feet. She wished she had worn a heavier robe, but she was not chilled enough to retreat into the house. She huddled on a cushion and settled to await the dawn. Soon a crimson ball would rise from the desert and paint the eastern sky with streaks of pink and lavender and gold.

Bryna nibbled a piece of bread. Now that her stomach was calmer, she was actually hungry. Smiling as she reached for another piece of bread, she thought she was soon going to be as bad as Pamela.

Pamela? The memory stopped her short. She saw a girl in her mind's eye with blond hair and brown eyes. The girl from her dreams. She remembered now. Pamela had been pregnant, her bulky body swathed in a black burnoose.

I knew this foreign woman, Bryna thought certainly. But how? And where? And when? She tried in vain to remember until, finally, her head began to ache from the effort.

Faisal had said it would take time for her memory to return, Bryna reminded herself. *Insh'allah.* Do not worry about yesterday. Resolutely she turned her attention to the pastel-hued sky and the serenity of the morning. Hugging her body for warmth against the chill, she relished this moment of privacy.

Soon her nocturnal meals would be the rule rather than the exception, shared by every member of the household, for Ramadan was approaching, when all good Moslems fasted from sunup to sundown. For the wealthy in particular, the pattern of life reversed itself during that month. Their day would begin at sunset. Just after midnight *sahúr*, the early breakfast, would be served, followed by hours of visiting with family and telling stories on the rooftop. Each night's festivities would end with dawn prayers, then those who could afford to rest from dawn until midday would sleep. In the afternoons much time would be given to worship.

"Farha!" Bryna started almost guiltily when Sharif's concerned voice spoke from behind her. She had not heard his footsteps on the stairs. "What are you doing up here?"

"Just waiting for the dawn," she replied without turning.

"You will catch a cold." She heard a rustle as Sharif stepped toward her and removed his heavy woolen aba. Then she felt the weight of it on her shoulders.

"You could not sleep either?" he asked, sitting on a cushion behind her. "Was it another nightmare?"

"How do you know?" she asked over her shoulder.

"Abla told me."

"I asked her not to." She wished he had positioned himself so she could see his face.

"You asked her not to wake me," the man corrected, pulling her back gently so she rested, warm and comfortable, against his chest. His arm was crooked loosely around her neck. He nestled his face against her hair, breathing in her sweet scent. As always he felt a stir of desire, but he sat motionless and silent.

After a long moment she stirred in his embrace, and to his surprise she rubbed her cheek against his hand, which rested on her shoulder. "I have missed you, my lord." Her voice was a sigh carried on the breeze.

"And I have missed you, Farha."

"Why have you not visited me in the harem?"

"I did not wish to force my company on you," he answered stiffly. Even though he had not released her, he seemed distant and withdrawn as he remembered their differences.

Bryna twisted in his loose grasp to face him, her expression puzzled. "How can you say that?"

"Did you think I could ignore your reaction to my proposal? It is a powerful blow to a man's pride when his beloved finds the idea of marriage to him so distasteful that she swoons at the thought."

"So that is what has been wrong between us," she murmured, her relief showing plainly in her blue eyes. "Please believe me, Sharif, it was not your proposal that made me faint. It was that I was remembering."

His arm tightened convulsively, then relaxed as he forced himself to ask, "What is it you remembered, Farha?"

"Only a bit of a conversation. And I do not know who the speaker was. But the words you spoke that night—I think I had heard them before. I just can't remember . . . " Her voice trailed off helplessly.

Sharif felt an irrational flash of jealousy. Though he hated to think of it, it was possible that someone had proposed to Bryna before, that he was not the first. But had she accepted this other suitor? Had she loved him?

"Please do not be angry, my sheik." Bryna gazed up at his stony face pleadingly. "But you must understand that I cannot marry you now. These jolts of memory strike and they leave me disoriented and uncertain. If I am not sure of myself, how can you ever be sure of me?"

"I am sure you are my love and my joy." Easing the girl back so she leaned against him again, Sharif kissed the top of her head. "We will work these things out together. Do not worry."

They sat together contentedly in the dawn until the muezzin summoned the faithful to mosque. As Sharif held her, Bryna considered revealing that she carried his child, but she waited. Another week should tell, and now that he seemed happy again, she could not bear to raise his hopes only to dash them.

In the days that followed, Sharif forgot his hurt and spent every possible moment with Bryna. After their week's estrangement, she had a new appreciation for his tender thoughtfulness. He was as he had always been, she realized. She had changed. The spark of attraction she had felt since the moment she'd awakened from her delirium to find him sitting beside her bed had ignited. Now she felt more than desire. She loved Sharif Al Selim as she had never dreamed possible.

When the month of fasting started, Sharif watched Bryna carefully, concerned that she might not yet be strong enough for the ritual after her ordeal in the desert. But the sheik worried for more than her physical well-being. His gray eyes never seemed to leave her when a steady stream of guests began to appear at the Selim house each evening for the customary sunset breakfast parties and *sahúrs*.

"Every year may you be well," Bryna greeted everyone with the proper salutation of Ramadan when she was reintroduced to Sharif's family, gathered each night on the rooftop. He watched warily as she tried to recall each person's name and relationship, but to his relief nothing seemed to jar her into remembering her past.

In the time of fasting and sexual abstinence, Bryna seemed to become more beautiful each day. Her pregnancy did not yet show, but she seemed to glow with an inner light, partly because of her pleasant secret and partly because of her newly discovered love for Sharif. She wanted to tell him, but they never seemed to have a moment to themselves. When they were not hosting a supper, they were guests in someone else's home. Aching with longing for her, the man often remembered an irreverent story his grandfather, the sultan, had told him years before.

"In trying to teach his apprentice how to make gold, the sorcerer warned him not to think of pink elephants during the complex process. Though he tried, the apprentice could not keep the forbidden subject from his thoughts. At last he gave up his attempts at alchemy, saying sadly to his master, 'Why did you tell me not to think of pink elephants? If you had not told me, I would have never thought of them.'

"And so it is with women during Ramadan," the old man had cackled wickedly. "If they were not forbidden, I would not even think of them at my age."

Even without Ramadan, he thought of Bryna constantly, Sharif reflected wryly. During those long evenings, his eyes often found her sitting among the women. Above the half veil she wore among family, he could easily see the smile in her eyes when she looked at him. He wished that they could be alone, never knowing how fervently she wished the same thing. She wanted to tell him that she would marry him. She wanted to tell him everything, now that she was sure.

But when the opportunity presented itself, Bryna was as unprepared for Sharif's reaction as he was for her news.

For the first time in nearly a month, the couple was alone in the garden. Sharif sat, his back against a tree trunk, with Bryna cradled in front of him. As they watched the stars, she told him that she was going to have a child. To her amazement, he released her abruptly and jumped to his feet, pacing and far from delighted. His mind seemed to be working rapidly, calculatingly.

"We must marry as soon as possible," he muttered more to himself than to her.

"What do you mean we must?" She had risen to her feet as well and was watching him with a dangerous glint in her blue eyes.

He stopped pacing and looked at her. "We must, because it is the only honorable thing to do," he explained as if he were talking to a half-wit.

Bryna stared at him disbelievingly. He was not excited in the least that she might bear him a son.

"I refuse to marry to appease your sense of duty," she declared, struggling to keep her voice steady.

"But you are with child," he argued reasonably.

Her chin rising, she snapped, "Just because I am with child doesn't mean I must marry, Sharif."

Sheer astonishment revealed itself in the sheik's gray eyes. Never had a woman spoken to him in such a way. The astonishment turned to anger and his eyes to bits of flint as she glared up at him defiantly. Muttering dire curses under his breath, he whirled and stormed from the house without a backward look, leaving Bryna weeping behind him.

At dawn Sharif roused a few disgruntled retainers, who would have preferred to sleep the hot morning away, and rode into the desert with his falcon. The clean air of the desert would clear his mind, the sheik thought. There he could sort through his problem and arrive at a decision.

While he flew his mighty little *hurr* falcon, Sharif's thoughts returned to Riyadh. Bryna was pregnant through no fault of her own. It was his fault, he reproached himself. He had known what could happen between a man and a woman when he wandered through the harem each night and looked in at her sleeping figure. But still, in the back of his mind, lurked the thought that the unborn baby might not be his at all. A man did not speak to a woman of her flux. How was he to know who the father was?

If the child was Nassar's, it was his duty as head of his family to bring it up, Sharif brooded. But what if it belonged to one of the marauders? He did not know what had happened in the desert, but the fact remained that Bryna had not been a virgin when he had gone to her bed, he reminded himself, feeling disloyal even for thinking it.

Returning the bird to its handler, the sheik wheeled his mare and galloped back toward the city. Why was he thinking again of honor when love was at stake? he asked himself savagely. To whom the child belonged did not change Bryna or his feelings for her. He would always love her.

But could he rear the son of a Bedu raider or his worthless nephew and accept it as his own? The proud man forced himself to deal with the painful question on the long ride back to Riyadh. But by the time he reached home, his mind was made up. He had told Faisal he would marry the girl even if she could have no children. Now it was proven she was not barren. This child would be the first of many. He would marry Bryna and damn the consequences. She thought the child was his. Let the world think it as well.

He found the unhappy woman in the harem garden. He watched her, undetected, for a moment from the door. She sat listlessly under the peach tree with her head against the trunk and her eyes closed. Unnoticed, her embroidery slid from her loose grip.

"Beloved," he murmured repentantly, making his presence known.

Skeins of thread left a bright trail on the ground as Bryna fled to his arms. "Do not say anything, Sharif." She silenced him with a gentle kiss. "I am sorry for my harsh words. You are right. We should not have done what we did, but *Insh'allah,* as you tell me yourself. We do have a responsibility for the child. If you still want me, I will marry you."

"Of course I want you," he assured her, but his heart ached. Now it was Bryna who spoke of duty and not of love. "There is nothing to prevent our marriage. You have made your *shahada.* We will marry during Eed al Fitr, the end of Ramadan."

When he had gone, Bryna realized the sheik had rendered his decision regarding their marriage as emotionlessly as he delivered a judgment in *majlis.* She was not able to gauge his mood in the days that followed. A whirl of activity kept the engaged couple apart most of the time.

When they were together, Sharif was kind and solicitous, but Bryna sensed his aloofness as he struggled with his conflicting feelings. With all the conviction of a pregnant woman, she was certain she had lost his love. Amid the joyful preparations for her wedding, she became downcast.

She approached the day of her marriage with growing resentment. He had wanted to marry her and now that she had agreed, Sharif seemed to consider her nothing more than an obligation. She knew that part of the reason she loved him was that he was an honorable man, but she could not bear the thought of being just another duty. She longed to talk with him, but he avoided her company.

On the morning of her wedding, Bryna miserably allowed herself to be bathed and prepared for the ceremony by Sharif's female relatives, balking only when they wanted to paint her arms and legs with henna. She was dressed in a magnificent wedding gown of dark blue velvet, lavishly embroidered with gold thread, with pearl buttons from neck to hem. On her ears she wore earrings of huge al Hasa pearls Sharif had bought for her. Her *ghata* was of rich striped silk, and on her forehead was placed another gift from Sharif, a heavy chain of riyals, the golden coins overlapping in their abundance.

While her soon-to-be relatives, all dressed in new holiday clothes, chattered behind her, Bryna stood alone beside the window looking out into the garden. She presented the picture of a docile bride. No one could know her misgivings as she waited to be taken to her husband.

If Bryna was a reticent bride, certainly Sharif seemed the reluctant groom. He scarcely looked at her when she was led to him in the tent pavilion pitched behind the house. He stared straight ahead, his handsome face serious as he grappled with his private thoughts. She still did not really wish to marry him, he thought bitterly, when he had tried so hard to win her. How could he do more for her than he was doing at this very moment? Would it always be that his love counted for nothing with her?

Bryna was relieved the ceremony was brief. The wedding feast followed, then the men of the tribe danced the ardha as the women clapped their hennaed palms. The celebration was especially festive, occurring on the great festival, but the nuptial couple seemed subdued. Little was said between them beyond what was required. At the end of the evening, the sura to end Ramadan was recited and the last line seemed to linger in the air: "Peace until the rising of the dawn."

Then, in strained silence, the couple was taken to the women's quarters. The door was scarcely shut behind them when Bryna turned to Sharif entreatingly. "Please, my lord, I think we have made a great mistake."

"Hold your tongue," he ordered quietly, scowling down at her. "The women listen just outside."

She nodded, knowing it was true, and stepped away from the door to the middle of the lamplit room. Having been instructed on the proper behavior of a bride on her wedding night, Bryna knew she was expected to protect her *ird,* or feminine honor. The longer the struggle against her groom, the greater the honor. The women waited to bear the report to the men. But first she must speak to the man she had just married.

Coming to stand beside her, Sharif asked curtly, "What is it you wish to say, Farha?"

"Couldn't you put me away for some reason?" she whispered urgently. "I know it can be done."

"Not usually so soon after the wedding," he retorted, "even if I wanted to."

"Couldn't you tell them you are not pleased with me or that I . . . I am not a virgin."

"Wallahi, are you mad? Why would I do that?"

"It may be honorable that we married, Sharif, but it was wrong."

"What is wrong with giving the child a home?"

"But what kind of home will it be without love?" Bryna's voice began to rise as she blurted, "Don't you understand? I want to love you and to be loved in return."

The words seemed familiar somehow, but she did not examine them. She was more concerned that she was about to cry in front of her new husband. Turning a rigid back to him, she blinked back angry tears.

She kept her face stubbornly averted when the

man gently turned her to face him. With one crooked finger he lifted her chin, and she saw for the first time the light of hope her words had kindled in his eyes. "Do you love me, Farha?" he asked warily.

"Yes," she moaned, suddenly bursting into tears. Chagrined, she buried her face against his shoulder and wept, her shoulders heaving with sobs.

"And I love you, *maddamti*, my lady wife." Sharif embraced her blissfully, planting quick glad kisses on her lustrous hair, on her tear-wet face, and, lingeringly, on her willing lips.

"We love each other." He laughed aloud, thrilled by the discovery. "We love each other, and that is all that matters."

Suddenly he released her and led her over to sit on the bed. "The women still wait," he reminded her quietly, sitting beside her. "You must scream now so they know you fight for your honor."

She felt foolish, but she obeyed. She could not allow her husband to lose face. Tentatively she cried out, the volume rising until it was a resistant wail. At last unearthly shrieks of protest rose to a shattering crescendo. As it ebbed finally to terrified whimpers, the couple in the bedchamber heard the women run downstairs, almost tripping over each other in their haste to inform the others of the great battle.

Dissolving into gales of laughter, the sheik and his new wife fell into each other's arms, the strain between them past.

When their eyes met, their faces sobered. Deliberately Sharif blew out the lamp. Then he eased Bryna back so she lay across the bed. Leaning over her, he murmured, "Now that the business of honor is done, let us get to the important task of making you my own."

"I am yours," she whispered, her arms sliding around his neck.

"Just as I am yours," he answered, his voice thick with passion. He kissed her tenderly at first, but then with more urgency as his desire grew. Gently he stroked the slender column of her neck, feeling the flutter of her heart under the ivory skin. She moaned softly against his mouth and laced her fingers through his long thick hair, seeking to draw him closer still.

Sharif ran a hand over Bryna's shoulder and cupped one of her breasts, savoring for a moment the prickly feel of the velvet against his palm. But, determined to feel the satiny softness of her body, he quickly began to unbutton her dress. In her pregnancy her breasts were fuller than he had remembered, and he delighted in their instant response to his caresses.

It seemed Bryna also longed for the feel of warm, bare skin. Sharif's breath caught as her fingers slid into the deep neckline of his *thobe* and traced the scar on his chest. Nearly trembling with desire, he stood and rapidly removed his *thobe*. Then, bending over her, he finished unbuttoning her dress, and arranged it so the length of her body was bared. She lay in a pool of moonlight, her skin very white against the blue velvet.

"Thou art beautiful, my beloved," he whispered, coming to lie beside her again.

"And thou, my husband." Bryna's voice was husky with desire as she reached out to him. Eagerly, she molded her body to his hard length and her fingernails etched delicate patterns on his back. His hands stroked and caressed her slim hips and thighs before finding what he sought. She gasped but soon relaxed under his skillful hand. She exulted in the feel of skin against skin and wished to feel every part of his firm body. When her fingers, cool and gentle, curled around his heated shaft, the man murmured with delight, entranced with both giving and receiving pleasure.

When they could no longer stem the tide of desire, they united, reveling in sensation and the release their joining gave them. Finally Bryna slept, her head on her husband's shoulder. Sharif pulled her close against his body and, before he slept, thanked Allah for his fortune.

When Bryna rose to bathe the next morning, her husband lingered in bed. Cutting his arm with his dagger where the wound would not be seen, he allowed the blood to drip onto the sheets. Only Faisal knew Bryna was not a virgin, and the secret was safe with him. What he did was shameful, Sharif thought soberly, but no one else must know the sheik's wife was not chaste when she came to him.

The bride was radiant and the groom a contented man when Bryna and Sharif rejoined the Selims for the week-long wedding celebration. When the household settled back into the everyday routines, `Abla was delighted to have a new *umm,* and Bryna relished family life, savoring every mood of pregnancy.

Still, sometimes she sensed a brooding uneasiness in her new husband. She knew that Sharif loved her, but at times he seemed distant and reserved. During those times Bryna realized how little she knew him. Perhaps the child growing inside her would bring him closer to her. She wanted so much to give him a son.

But Bryna's ardent desire to please her husband was not to be realized. Three months into her term, she was taken suddenly with a severe case of cramps. Retching and doubled over with pain, she was carried to her bedchamber and the hakim was summoned. Before Faisal could arrive, her body ejected the child she carried.

After the doctor had seen her and given her a sleeping draft, Sharif went to Bryna. His rugged face, made young by love, looked lined and haggard from worry. He feared his wife would die.

Bryna's face was pale and lifeless against the cushion. Her dark hair streamed out onto the pillow in the dying sunlight. A muezzin shouted from a nearby mosque as Sharif entered her room, but he ignored the call to prayers and went to kneel at her bedside.

She opened her eyes drowsily and seemed surprised to see him. One hand lifted weakly to smooth his hair. "Did you not hear the call to prayer, my husband?"

"I would rather be with you." He took the hand in his.

"I lost the baby, Sharif," she whispered painfully.

"I know, my joy."

"I am so sorry," she choked through unshed tears.

"Oh, Farha, there will be other children—boys, girls, it makes no difference. Do you not know that I love you?"

"Do not stop loving me, Sharif." She wept against his shoulder. "I do not think I could endure it. I have lost the baby. I have lost my past. I have lost everything but you."

"I will never stop loving you, my own. You are a part of me now."

He stayed with her as she slept through the evening prayers. It was only a matter of time before her memory returned, he thought bleakly. What would happen then? Would she be content to be his wife, or would she want to return to her old life? Would she hate him for doing what he had done to keep her beside him? The sheik brooded beside her bed until the night sky was touched with the dawn of a new day.

When Bryna awoke, her manner reminded her husband of the way he had found her in the desert, numbed and docile. She quickly regained her strength, but she was not the same. Not Sharif, not Taman, not even `Abla could chase away the sadness. She no longer slept at night, hoping to elude the nightmares that returned with frightening regularity. She fretted, trying to recall names, faces, places. But she could not make the puzzle fit together.

Sharif could not bear to watch her pain. Feeling twinges of guilt, he considered telling her of her past, but he hesitated. What did he know? Her name, her age, that she had a father who might one day appear to claim her.

At last, when he felt his wife had recovered enough, Sharif desperately suggested a change of scenery—Mecca, where they could seek the blessings of Allah and his wife could drink the magical, curing waters of Zem-Zem.

He was surprised when she balked at the idea until he understood she was fearful to return to the desert. He explained that after their successful raid on their enemies, the Selims had nothing to fear in the desert. They would take no more than half a dozen retainers and ride for the holy city.

Reassured, Bryna was cheered. The shadows left her eyes for a time and the entire household gladly set about making the necessary arrangements for the journey.

Giving her something to keep her mind busy might not benefit him forever, the sheik realized bleakly, but perhaps it would postpone what he feared most—the return of Bryna's memory.

CHAPTER

✦✦✦✦✦ **21** ✦✦✦✦✦

THREE MEN IN ALGERIAN DRESS STOOD ACROSS from Sharif Al Selim's home, watching the bustling servants in the courtyard.

"You are sure this is the right house?" Blaine asked impatiently.

"It is, but we cannot simply storm the gates," Ernst responded. "We are not even certain your daughter is here, O'Toole Effendi. Besides, these Aribi are very possessive with what is theirs."

"Bryna is not theirs. She is a free woman," Derek snapped.

"One of the Selims paid for her, and he is not likely to see it your way," the guide maintained reasonably. "If she is in the house and he does not wish to surrender her, there is not a lot we can do . . . legally."

"All the more reason to go in after her," Derek muttered, hating the helplessness he felt.

"How many times . . . " Blaine began ominously.

Ernst eyed them balefully and admonished, "My plan is still the best. You must wait until I can get inside and find out what is going on from one of the servants."

"I am not sure they'll let a tinker into that palace," Derek said derisively.

"Then it's just as well he's a seller of knives and blades," Blaine retorted, running out of patience. "A great sheik will be interested in what he has to sell. Why do you think he decided on that disguise?"

"Before I visit the sheik, I will visit the souk to see what information I can gather," Ernst intervened. "You should go to the coffeehouse to meet Mustafa. He's probably found lodgings for us by now."

As the men parted company, Blaine and Derek cast one last, hopeful glance toward the palatial house. Then in gloomy silence they walked to the coffeehouse, but when they arrived Mustafa was nowhere to be seen. Hot and disgruntled, they dropped onto a bench outside to wait.

"What time is it?" Blaine asked in the French they had used since Tripoli.

"Must be past four," Derek replied, fishing for the ornate watch he carried. As he pulled it from the front of his *thobe,* the scrap of green cloth in which it had been wrapped fluttered onto his lap. "It's half-past," he pronounced with satisfaction.

Glancing over at him, Blaine said, "I thought we never would get rid of the suspicious old coot who sold that watch to you. I think he would have crossed the desert on foot, just for the pleasure of quizzing us."

"We wouldn't have gotten rid of the worthy sayyid if I had not bought the watch and financed his return to Jidda." Absently Derek picked up the green cloth and mopped his perspiring face with it. "*Zut,* but it is hot," he complained.

"Kaffir! Blasphemer!" a furious voice roared behind them, and a stout rod whistled through the air to descend on Derek's back.

Shielding himself from a rain of blows, the Englishman struggled to his feet as the *muttawwah* swooped down upon him. The furious Arab yanked the cloth from Derek's hand and waved it under his nose.

"How dare you wipe your worthless face, using the sacred color of the Prophet?" he demanded shrilly. "Bear witness, people," he addressed the curious crowd that began to gather, "Allah punishes those who defile the memory of his messenger." The old man applied the rod vigorously across Derek's shoulders several more times.

The young soldier did not understand why he was being beaten; he knew only that he was under attack. With a bellow, he charged the *muttawwah,* intent on returning the abuse.

"Derek, don't." Blaine grappled with him futilely. "He is one of their holy men. You will get us killed."

"What is this language they speak?" the *muttawwah* shouted, wild-eyed. "They are indeed kaffirs—foreigners! One blasphemes and the other has the blue eyes of a sorcerer. Hold them lest they use evil magic to escape."

Filled with holy purpose, the bystanders rushed toward them.

A little way down the narrow street, two litters

approached the market, bound for a last-minute shopping trip. Their procession, led by a slave bearing a pot of smoldering incense to sweeten his mistress's progress, slowed when the bearers were forced to sidestep avid spectators hurrying toward the commotion ahead.

In the lead litter, the curtains stirred slightly as Farha Al Selim, wife of the great sheik, called out to the old servant who walked beside her conveyance, "What is going on in the street ahead? I hope it is not another public execution."

"Perhaps there will be a beheading later. They say two kaffirs struck a *muttawwah*," Abu Ahmad replied disapprovingly. "They will be taken to jail in a moment and then we can get through."

Bryna settled back, sweltering in the closed vehicle. After removing her *burqu* in the privacy of her litter, she fanned herself with the stiff veil. The delay was a minor annoyance, but she wondered how her impatient stepdaughter was faring in the litter behind her.

They inched through the milling throng until Bryna's litter was almost even with the *muttawwah* and his prisoner. She peeped through the curtain, but the crowd blocked her view. Gawking bystanders jumped at the back ranks in an effort to witness the foreigners' arrest. One of the observers leapt up, coming down on the foot of one of her bearers, bringing all of them to a halt while the injured one yelped in pain.

Bryna clung to the frame as the litter jostled and swayed. Her bearers were experienced, and the litter was not in danger of upset. Abu Ahmad shouted at them nevertheless not to drop his mistress.

Somehow the old man's shouts caught Blaine's attention as he fought the crowd closing around him. The big Irishman glanced at the wobbling litter making its way past the crowd, just as the curtains opened slightly, permitting the barest glimpse of the occupant. "Bryna," he breathed.

"Bryna!" he shouted, giving up the fight to shove through the throng toward the litter. "Bryna, wait!"

His voice reached the occupant of the litter faintly. Who was that? she wondered. The voice sounded familiar, but she did not understand the words. Peering carefully between the curtains again, she saw nothing except the crowd that they were rapidly leaving behind.

In the midst of the confusion, Blaine struggled to reach her in vain.

"Seize him! Do not let the other kaffir get away," someone in the mob shouted. Blaine was dragged to where the *muttawwah* stood with a bruised and battered Derek. The Arabs who flanked the English soldier looked no better, for he had given them a good fight.

"You might have escaped. Why did you shout and draw attention to yourself?" Derek asked exasperatedly through swollen lips.

"Because I saw her—I saw Bryna—in a litter. She is here, Ashburn. She was so close I could have touched her, and I didn't know until it was too late."

"Did she see you?"

"I don't know. She might have."

"If it was Bryna, why didn't she stop?"

"Silence!" the *muttawwah* roared. "No more of your infidel babbling. Let us take them to the jail," he ordered pompously. The eager Arabs obeyed, hauling their unfortunate captives to a formidable stone prison, where they spent a sleepless night.

Just after dawn Sharif's small party departed for Mecca. Mounted on swift camels with their horses on lead ropes, they traveled light. On the way out of town, Bryna shed a few tears at leaving `Abla and Taman behind. She had bade both of them good-bye the night before and given `Abla a silver bracelet that she had bought in the souk. Bryna had loved it from the moment she saw it because its exquisite rose engraving dimly reminded her of something she had once known. She did not know why, but it seemed to bespeak warmth and love, and she wanted the little girl to have it.

The Selims rode out of Riyadh past early risers and laborers. Passing the constabulary, they did not notice the anxious man who entered to do business there. Mustafa beseeched the officials to release the Algerians whose ways were different from the Wahabis. The jailer was unswayed until baksheesh was produced. Many coins changed hands before the foreigners saw the light of day, but at last they were released with an admonition to leave Riyadh at once. Nothing would please them better. All that remained was to rescue Bryna.

Mustafa took his exhausted charges to the lodgings he had found, a meager apartment of uncomfortable rooms. There they waited for Ernst, who had already departed for the house of Al Selim, disguised as a Syrian merchant and laden with fine Ajami and Hindi knives.

While the Swiss guide was away, Blaine paced, unable to rest even after the nightmarish stay in the Arabian prison. "Ernst will find her," he asserted, as much to convince himself as the other men. "She is here. I saw her."

"If you are sure it was Bryna, why don't we just go and get her?" Derek asked, as ready as ever for action despite what Ernst had told them.

"Please, young effendi, do not speak foolishly," Mustafa entreated. "You must be patient." The Egyptian watched them nervously until the other guide's footstep was heard on the stairs. Relieved, he opened the door for him.

"She was here," Ernst announced without preamble, unburdening himself of his wares.

"What do you mean, 'was'?" Blaine shouted. "I saw her myself only yesterday."

"She left this morning with a small party bound for Mecca."

"She wouldn't have done that," he argued hotly. "She peeped out. She must have seen me."

"All the same, she has gone."

"Perhaps she did not recognize you, *sidi*," Mustafa suggested. "You look very different with a beard."

"Perhaps," he agreed, unconvinced.

"Or perhaps she does not wish to be rescued," Derek muttered, voicing his fears for the first time.

"There is something to what you say," Ernst interjected unexpectedly.

"What!" Both men wheeled on the guide.

"Al Selim's cook fancies himself a teller of tales, and Bryna's romantic story greatly appeals to him," the guide said.

"What romantic story?" her father roared.

Ernst was not intimidated. "She was a slave who lost her memory during a raid in the desert. When the sheik rescued her and brought her to Riyadh, he was not eager for her to remember her past. He is, it seems, a man in love. His actions have brought doubts to the minds of his own tribesmen, but he has even expressed a willingness to give up his position for her. This woman means a great deal to him."

"What of Bryna?" Blaine asked, his deep voice soft.

"The servants say Farha, as she is now called, is sometimes despondent but strives to make a new life for herself. She apparently returns the sheik's affection enough to become a Moslem."

"My daughter is convent bred. She would not embrace Islam," Blaine protested.

"Surely not," Derek agreed. "She is too strong-willed to be bullied into such a thing. Why should she become a Moslem?"

Ernst looked back and forth between the hostile faces before answering reluctantly, "She would become a Moslem so they could marry, my friends."

"Bryna is going to marry someone else?" the young Englishman said disbelievingly.

"I am sorry, Lieutenant. She already has. So you must consider that even if we were to find her, she may not wish to go with us," the guide said gently.

"She loves me, I know it," Derek protested hoarsely. "We are to be married. I will not believe she loves another until she tells me herself. We must go after her."

"We will, lad, we will," Blaine muttered, his face aged and stricken. "We've come too far to give up now."

"Do you know what you are saying, *sidis?*" Mustafa cut in worriedly. "If we did not overtake their party in the desert, we would have to go all the way to Mecca to find them."

"I know," the Irishman answered wearily.

Only Ernst appeared excited at the possibility. "Mecca . . . hmmm . . . yes. We might be able to pass for foreign pilgrims. Our disguises have held for months." The idea clearly appealed to him, despite its obvious danger.

"But, effendi," Mustafa argued. "All of Arabia is dangerous for kaffirs. Although I have tried to convert you to the god of Muhammad, you have not cooperated. You cannot go to the holy city. You would not know what to say, what to do. If it was discovered you were an infidel, it would mean immediate execution. Have you not heard of the Jewish horse trader who tried to pass himself off as Moslem? They hung his body from the Hail gate for all to see and take warning."

"Then it is up to you to teach us what we need to know and to make sure we are not found out,"

Ernst informed the Egyptian, "for we do not want to decorate the gates of Mecca."

"Up to me to perform the impossible? Allah protect me from the devil! I am a simple Moslem, not a *derwish*, not a worker of miracles. I would be killed first if it was discovered I brought you there. No amount of money in the world could convince me to undertake such a foolish task."

"Surely some amount could," Ernst retorted knowingly.

"Cursed of your two parents, you think to bribe me?"

"Of course." The guide laughed. "But you are indeed blessed of Allah. Not only will you become a rich man, Mustafa, but you will have visited the holy city, and you will have further opportunity to convert not one, but three infidels."

"Perhaps," the Arab servant replied grudgingly. "I must think on it."

"While you think, let's get ready for departure," Blaine instructed. "We will be leaving immediately."

Feeling happy and free, Bryna wondered why she had been afraid to return to the desert. Accompanied by only a few of Sharif's tribesmen, she was allowed to wear a light veil and trousers under her *thobe* to make riding easier.

She managed to keep up with the men, enjoying their easy camaraderie, even though she could not participate in it. She rode uncomplainingly for hours on camelback, with Rih running gladly beside her. At the end of the day's march, she drew from unremembered habit and set up Sharif's tent, reveling in it, for it showed she was his woman.

Despite what his men might think, Sharif ate dinner with his wife each evening in their tent. Behind the goat-hair panels, the couple dined together, speaking in low, intimate tones. Often the sheik reclined, his head in Bryna's lap, and smilingly allowed her to feed him choice morsels. They could hear the laughter of the men outside where they pulled the bread from the embers with their fingers and drew lots for the meat. So generous were the Bedu that each insisted the others take the largest portions. Lottery was the only solution to the problem.

After dinner Bryna sat quietly behind her husband at the campfire, observing the age-old ritual while coffee was prepared and served. Under the starlit Arabian sky with Rih curled at her side, she listened to qasidah. She felt she had experienced nights such as these before, but the perception brought no jarring memories, only comfortable glimpses of other campfires.

Sharif took part in the recitations as expected and told stories from his childhood among the Ottomans. But each night he retired as soon as possible with his young wife, leaving the others to exchange knowing looks over the camel-dung fire.

On their pallet in the dark tent, Bryna snuggled happily against Sharif's side, content to have his strong arms around her. In the desert she found unexpected peace. No longer plagued by dreams, she slept the sleep of the untroubled.

After a week's travel, they came upon a young shepherd camped near good grazing. While the boy napped under a saf, his cloak fluttered on the staff he had driven into the soft sand to give the sheep the sense they were being watched over and keep them from straying too far. Hearing the riders approach, the lad stood up and greeted the sheik respectfully.

"*Fen el-Arab?* Where are your people?" Sharif called when he had ascertained the boy's tribe, the Al Shammar, was friendly to the Selims.

The shepherd answered they were some distance away and pointed to the south. Because the camp was out of their way, the sheik sent most of his *smala* on toward Mecca, entrusting his wife's welfare to Abu Ahmad while he rode with a few men to visit the other chieftain. In a time of political unrest, it was wise to keep as many friends as possible.

When the tiny caravan finally stopped for the night, the men settled to wait for their sheik. Though the hour grew late, they did not eat or drink, for it would be impolite to do so before their companions had returned. When Sharif rode into the camp well after midnight, Bryna already slept in the women's quarters, so he did not disturb her.

Rising in the cold dawn, she donned a heavy aba of black-and-white-and-red striped wool and a scarlet *ghata* and veil and went out immediately. The men were finishing a breakfast of dates and camel milk, and she ate hungrily. She waited, but

Sharif said nothing of *ráhla*. Instead he announced his intention to ride to a nearby well to refill the water skins. To the surprise of everyone in the party, he invited his wife to ride with him. Eagerly she accepted.

Bryna's surprise was compounded when one of the men brought a dainty prancing bay mare with a fine leather saddle to the front of the tent.

"The well is not far. We will go by horseback," Sharif explained gruffly. "This one is yours."

"Mine?" she asked wonderingly, her eyes wide over her veil. So taken was she with the graceful animal, she was completely unaware of the under-current of disapproval that ran through the tiny camp. Truly their chieftain must be bewitched, the men grumbled under their breath. Though the lady Farha was docile and kind, to give a woman a fine mare was an unheard-of extravagance.

"I bought her for you last night when I visited the Al Shammar. They breed the finest horses in Arabia. Consider her a belated Eed al Fitr gift." Sharif handed her the reins, chagrined by his retainers' rapt attention to the exchange between them.

"Oh, Sharif . . ." Bryna's voice trailed off as she patted the mare's velvety nose. The little horse nickered softly but did not pull away. While she stroked the animal's neck, Bryna wished she could tell her husband how happy she was with his gift, but she would convey just how happy when they were alone, she decided.

"*Mashallah*. What is her name?" she asked, for

Arabs did name their horses.

"That is for you to decide."

"Then I would like to call her Scheherazade."

Her husband chuckled at her whimsy. "For the stories I tell you?"

"Yes, they carry me to strange, faraway places. Perhaps Scheherazade will carry me away, too." She was enchanted by the beautiful animal.

"Not too far away, and not without me." Sharif still smiled, but his eyes were serious. "But I did not even ask you, can you ride a horse? You do well enough on a camel."

"I think I have ridden before." Bryna pulled up her *thobe* enough to place her foot in the stirrup and swung into the saddle naturally. The mare pranced, but the young woman quickly controlled her. Her face aglow with pleasure, she effortlessly trotted the horse around the camp, starting, stopping, backing up.

"Mashallah," Sharif's men called. Warmed by Bryna's delight and her skill, they forgot their disapproval.

The sun was still low in the eastern sky when Sharif and Bryna set out for the oasis, leading two pack horses behind them. Held tightly in Abu Ahmad's arms, Rih whimpered and watched sadly as the couple rode out of sight.

A cool breeze whipped their robes and tore at Bryna's veil, lifting it and, finally, ripping the sheer silk from her face. With a surprised cry, she reined her horse to a halt and grabbed at the scarf as it floated on the wind across the sand. Immediately

Sharif wheeled his horse and galloped back for it. Swooping down, he leaned from the saddle and picked it up with one graceful, practiced motion, shoving it into the front of his *thobe* so the red silk peeped out.

"What a skilled rider you are, my lord," his wife complimented him as he trotted back to where she waited.

"It is nothing," Sharif said curtly, but pleasure at her admiration shone in his eyes as they continued their ride.

"May I have my veil?" she asked after a while, holding out her hand expectantly.

He seemed to consider her question before shoving the scarf even deeper into his *thobe*. "I think not. We are alone, and if we were to come across someone here in the desert, we would see him long before he reached us. You would have plenty of time to veil yourself. Stay as you are, Farha. It pleases me to see your face."

Bryna smiled, overjoyed by his decision. Without the constricting veil to hold it into place, her *ghata* blew freely in the wind and her dark tresses lifted on her shoulders. Sharif rode beside her, captivated by her windswept beauty.

After several hours they neared the oasis, surrounded by date palms. Sniffing the wind and pricking up their ears, the horses quickened their step. The day had grown hot, and a drink of fresh water would be welcome. Suddenly Bryna urged her mare to a gallop.

"Come, my lord," she called gaily, "it is but a

short run. Let us see if my Scheherazade is as fleet as your Târiq."

With an indulgent chuckle and a shake of his head, the sheik followed his impetuous young wife across the sand.

After the horses had been watered, Bryna and Sharif drank their fill and ate the food they had brought along. Then Sharif hiked his *thobe* around his knees, belted it, and waded into the water. Working together, with Bryna on the bank, they quickly filled the water skins. All the while she eyed the shaded pool longingly.

"Let's go swimming, Sharif," she implored when the full skins wobbled in a pile beside the horses.

"Swimming?" The Arab exploded with laughter. "Farha, sometimes I do not know where you get your ideas."

"It is a good idea. It's very hot."

"Do you know how to swim?"

"I believe I do. I'll be careful. Please, Sharif, no one will see us. You said yourself we would see anyone who approached long before he reached us."

"I know, but . . . " He faltered, unable to deny his bride almost anything she asked.

Taking his hesitation as consent, she immediately sat down on the bank and began to tug at her red leather boots. "Besides," she teased, grinning up at her husband, "I enjoyed seeing your legs, and I want to return the favor."

"Farha," he sputtered in embarrassment. Then he too smiled and began to shed his clothing.

When she was naked, Bryna poised at the edge of the shallow pool. Beckoning her husband to follow, she slipped contentedly into the warm water, tucking at the waist to dive below the surface. She swam gracefully, gliding through the pool as if she were a playful water creature.

Sharif quickly joined her underwater. His boyhood swims in pools in the Ottoman court came back to him, and his athletic training served him well. He was a powerful swimmer, his muscular body cutting through the water like a blade. Beneath the surface his arms wrapped around his wife and pulled her to him, his lips seeking hers. When they could no longer hold their breath, they ceased their kissing and their dark heads burst from the water.

Finding his footing on the mossy bottom of the pool, Sharif guided Bryna to a sheltered spot, where they stood, facing each other, waist deep in water. She could feel his hardness jutting against her as he licked away the drops of water that collected on her breasts. Joyfully she returned his caresses and wrapped her long slender legs around his waist. Buoyed by the water, they made love, slowly and tenderly.

When their lovemaking was complete and Sharif cradled his wife against his chest, Bryna pushed away gently to float a few feet away on her back. He caught her ankle and pulled her toward him across the placid surface of the pool. Gathering her in his arms, he waded to the sun-dappled bank. He laid her on his aba and stretched out beside her.

Warm and drowsy, they basked luxuriously.

"This is my *kayf*," Sharif murmured, pulling her close, "my time of tranquillity and pure pleasure of which the poets write."

"I am glad I please you, my husband," she whispered.

"You do much more than please me, *maddamti*. It seems sometimes as if I did not live at all before you came into my life."

"In Taif?"

Sharif lifted his head to stare down at her. "You remember Taif?" he asked apprehensively.

"I remember the mountains and the house—well, not the house as much as a garden."

"Ah, the harem garden. I watched you there often."

"Yes, from the balcony, I remember," she cried gladly.

"What else do you remember?" Sharif tried not to sound anxious.

"Not very much." She frowned in concentration.

"What do you think of Scheherazade?" he asked abruptly, desperate to change the subject.

"Oh, Sharif, I think she is wonderful," Bryna exclaimed excitedly, propping herself on an elbow. Swooping down on him, she rained kisses over his face. "And I think you are the best husband a woman could have."

"You are not a woman." He man laughed, dodging the shower of kisses.

"What then?"

"A houri sent from heaven to comfort me in my old age."

"You are not old," his wife protested.

"I will be if I spend many more afternoons thus. A lifetime could slip away and I would not know it. It grows late and we must go."

"Can we not stay just a little longer? I love the water."

"No, Farha, my men wait for us at camp," Sharif refused firmly.

Her face thoughtful, Bryna was silent while they dressed. "Have you ever seen the sea, my lord?" she asked at last.

"Yes." Sharif grunted as he loaded the water skins on the horses.

"I would like to see the sea," she said with a wistful sigh. "I think I have seen it before. Perhaps it would help me remember."

"Farha!" Sharif strode around the horses and seized her. His face was a mask of pain as he looked down at her. "Can you not be happy with me, with our life together?"

Bryna stared up at him in genuine surprise. "Of course I can. I am happy with you, Sharif."

"Alhamdillah!" Relief replaced the cold steel in the sheik's gray eyes, and he embraced her. "Let us go home, then, to our house of hair."

"My veil first, my sheik," she reminded him, arranging her *ghata* over her damp hair.

"In return for a kiss," he teased, whipping the silken square from the front of his *thobe* to wave under her nose. When he pulled it out, her locket dropped into the dust at his feet. Instantly he thrust the veil into her hand and stooped to pick up the necklace, hoping she had not seen it.

She had not. "What was that?" she asked absently as she pinned her veil in place.

"Nothing . . . I just dropped something," Sharif answered vaguely, thrusting the locket back into his *thobe*. "Let's get back to camp."

His lie haunting him, the guilt-stricken man rode with his wife across the desert. He had vowed to tell Bryna the truth when she asked, and now he hid her only link with the past. What a wretch he was, he thought miserably, but how could he bear to lose her?

CHAPTER

✧✧✧✧✧ **22** ✧✧✧✧✧

RESENTFULLY BRYNA EYED HER HUSBAND'S sturdy back as he guided Târiq along the rocky path in front of her. Although he did not seem to be angry, Sharif had been moody and withdrawn for three days. At first she had tried to be understanding, but now her patience was wearing thin.

This is how it has been since we made love at the oasis, she thought sadly. When they had returned to camp, Sharif seemed relieved to seek the company of his men and avoid her. Certain at first that she had done something wrong, she'd tried to talk to him, but he'd rebuffed every attempt to discuss the growing gap between them. The more uncommunicative Sharif's behavior, the more furious Bryna had become. In turn he had reacted to her rancor with wary reserve. Now they were at odds and she still did not know why.

Though his wife chafed at the brusqueness of his order this morning, she was riding with him to Taif while the rest of the *smala* rode on toward Mecca. All Sharif would tell her of his change of plans was that he must see to some unfinished business there and he would have her go with him. He did not say that he needed Alima's counsel more than he had ever needed it in his life.

The couple had ridden for hours in silence, saying no more than a dozen words between them, never slacking their pace. They had left the desert sands behind and now pushed on toward the mountains, purple in the distance. Bryna kept pace with Sharif, though she was hot and weary and thirsty. She would say nothing, do nothing, to slow them. He did not seem to notice her wrathful silence, so occupied was he with his own brooding. She trailed behind him, as grimly determined not to speak as he, her temper rising.

Halting suddenly beside a small mountain stream, the sheik dismounted and announced, "We will camp here."

He set out at once to gather firewood, missing the mutinous stare his wife directed at him.

Efficiently they set up camp, a silent team of two very independent members. Bryna built their small tent, and Sharif started a fire. Then she cooked dinner while the man made coffee. When his wife set his food in front of him without a word, he looked up at her as if seeing her for the first time that day.

"What is wrong, Farha?" he asked, frowning in puzzlement.

"Whatever could be wrong?" An icy smile on her face, a portent of the evening to come, she turned on her heel and disappeared into the tent.

Sharif sat beside the campfire for a few

moments, debating whether he should try to make peace with his wife. He had thought she would like a trip to Taif. Why should she be upset? He had said nothing to disturb her. Then he realized he had said nothing to her at all for most of the day. For most of several days, in fact. He grimaced at the realization. No wonder she was angry. The emotions with which he wrestled were not her fault.

Drawing a deep breath in preparation, the man rose and went inside, where he found Bryna spreading his pallet.

"I realize I have been somewhat, er, preoccupied the past few days," he began stiffly, unaccustomed to apologizing. "But I have many problems on my mind. They are for me to solve, and you must not let them worry you, Farha."

"At first I was worried, Sharif, and angry," she responded coldly. "Now I am just angry."

"Angry? At me?" He blinked his gray eyes in surprise.

"Yes, at you."

"I do not understand. Why?"

"Why?" She glared at him, nearly speechless with fury. "Because, my husband, you have done nothing but order me around for the past three days. You will not talk to me. When I try to talk to you, you say, 'This is my problem. There is nothing you can do to help.'"

"And there is not. I explained that to you."

"You explained nothing! I don't even know what the problem is. You wouldn't talk to me. It was as if you did not even know I was here," she stormed.

"You shut me out completely."

In the face of his wife's temper, Sharif struggled to control his own. "A man seeks solace in his tent, not a nagging wife," he warned in quiet, measured tones.

But his stern stare did not intimidate her. Bryna's chin lifted rebelliously. "Tonight, Sharif Al Selim, you will have neither solace nor a wife. I am sleeping outside," she declared, gathering her sleeping rug and blankets.

"I would not do that if I were you," he advised dangerously, catching the fringe of the rug to stay her.

"Why?" she snapped, yanking it from his grip. "Because you wish suddenly to sleep with me? It will be the first time in three days. All I have done is to follow where you lead—"

"I am your husband," he exploded.

She would not be deterred. "I have set up your tent, cooked your meals, broken your camp. I might as well be a slave."

"Slaves have been known to warm their masters' beds more willingly than you would tonight."

"Not even Nassar forced me to sleep with him," she snapped hatefully.

Suddenly Bryna stiffened and dropped her burden, staring at Sharif in horrified disbelief.

"Nassar," she repeated in a whisper. The argument forgotten, she sank weakly to sit on the ground. "Nassar bin Hamza . . . you told me he was my intended."

"He was," Sharif insisted hoarsely.

"But I was his slave, wasn't I?" Her blue eyes searched the man's stricken face apprehensively, finding the answer there he did not wish to speak. "It is true, isn't it? Why didn't you tell me?"

"Because I love you." He sat down beside her and touched her shoulder gently, encouraged when she did not shrink away. Stroking her hair, he spoke urgently. "Try to understand, Farha. You are a beautiful and spirited woman. I did not want you to remember that you had ever been bought or sold."

She looked away beyond the tent to the limitless horizon, her blue eyes brimming with tears. "I am trying to remember, Sharif, but I cannot. Was I always . . . a slave?" The word was a sob, torn from her.

"Since I have known you, yes."

"Just tell me one thing." She lifted her tortured gaze to his. "When Nassar died, did I become your slave?"

"No, my joy, I became yours." Gathering his wife into his arms, the sheik silenced her questions tenderly, his mouth seeking hers.

That night as Bryna slept, nestled against his chest, Sharif stared into the darkness. She would remember everything one day. Perhaps he should have told her all he knew, but he could not. He was running a great risk by taking Bryna to Taif, but they must return to his home there someday. Even more important at the moment, he was compelled to share this inner strife with the only person who would understand. He had to talk to Alima.

Bryna was over her anger the next morning, but she was subdued as they rode to Taif. It was not difficult to gauge her abstraction when they approached more populated areas and she donned her hated *burqu* without comment. Sharif could see her straining to recognize landmarks, looking for anything that would give her a clue to her past.

A sense of dread nearly overcame him when they reached the outskirts of the mountain town in the afternoon. Sharif watched Bryna carefully as they rode past his unoccupied villa, but she did not show even a glimmer of recognition. Relieved that she exhibited none of the distress that memories often brought her, he was strangely saddened that she had not known his home, for it had been the place where they had first met.

Dismounting in front of Alima's house, Sharif took his wife by the hand and led her into the courtyard, where his aunt waited, distinguished and regal, with her tiny staff. In her own home Alima wore no veil, and her smile was genuine and welcoming.

"Peace be unto you, my sheik," the old woman greeted her nephew graciously. "What an unexpected pleasure."

"And unto you be peace, Alima." He kissed her on the cheek.

"I heard of your sad losses, Sharif." She peered up at him sympathetically. "You have seen too many such losses, and I'm sorry."

Sharif was touched by her words, but, unwilling to show emotion before the assembled servants, he responded decorously, "It was Allah's will. May He keep such and all hateful things from you."

"And you." Alima's bright eyes lit on the black-cloaked figure who lingered behind Sharif. Bryna bint Blaine's blue eyes were unmistakable behind her concealing *burqu.* "Whom have you brought to visit me, nephew?" she asked cordially, hardly prepared for his reply.

"I want you to meet my new wife, Alima . . . the lady Farha."

If the old woman faltered, it was not discernible. Without pause she greeted Bryna warmly. "Peace be unto you, niece. Welcome to my home."

"And unto you be peace, my lady."

"Call me Alima, please. Now I am your aunt as well as Sharif's. Come into the house, my children. I am sure you are weary after your travels."

Her ancient eunuch showed Sharif to his apartment while Alima settled Bryna in the harem, commanding her maids to see to the young woman's every need. Then she hurried to the *majlis,* where she knew she would find her nephew. She carried with her a tray of coffee, dismissing the servants for the sake of privacy.

Already seated on a divan, Sharif greeted her without surprise, waiting silently while she sat down and poured the coffee.

Once she was satisfied her guest was comfortable, Alima broached the subject. "Well, my nephew, while your wife— What is it you call her, Farha? A suitable name, I think. While Farha is in the baths, let us speak openly."

"I knew you would waste little time, but I had forgotten how blunt you can be, Alima. Very well, say what you must say." The man seemed to steel himself for her lecture.

"No, I think perhaps it is you who should speak, Sharif," his aunt urged gently. "What's wrong? I can see you are disturbed. Did you find that you do not love this woman after all?"

For a long moment she wondered if he would answer. Sharif seemed oblivious of her presence. He stared straight ahead, his handsome face solemn as he gathered his thoughts.

"I find I love her too much, Alima," he said at last, still refusing to look at her. "And sometimes it makes me afraid."

"You, afraid?" The woman drew a quick breath at the admission the sheik would make to no one else. "What can you fear? That the American girl does not love you in return? She does. I can see it in her eyes."

"Farha loves me now, or she thinks she does, but will she love me when her memory returns?"

"Ah, yes, her memory." Alima nodded wisely. "And is it returning?"

"More and more every day."

"Why have you not told her of her past, my lord?"

Too tense to sit still, Sharif rose to pace the length of the *majlis*. His robes fluttered softly behind him at every turn while he searched for the words to explain. "In the beginning, it seemed a miracle that Bryna did not remember her old life.

You see, I did not want her to remember it or to long to return to it. I wanted her to believe she belonged with me, forever. I knew, with time, she would grow to love me as I loved her."

"And hasn't she?" the old woman interjected.

"I told you. Farha loves me, but what of Bryna bint Blaine?"

"I see the problem," she murmured. "As I recall, Bryna is a woman of great spirit."

"Indeed." Sharif halted before his aunt's divan and looked down at her with a troubled frown. "What will happen when she remembers all, as she surely will? Perhaps not today or tomorrow, but one day she will remember. And she will realize that I had it in my power to free her or to tell her what I knew of her past all the time. She will hate me."

"What would happen if you told her now?" She met his gaze challengingly.

"It's too late," he said sadly. "You once told me that when I loved again, it would be Allah's greatest blessing, Alima. Instead I am cursed to love her so. I cannot bear her loss, yet I know I will not be able to keep her if she hates me."

"Oh, my nephew, what a web you have woven for yourself," the woman sighed. "But there must be something . . . "

"There is nothing I can do about it," he countered harshly. "*Insh'allah*."

"Do not be a fool, Sharif," she said sharply. "You can continue to love Farha as you've always loved her, from the first moment you saw her. You say you fear—all men, even great men, fear, but they overcome it. You can do something. It will take a great deal of courage, but if you love Bryna, you will fight to keep her. And you will win her."

"I hope what you say is true, Aunt," he replied hoarsely, "for I love her as I have loved no other."

"Sharif . . . "

"There is nothing more to say." The proud man wheeled and strode from the *majlis*, leaving Alima with her own thoughts.

No, my nephew, we will not say what you already know, she reflected pensively. *You have loved this woman more than honor, and you have found what your heart wills, just as the prophecy said. Now let us see if you have the courage to keep her.*

Hirfa trudged along the corridor, grumbling to herself. It was near midnight, but she must come when her mistress called. Stopping before the closed door to Alima's private apartment, the old servant scratched softly and was admitted immediately.

Clad in a white robe with her silver hair unbound, Alima resembled a ghost in the flickering lamplight. Peering around the room uneasily, Hirfa said, "You wished to see me, my lady?"

"Yes, I need for you to read the sands, for the lady Farha."

"Will she join us?" The maid's eyes strained to see into the dark corners as if she sought Bryna in the shadows.

"She will not. She and my nephew are asleep

432

now. They leave early tomorrow for Mecca. Just tell me what you see for her."

"If it is the will of Allah," the old woman muttered, setting her tray on a low table and taking out a tiny bag of sand.

She knew why I beckoned before I told her, Alima thought uncomfortably as she watched Hirfa sprinkle the sand onto the tray.

The fortune-teller sat down at the table and hunched over the tray, frowning in deep concentration, mumbling under her breath. At last she sat up, her eyes still on the rippled surface of the sand, and shook her head sadly. "I'm sorry. I cannot tell what the future holds for the sheik's lady. The sands are unclear. I see much confusion for her."

"That is hardly a revelation for a woman who has forgotten her past," her mistress retorted dryly. "Do you not see anything else?"

"Turmoil . . . great turmoil. The lady Farha must make a difficult choice, one that will change her life."

Alima's heart skipped a beat and she leaned across the table to ask breathlessly. "Tell me, what is the choice?"

"I do not know, but—"

"But?"

"But I see that she too will find what her heart wills," the maid announced with satisfaction.

Alima rocked back on her cushions and sighed gustily. What kinds of portents were these? Both Sharif and Bryna will find what their hearts will? What if both hearts did not share the same will?

She still did not know whether Sharif would be happy.

"Surely there is more?" the sheik's aunt asked finally.

"Nothing." Hirfa answered with a definite shake of her white head.

"Then I suppose we must trust that all will be well," Alima muttered to herself. "*Insh'allah* . . . You may go." She dismissed the maid with a nod. "But Hirfa . . . "

"Yes, my lady?"

"Say nothing of this to anyone else."

When Alima rose to see Sharif and Bryna off the next morning, she was relieved to see that all seemed to be well between them. Her nephew behaved as if nothing were amiss, his tenderness for his young wife apparent in his gray eyes. Despite a haunted sadness in her own eyes, Bryna returned his love with every look, every gesture.

Sadly the old woman watched them ride away together, hoping they would realize that what their hearts willed, they had already found in each other.

CHAPTER

✧✧✧✧✧ **23** ✧✧✧✧✧

EVENING HAD FALLEN WHEN BLAINE AND DEREK and their guides cautiously entered Mecca. Their robes crusted with dust, the travelers paused for a moment to greet the idlers at the gate and to buy water from a vendor, then urged their tired camels through noisy streets, teeming with pilgrims from throughout the world, past the Beit Allah, or Great Mosque, where the Kaaba, the huge black stone monument that is the heart of Islam, stood.

Within the walls of the mosque, thousands of supplicants milled around the courtyard, despite the lateness of the hour. Legend maintained the walls would expand to hold as many pilgrims as had come to worship. Tonight many sought not to revere the sanctuary, but to sleep in the relative safety of its confines.

The foreigners filed past the elegant homes of the nobility and Blaine and Derek gazed longingly at the big stone house of the Selims, knowing that Bryna was probably inside.

Blaine, Derek, and Ernst waited wearily in the street, lounging against their couched camels while

Mustafa found lodgings for them above the shop of an olive merchant near the immense souk. Leading the fatigued animals to a dusty courtyard behind the building, they allowed the beasts to drink from a shabby fountain while they inspected their surroundings, warily noting the unreliable-looking staircase ranging along the back of the house.

Fearful that the men might get lost in the Moslem stronghold and meet the terrible fate of impostors, Ernst took them around to the front entrance of the apartment so they could identify their lodgings from the street. They halted before a narrow doorway that was almost blocked by barrels of olive oil that had been unloaded in the crowded street. Peering through the darkness, they discerned cramped stairs that led from the street to a small suite of rooms. Up that staircase came the pungent smell of olives and oil from the merchant's warehouse below.

Not even their clever Swiss guide had a clear plan in mind about how to approach the wife of a sheik without losing their lives, so the foreigners spent their first few days in Mecca watching the gate of the house in which Bryna lived. Enclosed litters came and went, accompanied by the armed Selim retinue, but they caught no glimpse of Bryna.

Blaine and Derek also searched the bazaar each day in hopes they would see the girl. Perhaps they passed her in the crowd, they agonized, but how could they recognize her under the concealing veil the women wore? If Bryna saw them, she behaved as a good Moslem wife should and paid no special note to the Algerian pilgrims.

In the huge house near the Great Mosque, Bryna did indeed work at being a good Moslem wife. But soon the boredom of her isolation overcame her. At first it had not mattered that she knew no one in Mecca, for Sharif had taken her to tour the city. Even though it was not officially hajj, the time of pilgrimage, he had taken her to see Hagar's well, Zem-Zem, and drink the curative waters. She had sipped, nearly gagging on the bitter, salty taste, but she drank to please her husband, who watched anxiously. Then they had strolled through the souks, where souvenirs of the holy city were offered for sale, pausing to admire elaborate *tespis* made of turquoise and coral and mother-of-pearl.

But now the sheik's leisure was at an end. It was necessary for him, as a sayyid, to don his green turban and join the ulema, the Islamic court, as custom dictated. Regretfully he left his wife to her own devices. Sharif employed only a few servants during their stay in Mecca, but there was still little for his wife to do in the huge house. She frequently spent her afternoons in the market, escaping her loneliness in the company of Abu Ahmad.

It was for the old warrior Bryna waited this afternoon. When he finished carrying a message for his master, he would return for her and they would go to the bazaar. As restless as she at the inactivity, he had readily agreed to accompany her, even though the sun was low in the sky.

Looking for something to occupy her until he arrived, she prowled the big house restlessly. At last, remembering a rip she had noticed in the sleeve of one of Sharif's *thobes,* she went upstairs to his room to find the garment.

Although Sharif spent a great deal of time in the women's quarters, Bryna had only visited his bed-chamber once or twice. But she did not feel like an intruder. Her husband's personality seemed to be revealed in the simple room. It was a study in con-trasts. Colorful tiles decorated the walls, but the furnishings were plain and few. His rifle hung by its cord from a peg on the wall, but below it, on a low table, an ornate copy of the Koran lay open. His heavy saddlebags were stacked in a corner, but the open door to the balcony gave the room an airy, pleasant feel.

She crossed to the carved wooden chest and lifted the lid. The scent of the incense used to per-fume the hair and beard after the coffee ritual waft-ed up to her. Smiling to herself, she sorted among her husband's clothing until she found what she sought.

As Bryna pulled the *thobe* from the chest, a bright metallic gleam underneath it caught her eye. She picked up a shiny golden oval engraved with flowers. Where had Sharif gotten this? It seemed familiar somehow. She turned it over in her hands, discovering it was hinged. But before she could open it, Abu Ahmad's voice reached her from the stairs.

"Al-Kibirah, are you there?"

"I am here," she answered, hastily dropping the locket into an embroidered bag she wore on her belt. She wanted to examine the necklace further, but as she secreted it away, she felt guilty, as if she had been caught doing something she should not have done. Picking up Sharif's *thobe,* she closed the lid of the chest and hurried out to meet the servant.

"I was just looking for this . . . I want to mend it," she blurted before he could speak.

"I will summon a maid to take it to your apartment, my lady." He flashed her a mostly toothless smile in approval. The lady Farha was a good wife for his master. "If we are to go to the souk, we must leave now. It's getting late."

They walked toward the souk at a leisurely pace, skirting the slave market. Bryna could not bear to walk on the long broad street, where men and women sat on banks of benches under a roof of matting, awaiting an uncertain future as servants and concubines.

As Bryna and Abu Ahmad wandered, she was moody at first, thinking of the locket in her bag, but she soon forgot it. There was too much to see. The streets were clogged with pilgrims, and she was content to be a sightseer. Occupied with listening to the many languages, seeing the costumes of countless nationalities, she could almost ignore the heat and filth and stench of closely packed humanity.

At the edge of a souk, where foodstuffs were sold, they came across a busy fruit stall.

"Look at those pomegranates, my lady," the old man exclaimed, pointing a gnarled finger, "the best I have seen in years."

"Perhaps you should buy some before the very best are gone, Abu Ahmad," Bryna responded with a smile, handing him some coins. The servant hurried to do his mistress's bidding, leaving her to wait in the shade of a stack of small casks.

While she waited, Bryna heard voices from nearby. Meccans were notoriously loud and foulmouthed, but these voices spoke a language she dimly understood. Curiously she cocked an ear to a chink in the wall of barrels.

"I do not understand why we search the marketplace every day, Colonel. Even if we saw her, how would we know her under a veil? There must be a better way." Derek and his companion stood on the bottom step of the stairs to their lodgings and watched the throng in discouragement.

"Do you still insist we should march into the sheik's courtyard and demand her return?" Blaine asked dryly. "Ernst says this is the best place to start if we do not wish to lose our heads."

"I know, I know. If we see her, if we recognize her . . . If, if, if," the Englishman suddenly exploded.

Blaine scowled at him. "We have come a long way on ifs, lad, and don't forget it."

Unnoticed by Abu Ahmad, Bryna wandered to the end of the line of barrels and peeped around them. In the shadowy doorway stood two men. She scrutinized them from behind her cover of barrels. One was young and slender, the other a tall, older man. They looked to be Arab, but what tribe were they? What was their language?

While she pondered, she was distracted by a boy who ran through the bazaar with a fat merchant at his heels. The boy hugged a melon against his chest. Perched backward on his shoulder was a monkey that chattered and waved its spindly arms at their pursuer as if taunting him.

Made awkward by his burden, the child lurched against Bryna, then careened into the olive oil barrels behind her. As the monkey fought to maintain its balance, it grabbed at anything that might steady it. Its grasping paw ripped the *burqu* from Bryna's face as she staggered against the tottering kegs. The unsteady stack of barrels collapsed with a deafening crash. Small casks rolled through the marketplace, bowling over pedestrians and crashing into stalls, bringing their canvas roofs down on merchants and shoppers alike.

In the pandemonium Bryna fell, knocked unconscious by a falling cask, nearly at the feet of the two men in the doorway. Blaine and Derek rushed to aid the injured woman. Kneeling beside her, they turned her black-clad figure over, and neither man could believe his eyes.

"Petite maîtresse," Blaine breathed in wonder.

"Bryna!" She was more beautiful than Derek had remembered. Her parted lips were painted red, and her closed eyes were shadowed and lined with kohl, enhancing her exotic appearance, but she was Bryna. How often had he dreamed of her in the past months. But he had known a girl, the girl he had planned to marry in Tangier. This Bryna was a woman.

"Bryna!" Blaine leaned over her urgently. "Speak to me. Are you all right?"

A moan was the only response. Derek looked

around furtively. No one was watching them in the confusion. He peeped around what remained of the stack of barrels into the thoroughfare. No one paid the slightest attention to him.

"Hurry," he instructed the other man briskly. "Get her inside before someone notices. We do not want a repeat of that fiasco in Riyadh—or worse."

Blaine wasted no time, scooping his unconscious daughter into his arms and running upstairs.

Derek lingered on the steps, watching the dying furor in the market. Apparently the young thief had escaped, for the disgruntled merchant walked back to his own stall without his melon. Other vendors righted overturned baskets and repaired their damaged canopies. Derek watched a grizzled old man going anxiously from stall to stall, speaking to every merchant, urgently stopping passersby in the street to question them. But no one approached the Algerian who loitered beside the olive merchant's shop.

Upstairs, Blaine carried Bryna's limp form through the *majlis* to the bedchamber, where he laid her down and examined her injury with gentle hands. She would be all right, he realized with relief. She had a small lump on the back of her head, but no blood seeped through her hair.

He removed her aba and *ghata* against the heat. After the din in the souk, the heavy chain of coins she wore on her forehead clinked loudly in the silence of the room when he removed them. As he loosened her belt, the golden locket slipped from her bag and dropped onto the bed beside her.

Blaine picked it up, surprised she carried this

reminder of her past. Had she remembered? Or was this proof that her memory was gone entirely? Worriedly he bathed her face with a damp cloth, heedlessly smearing her carefully applied cosmetics, but she did not awaken.

"Ah, *chère*, what you must have been through," her father said regretfully. Brushing back her hair, he planted a light kiss on her forehead and sat down to wait for her to awaken in her own time.

After a few minutes the door opened softly and Derek peered inside. "How is she?" he whispered.

"Still unconscious," Blaine answered in a low voice. "Is Mustafa out there?"

"No."

"Then you must go find Ernst. We have to get out of Mecca as soon as possible."

"But what if Bryna awakens before I return?" the young man objected.

"She will need some time. She may not recognize us at all."

"Surely she will when she sees us face to face."

"I don't know," the Irishman answered soberly, fingering the locket he held.

"She must remember me," Derek muttered. "I must speak to her, must make her remember."

"Don't worry, lad. You'll have your chance. We did not come all this way for nothing."

The young Englishman tarried a moment longer in the doorway, then withdrew and closed the door.

In the outer room he paced, trying to collect himself before he departed on his errand. He grappled with the questions he had asked himself so many times since Riyadh. What would happen now that they had found Bryna? Would her memory return? Would she go with them, or would she prefer to stay with her sheik?

Now another, more urgent doubt plagued the proud young man. Even if she chose him, could he forget she had given herself to another man? Would the specter of Sharif Al Selim, her Arab husband, haunt him forever?

The room was dusky when Bryna stirred at last. Blaine sat very still, watching her, almost afraid to breathe. Her eyes opened and she stared at the ceiling, blinking at the ache of her head.

Where am I? she wondered dully. The last thing she remembered was pain as the small kegs tumbled down around her head. And now she was in a strange room. Sensing another person nearby, she lifted her head, causing a sharp pain to ricochet in her skull.

She lay back on the pillow with a groan. A powerful-looking man leaned over her. Lit from behind by light coming in from the windows and the glow of a lamp on the table, his face was in the shadows. Though she could tell his lips moved, she could not hear for the blood roaring in her temples.

Who was he? He seemed somehow familiar. Where had she seen him before? Sharif had killed her kidnappers in the desert. Suddenly she knew that. Was this man another abductor? Was he the reason Sharif had wanted her to be guarded?

Sitting up slowly, she watched the big man warily. He nodded in encouragement but made no move to touch her. Scooting over near the wall, she increased the distance between them.

Seemingly unperturbed, he crooned in the strangely familiar language, "It's all right, *chère*. Don't be afraid."

"Who are you?" she demanded in Arabic. "What do you want?"

Blaine tried not to show the chagrin he felt in the face of her hostility. "Try to remember," he implored softly in French. "Your name is Bryna. I am your father." Carefully he reached to the table behind him and slid the lamp over so it lit his face.

Bryna's puzzled gaze examined his bearded face. There was something familiar, she thought distractedly, chewing her lower lip. Then she gasped. His eyes were blue, like hers.

Belatedly Blaine remembered the turban he wore and raked it off his head. As if mesmerized, she stared at his auburn hair, glinting in the lamplight.

"I . . . I cannot remember," she said in Arabic, shaking her head.

Wordlessly he handed her the open locket. She took it and looked down at two miniatures, one of a beautiful young woman, the other of a handsome man. She scrutinized each one. Then she looked up at the man who sat beside her breathlessly, then at the tiny portrait. At last her gaze searched his face with dawning recognition. Bryna felt as if she had awakened from a long dream to totter at the brink of memory.

"Père?" The word came unbidden to her lips.

"Thank *le bon Dieu*, you remember." Blaine

sighed in relief. He put his hand out as if he would touch her, then thought better of it. "I don't want to frighten you. You do remember, don't you, Bryna?"

"My name is not . . . Farha?" she asked uncertainly, her tongue stumbling over the long-unused French syllables.

"*Non*, your name is Bryna Jean-Marie O'Toole. You are my daughter, and you were kidnapped from my home in Tangier."

"I thought I would never see you again." With a strangled sob, Bryna buried her face in her hands and began to cry.

" 'Tis all right now. I've come to take you home." Her father took her gently in his powerful, protective arms while she wept. His deep, comforting voice murmuring in her ear brought a flood of lost memories that had nothing to do with him.

She did remember . . . Nejm, Suleiman, Pamela. Images of humiliation, suffering, and death raced through her mind. But there had been joys as well. And through most of it, there had been Sharif.

Sharif, Bryna thought with a sharp stab of pain. Why had he never told her the truth, not even her own name? He had allowed her to suffer months of torment, not knowing who she was. But the months had been filled with happiness as well, she admitted to herself. What was she to do?

"What is wrong, *chère?*" Blaine asked, feeling Bryna's body stiffen in his embrace.

"So much has happened since I was taken. There are things you do not know . . . " She faltered, uncertain how to proceed.

"I know about your sheik, Bryna," her father said gently.

"You do?" Her voice quavered, and she regarded him anxiously. "Then you understand? I do not know what to do. You are my father and I love you. But Sharif is good to me. He loves me. He saved my life. He took me in when I was all alone in the world. He risked everything to marry me. I do care for him, I cannot deny it. I don't know what to do," she repeated bleakly.

"And I can't tell you," Blaine said almost sadly. "I came to take you home, but I will not insist you come out of a sense of duty. 'Duty' was the reason I left your mother, and I've regretted it every day since. Al Selim sounds like a good man, and I think he must love you very much. Do you love him?"

"Yes, I mean, I believe so." She looked at her father miserably, her face splotchy from crying. "I don't know. I am so confused."

"This is not going to be easy. Come here," Blaine ordered gently. He led his daughter to a small basin of water and washed her face tenderly as if she were a child. "Bryna, there is someone else who loves you," he said, "and you cannot dismiss him without hearing what he has come all this way to say."

"Derek? He is here, isn't he?" she asked apprehensively. She'd loved him once, or thought she did. Did she love him still?

"Yes." He watched his daughter carefully. From Riyadh to Mecca, he had tried to prepare himself for this moment. He had suspected Bryna would have a choice to make when they found her, and he intended to see she had the freedom to make it.

He opened the door. Bryna could hear the Englishman's cultured voice ask worriedly from the outer room, "Is she . . . is she ready to see me yet, Colonel?"

"Aye." The wooden panel swung back to reveal the slender man. Even though she had expected to see him, Bryna's breath caught. Under the beard and the turban and the shaggy brown hair was the same handsome young man who had haunted her dreams—Derek.

He poised in the doorway, his hazel eyes locked on Bryna's. The instant he saw the recognition on her face, he uttered a choked cry of relief and strode into the room, taking her into his arms. Neither seemed to notice when Blaine left, closing the door behind him.

"Bryna, my love," he murmured, his voice thick with emotion. "We've found you at last." Before she could speak, he kissed her.

The feel of Derek's lips on hers was pleasant and familiar. When he kissed her, Bryna was not unmoved, but his nearness did not stir the emotions in her it once had. So much had changed. He seemed more serious, and his face had an attractive, new maturity. And she knew she was a different person from that girl in Tangier.

Drawing back, she gazed up at him with troubled eyes. "Derek, you do not know . . . many things have changed," she began painfully.

"I love you. That has not changed," he interrupted, putting a silencing finger to her lips as he had months ago when he had proposed. "Do you remember how I feel about you?"

"You said you loved me," she confirmed softly.

"And that I wanted to marry you, I still do. Please say you will be my wife as soon as we can get out of this godforsaken country."

"I am already married," she said because she did not know what else to do.

Bryna felt his arms tense around her before he released her, but the young Englishman's manner was tolerant. "If it will make you feel better, we'll have your Moslem marriage set aside when we get back to civilization. It means nothing. I won't let Al Selim keep you here against your will anymore."

"Sharif would not do that," Bryna protested, shocked that he would think such a thing.

"What do you call locking a woman in a harem?" Derek asked, his voice becoming harsh as he paced. "Or giving her a different name? Or marrying her under false pretenses?"

Suddenly Bryna felt weary, and the aching in her head returned with greater force than before. "I don't know . . . I don't know."

"I am sorry, darling. It is just that I have waited so long to find you, to know that you are mine." Taking her hand, he said solicitously, "I know you are tired and you've had a terrible shock today. I can wait a little longer. I won't press you."

"*Merci,*" she whispered, gently reclaiming her hand.

When they joined the others in the outer room,

Ernst looked up from the camel's bridle he was mending and smiled approvingly, *"Mashallah,* now I see the reason we have searched all Arabia."

"Oui," Blaine agreed, beaming at his daughter with paternal pride.

"Bon soir, Mademoiselle O'Toole." The Swiss guide rose and presented himself with a courtly bow. "I am Ernst Mann, guide and traveling companion of these demented kaffirs."

"How do you do, Monsieur Mann," she greeted him. But her gracious smile faded when she heard the call to evening prayers from a nearby minaret. "I must send a message to Sharif," she said to her father. "He is probably out of his mind with worry."

"You cannot, mademoiselle," Ernst interjected, "if you do not wish to endanger our lives."

"Sheik Al Selim would not harm you." Again Bryna found herself in the uncomfortable position of having to defend her husband.

"No, but could he keep others from doing so? We are infidels—kaffirs—in the holy city of the Moslems."

"What he says is true, my lady," a wiry man spoke in Arabic from the landing, where he had halted to listen to the conversation in the room above. "They would die terrible deaths, and so would I, for bringing them here. I beg you to reconsider."

"This is Mustafa, who is bringing our dinner. May I suggest that we eat, then talk of business?" Ernst said.

Dinner was a noisy affair, with conversation

conducted in French, English, and Arabic, depending on the pairings. Despite his initial disapproval of the unveiled woman, Mustafa took a liking to Bryna and was ecstatic to have someone new to talk to. Throughout the meal the four men regaled Bryna with tales of their adventures. When the meal was finished and they sipped their coffee, the conversation turned to plans for departure.

"Whether you go or stay, mademoiselle, it will be better for the rest of us to go quickly," Ernst said summing up their situation.

"You cannot consider staying," Derek objected at once, "not now that you have a chance to go home."

"I do not know what to do," Bryna confessed miserably. "I do not think I've ever been so confused. Not even when I couldn't remember who I was. I must speak to Sharif."

"And so you shall," her father declared firmly. "We both will . . . tomorrow."

CHAPTER

✦✦✦✦ **24** ✦✦✦✦✦

NO ONE SLEPT IN THE SELIM HOUSEHOLD. IT was nearly dawn when Sharif questioned the figure kneeling before him in his *majlis*. "Tell me once more, Abu Ahmad," he interrogated the aged servant again. "You never saw her again after the boy ran through the market?"

"No, my sheik. One moment the lady Farha was there, the next moment she was not. I saw no one following us, no one who wished to do us harm, I swear by the Prophet. I searched the bazaar, every stall, but no one saw her once the confusion started. And this was all I found to show she had been there at all." He held out Bryna's *burqu* toward the man.

"Where can she be?" Sharif's face was agonized. "Who could wish to harm her?"

In a panic when Bryna had not returned that night, the sheik himself had searched the bazaar. Wise men said that evil lives in the two holy cities, for no sooner were pilgrims forgiven their sins than they sought others to take their place.

He had frantically combed the deserted maze of streets that were Mecca, past the doors of coffeehouses closed for the night; past sleeping households; past mosques, where beggars and pilgrims slept, lining the walls. At last he had found Abu Ahmad seeking shelter in one of the mosques near the souk. The intrepid old warrior had feared to face the sheik's fury if he came home without his mistress.

"Please, my lord," Abu Ahmad entreated, "fear not. As soon as it is light, I will search the market again. Surely someone saw something."

"My men and I will search with you," the sheik said grimly. "We will find Farha if we must take Mecca apart."

"Insh'allah," muttered one of his retainers. "And the dogs who have taken her will die this day."

"Perhaps no one has taken her," Sharif mumbled more to himself than to the others, "Perhaps her memory has failed her once again."

Or perhaps, he thought wretchedly, it has returned.

That morning, while Sharif and his men combed the souk, Abu Ahmad returned to the spot where he had lost his mistress. Nearby he found a stooped old crone who sold baskets, sitting in the sun. She rose respectfully when the man approached her. Yes, she thought she remembered the woman who stood near the barrels before they fell. But no, she had seen nothing else, only the excitement of the chase.

"She was hurt when the barrels fell, *sidi*," the woman's grandson volunteered helpfully. "I saw it. Two men took care of her."

"What men?"

"Two of the ones who are staying above the shop of the olive merchant." The boy nodded to a doorway across the street. "I think she is there yet."

So that was how she had disappeared so quickly, Abu Ahmad realized with relief. She was simply taken in when she was injured. Then he scowled darkly. Two men helped her? He must tell his master immediately so Sharif could reclaim his wife before any harm was done.

Bryna awakened slowly to the rhythmic pounding from the other room as Mustafa prepared the morning coffee. Soon other noises drifted in from the street. Mecca was awake and beginning a new day. Sluggish after a poor night's sleep, she rose and dressed, then went out to meet the others.

In the *majlis* she found the air electric with tension. Mustafa fussed over breakfast, advising fretfully that the sheik's men were already searching the market. Ernst did not seem to hear him. He ate silently, his mind full of plans for departure. Blaine sipped coffee and watched his daughter. Although he lounged on a cushion, he was poised, as if ready for action at an instant's notice. But it was on Derek that Bryna's gaze rested worriedly. He had already honed his sword this morning, and now he oiled his pistol, a preoccupied frown on his face. It was as if he were preparing for war instead of flight.

After breakfast Ernst and Mustafa went to oversee the loading of the camels and Blaine disappeared into the bedchamber to gather his belongings. Sheathing his sword and tucking his pistol into his belt, Derek came to stand beside Bryna.

She accepted the hand he offered and allowed him to pull her to her feet. The young man stood very close, but he did not touch her.

"Bryna, I have been thinking," he said huskily. "You are right. We've both changed a great deal in the past year. In fact, it seems a lifetime ago since that night on the *Mab* and half a lifetime since I proposed to you in Tangier.

"I don't know if we will get out of Arabia alive, but I'm not sorry I came. I've learned a lot, about friendship and loyalty and love. You must believe me. It was not money or position or influence that brought me here, not all this way. I came for you. And somewhere on the journey, I realized why I had to find you, because I want to give instead of always taking, because I want what is best for you, because I love you."

"Oh, Derek," she whispered, her eyes brimming with tears. She did not know what to say.

But the young man did not seem to expect an answer. He drew her into his arms and kissed her tenderly, savoring the feel of her in his arms. Then he released her and went outside without a backward look to prepare for the trip to Jidda.

Turning, Bryna saw her father in the doorway, and her face crumpled. "I am so afraid I will do the wrong thing." She wept, accepting the handkerchief he offered.

"I know, *chère.* I worry for you, too," Blaine said

sympathetically, putting his arm around her shoulders. "But all will be well if you follow your heart. Whatever happens . . . *Insh'allah.* Your sheik would tell you so himself."

"Insh'allah," she repeated doggedly.

As her father opened the door to the stairs at the back of the building, the sound of horsemen reached their ears.

"It is Sharif," Bryna said positively.

"Stay here," Blaine ordered. He paused just outside, blocking her way. "I do not want this sheik to haul you onto his horse and gallop away with you. He and I have a few things to discuss."

Over Blaine's shoulder, Bryna could see Sharif and his men gallop into the dusty stable yard. The sheik led the way, Târiq rearing in the center, while his men ranged around the enclosure, cutting off Derek, Ernst, and Mustafa from the building.

Sharif wasted no time in polite greeting. "I have come for my lady, Farha Al Selim." His glare swept the courtyard. His retainers pulled their swords and brandished them in murderous warning at the men beside the camels. "Give her to me or you will surely die."

"Let me talk to him," Bryna whispered from the dark doorway behind her father.

"Of course, *chère,* but in privacy," Blaine murmured under his breath. "What you have to say is between the two of you.

"As salaam 'alaykum, sayyid," he called down to the man in careful Arabic.

Sharif wheeled his horse and glared up at the

big man who slowly descended the stairs.

"You must be Sheik Sharif Al Selim," Blaine greeted him cordially. "Please, will you come inside? We must talk."

"I did not come to talk, so do not speak to me of ransom, kaffir," the Arab shouted. "I do not pay for what is mine."

"I seek no ransom," Blaine answered quietly, lowering his voice in hopes no one could overhear, "but I must tell you that Bryna is not yours unless she says she is."

"Who are you?" A look of fear crossed Sharif's face.

"My name is Blaine O'Toole. I'm Bryna's father. Now please come inside where the two of you can talk privately," the big man insisted.

"There is nothing to talk about. She is my wife. She belongs with me."

"She does not belong to you, you bastard," Derek bellowed, breaking away from the others. "Bryna is going to marry me. You can't have her."

"No," Sharif roared, leaping from his horse at the other man's throat.

Maddened by the thought of losing Bryna, Sharif paid no heed to the sword he held in one hand while the other grasped Derek's throat. He wanted to choke this foreigner with his bare hands.

"Where is she?" he demanded. "Where is Bryna?"

Sharif did not hear her call his name or see her as she shoved past her father to dart down the stairs. He only heard the angry rush of blood in his ears and saw the contorted face of his enemy as the Inglayzi fought for air.

One of Sharif's men captured the weeping woman by the arm and kept her from the fray as Derek broke Sharif's infuriated grip and they circled each other in the dust.

Sharif recovered himself and raced toward his opponent, his sword drawn back for a brutal blow. Just as the sword descended, Derek drew his own weapon and parried the blow.

The courtyard was silent except for the clanking of the swords and the grunting of the men as they fought, circling the fountain. Sharif was a desperate man, slashing his blade in a frenzy. Derek fenced skillfully, managing to nick the Arab's shoulder and bring blood.

At that moment the young Englishman glanced toward Bryna and was rocked by the stricken look on her face as she strained against the man who held her. She loved Al Selim, he realized bitterly. If he killed the sheik, she would never forgive him. With a look of grim resignation, he began to advance rapidly, hoping to tire his opponent and disarm him before any more blood was shed.

But Sharif seemed inexhaustible in his fury. He fought as if possessed, attacking savagely, cornering the Englishman against the stairs. As he drew back his sword to deliver the death blow, Bryna broke free from her captor to throw herself across Derek's body.

"No, Sharif, do not kill him!" she shouted in French.

"Get out of the way, Bryna!" both men shouted.

"If you love me, my lord, you will not kill him," she pleaded.

The sheik's shoulders slumped dejectedly and he lowered his sword. "You care for this man?" he asked, looking as if his heart would break.

"*Oui.*" Bryna affirmed gently. "I do not want you to kill him."

"You have your memory back, then?"

"Yes."

"Allah grant me strength, it is as I feared," Sharif said. "You are right, monsieur." He turned to Blaine wearily. "We must go upstairs, where we can talk."

"You go with him." Blaine nodded to Bryna. "You don't need me for this."

Solicitously she held her husband's arm and led him up to the meager rooms. The mighty chieftain stood with his head bowed and his back to her as she closed the door.

"Let me tend your wound, my sheik," she said, coming behind him to touch his shoulder.

"It is nothing." He shrugged off her hand. "A man must have his pride, even if he loses all else. It is as the old woman predicted, my honor was your bride price. I have lost even that."

"I cannot believe that," she disagreed softly. "But what of a woman who loses her past, Sharif? Why did you not tell me the truth?"

"I feared losing you."

"So much that you never let me make my own choice? Didn't you know I would have never hurt you?"

"How is it then that I feel such pain, woman?" he asked savagely. "Your father has come to take you away. And this boy . . . he says you will marry him. You should have let me kill him." He whirled to look at her for the first time, his eyes two cold points of hard steel.

"You do not mean that."

"No, it is not the way of Allah." He sighed. "But I will pay him a fortune to leave us. I will reimburse the bride price he paid for you, and I will pay your father."

"You are talking about buying me," she accused.

"I am talking about your true bride price," he snapped.

Her chest heaving, she managed to control her temper and say with dignity, "I will not be bought or sold again, Sharif."

"Because it is not the way of your country?"

"No, because—"

"Because you love the kaffir?" His voice was flat.

"No," she answered hotly, "because I must go where I choose. I must decide. And you must allow me."

Pain and comprehension on his face, Sharif said with hoarse intensity, "You say you want your freedom, but it is already yours. You ceased to be a slave when Nassar died. The only bonds that hold you now are the bonds of our marriage.

"What must I do to make you happy? Must I release you? Then, before Allah, I will do it. But first

I must ask you . . . " The sheik's craggy face looked as if it were carved from stone as he stared into the distance, unwilling to meet her eyes. He did not see the blaze of joy in them at his words.

He loved her enough to let her go! With such logic she must be mad, Bryna thought. But she was not mad. She was ecstatic, and she felt as if her heart would burst with happiness.

"Sharif . . . "

"No, I must know," he insisted, "did you ever love me?"

"Oh, yes, my lord," she murmured, "but never more than this moment."

His tortured gray eyes met hers at last. Drawing her into his arms, he held her lovingly. "Then tell me and I will let you go."

"I love you, my husband," she whispered as his lips found hers.

The kiss they shared was fiery and passionate. Sharif's touch was the touch of a man who knew there would be no tomorrow, the spilling out of all his emotion in one moment.

Releasing her abruptly, the sheik gazed down at his wife. "Allah grant you happiness, Bryna bint Blaine," he declared with great effort. "I divorce thee, I divorce thee, I—"

"No, Sharif, do not say it." She shook her head. "I must do what my heart wills."

"What your heart wills?" he repeated hopefully.

"With thee I will stay forever, my beloved," she said simply.

"And I with thee, my own." Laughing incredulously and crying at the same time, Sharif enfolded her joyfully in powerful arms and his lips claimed hers once again. When they parted, his rugged face was transformed by the love he saw reflected in her blue eyes.

An arm around her waist, the sheik smiled down at her as they walked toward the door. "Come," he invited, his voice rich and warm and tender, "my wife, my joy . . . my Bryna."

EPILOGUE

✦✦✦✦✦✦✦✦✦✦✦

BRYNA STOOD ON THE SHELTERED BALCONY OF Sharif's home in Jidda, looking out over the harbor, watching the crowded sambuk that was bearing her father back to Africa sail out to sea. Her mind returned to the morning three days ago when she had decided to stay.

When she and Sharif had emerged from the house, the Arabs and the foreigners were still ranged on opposite sides of the fountain as if positioned for battle. But all of the faces, light and dark, were turned toward them expectantly.

"The lady Bryna bint Blaine stays with the Selims," her husband announced to his men, hugging her close to his side.

A loud cheer rang out from one side of the courtyard. On the other, Derek swung into his saddle and grimly urged the camel to its feet. He did not have to speak Arabic to know Bryna had made her choice.

Riding close to the landing, he glared up at the Arab. "Do not ever hurt her, Al Selim," he roared.

Lifting a restraining hand to his hotheaded

men, who scowled ominously at the kaffir, the sheik called back, "I give you my word of honor, Inglayzi, I will make her happy."

"I'll come back and kill you if you don't."

"I believe you would," Sharif murmured. Drawing one of his jeweled daggers, he held it by the blade and tossed it to the young man. "If I do not keep my word, I deserve to die," he shouted.

Shoving it into his belt, Derek wheeled his camel and rode out of the courtyard.

"Follow him," Sharif ordered his men, "and take the others with you. They are to have safe conduct to Jidda."

His retainers hurried to obey, and the foreigners' camels bellowed and hissed at the hurried leave-taking. But when the dust cleared, Blaine remained in the courtyard.

"You will pardon me if I don't run off with the others," he said mildly, mounting the stairs to where the couple stood, "but I am not leaving Mecca until you and I have had a little talk . . . son-in-law."

They had gone to Sharif's huge home, where the men disappeared into the *majlis* for several hours, leaving Bryna to worry what the results would be when two such proud men met head on. When they emerged at last, Blaine was wearing the sheik's other dagger and both men were smiling in satisfaction. Relations were guarded between them, but congenial as Blaine, accompanied by Bryna and her husband, rode to Jidda.

At the dock, where Blaine would find Derek for

their voyage back to Africa, the farewell between the big Irishman and his daughter had been brief and tender and bittersweet.

Seeing his wife watching the harbor from the balcony, Sharif joined her, suddenly fearful that she might regret her decision to stay with him. Since that day they had talked for hours on end, getting to know each other, sorting out old emotions, laying to rest old fears. They spoke for the first time of the raid and of Bryna's ordeal in the Rub al Khali. He knew now she had come to their wedding bed untouched. But the sheik found to his amazement that, beyond relief that she had not suffered ill treatment at Nassar's hands or in the desert, the information made no difference in his feelings at all. He loved Bryna as she was, for all time, and he rejoiced that she loved him in return.

Silently now he went to stand behind her and slipped his arms around her waist, pulling her gently against his solid chest.

She tilted her head so it rested against his cheek and asked, "What did my father say to you to cause you to give him your other dagger, Sharif?"

"He wanted to know if I would follow the Moslem custom of having more than one wife," he murmured, more interested in nuzzling her hair and kissing her ear than in conversation.

"And what did you say?" she asked without real concern. She knew the answer.

"I told him that I want no other, that his daughter is the woman of my heart."

"And you gave your word?"

"I gave my word," he confirmed with a chuckle, "and my dagger." He tightened his arms and drew her nearer. "Are you happy, Bryna?"

"Very happy." She sighed in contentment. "I always said I would choose my own family. I would love them and never leave them. I chose you and `Abla, but now I know I will always have my father, too.

"Besides," she added sensibly, "I suspect he will be back this time next year."

"So soon?" Sharif momentarily forgot his ardor. He was not sure how he felt about sharing his wife with anyone, not even her father. His time spent with his newfound father-in-law had been tense until they'd gained a wary mutual respect for each other.

"A lot can happen in a year," Bryna was saying dreamily. "And he wants to see his only grandson before he is a man."

"Grandson?" Sharif turned his wife to face him and discovered she was beaming. "Bryna, my joy, you mean . . . "

"I mean grandson. Your son, Sharif. Surely our first child will be a boy."

"Allahu akbar!" the man cried exultantly, hugging her close.

"Yes, my sheik," she agreed softly, lifting her face for his kiss. "God is great. He gave us each other."

Karen Jones Delk is vice president and partner in a broadcast consulting firm. She's a former advertising copywriter and creative director. Writing as Kate Kingsley, she is the author of two other historical novels. She lives in Northern California with her husband.